THE RED BADGE
OF COURAGE

AN ANNOTATED TEXT

BACKGROUNDS AND SOURCES

ESSAYS IN CRITICISM

NORTON CRITICAL EDITIONS

≫ A NORTON CRITICAL EDITION ≪

STEPHEN CRANE

THE
RED BADGE OF COURAGE

AN ANNOTATED TEXT
BACKGROUNDS AND SOURCES
ESSAYS IN CRITICISM

≫ ≪

Edited by

SCULLEY BRADLEY
UNIVERSITY OF PENNSYLVANIA

RICHMOND CROOM BEATTY
LATE OF VANDERBILT UNIVERSITY

E. HUDSON LONG
BAYLOR UNIVERSITY

W · W · NORTON & COMPANY · INC · *New York*

W. W. NORTON & COMPANY, INC.
also publishes

THE NORTON ANTHOLOGY OF ENGLISH LITERATURE
edited by M. H. Abrams et al.

THE NORTON ANTHOLOGY OF POETRY
edited by Arthur M. Eastman et al.

WORLD MASTERPIECES
edited by Maynard Mack et al.

THE NORTON READER
edited by Arthur M. Eastman et al.

THE NORTON FACSIMILE OF
THE FIRST FOLIO OF SHAKESPEARE
prepared by Charlton Hinman

and the NORTON CRITICAL EDITIONS

ISBN   0   393   09543   6

ISBN   0   393   05320   2

PRINTED IN THE UNITED STATES OF AMERICA

3 4 5 6 7 8 9

Contents

Introduction

Among the avant-garde writers of the 1890's, Crane was most clearly the herald of twentieth-century literature. Had he written *Maggie: A Girl of the Streets* (1893) or *The Red Badge of Courage* (1895) twenty-five years later, he would still have been as much a pioneer as Sherwood Anderson then was. Crane made a clean break with the past. At nineteen, he wrote the first draft of *Maggie*, our first completely naturalistic novel. At twenty-four he had produced, in his earliest short stories and *The Red Badge of Courage*, the first examples of modern American impressionism. As a poet, he was the earliest to be influenced by the radical genius of Emily Dickinson, producing a volume of imagist impressionism twenty years in advance of the "imagist" poets. He was in every respect phenomenal. At twenty-two, he was living from hand to mouth and borrowing money to have *Maggie* printed; at twenty-four he was the author of a classic that was then, and still is, a best seller; at twenty-five he was a star feature writer for an important syndicate; and before he reached his twenty-ninth birthday he was dead, leaving writings that filled twelve volumes in a collected edition.

Stephen Crane was born on November 1, 1871, in Newark, New Jersey. The family lived in Jersey City, Bloomington, and Paterson, New Jersey, and in Port Jervis, New York, giving him the experience of small-city and small-town life that he utilized in his writing. In 1880 his father, a clergyman, died, and after several removals the family settled in 1882 at Asbury Park, a New Jersey resort town. An older brother, Townley, ran a news-reporting agency, and gave Stephen Crane his first newspaper experience, as a reporter of vacation news. He attended school at nearby Pennington Academy and later (1888–90) the Claverack College and Hudson River Institute, New York. His baseball apprenticeship on sand lots and at preparatory school led, in college, to a brief athletic distinction. After a term each at Lafayette and at Syracuse (1890–91) he brought his college days to an end, and relieved his family of a financial burden.

Crane turned to newspaper work as the natural and expedient means to earn a living. While in college he had sold sketches to the Detroit *Free Press*, and during the summers he had written news. However, in the three years from 1892 until the publication of *The*

Red Badge of Courage he experienced professional difficulty and economic hardship. He was a born journalist, but unfitted for the routine assignments then required of the cub. While still in college, during the spring of 1891, he had been able, as he reported, to complete a draft of *Maggie* in two days, but news reporting was something else. He managed to survive as a free-lance writer, and he learned the mean streets and poverty-ridden slums of New York, living among them himself with a group of young writers and painters. In 1893 he produced the first example of modern American realism with his rewritten version of *Maggie*, a naturalistic tragedy of a girl driven to prostitution and death in the slums of the city. But prudent publishers declined it, and he borrowed seven hundred dollars from his brother for a private printing, in yellow paper wrappers, under the pseudonym of "Johnston Smith." It did not sell. But it was noticed by Hamlin Garland, who became his friend, helped him to find markets for his sketches, and called the attention of Howells to the serial publication of *The Red Badge of Courage* in 1894. *Maggie* was regularly published in 1896.

Crane's first two novels and the early short stories expressed a creed which, if it came more directly from good journalism than from close study of the European naturalists, produced comparable results. He sought "truth," he said, apparently meaning to represent emotional actuality or being, at the expense of depiction if necessary. For this he discovered the methods of impressionism, which distinguished his work from that of such naturalists as Zola and Tolstoy, who had some initial influence on his work.

The influence of naturalistic determinism, as a view of man's fate, is clearly present in *Maggie* and in such early masterpieces among his short stories as "The Open Boat," "The Blue Hotel," and "The Monster." But this "minister's son" was no consistent amoralist; the spirit of an earlier critical realism appears in the ending of *The Red Badge* and increasingly in his later works. As the first great American impressionist, however, he never wavered. The fictional emotional experience, whether actually his own or only something apprehended through his projected sensitivity, became the dynamic center of his creative energies, communicating itself in action or character by extremes of paradox, dissociation, and other forms of shock or violence; or by images so striking that they rendered strict delineation superfluous—as in the image of the "red sun * * * pasted in the sky like a wafer" (*The Red Badge*, Chapter IX); or by almost metaphysical extremes of association; or by the personification of inanimate objects or the sudden attribution of fixity or rigidity to a person or other animate creature. Crane's true literary progeny were not to appear for more than two decades, in Sherwood Anderson, and in the generation of Hemingway, Faulkner and Dos Passos.

At once, on the appearance of the English edition of *The Red Badge* (1896), he won recognition in London, where his reputation was made, and where, or nearby, he made his home during the tragic four last years of his life. Prominent writers of that literary capital—Conrad, James, Garnett, Ford Madox Ford, Wells, and others—announced his surpassing merits, while he continued to tax his frail health in pursuit of his cult of experience, a creed which he himself had proved false by writing a great war book when he had never seen a war. So alternately he "covered" a war, wrote furiously, then took to his bed, dying of overstrain and tuberculosis. The last irony of his life was that his death on June 5, 1900, was hastened, if not caused, by the arduous journey to a health resort at Baden-weiler, Germany, undertaken on bad medical advice.

Crane's publications are listed in the Bibliography of this collection. The headnote to the text of *The Red Badge of Courage*, below, gives details of the publication and manuscript of that volume, and the text of the novel is annotated throughout.

In selecting the texts of critical articles and source studies we have had in mind the student primarily interested in the literary values inherent in the novel and the critical literature which it inspired. We have therefore simply selected the best criticism we can find, within space limitations, and arranged it in chronological order. We have not attempted to support our favorite view of *The Red Badge*, nor to solve or simplify its complexities, nor to illustrate any single theory of criticism. In selecting for quality, however, we find that we have represented several "schools" of criticism, and a considerable variety of opinion concerning Crane's novel. In short, we hope that we have made it possible for the reader to "listen to all sides and filter it" for himself, as Whitman said.

We have departed from the prevailing convention for such studies by selecting rather more than the usual amount from volume-length studies, which generally have a broader perspective than periodical writings. We have included passages dealing with works of Crane other than *The Red Badge* because they enriched the discussion, as a whole, with respect to the novel itself. We have selected certain biographical sketches and reminiscences because they contained knowledge of use to the critic; we have segregated the source studies because in the case of Crane's novel they show the possibilities for the genetic study of literature.

S. B., R. C. B., E. H. L.

A Note on the
Texts and Documentation

Since the editors share the concern for the teaching of scholarly fidelity in the documentation of research work, we list here the editorial principles we have followed in reproducing the source materials and critical essays included in this Critical Edition. The text for each selection is printed from a photographic facsimile of the original publication, and, in each case, the footnote numbers are those of the original. The first footnote for each title is a bibliographical record of the item, giving its source and the original page numbers. Occasional additional footnotes supplied by the editors are indicated by a dagger (†) and the bracketed word "[Editors]." Titles of selections not original with their authors have been enclosed in brackets.

The majority of the articles have been printed in their entirety. Where matter irrelevant to this book has been excluded, the deletion is indicated by three asterisks; where a deletion is extensive, we have usually noted the general subject of the deleted material.

The editors have not, in this Critical Edition, followed the practice of indicating the pagination of each original document within the texts as here printed. In our opinion, the principle to be taught is the scrupulous documentation of the present source of reference, whether it be the first or later edition or a transcript. The citation of the original source, if possible, should also be included for the benefit of others who may be able to consult it. In the use of this Critical Edition for documented themes, the researcher could be advised, in his first reference to any article in the collection, to give the location, the date, and the pagination of the original as shown in our first footnote, followed by the number of the page in the Critical Edition on which the quoted or designated matter appears. A second reference to the same article could be abbreviated to the author's name, with or without a short title, followed by the page number in the Critical Edition.

The Text of
The Red Badge
of Courage

The Red Badge of Courage first appeared in condensed serialized form in the Philadelphia *Press*, December 3–8, 1894. The full-length version was published as a book the following autumn by D. Appleton and Company, New York, in 1895, and reprinted in an English edition in 1896. The first American edition was proofread by Crane and reprinted several times without further revision before his death. During the next forty-five years this edition was reprinted almost annually, and successive issues accumulated minor corruptions still present in certain modern reprints. The present text is printed from a photographic facsimile of the first issue of the first American edition of 1895, in which obvious typographical errors have been corrected and noted.

Crane sent the complete manuscript as a keepsake to his friend Willis Brooks Hawkins (*cf.* letter of January 27, 1896, in *Stephen Crane: Letters*, ed. R. W. Stallman and L. Gilkes, 1960). This manuscript, reported as that of the first American edition, shows passages canceled by Crane before printing. Fifty-eight of the 176 pages of the final manuscript were written on the *verso* sides of an earlier draft, which also provides variants. Robert W. Stallman, in *Stephen Crane: An Omnibus* (1952), pp. 225–70, discusses the textual problems and shows them by footnotes in his text of *The Red Badge*. The final manuscript was first published in the Folio Society edition in 1951, but the text of that London edition is incomplete and erroneous. In *Omnibus* appeared for the first time both manuscripts of *The Red Badge*, the final holograph and the earlier draft, and here Mr. Stallman showed that certain uncanceled passages in the final manuscript were somehow omitted from the printed first edition of 1895. Mr. Stallman's *Omnibus* text shows 26 of these passages—uncanceled but not printed—by restoring them between square brackets wherever they appeared in the manuscript. We have preferred not to interrupt the text, but we have given a complete list of these interpolations in our section entitled "The Manuscript: Unpublished Passages" (see p. 113). The probable positions of these missing passages are given in our list with reference to page and line numbers in this volume. The dropping out of a number of these passages from the 1895 text definitely improved it; none of the omissions altered the meaning of the novel, but they have a certain interest for the critic. That Crane finally intended to retain them seems unlikely. Since after its publication Crane expressed the opinion that the novel was still "too long," he may have omitted these passages from the typescript made for the printer (*cf.* Stallman, *Omnibus*, p. 213) or he may have approved his editor's doing so. In his earlier novel, *Maggie*, Crane made significant revisions between 1893 and 1896, but *The Red Badge* remained unchanged during the five years between its publication and the author's death. They were busy and troubled years, of course, but pending further evidence, the text of 1895, reproduced in this volume, remains the authorized edition.

The Red
Badge of Courage [1]

Chapter I

The cold passed reluctantly from the earth, and the retiring fogs revealed an army stretched out on the hills, resting. As the landscape changed from brown to green, the army awakened, and began to tremble with eagerness at the noise of rumors. It cast its eyes upon the roads, which were growing from long troughs of liquid mud to proper thoroughfares. A river, amber-tinted in the shadow of its banks, purled at the army's feet; and at night, when the stream had become of a sorrowful blackness, one could see across it the red, eyelike gleam of hostile camp-fires set in the low brows of distant hills.

Once a certain tall soldier developed virtues and went resolutely to wash a shirt. He came flying back from a brook waving his garment bannerlike. He was swelled with a tale he had heard from a reliable friend, who had heard it from a truthful cavalryman, who had heard it from his trustworthy brother, one of the orderlies at division headquarters. He adopted the important air of a herald in red and gold.

"We're goin' t' move t' morrah—sure," he said pompously to a group in the company street. "We're goin' 'way up the river, cut across, an' come around in behint 'em."

To his attentive audience he drew a loud and elaborate plan of a very brilliant campaign. When he had finished, the blue-clothed men scattered into small arguing groups between the rows of squat brown huts. A negro teamster who had been dancing upon a cracker box with the hilarious encouragement of twoscore soldiers was deserted. He sat mournfully down. Smoke drifted lazily from a multitude of quaint chimneys.

"It's a lie! that's all it is—a thunderin' lie!" said another private loudly. His smooth face was flushed, and his hands were thrust sulkily into his trousers' pockets. He took the matter as an affront to him. "I don't believe the derned old army's ever going to move.

1. See the note on the text of the novel, preceding the Contents.

We're set. I've got ready to move eight times in the last two weeks, and we ain't moved yet."

The tall soldier[2] felt called upon to defend the truth of a rumor he himself had introduced. He and the loud one came near to fighting over it.

A corporal began to swear before the assemblage. He had just put a costly board floor in his house, he said. During the early spring he had refrained from adding extensively to the comfort of his environment because he had felt that the army might start on the march at any moment. Of late, however, he had been impressed that they were in a sort of eternal camp.

Many of the men engaged in a spirited debate. One outlined in a peculiarly lucid manner all the plans of the commanding general. He was opposed by men who advocated that there were other plans of campaign. They clamored at each other, numbers making futile bids for the popular attention. Meanwhile, the soldier who had fetched the rumor bustled about with much importance. He was continually assailed by questions.

"What's up, Jim?"

"Th' army's goin' t' move."

"Ah, what yeh talkin' about? How yeh know it is?"

"Well, yeh kin b'lieve me er not, jest as yeh like. I don't care a hang."

There was much food for thought in the manner in which he replied. He came near to convincing them by disdaining to produce proofs. They grew much excited over it.

There was a youthful private who listened with eager ears to the words of the tall soldier and to the varied comments of his comrades. After receiving a fill of discussions concerning marches and attacks, he went to his hut and crawled through an intricate hole that served it as a door. He wished to be alone with some new thoughts that had lately come to him.

He lay down on a wide bunk[3] that stretched across the end of the room. In the other end, cracker boxes were made to serve as furniture. They were grouped about the fireplace. A picture from an illustrated weekly was upon the log walls, and three rifles were paralleled on pegs. Equipment[4] hung on handy projections, and some tin dishes lay upon a small pile of firewood. A folded tent was serving as a room. The sunlight, without, beating upon it, made it glow a light yellow shade. A small window shot an oblique square

---

2. Crane identifies the principal characters by the device of Homeric attribution: "the tall soldier," "the loud soldier," "the youth." On a few occasions we distinguish these respectively as Jim Conklin, Wilson, and Henry Fleming, the protagonist. "The tattered man" remains anonymous. The device heightens the impression of a generalized allegory of warfare.
3. Misprinted as "bank" in 1895.
4. Printed as "Equipments" in 1895.

of whiter light upon the cluttered floor. The smoke from the fire at times neglected the clay chimney and wreathed into the room, and this flimsy chimney of clay and sticks made endless threats to set ablaze the whole establishment.

The youth was in a little trance of astonishment. So they were at last going to fight. On the morrow, perhaps, there would be a battle, and he would be in it. For a time he was obliged to labor to make himself believe. He could not accept with assurance an omen that he was about to mingle in one of those great affairs of the earth.

He had, of course, dreamed of battles all his life—of vague and bloody conflicts that had thrilled him with their sweep and fire. In visions he had seen himself in many struggles. He had imagined peoples secure in the shadow of his eagle-eyed prowess. But awake he had regarded battles as crimson blotches on the pages of the past. He had put them as things of the bygone with his thought-images of heavy crowns and high castles. There was a portion of the world's history which he had regarded as the time of wars, but it, he thought, had been long gone over the horizon and had disappeared forever.

From his home his youthful eyes had looked upon the war in his own country with distrust. It must be some sort of a play affair. He had long despaired of witnessing a Greeklike struggle. Such would be no more, he had said. Men were better, or more timid. Secular and religious education had effaced the throat-grappling instinct, or else firm finance held in check the passions.

He had burned several times to enlist. Tales of great movements shook the land. They might not be distinctly Homeric, but there seemed to be much glory in them. He had read of marches, sieges, conflicts, and he had longed to see it all. His busy mind had drawn for him large pictures extravagant in color, lurid with breathless deeds.

But his mother had discouraged him. She had affected to look with some contempt upon the quality of his war ardor and patriotism. She could calmly seat herself and with no apparent difficulty give him many hundreds of reasons why he was of vastly more importance on the farm than on the field of battle. She had had certain ways of expression that told him that her statements on the subject came from a deep conviction. Moreover, on her side, was his belief that her ethical motive in the argument was impregnable.

At last, however, he had made firm rebellion against this yellow light thrown upon the color of his ambitions. The newspapers, the gossip of the village, his own picturings, had aroused him to an uncheckable degree. They were in truth fighting finely down there.

Almost every day the newspapers printed accounts of a decisive victory.

One night, as he lay in bed, the winds had carried to him the clangoring of the church bell as some enthusiast jerked the rope frantically to tell the twisted news of a great battle.[5] This voice of the people rejoicing in the night had made him shiver in a prolonged ecstasy of excitement. Later, he had gone down to his mother's room and had spoken thus: "Ma, I'm going to enlist."

"Henry, don't you be a fool," his mother had replied. She had then covered her face with the quilt. There was an end to the matter for that night.

Nevertheless, the next morning he had gone to a town that was near his mother's farm and had enlisted in a company that was forming there. When he had returned home his mother was milking the brindle cow. Four others stood waiting. "Ma, I've enlisted," he had said to her diffidently. There was a short silence. "The Lord's will be done, Henry," she had finally replied, and had then continued to milk the brindle cow.

When he had stood in the doorway with his soldier's clothes on his back, and with the light of excitement and expectancy in his eyes almost defeating the glow of regret for the home bonds, he had seen two tears leaving their trails on his mother's scarred cheeks.

Still, she had disappointed him by saying nothing whatever about returning with his shield or on it.[6] He had privately primed himself for a beautiful scene. He had prepared certain sentences which he thought could be used with touching effect. But her words destroyed his plans. She had doggedly peeled potatoes and addressed him as follows: "You watch out, Henry, an' take good care of yerself in this here fighting business—you watch out, an' take good care of yerself. Don't go a-thinkin' you can lick the hull rebel army at the start, because yeh can't. Yer jest one little feller amongst a hull lot of others, and yeh've got to keep quiet an' do what they tell yeh. I know how you are, Henry.

"I've knet yeh eight pair of socks, Henry, and I've put in all yer best shirts, because I want my boy to be jest as warm and comf'able as anybody in the army. Whenever they get holes in 'em, I want yeh to send 'em right-away back to me, so's I kin dern 'em.

"An' allus be careful an' choose yer comp'ny. There's lots of bad men in the army, Henry. The army makes 'em wild, and they like nothing better than the job of leading off a young feller like

5. These false rumors of victory, in the early spring of 1863, reflected the anxious hopes of the North for a change of fortune. Chancellorsville, May 2 to 4, the unacknowledged setting of this novel, was another lost battle.
6. A traditional injunction to the young warrior in Greek heroic literature.

you, as ain't never been away from home much and has allus had
a mother, an' a-learning 'em to drink and swear. Keep clear of them
folks, Henry. I don't want yeh to ever do anything, Henry, that
yeh would be 'shamed to let me know about. Jest think as if I was
a-watchin' yeh. If yeh keep that in yer mind allus, I guess yeh'll
come out about right.

"Yeh must allus remember yer father, too, child, an' remember
he never drunk a drop of licker in his life, and seldom swore a
cross oath.

"I don't know what else to tell yeh, Henry, excepting that yeh
must never do no shirking, child, on my account. If so be a time
comes when yeh have to be kilt or do a mean thing, why, Henry,
don't think of anything 'cept what's right, because there's many a
woman has to bear up 'ginst sech things these times, and the Lord
'll take keer of us all.

"Don't forgit about the socks and the shirts, child; and I've put
a cup of blackberry jam with yer bundle, because I know yeh like
it above all things. Good-by, Henry. Watch out, and be a good
boy."

He had, of course, been impatient under the ordeal of this
speech. It had not been quite what he expected, and he had borne
it with an air of irritation. He departed feeling vague relief.

Still, when he had looked back from the gate, he had seen his
mother kneeling among the potato parings. Her brown face, upraised, was stained with tears, and her spare form was quivering.
He bowed his head and went on, feeling suddenly ashamed of
his purposes.[7]

From his home he had gone to the seminary[8] to bid adieu to
many schoolmates. They had thronged about him with wonder
and admiration. He had felt the gulf now between them and had
swelled with calm pride. He and some of his fellows who had
donned blue were quite overwhelmed with privileges for all of one
afternoon, and it had been a very delicious thing. They had strutted.

A certain light-haired girl had made vivacious fun at his martial
spirit, but there was another and darker girl whom he had gazed
at steadfastly, and he thought she grew demure and sad at sight
of his blue and brass. As he had walked down the path between
the rows of oaks, he had turned his head and detected her at a
window watching his departure. As he perceived her, she had immediately begun to stare up through the high tree branches at the

---

7. In structure this novel is a sequence
of such episodes as that just concluded.
They may occur in cycles, as in the
noteworthy cycle of Chapters VI
through XII. Renaissance ancestors of
the novel are generally episodic, as

are the works of such British progeni-
tors as Daniel Defoe, Tobias Smollett,
and Laurence Sterne; *cf.* Mark Twain
and his frontier forerunners.
8. A local school, not then necessarily
a school of theology.

sky. He had seen a good deal of flurry and haste in her movement as she changed her attitude. He often thought of it.

On the way to Washington his spirit had soared. The regiment was fed and caressed at station after station until the youth had believed that he must be a hero. There was a lavish expenditure of bread and cold meats, coffee, and pickles and cheese. As he basked in the smiles of the girls and was patted and complimented by the old men, he had felt growing within him the strength to do mighty deeds of arms.

After complicated journeyings with many pauses, there had come months of monotonous life in a camp. He had had the belief that real war was a series of death struggles with small time in between for sleep and meals; but since his regiment had come to the field the army had done little but sit still and try to keep warm.

He was brought then gradually back to his old ideas. Greeklike struggles would be no more. Men were better, or more timid. Secular and religious education had effaced the throat-grappling instinct, or else firm finance held in check the passions.

He had grown to regard himself merely as a part of a vast blue demonstration. His province was to look out, as far as he could, for his personal comfort. For recreation he could twiddle his thumbs and speculate on the thoughts which must agitate the minds of the generals. Also, he was drilled and drilled and reviewed, and drilled and drilled and reviewed.

The only foes he had seen were some pickets along the river bank. They were a sun-tanned, philosophical lot, who sometimes shot reflectively at the blue pickets. When reproached for this afterward, they usually expressed sorrow, and swore by their gods that the guns had exploded without their permission. The youth, on guard duty one night, conversed across the stream with one of them. He was a slightly ragged man, who spat skillfully between his shoes and possessed a great fund of bland and infantile assurance. The youth liked him personally.

"Yank," the other had informed him, "yer a right dum good feller." This sentiment, floating to him upon the still air, had made him temporarily regret war.

Various veterans had told him tales. Some talked of gray, be-whiskered hordes who were advancing with relentless curses and chewing tobacco with unspeakable valor; tremendous bodies of fierce soldiery who were sweeping along like the Huns.[9] Others spoke of tattered and eternally hungry men who fired despondent powders. "They'll charge through hell's fire an' brimstone t' git

9. A fierce Asiatic people whose brutal raids terrorized Europe in the fourth and fifth centuries.

a holt on a haversack, an' sech stomachs ain't a-lastin' long," he was told. From the stories, the youth imagined the red, live bones sticking out through slits in the faded uniforms.

Still, he could not put a whole faith in veterans' tales, for recruits were their prey. They talked much of smoke, fire, and blood, but he could not tell how much might be lies. They persistently yelled "Fresh fish!" at him, and were in no wise to be trusted.

However, he perceived now that it did not greatly matter what kind of soldiers he was going to fight, so long as they fought, which fact no one disputed. There was a more serious problem. He lay in his bunk pondering upon it. He tried to mathematically prove to himself that he would not run from a battle.

Previously he had never felt obliged to wrestle too seriously with this question. In his life he had taken certain things for granted, never challenging his belief in ultimate success, and bothering little about means and roads. But here he was confronted with a thing of moment. It had suddenly appeared to him that perhaps in a battle he might run. He was forced to admit that as far as war was concerned he knew nothing of himself.

A sufficient time before he would have allowed the problem to kick its heels at the outer portals of his mind, but now he felt compelled to give serious attention to it.

A little panic-fear grew in his mind. As his imagination went forward to a fight, he saw hideous possibilities. He contemplated the lurking menaces of the future, and failed in an effort to see himself standing stoutly in the midst of them. He recalled his visions of broken-bladed glory, but in the shadow of the impending tumult he suspected them to be impossible pictures.

He sprang from the bunk and began to pace nervously to and fro. "Good Lord, what's th' matter with me?" he said aloud.

He felt that in this crisis his laws of life were useless. Whatever he had learned of himself was here of no avail. He was an unknown quantity. He saw that he would again be obliged to experiment as he had in early youth. He must accumulate information of himself, and meanwhile he resolved to remain close upon his guard lest those qualities of which he knew nothing should everlastingly disgrace him. "Good Lord!" he repeated in dismay.

After a time the tall soldier slid dexterously through the hole. The loud private followed. They were wrangling.

"That's all right," said the tall soldier as he entered. He waved his hand expressively. "You can believe me or not, jest as you like. All you got to do is to sit down and wait as quiet as you can. Then pretty soon you'll find out I was right."

His comrade grunted stubbornly. For a moment he seemed to be searching for a formidable reply. Finally he said: "Well, you don't know everything in the world, do you?"

"Didn't say I knew everything in the world," retorted the other sharply. He began to stow various articles snugly into his knapsack.

The youth, pausing in his nervous walk, looked down at the busy figure. "Going to be a battle, sure, is there, Jim?" he asked.

"Of course there is," replied the tall soldier. "Of course there is. You jest wait 'til to-morrow, and you'll see one of the biggest battles ever was. You jest wait."

"Thunder!" said the youth.

"Oh, you'll see fighting this time, my boy, what'll be regular out-and-out fighting," added the tall soldier, with the air of a man who is about to exhibit a battle for the benefit of his friends.

"Huh!" said the loud one from a corner.

"Well," remarked the youth, "like as not this story'll turn out jest like them others did."

"Not much it won't," replied the tall soldier, exasperated. "Not much it won't. Didn't the cavalry all start this morning?" He glared about him. No one denied his statement. "The cavalry started this morning," he continued. "They say there ain't hardly any cavalry left in camp. They're going to Richmond, or some place, while we fight all the Johnnies.[1] It's some dodge like that. The regiment's got orders, too. A feller what seen 'em go to headquarters told me a little while ago. And they're raising blazes all over camp—anybody can see that."

"Shucks!" said the loud one.

The youth remained silent for a time. At last he spoke to the tall soldier. "Jim!"

"What?"

"How do you think the reg'ment 'll do?"

"Oh, they'll fight all right, I guess, after they once get into it," said the other with cold judgment. He made a fine use of the third person. "There's been heaps of fun poked at 'em because they're new, of course, and all that; but they'll fight all right, I guess."

"Think any of the boys 'll run?" persisted the youth.

"Oh, there may be a few of 'em run, but there's them kind in every regiment, 'specially when they first goes under fire," said the other in a tolerant way. "Of course it might happen that the hull kit-and-boodle might start and run, if some big fighting came first-off, and then again they might stay and fight like fun. But you can't bet on nothing. Of course they ain't never been under fire yet, and it ain't likely they'll lick the hull rebel army all-to-oncet

1. "Johnny Rebs," or Confederate soldiers.

the first time; but I think they'll fight better than some, if worse than others. That's the way I figger. They call the reg'ment 'Fresh fish' and everything; but the boys come of good stock, and most of 'em 'll fight like sin after they oncet git shootin'," he added, with a mighty emphasis on the last four words.

"Oh, you think you know——" began the loud soldier with scorn.

The other turned savagely upon him. They had a rapid altercation, in which they fastened upon each other various strange epithets.

The youth at last interrupted them. "Did you ever think you might run yourself, Jim?" he asked. On concluding the sentence he laughed as if he had meant to aim a joke. The loud soldier also giggled.

The tall private waved his hand. "Well," said he profoundly, "I've thought it might get too hot for Jim Conklin[2] in some of them scrimmages, and if a whole lot of boys started and run, why, I s'pose I'd start and run. And if I once started to run, I'd run like the devil, and no mistake. But if everybody was a-standing and a-fighting, why, I'd stand and fight. Be jiminey, I would. I'll bet on it."

"Huh!" said the loud one.

The youth of this tale felt gratitude for these words of his comrade. He had feared that all of the untried men possessed a great and correct confidence. He now was in a measure reassured.

Chapter II

The next morning the youth discovered that his tall comrade had been the fast-flying messenger of a mistake. There was much scoffing at the latter by those who had yesterday been firm adherents of his views, and there was even a little sneering by men who had never believed the rumor. The tall one fought with a man from Chatfield Corners[3] and beat him severely.

The youth felt, however, that his problem was in no wise lifted from him. There was, on the contrary, an irritating prolongation. The tale had created in him a great concern for himself. Now, with the newborn question in his mind, he was compelled to sink back into his old place as part of a blue demonstration.

For days he made ceaseless calculations, but they were all wondrously unsatisfactory. He found that he could establish nothing.

2. *I.e.*, the tall soldier himself. Certain critics regard this character as a principal instrument of the author's meaning.

3. Unidentified town, the fictitious regiment may be from New York. See p. 62, the last line.

He finally concluded that the only way to prove himself was to go into the blaze, and then figuratively to watch his legs[4] to discover their merits and faults. He reluctantly admitted that he could not sit still and with a mental slate and pencil derive an answer. To gain it, he must have blaze, blood, and danger, even as a chemist requires this, that, and the other. So he fretted for an opportunity.

Meanwhile he continually tried to measure himself by his comrades. The tall soldier, for one, gave him some assurance. This man's serene unconcern dealt him a measure of confidence, for he had known him since childhood, and from his intimate knowledge he did not see how he could be capable of anything that was beyond him, the youth. Still, he thought that his comrade might be mistaken about himself. Or, on the other hand, he might be a man heretofore doomed to peace and obscurity, but, in reality, made to shine in war.

The youth would have liked to have discovered another who suspected himself. A sympathetic comparison of mental notes would have been a joy to him.

He occasionally tried to fathom a comrade with seductive sentences. He looked about to find men in the proper mood. All attempts failed to bring forth any statement which looked in any way like a confession to those doubts which he privately acknowledged in himself. He was afraid to make an open declaration of his concern, because he dreaded to place some unscrupulous confidant upon the high plane of the unconfessed from which elevation he could be derided.

In regard to his companions his mind wavered between two opinions, according to his mood. Sometimes he inclined to believing them all heroes. In fact, he usually admitted in secret the superior development of the higher qualities in others. He could conceive of men going very insignificantly about the world bearing a load of courage unseen, and although he had known many of his comrades through boyhood, he began to fear that his judgment of them had been blind. Then, in other moments, he flouted these theories, and assured himself that his fellows were all privately wondering and quaking.

His emotions made him feel strange in the presence of men who talked excitedly of a prospective battle as of a drama they were about to witness, with nothing but eagerness and curiosity apparent in their faces. It was often that he suspected them to be liars.

4. Crane's naturalistic inclination suggested images representing the soldiers' acts as mechanical responses not controlled by moral judgment or choice, while inanimate things and machines, especially weapons, are personified.

He did not pass such thoughts without severe condemnation of himself. He dinned reproaches at times. He was convicted by himself of many shameful crimes against the gods of traditions.

In his great anxiety his heart was continually clamoring at what he considered the intolerable slowness of the generals. They seemed content to perch tranquilly on the river bank, and leave him bowed down by the weight of a great problem. He wanted it settled forthwith. He could not long bear such a load, he said. Sometimes his anger at the commanders reached an acute stage, and he grumbled about the camp like a veteran.

One morning, however, he found himself in the ranks of his prepared regiment. The men were whispering speculations and recounting the old rumors. In the gloom before the break of the day their uniforms glowed a deep purple hue. From across the river the red eyes were still peering.[5] In the eastern sky there was a yellow patch like a rug laid for the feet of the coming sun; and against it, black and patternlike, loomed the gigantic figure of the colonel on a gigantic horse.

From off in the darkness came the trampling of feet. The youth could occasionally see dark shadows that moved like monsters. The regiment stood at rest for what seemed a long time. The youth grew impatient. It was unendurable the way these affairs were managed. He wondered how long they were to be kept waiting.

As he looked all about him and pondered upon the mystic gloom, he began to believe that at any moment the ominous distance might be aflare, and the rolling crashes of an engagement come to his ears. Staring once at the red eyes across the river, he conceived them to be growing larger, as the orbs of a row of dragons advancing. He turned toward the colonel and saw him lift his gigantic arm and calmly stroke his mustache.

At last he heard from along the road at the foot of the hill the clatter of a horse's galloping hoofs. It must be the coming of orders. He bent forward, scarce breathing. The exciting clickety-click, as it grew louder and louder, seemed to be beating upon his soul. Presently a horseman with jangling equipment drew rein before the colonel of the regiment. The two held a short, sharp-worded conversation. The men in the foremost ranks craned their necks.

As the horseman wheeled his animal and galloped away he turned to shout over his shoulder, "Don't forget that box of cigars!" The colonel mumbled in reply. The youth wondered what a box of cigars had to do with war.

A moment later the regiment went swinging off into the dark-

---

5. Sentries of the Confederate army, on the opposite shore of the Rappa- hannock (*cf.* "the red, eyelike gleam of hostile camp-fires" in Chapter I).

ness. It was now like one of those moving monsters wending with many feet. The air was heavy, and cold with dew. A mass of wet grass, marched upon, rustled like silk.

There was an occasional flash and glimmer of steel from the backs of all these huge crawling reptiles. From the road came creakings and grumblings as some surly guns were dragged away.[6]

The men stumbled along still muttering speculations. There was a subdued debate. Once a man fell down, and as he reached for his rifle a comrade, unseeing, trod upon his hand. He of the injured fingers swore bitterly and aloud. A low, tittering laugh went among his fellows.

Presently they passed into a roadway and marched forward with easy strides. A dark regiment moved before them, and from behind also came the tinkle of equipments on the bodies of marching men.

The rushing yellow of the developing day went on behind their backs. When the sunrays at last struck full and mellowingly upon the earth, the youth saw that the landscape was streaked with two long, thin, black columns which disappeared on the brow of a hill in front and rearward vanished in a wood. They were like two serpents crawling from the cavern of the night.

The river was not in view. The tall soldier burst into praises of what he thought to be his powers of perception.

Some of the tall one's companions cried with emphasis that they, too, had evolved the same thing, and they congratulated themselves upon it. But there were others who said that the tall one's plan was not the true one at all. They persisted with other theories. There was a vigorous discussion.

The youth took no part in them. As he walked along in careless line he was engaged with his own eternal debate. He could not hinder himself from dwelling upon it. He was despondent and sullen, and threw shifting glances about him. He looked ahead, often expecting to hear from the advance the rattle of firing.

But the long serpents crawled slowly from hill to hill without bluster of smoke. A dun-colored cloud of dust floated away to the right. The sky overhead was of a fairy blue.

The youth studied the faces of his companions, ever on the watch to detect kindred emotions. He suffered disappointment. Some ardor of the air which was causing the veteran commands to move with glee—almost with song—had infected the new regiment. The men began to speak of victory as of a thing they knew. Also, the tall soldier received his vindication. They were certainly going to come around in behind the enemy. They expressed commiseration for that part of the enemy which had been left upon the river bank,

6. Animal images of soldiers and weapons often appear.

felicitating themselves upon being a part of a blasting host.

The youth, considering himself as separated from the others, was saddened by the blithe and merry speeches that went from rank to rank. The company wags all made their best endeavors. The regiment tramped to the tune of laughter.

The blatant soldier often convulsed whole files by his biting sarcasms aimed at the tall one.

And it was not long before all the men seemed to forget their mission. Whole brigades grinned in unison, and regiments laughed.[7]

A rather fat soldier attempted to pilfer a horse from a dooryard. He planned to load his knapsack upon it. He was escaping with his prize when a young girl rushed from the house and grabbed the animal's mane. There followed a wrangle. The young girl, with pink cheeks and shining eyes, stood like a dauntless statue.

The observant regiment, standing at rest in the roadway, whooped at once, and entered whole-souled upon the side of the maiden. The men became so engrossed in this affair that they entirely ceased to remember their own large war. They jeered the piratical private, and called attention to various defects in his personal appearance; and they were wildly enthusiastic in support of the young girl.

To her, from some distance, came bold advice. "Hit him with a stick."

There were crows and catcalls showered upon him when he retreated without the horse. The regiment rejoiced at his downfall. Loud and vociferous congratulations were showered upon the maiden, who stood panting and regarding the troops with defiance.

At nightfall the column broke into regimental pieces, and the fragments went into the fields to camp. Tents sprang up like strange plants. Campfires, like red, peculiar blossoms, dotted the night.

The youth kept from intercourse with his companions as much as circumstances would allow him. In the evening he wandered a few paces into the gloom. From this little distance the many fires, with the black forms of men passing to and fro before the crimson rays, made weird and satanic effects.

He lay down in the grass. The blades pressed tenderly against his cheek. The moon had been lighted and was hung in a treetop. The liquid stillness of the night enveloping him made him feel vast pity for himself. There was a caress in the soft winds; and the whole mood of the darkness, he thought, was one of sympathy for himself in his distress.[8]

He wished, without reserve, that he was at home again making

7. A characteristic example of Crane's depersonalized image of the individual as soldier.
8. Figures of speech in this paragraph represent the "pathetic fallacy"—illogical association of the emotions with external objects—an impressionistic device then condemned by purists.

the endless rounds from the house to the barn, from the barn to the fields, from the fields to the barn, from the barn to the house. He remembered he had often cursed the brindle cow and her mates, and had sometimes flung milking stools. But, from his present point of view, there was a halo of happiness about each of their heads, and he would have sacrificed all the brass buttons on the continent to have been enabled to return to them. He told himself that he was not formed for a soldier. And he mused seriously upon the radical differences between himself and those men who were dodging implike around the fires.

As he mused thus he heard the rustle of grass, and, upon turning his head, discovered the loud soldier. He called out, "Oh, Wilson!"[9]

The latter approached and looked down. "Why, hello, Henry; is it you? What you doing here?"

"Oh, thinking," said the youth.

The other sat down and carefully lighted his pipe. "You're getting blue, my boy. You're looking thundering peeked. What the dickens is wrong with you?"

"Oh, nothing," said the youth.

The loud soldier launched them into the subject of the anticipated fight. "Oh, we've got 'em now!" As he spoke his boyish face was wreathed in a gleeful smile, and his voice had an exultant ring. "We've got 'em now. At last, by the eternal thunders, we'll lick 'em good!"

"If the truth was known," he added, more soberly, *"they've* licked *us* about every clip up to now; but this time—this time— we'll lick 'em good!"

"I thought you was objecting to this march a little while ago," said the youth coldly.

"Oh, it wasn't that," explained the other. "I don't mind marching, if there's going to be fighting at the end of it. What I hate is this getting moved here and moved there, with no good coming of it, as far as I can see, excepting sore feet and damned short rations."

"Well, Jim Conklin says we'll get a plenty of fighting this time."

"He's right for once, I guess, though I can't see how it come. This time we're in for a big battle, and we've got the best end of it, certain sure. Gee rod![10] how we will thump 'em!"

He arose and began to pace to and fro excitedly. The thrill of this enthusiasm made him walk with an elastic step. He was sprightly, vigorous, fiery in his belief in success. He looked into the future with clear, proud eye, and he swore with the air of an old soldier.

9. Here "the loud soldier" is first called by name.
10. Readers are assured that many soldiers probably "swore like troopers"; but prevailing taste decreed euphemisms for profanity.

The youth watched him for a moment in silence. When he finally spoke his voice was as bitter as dregs. "Oh, you're going to do great things, I s'pose!"

The loud soldier blew a thoughtful cloud of smoke from his pipe. "Oh, I don't know," he remarked with dignity; "I don't know. I s'pose I'll do as well as the rest. I'm going to try like thunder." He evidently complimented himself upon the modesty of this statement.

"How do you know you won't run when the time comes?" asked the youth.

"Run?" said the loud one; "run?—of course not!" He laughed.

"Well," continued the youth, "lots of good-a-'nough men have thought they was going to do great things before the fight, but when the time come they skedaddled."

"Oh, that's all true, I s'pose," replied the other; "but I'm not going to skedaddle. The man that bets on my running will lose his money, that's all." He nodded confidently.

"Oh, shucks!" said the youth. "You ain't the bravest man in the world, are you?"

"No, I ain't," exclaimed the loud soldier indignantly; "and I didn't say I was the bravest man in the world, either. I said I was going to do my share of fighting—that's what I said. And I am, too. Who are you, anyhow? You talk as if you thought you was Napoleon Bonaparte." He glared at the youth for a moment, and then strode away.

The youth called in a savage voice after his comrade: "Well, you needn't git mad about it!" But the other continued on his way and made no reply.

He felt alone in space when his injured comrade had disappeared. His failure to discover any mite of resemblance in their viewpoints made him more miserable than before. No one seemed to be wrestling with such a terrific personal problem. He was a mental outcast.

He went slowly to his tent and stretched himself on a blanket by the side of the snoring tall soldier. In the darkness he saw visions of a thousand-tongued fear that would babble at his back and cause him to flee, while others were going coolly about their country's business. He admitted that he would not be able to cope with this monster. He felt that every nerve in his body would be an ear to hear the voices, while other men would remain stolid and deaf.

And as he sweated with the pain of these thoughts, he could hear low, serene sentences. "I'll bid five." "Make it six." "Seven." "Seven goes."

He stared at the red, shivering reflection of a fire on the white wall of his tent until, exhausted and ill from the monotony of his suffering, he fell asleep.

Chapter III

When another night came the columns, changed to purple streaks, filed across two pontoon bridges.[1] A glaring fire wine-tinted the waters of the river. Its rays, shining upon the moving masses of troops, brought forth here and there sudden gleams of silver or gold. Upon the other shore a dark and mysterious range of hills was curved against the sky. The insect voices of the night sang solemnly.

After this crossing the youth assured himself that at any moment they might be suddenly and fearfully assaulted from the caves of the lowering woods. He kept his eyes watchfully upon the darkness.

But his regiment went unmolested to a camping place, and its soldiers slept the brave sleep of wearied men. In the morning they were routed out with early energy, and hustled along a narrow road that led deep into the forest.

It was during this rapid march that the regiment lost many of the marks of a new command.

The men had begun to count the miles upon their fingers, and they grew tired. "Sore feet an' damned short rations, that's all," said the loud soldier. There was[2] perspiration and grumblings. After a time they began to shed their knapsacks. Some tossed them unconcernedly down; others hid them carefully, asserting their plans to return for them at some convenient time. Men extricated themselves from thick shirts. Presently few carried anything but their necessary clothing, blankets, haversacks, canteens, and arms and ammunition. "You can now eat and shoot," said the tall soldier to the youth. "That's all you want to do."

There was sudden change from the ponderous infantry of theory to the light and speedy infantry of practice. The regiment, relieved of a burden, received a new impetus. But there was much loss of valuable knapsacks, and, on the whole, very good shirts.

But the regiment was not yet veteranlike in appearance. Veteran regiments in the army were likely to be very small aggregations of men. Once, when the command had first come to the field, some perambulating veterans, noting the length of their column, had accosted them thus: "Hey, fellers, what brigade is that?" And when the men had replied that they formed a regiment and not a brigade,[3]

---

1. General Burnside's army, camped on the east bank of the Rappahannock opposite the Confederate army of Lee and Jackson, slipped down the river beyond the Southerners, and crossed by night on temporary bridges in order to attack.
2. So printed in 1895.
3. A brigade comprises two or more regiments.

the older soldiers had laughed, and said, "O Gawd!"

Also, there was too great a similarity in the hats. The hats of a regiment should properly represent the history of headgear for a period of years. And, moreover, there were no letters of faded gold speaking from the colors. They were new and beautiful, and the color bearer habitually oiled the pole.

Presently the army again sat down to think. The odor of the peaceful pines was in the men's nostrils. The sound of monotonous axe blows rang through the forest, and the insects, nodding upon their perches, crooned like old women. The youth returned to his theory of a blue demonstration.

One gray dawn, however, he was kicked in the leg by the tall soldier, and then, before he was entirely awake, he found himself running down a wood road in the midst of men who were panting from the first effects of speed. His canteen banged rhythmically upon his thigh, and his haversack bobbed softly. His musket bounced a trifle from his shoulder at each stride and made his cap feel uncertain upon his head.

He could hear the men whisper jerky sentences: "Say—what's all this—about?" "What th' thunder—we—skedaddlin' this way fer?" "Billie—keep off m' feet. Yeh run—like a cow." And the loud soldier's shrill voice could be heard: "What th' devil they in sich a hurry for?"

The youth thought the damp fog of early morning moved from the rush of a great body of troops. From the distance came a sudden spatter of firing.

He was bewildered. As he ran with his comrades he strenuously tried to think, but all he knew was that if he fell down those coming behind would tread upon him. All his faculties seemed to be needed to guide him over and past obstructions. He felt carried along by a mob.

The sun spread disclosing rays, and, one by one, regiments burst into view like armed men just born of the earth. The youth perceived that the time had come. He was about to be measured. For a moment he felt in the face of his great trial like a babe, and the flesh over his heart seemed very thin. He seized time to look about him calculatingly.

But he instantly saw that it would be impossible for him to escape from the regiment. It inclosed him. And there were iron laws of tradition and law on four sides. He was in a moving box.

As he perceived this fact it occurred to him that he had never wished to come to the war. He had not enlisted of his free will. He had been dragged by the merciless government. And now they were taking him out to be slaughtered.

The regiment slid down a bank and wallowed across a little stream. The mournful current moved slowly on, and from the water, shaded black, some white bubble eyes[4] looked at the men.

As they climbed the hill on the farther side artillery began to boom. Here the youth forgot many things as he felt a sudden impulse of curiosity. He scrambled up the bank with a speed that could not be exceeded by a bloodthirsty man.

He expected a battle scene.

There were some little fields girted and squeezed by a forest. Spread over the grass and in among the tree trunks, he could see knots and waving lines of skirmishers who were running hither and thither and firing at the landscape. A dark battle line lay upon a sunstruck clearing that gleamed orange color. A flag fluttered.

Other regiments floundered up the bank. The brigade was formed in line of battle, and after a pause started slowly through the woods in the rear of the receding skirmishers, who were continually melting into the scene to appear again farther on. They were always busy as bees, deeply absorbed in their little combats.

The youth tried to observe everything. He did not use care to avoid trees and branches, and his forgotten feet were constantly knocking against stones or getting entangled in briers. He was aware that these battalions with their commotions were woven red and startling into the gentle fabric of softened greens and browns. It looked to be a wrong place for a battle field.

The skirmishers in advance fascinated him. Their shots into thickets and at distant and prominent trees spoke to him of tragedies —hidden, mysterious, solemn.

Once the line encountered the body of a dead soldier. He lay upon his back staring at the sky. He was dressed in an awkward suit of yellowish brown. The youth could see that the soles of his shoes had been worn to the thinness of writing paper, and from a great rent in one the dead foot projected piteously. And it was as if fate had betrayed the soldier. In death it exposed to his enemies that poverty which in life he had perhaps concealed from his friends.

The ranks opened covertly to avoid the corpse. The invulnerable dead man forced a way for himself. The youth looked keenly at the ashen face. The wind raised the tawny beard. It moved as if a hand were stroking it. He vaguely desired to walk around and around the body and stare; the impulse of the living to try to read in dead eyes the answer to the Question.[5]

During the march the ardor which the youth had acquired when out of view of the field rapidly faded to nothing. His curiosity was

---

4. *Cf.* above, "the red eyes" of the enemy.

5. Crane's symbolic images of the dead soldier have won praise—here for the cumulative impact of "poverty," "invulnerability," and the final "Question."

quite easily satisfied. If an intense scene had caught him with its wild swing as he came to the top of the bank, he might have gone roaring on. This advance upon Nature was too calm. He had opportunity to reflect. He had time in which to wonder about himself and to attempt to probe his sensations.

Absurd ideas took hold upon him. He thought that he did not relish the landscape. It threatened him. A coldness swept over his back, and it is true that his trousers felt to him that they were no fit for his legs at all.

A house standing placidly in distant fields had to him an ominous look. The shadows of the woods were formidable. He was certain that in this vista there lurked fierce-eyed hosts. The swift thought came to him that the generals did not know what they were about. It was all a trap. Suddenly those close forests would bristle with rifle barrels. Ironlike brigades would appear in the rear. They were all going to be sacrificed. The generals were stupids. The enemy would presently swallow the whole command. He glared about him, expecting to see the stealthy approach of his death.

He thought that he must break from the ranks and harangue his comrades. They must not all be killed like pigs; and he was sure it would come to pass unless they were informed of these dangers. The generals were idiots to send them marching into a regular pen. There was but one pair of eyes in the corps. He would step forth and make a speech. Shrill and passionate words came to his lips.

The line, broken into moving fragments by the ground, went calmly on through fields and woods. The youth looked at the men nearest him, and saw, for the most part, expressions of deep interest, as if they were investigating something that had fascinated them. One or two stepped with overvaliant airs as if they were already plunged into war. Others walked as upon thin ice. The greater part of the untested men appeared quiet and absorbed. They were going to look at war, the red animal—war, the blood-swollen god. And they were deeply engrossed in this march.

As he looked the youth gripped his outcry at his throat. He saw that even if the men were tottering with fear they would laugh at his warning. They would jeer him, and, if practicable, pelt him with missiles. Admitting that he might be wrong, a frenzied declamation of the kind would turn him into a worm.

He assumed, then, the demeanor of one who knows that he is doomed alone to unwritten responsibilities. He lagged, with tragic glances at the sky.

He was surprised presently by the young lieutenant of his company, who began heartily to beat him with a sword, calling out in a loud and insolent voice: "Come, young man, get up into ranks there. No skulking 'll do here." He mended his pace with suitable haste. And he hated the lieutenant, who had no appreciation of fine minds. He was a mere brute.

After a time the brigade was halted in the cathedral light of a forest. The busy skirmishers were still popping. Through the aisles of the wood could be seen the floating smoke from their rifles. Sometimes it went up in little balls, white and compact.

During this halt many men in the regiment began erecting tiny hills in front of them. They used stones, sticks, earth, and anything they thought might turn a bullet. Some built comparatively large ones, while others seemed content with little ones.

This procedure caused a discussion among the men. Some wished to fight like duelists, believing it to be correct to stand erect and be, from their feet to their foreheads, a mark. They said they scorned the devices of the cautious. But the others scoffed in reply, and pointed to the veterans on the flanks who were digging at the ground like terriers. In a short time there was quite a barricade along the regimental fronts. Directly, however, they were ordered to withdraw from that place.

This astounded the youth. He forgot his stewing over the advance movement. "Well, then, what did they march us out here for?" he demanded of the tall soldier. The latter with calm faith began a heavy explanation, although he had been compelled to leave a little protection of stones and dirt to which he had devoted much care and skill.

When the regiment was aligned in another position each man's regard for his safety caused another line of small intrenchments. They ate their noon meal behind a third one. They were moved from this one also. They were marched from place to place with apparent aimlessness.

The youth had been taught that a man became another thing in a battle. He saw his salvation in such a change. Hence this waiting was an ordeal to him. He was in a fever of impatience. He considered that there was denoted a lack of purpose on the part of the generals. He began to complain to the tall soldier. "I can't stand this much longer," he cried. "I don't see what good it does to make us wear out our legs for nothin'." He wished to return to camp, knowing that this affair was a blue demonstration; or else to go into battle and discover that he had been a fool in his doubts, and was, in truth, a man of traditional courage. The strain of present circumstances he felt to be intolerable.

The philosophical tall soldier measured a sandwich of cracker[6]

6. Hardtack, a large hard biscuit.

and pork and swallowed it in a nonchalant manner. "Oh, I suppose we must go reconnoitering around the country jest to keep 'em from getting too close, or to develop 'em, or something."

"Huh!" said the loud soldier.

"Well," cried the youth, still fidgeting, "I'd rather do anything most than go tramping 'round the country all day doing no good to nobody and jest tiring ourselves out."

"So would I," said the loud soldier. "It ain't right. I tell you if anybody with any sense was a-runnin' this army it——"

"Oh, shut up!" roared the tall private. "You little fool. You little damn' cuss. You ain't had that there coat and them pants on for six months, and yet you talk as if——"

"Well, I wanta do some fighting anyway," interrupted the other. "I didn't come here to walk. I could 'ave walked to home—'round an' 'round the barn, if I jest wanted to walk."

The tall one, red-faced, swallowed another sandwich as if taking poison in despair.

But gradually, as he chewed, his face became again quiet and contented. He could not rage in fierce argument in the presence of such sandwiches. During his meals he always wore an air of blissful contemplation of the food he had swallowed. His spirit seemed then to be communing with the viands.

He accepted new environment and circumstance with great coolness, eating from his haversack at every opportunity. On the march he went along with the stride of a hunter, objecting to neither gait nor distance. And he had not raised his voice when he had been ordered away from three little protective piles of earth and stone, each of which had been an engineering feat worthy of being made sacred to the name of his grandmother.

In the afternoon the regiment went out over the same ground it had taken in the morning. The landscape then ceased to threaten the youth. He had been close to it and become familiar with it. When, however, they began to pass into a new region, his old fears of stupidity and incompetence reassailed him, but this time he doggedly let them babble. He was occupied with his problem, and in his desperation he concluded that the stupidity did not greatly matter.

Once he thought he had concluded that it would be better to get killed directly and end his troubles. Regarding death thus out of the corner of his eye, he conceived it to be nothing but rest, and he was filled with a momentary astonishment that he should have made an extraordinary commotion over the mere matter of getting killed. He would die; he would go to some place where he would be understood. It was useless to expect appreciation of his profound and fine senses from such men as the lieutenant. He must look to the grave for comprehension.

The skirmish fire increased to a long clattering sound. With it was mingled far-away cheering. A battery spoke.

Directly the youth would see the skirmishers running. They were pursued by the sound of musketry fire. After a time the hot, dangerous flashes of the rifles were visible. Smoke clouds went slowly and insolently across the fields like observant phantoms. The din became crescendo, like the roar of an oncoming train.

A brigade ahead of them and on the right went into action with a rending roar. It was as if it had exploded. And thereafter it lay stretched in the distance behind a long gray wall, that one was obliged to look twice at to make sure that it was smoke.

The youth, forgetting his neat plan of getting killed, gazed spellbound. His eyes grew wide and busy with the action of the scene. His mouth was a little ways open.

Of a sudden he felt a heavy and sad hand laid upon his shoulder. Awakening from his trance of observation he turned and beheld the loud soldier.

"It's my first and last battle, old boy," said the latter, with intense gloom. He was quite pale and his girlish lip was trembling.

"Eh?" murmured the youth in great astonishment.

"It's my first and last battle, old boy," continued the loud soldier. "Something tells me——"

"What?"

"I'm a gone coon this first time and—and I w-want you to take these here things—to—my—folks." He ended in a quavering sob of pity for himself. He handed the youth a little packet done up in a yellow envelope.

"Why, what the devil——" began the youth again.

But the other gave him a glance as from the depths of a tomb, and raised his limp hand in a prophetic manner and turned away.

Chapter IV

The brigade was halted in the fringe of a grove. The men crouched among the trees and pointed their restless guns out at the fields. They tried to look beyond the smoke.

Out of this haze they could see running men. Some shouted information and gestured as they hurried.

The men of the new regiment watched and listened eagerly, while their tongues ran on in gossip of the battle. They mouthed rumors that had flown like birds out of the unknown.

"They say Perry has been driven in with big loss."

"Yes, Carrott went t' th' hospital. He said he was sick. That smart lieutenant is commanding 'G' Company. Th' boys say they won't be under Carrott no more if they all have t' desert. They allus knew he was a——"

"Hannises' batt'ry is took."

"It ain't either. I saw Hannises' batt'ry off on th' left not more'n fifteen minutes ago."

"Well——"

"Th' general, he ses he is goin' t' take th' hull command of th' 304th when we go inteh action, an' then he ses we'll do sech fightin' as never another one reg'ment done."

"They say we're catchin' it over on th' left. They say th' enemy driv' our line inteh a devil of a swamp an' took Hannises' batt'ry."

"No sech thing. Hannises' batt'ry was 'long here 'bout a minute ago."

"That young Hasbrouck, he makes a good off'cer. He ain't afraid 'a nothin'."

"I met one of th' 148th Maine boys an' he ses his brigade fit th' hull rebel army fer four hours over on th' turnpike road an' killed about five thousand of 'em. He ses one more sech fight as that an' th' war 'll be over."

"Bill wasn't scared either. No, sir! It wasn't that. Bill ain't a-gittin' scared easy. He was jest mad, that's what he was. When that feller trod on his hand, he up an' sed that he was willin' t' give his hand t' his country, but he be dumbed if he was goin' t' have every dumb bushwhacker[7] in th' kentry walkin' 'round on it. Se he went t' th' hospital disregardless of th' fight. Three fingers was crunched. Th' dern doctor wanted t' amputate 'm, an' Bill, he raised a heluva row, I hear. He's a funny feller."

The din in front swelled to a tremendous chorus. The youth and his fellows were frozen to silence. They could see a flag that tossed in the smoke angrily. Near it were the blurred and agitated forms of troops. There came a turbulent stream of men across the fields. A battery changing position at a frantic gallop scattered the stragglers right and left.

A shell screaming like a storm banshee[8] went over the huddled heads of the reserves. It landed in the grove, and exploding redly flung the brown earth. There was a little shower of pine needles.

Bullets began to whistle among the branches and nip at the trees. Twigs and leaves came sailing down. It was as if a thousand axes, wee and invisible, were being wielded. Many of the men were constantly dodging and ducking their heads.

---

7. A guerrilla.

8. Gaelic folklore: a female spirit, warning of an approaching death.

The lieutenant of the youth's company was shot in the hand. He began to swear so wondrously that a nervous laugh went along the regimental line. The officer's profanity sounded conventional. It relieved the tightened senses of the new men. It was if he had hit his fingers with a tack hammer at home.

He held the wounded member carefully away from his side so that the blood would not drip upon his trousers.

The captain of the company, tucking his sword under his arm, produced a handkerchief and began to bind with it the lieutenant's wound. And they disputed as to how the binding should be done.

The battle flag in the distance jerked about madly. It seemed to be struggling to free itself from an agony. The billowing smoke was filled with horizontal flashes.

Men running swiftly emerged from it. They grew in numbers until it was seen that the whole command was fleeing. The flag suddenly sank down as if dying. Its motion as it fell was a gesture of despair.[9]

Wild yells came from behind the walls of smoke. A sketch in gray and red dissolved into a moblike body of men who galloped like wild horses.

The veteran regiments on the right and left of the 304th immediately began to jeer. With the passionate song of the bullets and the banshee shrieks of shells were mingled loud catcalls and bits of facetious advice concerning places of safety.

But the new regiment was breathless with horror. "Gawd! Saunders's got crushed!" whispered the man at the youth's elbow. They shrank back and crouched as if compelled to await a flood.

The youth shot a swift glance along the blue ranks of the regiment. The profiles were motionless, carven; and afterward he remembered that the color sergeant was standing with his legs apart, as if he expected to be pushed to the ground.

The following throng went whirling around the flank. Here and there were officers carried along on the stream like exasperated chips. They were striking about them with their swords and with their left fists, punching every head they could reach. They cursed like highwaymen.

A mounted officer displayed the furious anger of a spoiled child. He raged with his head, his arms, and his legs.

Another, the commander of the brigade, was galloping about bawling. His hat was gone and his clothes were awry. He resembled a man who has come from bed to go to a fire. The hoofs of his horse often threatened the heads of the running men, but

9. The bold personification of the inanimate flag is characteristic Crane imagery.

they scampered with singular fortune. In this rush they were apparently all deaf and blind. They heeded not the largest and longest of the oaths that were thrown at them from all directions.

Frequently over this tumult could be heard the grim jokes of the critical veterans; but the retreating men apparently were not even conscious of the presence of an audience.

The battle reflection that shone for an instant in the faces on the mad current made the youth feel that forceful hands from heaven would not have been able to have held him in place if he could have got intelligent control of his legs.

There was an appalling imprint upon these faces. The struggle in the smoke had pictured an exaggeration of itself on the bleached cheeks and in the eyes wild with one desire.

The sight of this stampede exerted a floodlike force that seemed able to drag sticks and stones and men from the ground. They of the reserves had to hold on. They grew pale and firm, and red and quaking.

The youth achieved one little thought in the midst of this chaos. The composite monster which had caused the other troops to flee had not then appeared. He resolved to get a view of it, and then, he thought he might very likely run better than the best of them.

Chapter V

There were moments of waiting. The youth thought of the village street at home before the arrival of the circus parade on a day in the spring. He remembered how he had stood, a small, thrillful boy, prepared to follow the dingy lady upon the white horse, or the band in its faded chariot. He saw the yellow road, the lines of expectant people, and the sober houses. He particularly remembered an old fellow who used to sit upon a cracker box in front of the store and feign to despise such exhibitions. A thousand details of color and form surged in his mind. The old fellow upon the cracker box appeared in middle prominence.

Some one cried, "Here they come!"

There was rustling and muttering among the men. They displayed a feverish desire to have every possible cartridge ready to their hands. The boxes were pulled around into various positions, and adjusted with great care. It was as if seven hundred new bonnets were being tried on.

The tall soldier, having prepared his rifle, produced a red handkerchief of some kind. He was engaged in knitting it about his throat with exquisite attention to its position, when the cry was repeated up and down the line in a muffled roar of sound.

"Here they come! Here they come!" Gun locks clicked.

Across the smoke-infested fields came a brown swarm of running men who were giving shrill yells. They came on, stooping and swinging their rifles at all angles. A flag, tilted forward, sped near the front.

As he caught sight of them the youth was momentarily startled by a thought that perhaps his gun was not loaded. He stood trying to rally his faltering intellect so that he might recollect the moment when he had loaded, but he could not.

A hatless general pulled his dripping horse to a stand near the colonel of the 304th. He shook his fist in the other's face. "You've got to hold 'em back!" he shouted, savagely; "you've got to hold 'em back!"

In his agitation the colonel began to stammer. "A-all r-right, General, all right, by Gawd! We-we'll do our—we-we'll d-d-do—do our best, General." The general made a passionate gesture and galloped away. The colonel, perchance to relieve his feelings, began to scold like a wet parrot. The youth, turning swiftly to make sure that the rear was unmolested, saw the commander regarding his men in a highly resentful manner, as if he regretted above everything his association with them.

The man at the youth's elbow was mumbling, as if to himself: "Oh, we're in for it now! oh, we're in for it now!"

The captain of the company had been pacing excitedly to and fro in the rear. He coaxed in schoolmistress fashion, as to a congregation of boys with primers. His talk was an endless repetition. "Reserve your fire, boys—don't shoot till I tell you—save your fire—wait till they get close up—don't be damned fools——"

Perspiration streamed down the youth's face, which was soiled like that of a weeping urchin. He frequently, with a nervous movement, wiped his eyes with his coat sleeve. His mouth was still a little ways open.

He got the one glance at the foe-swarming field in front of him, and instantly ceased to debate the question of his piece being loaded. Before he was ready to begin—before he had announced to himself that he was about to fight—he threw the obedient, well-balanced rifle into position and fired a first wild shot. Directly he was working at his weapon like an automatic affair.

He suddenly lost concern for himself, and forgot to look at a menacing fate. He became not a man but a member. He felt that something of which he was a part—a regiment, an army, a cause, or a country—was in a crisis. He was welded into a common personality which was dominated by a single desire. For some moments he could not flee no more than a little finger can commit a revolution from a hand.[10]

If he had thought the regiment was about to be annihilated perhaps he could have amputated himself from it. But its noise gave him assurance. The regiment was like a firework that, once ignited, proceeds superior to circumstances until its blazing vitality fades. It wheezed and banged with a mighty power. He pictured the ground before it as strewn with the discomfited.

There was a consciousness always of the presence of his comrades about him. He felt the subtle battle brotherhood more potent even than the cause for which they were fighting. It was a mysterious fraternity born of the smoke and danger of death.

He was at a task. He was like a carpenter who has made many boxes, making still another box, only there was furious haste in his movements. He, in his thought, was careering off in other places, even as the carpenter who as he works whistles and thinks of his friend or his enemy, his home or a saloon. And these jolted dreams were never perfect to him afterward, but remained a mass of blurred shapes.

Presently he began to feel the effects of the war atmosphere—a blistering sweat, a sensation that his eyeballs were about to crack like hot stones. A burning roar filled his ears.

Following this came a red rage. He developed the acute exasperation of a pestered animal, a well-meaning cow worried by dogs. He had a mad feeling against his rifle, which could only be used against one life at a time. He wished to rush forward and strangle with his fingers. He craved a power that would enable him to make a world-sweeping gesture and brush all back. His impotency appeared to him, and made his rage into that of a driven beast.

Buried in the smoke of many rifles his anger was directed not so much against the men whom[11] he knew were rushing toward him as against the swirling battle phantoms which were choking him, stuffing their smoke robes down his parched throat. He fought frantically for respite for his senses, for air, as a babe being smothered attacks the deadly blankets.

There was a blare of heated rage mingled with a certain expression of intentness on all faces. Many of the men were making low-toned noises with their mouths, and these subdued cheers, snarls, imprecations, prayers, made a wild, barbaric song that went as an undercurrent of sound, strange and chantlike with the resounding chords of the war march. The man at the youth's elbow was babbling. In it there was something soft and tender like the mono-

10. Conrad (*q.v.*) called this a primary motivation in this novel.   11. So printed in 1895.

logue of a babe. The tall soldier was swearing in a loud voice. From his lips came a black procession of curious oaths. Of a sudden another broke out in a querulous way like a man who has mislaid his hat. "Well, why don't they support us? Why don't they send supports? Do they think——"

The youth in his battle sleep heard this as one who dozes hears.

There was a singular absence of heroic poses. The men bending and surging in their haste and rage were in every impossible attitude. The steel ramrods clanked and clanged with incessant din as the men pounded them furiously into the hot rifle barrels. The flaps of the cartridge boxes were all unfastened, and bobbed idiotically with each movement. The rifles, once loaded, were jerked to the shoulder and fired without apparent aim into the smoke or at one of the blurred and shifting forms which upon the field before the regiment had been growing larger and larger like puppets under a magician's hand.

The officers, at their intervals, rearward, neglected to stand in picturesque attitudes. They were bobbing to and fro roaring directions and encouragements. The dimensions of their howls were extraordinary. They expended their lungs with prodigal wills. And often they nearly stood upon their heads in their anxiety to observe the enemy on the other side of the tumbling smoke.

The lieutenant of the youth's company had encountered a soldier who had fled screaming at the first volley of his comrades. Behind the lines these two were acting a little isolated scene. The man was blubbering and staring with sheeplike eyes at the lieutenant, who had seized him by the collar and was pommeling him. He drove him back into the ranks with many blows. The soldier went mechanically, dully, with his animal-like eyes upon the officer. Perhaps there was to him a divinity expressed in the voice of the other—stern, hard, with no reflection of fear in it. He tried to reload his gun, but his shaking hands prevented. The lieutenant was obliged to assist him.

The men dropped here and there like bundles. The captain of the youth's company had been killed in an early part of the action. His body lay stretched out in the position of a tired man resting, but upon his face there was an astonished and sorrowful look, as if he thought some friend had done him an ill turn. The babbling man was grazed by a shot that made the blood stream widely down his face. He clapped both hands to his head. "Oh!" he said, and ran. Another grunted suddenly as if he had been struck by a club in the stomach. He sat down and gazed ruefully. In his eyes there was mute, indefinite reproach. Farther up the line a man, standing behind a tree, had had his knee joint splintered by a ball.

Immediately he had dropped his rifle and gripped the tree with both arms. And there he remained, clinging desperately and crying for assistance that he might withdraw his hold upon the tree.

At last an exultant yell went along the quivering line. The firing dwindled from an uproar to a last vindictive popping. As the smoke slowly eddied away, the youth saw that the charge had been repulsed. The enemy were scattered into reluctant groups. He saw a man climb to the top of the fence, straddle the rail, and fire a parting shot. The waves had receded, leaving bits of dark *débris* upon the ground.

Some in the regiment began to whoop frenziedly. Many were silent. Apparently they were trying to contemplate themselves.

After the fever had left his veins, the youth thought that at last he was going to suffocate. He became aware of the foul atmosphere in which he had been struggling. He was grimy and dripping like a laborer in a foundry. He grasped his canteen and took a long swallow of the warmed water.

A sentence with variations went up and down the line. "Well, we've helt 'em back. We've helt 'em back; derned if we haven't." The men said it blissfully, leering at each other with dirty smiles.

The youth turned to look behind him and off to the right and off to the left. He experienced the joy of a man who at last finds leisure in which to look about him.

Under foot there were a few ghastly forms motionless. They lay twisted in fantastic contortions. Arms were bent and heads were turned in incredible ways. It seemed that the dead men must have fallen from some great height to get into such positions. They looked to be dumped out upon the ground from the sky.

From a position in the rear of the grove a battery was throwing shells over it. The flash of the guns startled the youth at first. He thought they were aimed directly at him. Through the trees he watched the black figures of the gunners as they worked swiftly and intently. Their labor seemed a complicated thing. He wondered how they could remember its formula in the midst of confusion.

The guns squatted in a row like savage chiefs. They argued with abrupt violence. It was a grim pow-wow.[1] Their busy servants ran hither and thither.

A small procession of wounded men were going drearily toward the rear. It was a flow of blood from the torn body of the brigade.

To the right and to left were the dark lines of other troops. Far in front he thought he could see lighter masses protruding in

---

1. This personification of cannon, noted by critics, also imitates cannonading in the sound of "pow-wow," a noisy conference.

points from the forest. They were suggestive of unnumbered thousands.

Once he saw a tiny battery go dashing along the line of the horizon. The tiny riders were beating the tiny horses.

From a sloping hill came the sound of cheerings and clashes. Smoke welled slowly through the leaves.

Batteries were speaking with thunderous oratorical effort. Here and there were flags, the red in the stripes dominating. They splashed bits of warm color upon the dark lines of troops.

The youth felt the old thrill at the sight of the emblem. They were like beautiful birds strangely undaunted in a storm.

As he listened to the din from the hillside, to a deep pulsating thunder that came from afar to the left, and to the lesser clamors which came from many directions, it occurred to him that they were fighting, too, over there, and over there, and over there. Heretofore he had supposed that all the battle was directly under his nose.

As he gazed around him the youth felt a flash of astonishment at the blue, pure sky and the sun gleamings on the trees and fields. It was surprising that Nature had gone tranquilly on with her golden process in the midst of so much devilment.[2]

Chapter VI

The youth awakened slowly. He came gradually back to a position from which he could regard himself. For moments he had been scrutinizing his person in a dazed way as if he had never before seen himself. Then he picked up his cap from the ground. He wriggled in his jacket to make a more comfortable fit, and kneeling relaced his shoe. He thoughtfully mopped his reeking features.

So it was all over at last! The supreme trial had been passed. The red, formidable difficulties of war had been vanquished.

He went into an ecstasy of self-satisfaction. He had the most delightful sensations of his life. Standing as if apart from himself, he viewed that last scene. He perceived that the man who had fought thus was magnificent.

He felt that he was a fine fellow. He saw himself even with those ideals which he had considered as far beyond him. He smiled in deep gratification.

Upon his fellows he beamed tenderness and good will. "Gee! ain't it hot, hey?" he said affably to a man who was polishing his

2. *Cf.* Whitman's "Look Down Fair Moon." Four of the twenty-four chapters of this novel (V, IX, XVII, and XXIV), each ending on a note of emotional tension, are climaxed by an unusual or portentous image referring to the appearance of the sun and sky.

streaming face with his coat sleeves.

"You bet!" said the other, grinning sociably. "I never seen sech dumb hotness." He sprawled out luxuriously on the ground. "Gee, yes! An' I hope we don't have no more fightin' till a week from Monday."

There were some handshakings and deep speeches with men whose features were familiar, but with whom the youth now felt the bonds of tied hearts. He helped a cursing comrade to bind up a wound of the shin.

But, of a sudden, cries of amazement broke out along the ranks of the new regiment. "Here they come ag'in! Here they come ag'in!" The man who had sprawled upon the ground started up and said, "Gosh!"

The youth turned quick eyes upon the field. He discerned forms begin to swell in masses out of a distant wood. He again saw the tilted flag speeding forward.

The shells, which had ceased to trouble the regiment for a time, came swirling again, and exploded in the grass or among the leaves of the trees. They looked to be strange war flowers bursting into fierce bloom.[3]

The men groaned. The luster faded from their eyes. Their smudged countenances now expressed a profound dejection. They moved their stiffened bodies slowly, and watched in sullen mood the frantic approach of the enemy. The slaves toiling in the temple of this god began to feel rebellion at his harsh tasks.

They fretted and complained each to each. "Oh, say, this is too much of a good thing! Why can't somebody send us supports?"

"We ain't never goin' to stand this second banging. I didn't come here to fight the hull damn' rebel army."

There was one who raised a doleful cry. "I wish Bill Smithers had trod on my hand, insteader me treddin' on his'n."[4] The sore joints of the regiment creaked as it painfully floundered into position to repulse.

The youth stared. Surely, he thought, this impossible thing was not about to happen. He waited as if he expected the enemy to suddenly stop, apologize, and retire bowing. It was all a mistake.

But the firing began somewhere on the regimental line and ripped along in both directions. The level sheets of flame developed great clouds of smoke that tumbled and tossed in the mild wind near the ground for a moment, and then rolled through the ranks as through a gate. The clouds were tinged an earthlike yellow in the sunrays and in the shadow were a sorry blue. The flag was

3. Again the ironic ascription of animate characteristics to engines of war. 4. Crane's purpose is in part sustained by the reiteration of a trivial incident, the recurrence of a familiar action, remark, or gesture.

sometimes eaten and lost in this mass of vapor, but more often it projected, sun-touched, resplendent.

Into the youth's eyes there came a look that one can see in the orbs of a jaded horse. His neck was quivering with nervous weakness and the muscles of his arms felt numb and bloodless. His hands, too, seemed large and awkward as if he was wearing invisible mittens. And there was a great uncertainty about his knee joints.

The words that comrades had uttered previous to the firing began to recur to him. "Oh, say, this is too much of a good thing! What do they take us for—why don't they send supports? I didn't come here to fight the hull damned rebel army."

He began to exaggerate the endurance, the skill, and the valor of those who were coming. Himself reeling from exhaustion, he was astonished beyond measure at such persistency. They must be machines of steel. It was very gloomy struggling against such affairs, wound up perhaps to fight until sundown.[5]

He slowly lifted his rifle and catching a glimpse of the thick-spread field he blazed at a cantering cluster. He stopped then and began to peer as best he could through the smoke. He caught changing views of the ground covered with men who were all running like pursued imps, and yelling.

To the youth it was an onslaught of redoubtable dragons. He became like the man who lost his legs at the approach of the red and green monster. He waited in a sort of a horrified, listening attitude. He seemed to shut his eyes and wait to be gobbled.

A man near him who up to this time had been working feverishly at his rifle suddenly stopped and ran with howls. A lad whose face had borne an expression of exalted courage, the majesty of him[6] who dares give his life, was, at an instant, smitten abject. He blanched like one who has come to the edge of a cliff at midnight and is suddenly made aware. There was a revelation. He, too, threw down his gun and fled. There was no shame in his face. He ran like a rabbit.

Others began to scamper away through the smoke. The youth turned his head, shaken from his trance by this movement as if the regiment was leaving him behind. He saw the few fleeting forms.

He yelled then with fright and swung about. For a moment, in the great clamor, he was like a proverbial chicken. He lost the direction of safety. Destruction threatened him from all points.

5. Depersonalized men, "machines of steel wound up," contrast with figures of animated machines—shells bursting like blooming war-flowers (page above) and guns squatted like savage chiefs in pow-wow (Chap. V).

6. Printed "he" in 1895.

Directly he began to speed toward the rear in great leaps. His rifle and cap were gone. His unbuttoned coat bulged in the wind. The flap of his cartridge box bobbed wildly, and his canteen, by its slender cord, swung out behind. On his face was all the horror of those things which he imagined.

The lieutenant sprang forward bawling. The youth saw his features wrathfully red, and saw him make a dab with his sword. His one thought of the incident was that the lieutenant was a peculiar creature to feel interested in such matters upon this occasion.

He ran like a blind man. Two or three times he fell down. Once he knocked his shoulder so heavily against a tree that he went headlong.

Since he had turned his back upon the fight his fears had been wondrously magnified. Death about to thrust him between the shoulder blades was far more dreadful than death about to smite him between the eyes. When he thought of it later, he conceived the impression that it is better to view the appalling than to be merely within hearing. The noises of the battle were like stones; he believed himself liable to be crushed.

As he ran on he mingled with others. He dimly saw men on his right and on his left, and he heard footsteps behind him. He thought that all the regiment was fleeing, pursued by these ominous crashes.

In his flight the sound of these following footsteps gave him his one meager relief. He felt vaguely that death must make a first choice of the men who were nearest; the initial morsels for the dragons would be then those who were following him. So he displayed the zeal of an insane sprinter in his purpose to keep them in the rear. There was a race.[7]

As he, leading, went across a little field, he found himself in a region of shells. They hurtled over his head with long wild screams. As he listened he imagined them to have rows of cruel teeth that grinned at him. Once one lit before him and the livid lightning of the explosion effectually barred the way in his chosen direction. He groveled on the ground and then springing up went careering off through some bushes.

He experienced a thrill of amazement when he came within view of a battery in action. The men there seemed to be in conventional moods, altogether unaware of the impending annihilation. The battery was disputing with a distant antagonist and

7. From this point through Chapter IX, a sequence of integrated episodes unifies the action, as Henry's craven desertion of his comrades in battle merges with successive revelations of death. This sequence merges, in turn, with another cycle, Chapters X–XII.

the gunners were wrapped in admiration of their shooting. They were continually bending in coaxing postures over the guns. They seemed to be patting them on the back and encouraging them with words. The guns, stolid and undaunted, spoke with dogged valor.

The precise gunners were coolly enthusiastic. They lifted their eyes every chance to the smoke-wreathed hillock from whence the hostile battery addressed them. The youth pitied them as he ran. Methodical idiots! Machine-like fools! The refined joy of planting shells in the midst of the other battery's formation would appear a little thing when the infantry came swooping out of the woods.

The face of a youthful rider, who was jerking his frantic horse with an abandon of temper he might display in a placid barnyard, was impressed deeply upon his mind. He knew that he looked upon a man who would presently be dead.

Too, he felt a pity for the guns, standing, six good comrades, in a bold row.

He saw a brigade going to the relief of its pestered fellows. He scrambled upon a wee hill and watched it sweeping finely, keeping formation in difficult places. The blue of the line was crusted with steel color, and the brilliant flags projected. Officers were shouting.

This sight also filled him with wonder. The brigade was hurrying briskly to be gulped into the infernal mouths of the war god. What manner of men were they, anyhow? Ah, it was some wondrous breed! Or else they didn't comprehend—the fools.

A furious order caused commotion in the artillery. An officer on a bounding horse made maniacal motions with his arms. The teams went swinging up from the rear, the guns were whirled about, and the battery scampered away. The cannon with their noses poked slantingly at the ground grunted and grumbled like stout men, brave but with objections to hurry.

The youth went on, moderating his pace since he had left the place of noises.

Later he came upon a general of division seated upon a horse that pricked its ears in an interested way at the battle. There was a great gleaming of yellow and patent leather about the saddle and bridle. The quiet man astride looked mouse-colored upon such a splendid charger.

A jingling staff was galloping hither and thither. Sometimes the general was surrounded by horsemen and at other times he was quite alone. He looked to be much harassed. He had the appearance of a business man whose market is swinging up and down.

The youth went slinking around this spot. He went as near as he dared trying to overhear words. Perhaps the general, unable to comprehend chaos, might call upon him for information. And he could tell him. He knew all concerning it. Of a surety the force was in a fix, and any fool could see that if they did not retreat while they had opportunity—why——

He felt that he would like to thrash the general, or at least approach and tell him in plain words exactly what he thought him to be. It was criminal to stay calmly in one spot and make no effort to stay destruction. He loitered in a fever of eagerness for the division commander to apply to him.

As he warily moved about, he heard the general call out irritably: "Tompkins, go over an' see Taylor, an' tell him not t' be in such an all-fired hurry; tell him t' halt his brigade in th' edge of th' woods; tell him t' detach a reg'ment—say I think th' center 'll break if we don't help it out some; tell him t' hurry up."

A slim youth on a fine chestnut horse caught these swift words from the mouth of his superior. He made his horse bound into a gallop almost from a walk in his haste to go upon his mission. There was a cloud of dust.

A moment later the youth saw the general bounce excitedly in his saddle.

"Yes, by heavens, they have!" The officer leaned forward. His face was aflame with excitement. "Yes, by heavens, they 've held 'im! They 've held 'im!"

He began to blithely roar at his staff: "We 'll wallop 'im now. We 'll wallop 'im now. We 've got 'em sure." He turned suddenly upon an aid: "Here—you—ones—quick—ride after Tompkins— see Taylor—tell him t' go in—everlastingly—like blazes—anything."

As another officer sped his horse after the first messenger, the general beamed upon the earth like a sun. In his eyes was a desire to chant a pæon. He kept repeating, "They 've held 'em, by heavens!"

His excitement made his horse plunge, and he merrily kicked and swore at it. He held a little carnival of joy on horseback.

Chapter VII

The youth cringed as if discovered in a crime. By heavens, they had won after all! The imbecile line had remained and become victors. He could hear cheering.

He lifted himself upon his toes and looked in the direction of the fight. A yellow fog lay wallowing on the treetops. From beneath it came the clatter of musketry. Hoarse cries told of an advance.

He turned away amazed and angry. He felt that he had been

wronged.

He had fled, he told himself, because annihilation approached. He had done a good part in saving himself, who was a little piece of the army. He had considered the time, he said, to be one in which it was the duty of every little piece to rescue itself if possible. Later the officers could fit the little pieces together again, and make a battle front. If none of the little pieces were wise enough to save themselves from the flurry of death at such a time, why, then, where would be the army?[8] It was all plain that he had proceeded according to very correct and commendable rules. His actions had been sagacious things. They had been full of strategy. They were the work of a master's legs.[9]

Thoughts of his comrades came to him. The brittle blue line had withstood the blows and won. He grew bitter over it. It seemed that the blind ignorance and stupidity of those little pieces had betrayed him. He had been overturned and crushed by their lack of sense in holding the position, when intelligent deliberation would have convinced them that it was impossible. He, the enlightened man who looks afar in the dark, had fled because of his superior perceptions and knowledge. He felt a great anger against his comrades. He knew it could be proved that they had been fools.

He wondered what they would remark when later he appeared in camp. His mind heard howls of derision. Their density would not enable them to understand his sharper point of view.

He began to pity himself acutely. He was ill used. He was trodden beneath the feet of an iron injustice. He had proceeded with wisdom and from the most righteous motives under heaven's blue only to be frustrated by hateful circumstances.

A dull, animal-like rebellion against his fellows, war in the abstract, and fate grew within him. He shambled along with bowed head, his brain in a tumult of agony and despair. When he looked loweringly up, quivering at each sound, his eyes had the expression of those of a criminal who thinks his guilt and his punishment great, and knows that he can find no words.

He went from the fields into a thick woods, as if resolved to bury himself. He wished to get out of hearing of the crackling shots which were to him like voices.

The ground was cluttered with vines and bushes, and the trees grew close and spread out like bouquets. He was obliged to force

---

8. Shaw's *Arms and the Man* opened on April 24, 1894, some six months before Crane's novel was serialized; its "hero" comically expressed identically the same philosophy of heroism as befitting a "professional" soldier.

9. Again the naturalistic dissociation of behavior from the responsible will or moral force. Yet moral force is present: note below, Henry's efforts to rationalize his desertion from the battle.

his way with much noise. The creepers, catching against his legs, cried out harshly as their sprays were torn from the barks of trees. The swishing saplings tried to make known his presence to the world. He could not conciliate the forest. As he made his way, it was always calling out protestations. When he separated embraces of trees and vines the disturbed foliages waved their arms and turned their face leaves toward him. He dreaded lest these noisy motions and cries should bring men to look at him. So he went far, seeking dark and intricate places.

After a time the sound of musketry grew faint and the cannon boomed in the distance. The sun, suddenly apparent, blazed among the trees. The insects were making rhythmical noises. They seemed to be grinding their teeth in unison. A woodpecker stuck his impudent head around the side of a tree. A bird flew on lighthearted wing.

Off was the rumble of death. It seemed now that Nature had no ears.

This landscape gave him assurance. A fair field holding life. It was the religion of peace. It would die if its timid eyes were compelled to see blood. He conceived Nature to be a woman with a deep aversion to tragedy.

He threw a pine cone at a jovial squirrel, and he ran with chattering fear. High in a treetop he stopped, and, poking his head cautiously from behind a branch, looked down with an air of trepidation.

The youth felt triumphant at this exhibition. There was the law, he said. Nature had given him a sign. The squirrel, immediately upon recognizing danger, had taken to his legs without ado. He did not stand stolidly baring his furry belly to the missile, and die with an upward glance at the sympathetic heavens. On the contrary, he had fled as fast as his legs could carry him; and he was but an ordinary squirrel, too—doubtless no philosopher of his race. The youth wended, feeling that Nature was of his mind. She reenforced his argument with proofs that lived where the sun shone.

Once he found himself almost into a swamp. He was obliged to walk upon bog tufts and watch his feet to keep from the oily mire. Pausing at one time to look about him he saw, out at some black water, a small animal pounce in and emerge directly with a gleaming fish.

The youth went again into the deep thickets. The brushed branches made a noise that drowned the sounds of cannon. He walked on, going from obscurity into promises of a greater obscurity.

At length he reached a place where the high, arching boughs

made a chapel. He softly pushed the green doors aside and entered. Pine needles were a gentle brown carpet. There was a religious half light.

Near the threshold he stopped, horror-stricken at the sight of a thing.

He was being looked at by a dead man who was seated with his back against a columnlike tree. The corpse was dressed in a uniform that once had been blue, but was now faded to a melancholy shade of green. The eyes, staring at the youth, had changed to the dull hue to be seen on the side of a dead fish. The mouth was open. Its red had changed to an appalling yellow. Over the gray skin of the face ran little ants. One was trundling some sort of a bundle along the upper lip.

The youth gave a shriek as he confronted the thing. He was for moments turned to stone before it. He remained staring into the liquid-looking eyes. The dead man and the living man exchanged a long look. Then the youth cautiously put one hand behind him and brought it against a tree. Leaning upon this he retreated, step by step, with his face still toward the thing. He feared that if he turned his back the body might spring up and stealthily pursue him.

The branches, pushing against him, threatened to throw him over upon it.[10] His unguided feet, too, caught aggravatingly in brambles; and with it all he received a subtle suggestion to touch the corpse. As he thought of his hand upon it he shuddered profoundly.

At last he burst the bonds which had fastened him to the spot and fled, unheeding the underbrush. He was pursued by a sight of the black ants swarming greedily upon the gray face and venturing horribly near to the eyes.

After a time he paused, and, breathless and panting, listened He imagined some strange voice would come from the dead throat and squawk after him in horrible menaces.

The trees about the portal of the chapel moved soughingly in a soft wind. A sad silence was upon the little guarding edifice.

Chapter VIII

The trees began softly to sing a hymn of twilight. The sun sank until slanted bronze rays struck the forest. There was a lull in the noises of insects as if they had bowed their beaks and were

10. In this chapter "the youth," hiding in the forest, held a discourse with Nature in three stages: first, he failed to "conciliate" her; next, her "aversion" to war led him to consider her as his friend; finally, exchanging "a long look" with the dead soldier sitting in the grove, he suddenly understood Nature's ultimate way with a man, whom small ants will bury—and he fled terrified, while branches and brambles grab "his unguided feet."

making a devotional pause. There was silence save for the chanted chorus of the trees.

Then, upon this stillness, there suddenly broke a tremendous clangor of sounds. A crimson roar came from the distance.

The youth stopped. He was transfixed by this terrific medley of all noises. It was as if worlds were being rended. There was the ripping sound of musketry and the breaking crash of the artillery.

His mind flew in all directions. He conceived the two armies to be at each other panther fashion. He listened for a time. Then he began to run in the direction of the battle. He saw that it was an ironical thing for him to be running thus toward that which he had been at such pains to avoid. But he said, in substance, to himself that if the earth and the moon were about to clash, many persons would doubtless plan to get upon the roofs to witness the collision.

As he ran, he became aware that the forest had stopped its music, as if at last becoming capable of hearing the foreign sounds. The trees hushed and stood motionless. Everything seemed to be listening to the crackle and clatter and ear-shaking thunder. The chorus pealed over the still earth.

It suddenly occurred to the youth that the fight in which he had been was, after all, but perfunctory popping. In the hearing of this present din he was doubtful if he had seen real battle scenes. This uproar explained a celestial battle; it was tumbling hordes a-struggle in the air.

Reflecting, he saw a sort of a humor in the point of view of himself and his fellows during the late encounter. They had taken themselves and the enemy very seriously and had imagined that they were deciding the war. Individuals must have supposed that they were cutting the letters of their names deep into everlasting tablets of brass, or enshrining their reputations forever in the hearts of their countrymen, while, as to fact, the affair would appear in printed reports under a meek and immaterial title. But he saw that it was good, else, he said, in battle every one would surely run save forlorn hopes and their ilk.

He went rapidly on. He wished to come to the edge of the forest that he might peer out.

As he hastened, there passed through his mind pictures of stupendous conflicts. His accumulated thought upon such subjects was used to form scenes. The noise was as the voice of an eloquent being, describing.

Sometimes the brambles formed chains and tried to hold him back. Trees, confronting him, stretched out their arms and forbade him to pass. After its previous hostility this new resistance of the forest filled him with a fine bitterness. It seemed that Nature could not be quite ready to kill him.

But he obstinately took roundabout ways, and presently he was where he could see long gray walls of vapor where lay battle lines. The voices of cannon shook him. The musketry sounded in long irregular surges that played havoc with his ears. He stood regardant for a moment. His eyes had an awestruck expression. He gawked in the direction of the fight.

Presently he proceeded again on his forward way. The battle was like the grinding of an immense and terrible machine to him. Its complexities and powers, its grim processes, fascinated him. He must go close and see it produce corpses.

He came to a fence and clambered over it. On the far side, the ground was littered with clothes and guns. A newspaper, folded up, lay in the dirt. A dead soldier was stretched with his face hidden in his arm. Farther off there was a group of four or five corpses keeping mournful company. A hot sun had blazed upon the spot.

In this place the youth felt that he was an invader. This forgotten part of the battle ground was owned by the dead men, and he hurried, in the vague apprehension that one of the swollen forms would rise and tell him to begone.

He came finally to a road from which he could see in the distance dark and agitated bodies of troops, smoke-fringed. In the lane was a blood-stained crowd streaming to the rear. The wounded men were cursing, groaning, and wailing. In the air, always, was a mighty swell of sound that it seemed could sway the earth. With the courageous words of the artillery and the spiteful sentences of the musketry mingled red cheers. And from this region of noises came the steady current of the maimed.

One of the wounded men had a shoeful of blood. He hopped like a schoolboy in a game. He was laughing hysterically.

One was swearing that he had been shot in the arm through the commanding general's mismanagement of the army. One was marching with an air imitative of some sublime drum major. Upon his features was an unholy mixture of merriment and agony. As he marched he sang a bit of doggerel in a high and quavering voice:

> "Sing a song 'a vic'try,
>   A pocketful 'a bullets,
> Five an' twenty dead men
>   Baked in a—pie."

Parts of the procession limped and staggered to this tune.

Another had the gray seal of death already upon his face. His lips were curled in hard lines and his teeth were clinched. His hands were bloody from where he had pressed them upon his wound. He seemed to be awaiting the moment when he should pitch headlong. He stalked like the specter of a soldier, his eyes burning with the power of a stare into the unknown.

There were some who proceeded sullenly, full of anger at their wounds, and ready to turn upon anything as an obscure cause.

An officer was carried along by two privates. He was peevish. "Don't joggle so, Johnson, yeh fool," he cried. "Think m' leg is made of iron? If yeh can't carry me decent, put me down an' let some one else do it."

He bellowed at the tottering crowd who blocked the quick march of his bearers. "Say, make way there, can't yeh? Make way, dickens take it all."

They sulkily parted and went to the roadsides. As he was carried past they made pert remarks to him. When he raged in reply and threatened them, they told him to be damned.

The shoulder of one of the tramping bearers knocked heavily against the spectral soldier who was staring into the unknown.

The youth joined this crowd and marched along with it. The torn bodies expressed the awful machinery in which the men had been entangled.

Orderlies and couriers occasionally broke through the throng in the roadway, scattering wounded men right and left, galloping on followed by howls. The melancholy march was continually disturbed by the messengers, and sometimes by bustling batteries that came swinging and thumping down upon them, the officers shouting order to clear the way.

There was a tattered man, fouled with dust, blood and powder stain from hair to shoes, who trudged quietly at the youth's side. He was listening with eagerness and much humility to the lurid descriptions of a bearded sergeant. His lean features wore an expression of awe and admiration. He was like a listener in a country store to wondrous tales told among the sugar barrels. He eyed the story-teller with unspeakable wonder. His mouth was agape in yokel fashion.

The sergeant, taking note of this, gave pause to his elaborate history while he administered a sardonic comment. "Be keerful, honey, you'll be a-ketchin' flies," he said.

The tattered man shrank back abashed.

After a time he began to sidle near to the youth, and in a different way try to make him a friend. His voice was gentle as a girl's voice and his eyes were pleading. The youth saw with surprise that the soldier had two wounds, one in the head, bound with a blood-soaked rag, and the other in the arm, making that member dangle like a broken bough.

After they had walked together for some time the tattered man mustered sufficient courage to speak. "Was pretty good fight, wa'n't it?" he timidly said. The youth, deep in thought, glanced up at the bloody and grim figure with its lamblike eyes. "What?"

"Was pretty good fight, wa'n't it?"

"Yes," said the youth shortly. He quickened his pace.

But the other hobbled industriously after him. There was an air of apology in his manner, but he evidently thought that he needed only to talk for a time, and the youth would perceive that he was a good fellow.

"Was pretty good fight, wa'n't it?" he began in a small voice, and then he achieved the fortitude to continue. "Dern me if I ever see fellers fight so. Laws, how they did fight! I knowed th' boys 'd like when they onct got square at it. Th' boys ain't had no fair chanct up t' now, but this time they showed what they was. I knowed it 'd turn out this way. Yeh can't lick them boys. No, sir! They 're fighters, they be."

He breathed a deep breath of humble admiration. He had looked at the youth for encouragement several times. He received none, but gradually he seemed to get absorbed in his subject.

"I was talkin' 'cross pickets with a boy from Georgie, onct, an' that boy, he ses, 'Your fellers 'll all run like hell when they onct hearn a gun,' he ses. 'Mebbe they will,' I ses, 'but I don't b'lieve none of it,' I ses; 'an' b'jiminey,' I ses back t' 'um, 'mebbe your fellers 'll all run like hell when they onct hearn a gun,' I ses. He larfed. Well, they didn't run t' day, did they, hey? No, sir! They fit, an' fit, an' fit."

His homely face was suffused with a light of love for the army which was to him all things beautiful and powerful.

After a time he turned to the youth. "Where yeh hit, ol' boy?" he asked in a brotherly tone.

The youth felt instant panic at this question, although at first its full import was not borne in upon him.

"What?" he asked.

"Where yeh hit?" repeated the tattered man.

"Why," began the youth, "I—I—that is—why—I——"

He turned away suddenly and slid through the crowd. His brow was heavily flushed, and his fingers were picking nervously at one of his buttons. He bent his head and fastened his eyes studiously upon the button as if it were a little problem.

The tattered man looked after him in astonishment.

Chapter IX

The youth fell back in the procession until the tattered soldier was not in sight. Then he started to walk on with the others.

But he was amid wounds. The mob of men was bleeding.[11] Because of the tattered soldier's question he now felt that his shame could be viewed. He was continually casting sidelong glances to see if the men were contemplating the letters of guilt he felt burned into his brow.

At times he regarded the wounded soldiers in an envious way. He conceived persons with torn bodies to be peculiarly happy. He wished that he, too, had a wound, a red badge of courage.[12]

The spectral soldier was at his side like a stalking reproach. The man's eyes were still fixed in a stare into the unknown. His gray, appalling face had attracted attention in the crowd, and men, slowing to his dreary pace, were walking with him. They were discussing his plight, questioning him and giving him advice. In a dogged way he repelled them, signing to them to go on and leave him alone. The shadows of his face were deepening and his tight lips seemed holding in check the moan of great despair. There could be seen a certain stiffness in the movements of his body, as if he were taking infinite care not to arouse the passion of his wounds. As he went on, he seemed always looking for a place, like one who goes to choose a grave.

Something in the gesture of the man as he waved the bloody and pitying soldiers away made the youth start as if bitten. He yelled in horror. Tottering forward he laid a quivering hand upon the man's arm. As the latter slowly turned his waxlike features toward him, the youth screamed:

"Gawd! Jim Conklin!" [1]

The tall soldier made a little commonplace smile. "Hello, Henry," he said.

The youth swayed on his legs and glared strangely. He stuttered and stammered. "Oh, Jim—oh, Jim—oh, Jim——"

The tall soldier held out his gory hand. There was a curious red and black combination of new blood and old blood upon it. "Where

11. *Cf.*, in Chapter V, "a flow of blood from the torn body of the brigade."
12. But is "the red badge" only "a wound"? See the final paragraphs of the novel; after the youth has touched "the great death," then "scars faded as flowers."
1. The death of "the tall soldier" dominates Chapters VIII and IX. Jim

Conklin is one of Crane's purposeful enigmas. His comrades acknowledge his leadership and perhaps his natural goodness. The impression of a mystical dedication is implied in the circumstances of Jim's death; note the critical debate on the theory that Jim's initials, "J. C.," are those of the Christ.

yeh been, Henry?" he asked. He continued in a monotonous voice, "I thought mebbe yeh got keeled over. There's been thunder t' pay t'-day. I was worryin' about it a good deal."

The youth still lamented. "Oh, Jim—oh, Jim—oh, Jim——"

"Yeh know," said the tall soldier, "I was out there." He made a careful gesture. "An', Lord, what a circus! An', b'jiminey, I got shot—I got shot. Yes, b'jiminey, I got shot." He reiterated this fact in a bewildered way, as if he did not know how it came about.

The youth put forth anxious arms to assist him, but the tall soldier went firmly on as if propelled. Since the youth's arrival as a guardian for his friend, the other wounded men had ceased to display much interest. They occupied themselves again in dragging their own tragedies toward the rear.

Suddenly, as the two friends marched on, the tall soldier seemed to be overcome by a terror. His face turned to a semblance of gray paste. He clutched the youth's arm and looked all about him, as if dreading to be overheard. Then he began to speak in a shaking whisper:

"I tell yeh what I'm 'fraid of, Henry—I 'll tell yeh what I 'm 'fraid of. I 'm 'fraid I 'll fall down—an' then yeh know—them damned artillery wagons—they like as not 'll run over me. That 's what I 'm 'fraid of——"

The youth cried out to him hysterically: "I 'll take care of yeh, Jim! I'll take care of yeh! I swear t' Gawd I will!"

"Sure—will yeh, Henry?" the tall soldier beseeched.

"Yes—yes—I tell yeh—I 'll take care of yeh, Jim!" protested the youth. He could not speak accurately because of the gulpings in his throat.

But the tall soldier continued to beg in a lowly way. He now hung babelike to the youth's arm. His eyes rolled in the wildness of his terror. "I was allus a good friend t' yeh, wa'n't I, Henry? I 've allus been a pretty good feller, ain't I? An' it ain't much t' ask, is it? Jes t' pull me along outer th' road? I 'd do it fer you, wouldn't I, Henry?"

He paused in piteous anxiety to await his friend's reply.

The youth had reached an anguish where the sobs scorched him. He strove to express his loyalty, but he could only make fantastic gestures.

However, the tall soldier seemed suddenly to forget all those fears. He became again the grim, stalking specter of a soldier. He went stonily forward. The youth wished his friend to lean upon him, but the other always shook his head and strangely protested. "No—no—no—leave me be—leave me be——"

His look was fixed again upon the unknown. He moved with

mysterious purpose, and all of the youth's offers he brushed aside. "No—no—leave me be—leave me be——"

The youth had to follow.

Presently the latter heard a voice talking softly near his shoulders. Turning he saw that it belong to the tattered soldier. "Ye 'd better take 'im outa th' road, pardner. There 's a batt'ry comin' helitywhoop down th' road an' he 'll git runned over. He 's a goner anyhow in about five minutes—yeh kin see that. Ye 'd better take 'im outa th' road. Where th' blazes does he git his stren'th from?"

"Lord knows!" cried the youth. He was shaking his hands helplessly.

He ran forward presently and grasped the tall soldier by the arm. "Jim! Jim!" he coaxed, "come with me."

The tall soldier weakly tried to wrench himself free. "Huh," he said vacantly. He stared at the youth for a moment. At last he spoke as if dimly comprehending. "Oh! Inteh th' fields? Oh!"

He started blindly through the grass.

The youth turned once to look at the lashing riders and jouncing guns of the battery. He was startled from this view by a shrill outcry from the tattered man.

"Gawd! He's runnin'!"

Turning his head swiftly, the youth saw his friend running in a staggering and stumbling way toward a little clump of bushes. His heart seemed to wrench itself almost free from his body at this sight. He made a noise of pain. He and the tattered man began a pursuit. There was a singular race.

When he overtook the tall soldier he began to plead with all the words he could find. "Jim—Jim—what are you doing—what makes you do this way—you 'll hurt yerself."

The same purpose was in the tall soldier's face. He protested in a dulled way, keeping his eyes fastened on the mystic place of his intentions. "No—no—don't tech me—leave me be—leave me be——"

The youth, aghast and filled with wonder at the tall soldier, began quaveringly to question him. "Where yeh goin', Jim? What you thinking about? Where you going? Tell me, won't you, Jim?"

The tall soldier faced about as upon relentless pursuers. In his eyes there was a great appeal. "Leave me be, can't yeh? Leave me be fer a minnit."

The youth recoiled. "Why, Jim," he said, in a dazed way, "what's the matter with you?"

The tall soldier turned and, lurching dangerously, went on. The youth and the tattered soldier followed, sneaking as if whipped, feeling unable to face the stricken man if he should again confront them. They began to have thoughts of a solemn ceremony. There was something ritelike in these movements of the doomed soldier. And there was a resemblance in him to a devotee of a mad religion, blood-sucking, muscle-wrenching, bone-crushing. They were awed and afraid. They hung back lest he have at command a dreadful weapon.

At last, they saw him stop and stand motionless. Hastening up, they perceived that his face wore an expression telling that he had at last found the place for which he had struggled. His spare figure was erect; his bloody hands were quietly at his side. He was waiting with patience for something that he had come to meet. He was at the rendezvous.[2] They paused and stood, expectant.

There was a silence.

Finally, the chest of the doomed soldier began to heave with a strained motion. It increased in violence until it was as if an animal was within and was kicking and tumbling furiously to be free.

This spectacle of gradual strangulation made the youth writhe, and once as his friend rolled his eyes, he saw something in them that made him sink wailing to the ground. He raised his voice in a last supreme call.

"Jim—Jim—Jim——"

The tall soldier opened his lips and spoke. He made a gesture. "Leave me be—don't tech me—leave me be——"

There was another silence while he waited.

Suddenly, his form stiffened and straightened. Then it was shaken by a prolonged ague. He stared into space. To the two watchers there was a curious and profound dignity in the firm lines of his awful face.

He was invaded by a creeping strangeness that slowly enveloped him. For a moment the tremor of his legs caused him to dance a sort of hideous hornpipe. His arms beat wildly about his head in expression of implike enthusiasm.

His tall figure stretched itself to its full height. There was a slight rending sound. Then it began to swing forward, slow and straight, in the manner of a falling tree. A swift muscular contortion made the left shoulder strike the ground first.

The body seemed to bounce a little way from the earth. "God!" said the tattered soldier.

The youth had watched, spellbound, this ceremony at the place of meeting. His face had been twisted into an expression of every agony he had imagined for his friend.

2. Hemingway, who had an early admiration for Crane's warbook, echoes as motivation for several memorable episodes a search for "the good place."

He now sprang to his feet and, going closer, gazed upon the pastelike face. The mouth was open and the teeth showed in a laugh.

As the flap of the blue jacket fell away from the body, he could see that the side looked as if it had been chewed by wolves.

The youth turned, with sudden, livid rage, toward the battlefield. He shook his fist. He seemed about to deliver a philippic.[3]

"Hell——"

The red sun was pasted in the sky like a wafer.[4]

Chapter X

The tattered man [5] stood musing.

"Well, he was reg'lar jim-dandy fer nerve, wa'n't he," said he finally in a little awestruck voice. "A reg'lar jim-dandy." He thoughtfully poked one of the docile hands with his foot. "I wonner where he got 'is stren'th from? I never seen a man do like that before. It was a funny thing. Well, he was a reg'lar jim-dandy."

The youth desired to screech out his grief. He was stabbed, but his tongue lay dead in the tomb of his mouth. He threw himself again upon the ground and began to brood.

The tattered man stood musing.

"Look-a-here, pardner," he said, after a time. He regarded the corpse as he spoke. "He 's up an' gone, ain't 'e, an' we might as well begin t' look out fer ol' number one. This here thing is all over. He 's up an' gone, ain't 'e? An' he 's all right here. Nobody won't bother 'im. An' I must say I ain't enjoying any great health m'self these days."

The youth, awakened by the tattered soldier's tone, looked quickly up. He saw that he was swinging uncertainly on his legs and that his face had turned to a shade of blue.

3. A speech characterized by strong denunciation, classically exemplified by the "Philippics" of Demosthenes to the Athenians against the invading Philip of Macedonia.
4. This figure of speech has been admired, also vigorously condemned as a strained and artificial image. In actuality either a heavy fog or battle smoke will produce this smoked-glass illusion of the sun. Some readers will recall ironically the old-fashioned seals or wafers pasted on apothecaries' bottles. To some the wafer, as the bread of the Eucharist, recalls the bloody hands and side of the "tall soldier," and his "ritelike" death. However, in the manuscript, the reading is "like a fierce wafer," a phrase not suggestive of the Christian Communion. (*cf.* Whitman,

"A Sight in Camp * * *"). Compare the effect on "the youth" of this death with that produced by the corpse in the woods (Chapter VII, note 10).
5. With this chapter another cycle of integrated episodes begins. The first cycle, which began in Chapter VI with Henry's desertion of his comrades, now merges with this sequence (Chapters X–XII) dealing with "the tattered man" and with the youth's final rescue and return to duty by one whose face he does not see. "The tattered man" is associated in death with "the tall soldier"; he might be the other side of the same coin, with his "lamblike eyes" suggesting sacrifice, and his homeliness "suffused with a light of love."

"Good Lord!" he cried, "you ain't goin' t'—not you, too."

The tattered man waved his hand. "Nary die," he said. "All I want is some pea soup an' a good bed. Some pea soup," he repeated dreamfully.

The youth arose from the ground. "I wonder where he came from. I left him over there." He pointed. "And now I find 'im here. And he was coming from over there, too." He indicated a new direction. They both turned toward the body as if to ask of it a question.[6]

"Well," at length spoke the tattered man, "there ain't no use in our stayin' here an' tryin' t' ask him anything."

The youth nodded an assent wearily. They both turned to gaze for a moment at the corpse.

The youth murmured something.

"Well, he was a jim-dandy, wa'n't 'e?" said the tattered man as if in response.

They turned their backs upon it and started away. For a time they stole softly, treading with their toes. It remained laughing there in the grass.

"I'm commencin' t' feel pretty bad," said the tattered man, suddenly breaking one of his little silences. "I'm commencin' t' feel pretty damn' bad."

The youth groaned. "O Lord!" He wondered if he was to be the tortured witness of another grim encounter.

But his companion waved his hand reassuringly. "Oh, I'm not goin' t' die yit! There too much dependin' on me fer me t' die yit. No, sir! Nary die! I *can't!* Ye'd oughta see th' swad a' chil'ren I've got, an' all like that."

The youth glancing at his companion could see by the shadow of a smile that he was making some kind of fun.

As they plodded on the tattered soldier continued to talk. "Besides, if I died, I wouldn't die th' way that feller did. That was th' funniest thing. I'd jest flop down, I would. I never seen a feller die th' way that feller did.

"Yeh know Tom Jamison, he lives next door t' me up home. He's a nice feller, he is, an' we was allus good friends. Smart, too. Smart as a steel trap. Well, when we was a-fightin' this afternoon, all-of-a-sudden he begin t' rip up an' cuss an' beller at me. 'Yer shot, yeh blamed infernal!'—he swear horrible—he ses t' me. I put up m' hand t' m' head an' when I looked at m' fingers, I seen, sure 'nough, I was shot. I give a holler an' began t' run, but b'fore I could git away another one hit me in th' arm an' whirl' me clean 'round. I got skeared when they was all ashootin' b'hind me an' I

6. Compare the awed questions here with Chapter III, note 5.

run t' beat all, but I cotch it pretty bad. I've an idee I'd a' been fightin' yit, if t'was n't fer Tom Jamison."

Then he made a calm announcement: "There's two of 'em—little ones—but they 're beginnin' t' have fun with me now. I don't b'lieve I kin walk much furder."

They went slowly on in silence. "Yeh look pretty peek-ed yerself," said the tattered man at last. "I bet yeh 've got a worser one than yeh think. Ye'd better take keer of yer hurt. It don't do t' let sech things go. It might be inside mostly, an' them plays thunder. Where is it located?" But he continued his harangue without waiting for a reply. "I see 'a feller git hit plum in th' head when my reg'ment was a-standin' at ease once. An' everybody yelled out to 'im: Hurt, John? Are yeh hurt much? 'No,' ses he. He looked kinder surprised, an' he went on tellin' 'em how he felt. He sed he didn't feel nothin'. But, by dad, th' first thing that feller knowed he was dead. Yes, he was dead—stone dead. So, yeh wanta watch out. Yeh might have some queer kind 'a hurt yerself. Yeh can't never tell. Where is your'n located?"

The youth had been wriggling since the introduction of this topic. He now gave a cry of exasperation and made a furious motion with his hand. "Oh, don't bother me!" he said. He was enraged against the tattered man, and could have strangled him. His companions seemed ever to play intolerable parts. They were ever upraising the ghost of shame on the stick of their curiosity. He turned toward the tattered man as one at bay. "Now, don't bother me," he repeated with desperate menace.

"Well, Lord knows I don't wanta bother anybody," said the other. There was a little accent of despair in his voice as he replied, "Lord knows I 've gota 'nough m' own t' tend to."

The youth, who had been holding a bitter debate with himself and casting glances of hatred and contempt at the tattered man, here spoke in a hard voice. "Good-by," he said.

The tattered man looked at him in gaping amazement. "Why—why, pardner, where yeh goin'?" he asked unsteadily. The youth looking at him, could see that he, too, like that other one, was beginning to act dumb and animal-like. His thoughts seemed to be floundering about in his head. "Now—now—look—a—here, you Tom Jamison—now—I won't have this—this here won't do. Where—where yeh goin'?"

The youth pointed vaguely. "Over there," he replied.

"Well, now look—a—here—now," said the tattered man, rambling on in idiot fashion. His head was hanging forward and his words were slurred. "This thing won't do, now, Tom Jamison. It won't do. I know yeh, yeh pig-headed devil. Yeh wanta go trompin' off with a bad hurt. It ain't right—now—Tom Jamison—it ain't. Yeh wanta leave me take keer of yeh, Tom Jamison. It ain't—right —it ain't—fer yeh t' go—trompin' off—with a bad hurt—it ain't —ain't—ain't right—it ain't."

In reply the youth climbed a fence and started away. He could hear the tattered man bleating plaintively.

Once he faced about angrily. "What?"

"Look—a—here, now, Tom Jamison—now—it ain't——"

The youth went on. Turning at a distance he saw the tattered man wandering about helplessly in the field.

He now thought that he wished he was dead. He believed that he envied those men whose bodies lay strewn over the grass of the fields and on the fallen leaves of the forest.[7]

The simple questions of the tattered man had been knife thrusts to him. They asserted a society that probes pitilessly at secrets until all is apparent. His late companion's chance persistency made him feel that he could not keep his crime concealed in his bosom. It was sure to be brought plain by one of those arrows which cloud the air and are constantly pricking, discovering, proclaiming those things which are willed to be forever hidden. He admitted that he could not defend himself against this agency. It was not within the power of viligance.

Chapter XI

He became aware that the furnace roar of the battle was growing louder. Great brown clouds had floated to the still heights of air before him. The noise, too, was approaching. The woods filtered men and the fields became dotted.

As he rounded a hillock, he perceived that the roadway was now a crying mass of wagons, teams, and men. From the heaving tangle issued exhortations, commands, imprecations. Fear was sweeping it all along. The cracking whips bit and horses plunged and tugged. The white-topped wagons strained and stumbled in their exertions like fat sheep.

The youth felt comforted in a measure by this sight. They were all retreating. Perhaps, then, he was not so bad after all. He seated himself and watched the terror-stricken wagons. They fled like soft, ungainly animals. All the roarers and lashers served to help him to magnify the dangers and horrors of the engagement that he might try to prove to himself that the thing with which men

7. In Henry's salvation as a man, his unforgettable craven failure in duty toward "the tattered man" may be as important an agent as the loftiness of Conklin's manhood in the face of death. See the ending of the last chapter of the novel.

could charge him was in truth a symmetrical act. There was an amount of pleasure to him in watching the wild march of this vindication.

Presently the calm head of a forward-going column of infantry appeared in the road. It came swiftly on. Avoiding the obstructions gave it the sinuous movement of a serpent. The men at the head butted mules with their musket stocks. They prodded teamsters indifferent to all howls. The men forced their way through parts of the dense mass by strength. The blunt head of the column pushed. The raving teamsters swore many strange oaths.

The commands to make way had the ring of a great importance in them. The men were going forward to the heart of the din. They were to confront the eager rush of the enemy. They felt the pride of their onward movement when the remainder of the army seemed trying to dribble down this road. They tumbled teams about with a fine feeling that it was no matter so long as their column got to the front in time. This importance made their faces grave and stern. And the backs of the officers were very rigid.

As the youth looked at them the black weight of his woe returned to him. He felt that he was regarding a procession of chosen beings. The separation was as great to him as if they had marched with weapons of flame and banners of sunlight. He could never be like them. He could have wept in his longings.

He searched about in his mind for an adequate malediction for the indefinite cause, the thing upon which men turn the words of final blame. It—whatever it was—was responsible for him, he said. There lay the fault.

The haste of the column to reach the battle seemed to the forlorn young man to be something much finer than stout fighting. Heroes, he thought, could find excuses in that long seething lane. They could retire with perfect self-respect and make excuses to the stars.

He wondered what those men had eaten that they could be in such haste to force their way to grim chances of death. As he watched his envy grew until he thought that he wished to change lives with one of them. He would have liked to have used a tremendous force, he said, throw off himself and become a better. Swift pictures of himself, apart, yet in himself, came to him—a blue desperate figure leading lurid charges with one knee forward and a broken blade high—a blue, determined figure standing before a crimson and steel assault, getting calmly killed on a high place before the eyes of all. He thought of the magnificent pathos of his dead body.

These thoughts uplifted him. He felt the quiver of war desire.

In his ears, he heard the ring of victory. He knew the frenzy of a rapid successful charge. The music of the trampling feet, the sharp voices, the clanking arms of the column near him made him soar on the red wings of war. For a few moments he was sublime.

He thought that he was about to start for the front. Indeed, he saw a picture of himself, dust-stained, haggard, panting, flying to the front at the proper moment to seize and throttle the dark, leering witch of calamity.

Then the difficulties of the thing began to drag at him. He hesitated, balancing awkwardly on one foot.

He had no rifle; he could not fight with his hands, said he resentfully to his plan. Well, rifles could be had for the picking. They were extraordinarily profuse.

Also, he continued, it would be a miracle if he found his regiment. Well, he could fight with any regiment.

He started forward slowly. He stepped as if he expected to tread upon some explosive thing. Doubts and he were struggling.

He would truly be a worm if any of his comrades should see him returning thus, the marks of his flight upon him. There was a reply that the intent fighters did not care for what happened rearward saving that no hostile bayonets appeared there. In the battle-blur his face would, in a way be hidden, like the face of a cowled man.

But then he said that his tireless fate would bring forth, when the strife lulled for a moment, a man to ask of him an explanation. In imagination he felt the scrutiny of his companions as he painfully labored through some lies.

Eventually, his courage expended itself upon these objections. The debates drained him of his fire.

He was not cast down by this defeat of his plan, for, upon studying the affair carefully, he could not but admit that the objections were very formidable.

Furthermore, various ailments had begun to cry out. In their presence he could not persist in flying high with the wings of war, they rendered it almost impossible for him to see himself in a heroic light. He tumbled headlong.

He discovered that he had a scorching thirst. His face was so dry and grimy that he thought he could feel his skin crackle. Each bone of his body had an ache in it, and seemingly threatened to break with each movement. His feet were like two sores. Also, his body was calling for food. It was more powerful than a direct hunger. There was a dull, weight like feeling in his stomach, and, when he tried to walk, his head swayed and he tottered. He could not see with distinctness. Small patches of green mist floated before his vision.

While he had been tossed by many emotions, he had not been aware of ailments. Now they beset him and made clamor. As he was at last compelled to pay attention to them, his capacity for self-hate was multiplied. In despair, he declared that he was not like those others. He now conceded it to be impossible that he should ever become a hero. He was a craven loon. Those pictures of glory were piteous things. He groaned from his heart and went staggering off.

A certain mothlike quality within him kept him in the vicinity of the battle. He had a great desire to see, and to get news. He wished to know who was winning.

He told himself that, despite his unprecedented suffering, he had never lost his greed for a victory, yet, he said, in a half-apologetic manner to his conscience, he could not but know that a defeat for the army this time might mean many favorable things for him. The blows of the enemy would splinter regiments into fragments. Thus, many men of courage, he considered, would be obliged to desert the colors and scurry like chickens. He would appear as one of them. They would be sullen brothers in distress, and he could then easily believe he had not run any farther or faster than they. And if he himself could believe in his virtuous perfection, he conceived that there would be small trouble in convincing all others.

He said, as if in excuse for this hope, that previously the army had encountered great defeats and in a few months had shaken off all blood and tradition of them, emerging as bright and valiant as a new one; thrusting out of sight the memory of disaster, and appearing with the valor and confidence of unconquered legions. The shrilling voices of the people at home would pipe dismally for a time, but various generals were usually compelled to listen to these ditties. He of course felt no compunctions for proposing a general as a sacrifice. He could not tell who the chosen for the barbs might be, so he could center no direct sympathy upon him. The people were afar and he did not conceive public opinion to be accurate at long range. It was quite probable they would hit the wrong man who, after he had recovered from his amazement would perhaps spend the rest of his days in writing replies to the songs of his alleged failure. It would be very unfortunate, no doubt, but in this case a general was of no consequence to the youth.

In a defeat there would be a roundabout vindication of himself. He thought it would prove, in a manner, that he had fled early because of his superior powers of perception. A serious prophet upon predicting a flood should be the first man to climb a tree.

This would demonstrate that he was indeed a seer.

A moral vindication was regarded by the youth as a very important thing. Without salve, he could not, he thought, wear the sore badge of his dishonor through life. With his heart continually assuring him that he was despicable, he could not exist without making it, through his actions, apparent to all men.

If the army had gone gloriously on he would be lost. If the din meant that now his army's flags were tilted forward he was a condemned wretch. He would be compelled to doom himself to isolation. If the men were advancing, their indifferent feet were trampling upon his chances for a successful life.

As these thoughts went rapidly through his mind, he turned upon them and tried to thrust them away. He denounced himself as a villain. He said that he was the most unutterably selfish man in existence. His mind pictured the soldiers who would place their defiant bodies before the spear of the yelling battle fiend, and as he saw their dripping corpses on an imagined field, he said that he was their murderer.

Again he thought that he wished he was dead. He believed that he envied a corpse. Thinking of the slain, he achieved a great contempt for some of them, as if they were guilty for thus becoming lifeless. They might have been killed by lucky chances, he said, before they had had opportunities to flee or before they had been really tested. Yet they would receive laurels from tradition. He cried out bitterly that their crowns were stolen and their robes of glorious memories were shams. However, he still said that it was a great pity he was not as they.

A defeat of the army had suggested itself to him as a means of escape from the consequences of his fall. He considered, now, however, that it was useless to think of such a possibility. His education had been that success for that mighty blue machine was certain; that it would make victories as a contrivance turns out buttons. He presently discarded all his speculations in the other direction. He returned to the creed of soldiers.

When he perceived again that it was not possible for the army to be defeated, he tried to bethink him of a fine tale which he could take back to his regiment, and with it turn the expected shafts of derision.

But, as he mortally feared these shafts, it became impossible for him to invent a tale he felt he could trust. He experimented with many schemes, but threw them aside one by one as flimsy. He was quick to see vulnerable places in them all.

Furthermore, he was much afraid that some arrow of scorn might lay him mentally low before he could raise his protecting tale.

He imagined the whole regiment saying: "Where's Henry Fleming? He run, didn't 'e? Oh, my!" He recalled various persons who
would be quite sure to leave him no peace about it. They would
doubtless question him with sneers, and laugh at his stammering
hesitation. In the next engagement they would try to keep watch
of him to discover when he would run.

Wherever he went in camp, he would encounter insolent and
lingeringly cruel stares. As he imagined himself passing near a crowd
of comrades, he could hear some one say, "There he goes!"

Then, as if the heads were moved by one muscle, all the faces
were turned toward him with wide, derisive grins. He seemed to
hear some one make a humorous remark in a low tone. At it the
others all crowed and cackled. He was a slang phrase.

Chapter XII

The column that had butted stoutly at the obstacles in the roadway was barely out of the youth's sight before he saw dark waves
of men come sweeping out of the woods and down through the
fields. He knew at once that the steel fibers had been washed from
their hearts. They were bursting from their coats and their equipments as from entanglements. They charged down upon him like
terrified buffaloes.

Behind them blue smoke curled and clouded above the treetops,
and through the thickets he could sometimes see a distant pink
glare. The voices of the cannon were clamoring in interminable
chorus.

The youth was horrorstricken. He stared in agony and amazement. He forgot that he was engaged in combating the universe.
He threw aside his mental pamphlets on the philosophy of the
retreated and rules for the guidance of the damned.

The fight was lost. The dragons were coming with invincible
strides. The army, helpless in the matted thickets and blinded by
the overhanging night, was going to be swallowed. War, the red
animal, war, the blood-swollen god, would have bloated fill.

Within him something bade to cry out. He had the impulse to
make a rallying speech, to sing a battle hymn, but he could only
get his tongue to call into the air: "Why—why—what—what 's th'
matter?"

Soon he was in the midst of them. They were leaping and
scampering all about him. Their blanched faces shone in the
dusk. They seemed, for the most part, to be very burly men. The
youth turned from one to another of them as they galloped along.
His incoherent questions were lost. They were heedless of his

appeals. They did not seem to see him.

They sometimes gabbled insanely. One huge man was asking of the sky: "Say, where de plank road? Where de plank road!" It was as if he had lost a child. He wept in his pain and dismay.

Presently, men were running hither and thither in all ways. The artillery booming, forward, rearward, and on the flanks made jumble of ideas of direction. Landmarks had vanished into the gathered gloom. The youth began to imagine that he had got into the center of the tremendous quarrel, and he could perceive no way out of it. From the mouths of the fleeing men came a thousand wild questions, but no one made answers.

The youth, after rushing about and throwing interrogations at the heedless bands of retreating infantry, finally clutched a man by the arm. They swung around face to face.

"Why—why——" stammered the youth struggling with his balking tongue.

The man screamed: "Let go me! Let go me!" His face was livid and his eyes were rolling uncontrolled. He was heaving and panting. He still grasped his rifle, perhaps having forgotten to release his hold upon it. He tugged frantically, and the youth being compelled to lean forward was dragged several paces.

"Let go me! Let go me!"

"Why—why——" stuttered the youth.

"Well, then!" bawled the man in a lurid rage. He adroitly and fiercely swung his rifle. It crushed upon the youth's head. The man ran on.

The youth's fingers had turned to paste upon the other's arm. The energy was smitten from his muscles. He saw the flaming wings of lightning flash before his vision. There was a deafening rumble of thunder within his head.

Suddenly his legs seemed to die. He sank writhing to the ground. He tried to arise. In his efforts against the numbing pain he was like a man wrestling with a creature of the air.

There was a sinister struggle.

Sometimes he would achieve a position half erect, battle with the air for a moment, and then fall again, grabbing at the grass. His face was of a clammy pallor. Deep groans were wrenched from him.

At last, with a twisting movement, he got upon his hands and knees, and from thence, like a babe trying to walk, to his feet. Pressing his hands to his temples he went lurching over the grass.

He fought an intense battle with his body. His dulled senses wished him to swoon and he opposed them stubbornly, his mind portraying unknown dangers and mutilations if he should fall upon the field. He went tall soldier fashion. He imagined secluded spots where he could fall and be unmolested. To search for one he strove against the tide of his pain.

Once he put his hand to the top of his head and timidly touched the wound. The scratching pain of the contact made him draw a long breath through his clinched teeth. His fingers were dabbled with blood. He regarded them with a fixed stare.

Around him he could hear the grumble of jolted cannon as the scurrying horses were lashed toward the front. Once, a young officer on a besplashed charger nearly ran him down. He turned and watehed the mass of guns, men, and horses sweeping in a wide curve toward a gap in a fence. The officer was making excited motions with a gauntleted hand. The guns followed the teams with an air of unwillingness, of being dragged by the heels.

Some officers of the scattered infantry were cursing and railing like fishwives. Their scolding voices could be heard above the din. Into the unspeakable jumble in the roadway rode a squadron of cavalry. The faded yellow of their facings shone bravely. There was a mighty altercation.

The artillery were assembling as if for a conference.

The blue haze of evening was upon the field. The lines of forest were long purple shadows. One cloud lay along the western sky partly smothering the red.

As the youth left the scene behind him, he heard the guns suddenly roar out. He imagined them shaking in black rage. They belched and howled like brass devils guarding a gate. The soft air was filled with the tremendous remonstrance. With it came the shattering peal of opposing infantry. Turning to look behind him, he could see sheets of orange light illumine the shadowy distance. There were subtle and sudden lightnings in the far air. At times he thought he could see heaving masses of men.

He hurried on in the dusk. The day had faded until he could barely distinguish place for his feet. The purple darkness was filled with men who lectured and jabbered. Sometimes he could see them gesticulating against the blue and somber sky. There seemed to be a great ruck of men and munitions spread about in the forest and in the fields.

The little narrow roadway now lay lifeless. There were overturned wagons like sun-dried bowlders. The bed of the former torrent was choked with the bodies of horses and splintered parts of war machines.

It had come to pass that his wound pained him but little. He was afraid to move rapidly, however, for a dread of disturbing it. He held his head very still and took many precautions against stumbling. He was filled with anxiety, and his face was pinched and drawn in anticipation of the pain of any sudden mistake of his feet in the gloom.

His thoughts, as he walked, fixed intently upon his hurt. There was a cool, liquid feeling about it and he imagined blood moving slowly down under his hair. His head seemed swollen to a size that made him think his neck to be inadequate.

The new silence of his wound made much worriment. The little blistering voices of pain that had called out from his scalp were, he thought definite in their expression of danger. By then he believed that he could measure his plight. But when they remained ominously silent he became frightened and imagined terrible fingers that clutched into his brain.

Amid it he began to reflect upon various incidents and conditions of the past. He bethought him of certain meals his mother had cooked at home, in which those dishes of which he was particularly fond had occupied prominent positions. He saw the spread table. The pine walls of the kitchen were glowing in the warm light from the stove. Too, he remembered how he and his companions used to go from the schoolhouse to the bank of a shaded pool. He saw his clothes in disorderly array upon the grass of the bank. He felt the swash of the fragrant water upon his body. The leaves of the overhanging maple rustled with melody in the wind of youthful summer.

He was overcome presently by a dragging weariness. His head hung forward and his shoulders were stooped as if he were bearing a great bundle. His feet shuffled along the ground.

He held continuous arguments as to whether he should lie down and sleep at some near spot, or force himself on until he reached a certain haven. He often tried to dismiss the question, but his body persisted in rebellion and his senses nagged at him like pampered babies.

At last he heard a cheery voice near his shoulder: "Yeh seem t' be in a pretty bad way, boy?"

The youth did not look up, but he assented with thick tongue. "Uh!"

The owner of the cheery voice took him firmly by the arm. "Well," he said, with a round laugh, "I'm goin' your way. Th' hull gang is goin' your way. An' I guess I kin give yeh a lift." They began to walk like a drunken man and his friend.

As they went along, the man questioned the youth and assisted him with the replies like one manipulating the mind of a child. Sometimes he interjected anecdotes. "What reg'ment do yeh b'long teh? Eh? What 's that? Th' 304th N' York? Why, what

corps is that in? Oh, it is? Why, I thought they wasn't engaged
t'-day—they 're 'way over in th' center. Oh, they was, eh? Well,
pretty nearly everybody got their share 'a fightin' t'-day. By dad,
I give myself up fer dead any number 'a times. There was shootin'
here an' shootin' there, an' hollerin' here an' hollerin' there, in th'
damn' darkness, until I couldn't tell t' save m' soul which side I
was on. Sometimes I thought I was sure 'nough from Ohier, an'
other times I could 'a swore I was from th' bitter end of Florida.
It was th' most mixed up dern thing I ever see. An' these here hull
woods is a reg'lar mess. It 'll be a miracle if we find our reg'ments
t'-night. Pretty soon, though, we 'll meet a-plenty of guards an'
provost-guards, an' one thing an' another. Ho! there they go with
an off'cer, I guess. Look at his hand a-draggin'. He 's got all th' war
he wants, I bet. He won't be talkin' so big about his reputation
an' all when they go t' sawin' off his leg. Poor feller! My brother 's
got whiskers jest like that. How did yeh git 'way over here, anyhow? Your reg'ment is a long way from here, ain't it? Well, I guess
we can find it. Yeh know there was a boy killed in my comp'ny
t'-day that I thought th' world an' all of. Jack was a nice feller:
By ginger, it hurt like thunder t' see ol' Jack jest git knocked flat.
We was a-standin' purty peaceable fer a spell, 'though there was
men runnin' ev'ry way all 'round us, an' while we was a-standin'
like that, 'long come a big fat feller. He began t' peck at Jack's
elbow, an' he ses: 'Say, where 's th' road t' th' river? An' Jack, he
never paid no attention, an' th' feller kept on a-peckin' at his
elbow an' saying': 'Say, where 's th' road t' th' river?' Jack was
a-lookin' ahead all th' time tryin' t' see th' Johnnies comin' through
th' woods, an' he never paid no attention t' this big fat feller fer a
long time, but at last he turned 'round an' he says: 'Ah, go t' hell
an' find th' road t' th' river!' An' jest then a shot slapped him
bang on th' side th' head. He was a sergeant, too. Them was his
last words. Thunder, I wish we was sure 'a findin' our reg'ments
t'-night. It 's goin' be long huntin'. But I guess we kin do it."

In the search which followed, the man of the cheery voice seemed
to the youth to possess a wand of a magic kind. He threaded the
mazes of the tangled forest with a strange fortune. In encounters
with guards and patrols he displayed the keenness of a detective
and the valor of a gamin. Obstacles fell before him and became of
assistance. The youth, with his chin still on his breast, stood woodenly by while his companion beat ways and means out of sullen
things.

The forest seemed a vast hive of men buzzing about in frantic
circles, but the cheery man conducted the youth without mistakes,
until at last he began to chuckle with glee and self-satisfaction. "Ah,

there yeh are! See that fire?"

The youth nodded stupidly.

"Well, there 's where your reg'ment is. An' now, good-by, ol' boy, good luck t' yeh."

A warm and strong hand clasped the youth's languid fingers for an instant, and then he heard a cheerful and audacious whistling as the man strode away. As he who had so befriended him was thus passing out of his life, it suddenly occurred to the youth that he had not once seen his face.[8]

Chapter XIII

The youth went slowly toward the fire indicated by his departed friend. As he reeled, he bethought him of the welcome his comrades would give him. He had a conviction that he would soon feel in his sore heart the barbed missiles of ridicule. He had no strength to invent a tale; he would be a soft target.

He made vague plans to go off into the deeper darkness and hide, but they were all destroyed by the voices of exhaustion and pain from his body. His ailments, clamoring, forced him to seek the place of food and rest, at whatever cost.

He swung unsteadily toward the fire. He could see the forms of men throwing black shadows in the red light, and as he went nearer it became known to him in some way that the ground was strewn with sleeping men.

Of a sudden he confronted a black and monstrous figure. A rifle barrel caught some glinting beams. "Halt! halt!" He was dismayed for a moment, but he presently thought that he recognized the nervous voice. As he stood tottering before the rifle barrel, he called out: "Why, hello, Wilson, you—you here?"

The rifle was lowered to a position of caution and the loud soldier came slowly forward. He peered into the youth's face. "That you, Henry?"

"Yes, it's—it's me."

"Well, well, ol' boy," said the other, "by ginger, I'm glad t' see yeh! I give yeh up fer a goner. I thought yeh was dead sure enough." There was husky emotion in his voice.

The youth found that now he could barely stand upon his feet. There was a sudden sinking of his forces. He thought he must hasten to produce his tale to protect him from the missiles already

8. Professor Stallman cites as basis for this episode Crane's meeting with an unrecognized and cheerful farmer who gave him help on a dark night on the road. The mystical suggestion that Henry "had not once seen his [rescuer's] face" recalls his bewilderment because the dying Conklin seemed to come simultaneously from three different places.

at the lips of his redoubtable comrades. So, staggering before the loud soldier, he began: "Yes, yes. I've—I've had an awful time. I've been all over. Way over on th' right. Ter'ble fightin' over there. I had an awful time. I got separated from th' reg'ment. Over on th' right, I got shot. In th' head. I never see sech fightin'. Awful time. I don't see how I could a' got separated from th' reg'ment. I got shot, too."

His friend had stepped forward quickly. "What? Got shot? Why didn't yeh say so first? Poor ol' boy, we must—hol' on a minnit; what am I doin'. I'll call Simpson."

Another figure at that moment loomed in the gloom. They could see that it was the corporal. "Who yeh talkin' to, Wilson?" he demanded. His voice was anger-toned. "Who yeh talkin' to? Yeh th' derndest sentinel—why—hello, Henry, you here? Why, I thought you was dead four hours ago! Great Jerusalem, they keep turnin' up every ten minutes or so! We thought we'd lost forty-two men by straight count, but if they keep on a-comin' this way, we'll git th' comp'ny all back by mornin' yit. Where was yeh?"

"Over on th' right. I got separated"—began the youth with considerable glibness.

But his friend had interrupted hastily. "Yes, an' he got shot in th' head an' he's in a fix, an' we must see t' him right away." He rested his rifle in the hollow of his left arm and his right around the youth's shoulder.

"Gee, it must hurt like thunder!" he said.

The youth leaned heavily upon his friend. "Yes, it hurts—hurts a good deal," he replied. There was a faltering in his voice.

"Oh," said the corporal. He linked his arm in the youth's and drew him forward. "Come on, Henry. I'll take keer 'a yeh."

As they went on together the loud private called out after them: "Put 'im t' sleep in my blanket, Simpson. An'—hol' on a minnit —here's my canteen. It's full 'a coffee. Look at his head by th' fire an' see how it looks. Maybe it's a pretty bad un. When I git relieved in a couple 'a minnits, I'll be over an' see t' him."

The youth's senses were so deadened that his friend's voice sounded from afar and he could scarcely feel the pressure of the corporal's arm. He submitted passively to the latter's directing strength. His head was in the old manner hanging forward upon his breast. His knees wobbled.

The corporal led him into the glare of the fire. "Now, Henry," he said, "let's have look at yer ol' head."

The youth sat down obediently and the corporal, laying aside his rifle, began to fumble in the bushy hair of his comrade. He was obliged to turn the other's head so that the full flush of the fire light would beam upon it. He puckered his mouth with a critical air. He drew back his lips and whistled through his teeth when his fingers came in contact with the splashed blood and the rare wound.

"Ah, here we are!" he said. He awkwardly made further investigations. "Jest as I thought," he added, presently. "Yeh've been grazed by a ball. It's raised a queer lump jest as if some feller had lammed yeh on th' head with a club. It stopped a-bleedin' long time ago. Th' most about it is that in th' mornin' yeh'll feel that a number ten hat wouldn't fit yeh. An' your head'll be all het up an' feel as dry as burnt pork. An' yeh may git a lot 'a other sicknesses, too, by mornin'. Yeh can't never tell. Still, I don't much think so. It's jest a damn' good belt on th' head, an' nothin' more. Now, you jest sit here an' don't move, while I go rout out th' relief. Then I'll send Wilson t' take keer 'a yeh."

The corporal went away. The youth remained on the ground like a parcel. He stared with a vacant look into the fire.

After a time he aroused, for some part, and the things about him began to take form. He saw that the ground in the deep shadows was cluttered with men, sprawling in every conceivable posture. Glancing narrowly into the more distant darkness, he caught occasional glimpses of visages that loomed pallid and ghostly, lit with a phosphorescent glow. These faces expressed in their lines the deep stupor of the tired soldiers. They made them appear like men drunk with wine. This bit of forest might have appeared to an ethereal wanderer as a scene of the result of some frightful debauch.

On the other side of the fire the youth observed an officer asleep, seated bolt upright, with his back against a tree. There was something perilous in his position. Badgered by dreams, perhaps, he swayed with little bounces and starts, like an old, toddy-stricken grandfather in a chimney corner. Dust and stains were upon his face. His lower jaw hung down as if lacking strength to assume its normal position. He was the picture of an exhausted soldier after a feast of war.

He had evidently gone to sleep with his sword in his arms. These two had slumbered in an embrace, but the weapon had been allowed in time to fall unheeded to the ground. The grass-mounted hilt lay in contact with some parts of the fire.

Within the gleam of rose and orange light from the burning sticks were other soldiers, snoring and heaving, or lying deathlike in slumber. A few pairs of legs were stuck forth, rigid and straight. The shoes displayed the mud or dust of marches and bits of rounded trousers, protruding from the blankets, showed rents and tears from hurried pitchings through the dense brambles.

The fire crackled musically. From it swelled light smoke. Overhead the foliage moved softly. The leaves, with their faces turned toward the blaze, were colored shifting hues of silver, often edged with red. Far off to the right, through a window in the forest could be seen a handful of stars lying, like glittering pebbles, on the black level of the night.

Occasionally, in this low-arched hall, a soldier would arouse and turn his body to a new position, the experience of his sleep having taught him of uneven and objectionable places upon the ground under him. Or, perhaps, he would lift himself to a sitting posture, blink at the fire for an unintelligent moment, throw a swift glance at his prostrate companion, and then cuddle down again with a grunt of sleepy content.

The youth sat in a forlorn heap until his friend the loud young soldier came, swinging two canteens by their light strings. "Well, now, Henry, ol' boy," said the latter, "we'll have yeh fixed up in jest about a minnit."

He had the bustling ways of an amateur nurse. He fussed around the fire and stirred the sticks to brilliant exertions. He made his patient drink largely from the canteen that contained the coffee. It was to the youth a delicious draught. He tilted his head afar back and held the canteen long to his lips. The cool mixture went caressingly down his blistered throat. Having finished, he sighed with comfortable delight.

The loud young soldier watched his comrade with an air of satisfaction. He later produced an extensive handkerchief from his pocket. He folded it into a manner of bandage and soused water from the other canteen upon the middle of it. This crude arrangement he bound over the youth's head, tying the ends in a queer knot at the back of the neck.

"There," he said, moving off and surveying his deed, "yeh look like th' devil, but I bet yeh feel better."

The youth contemplated his friend with grateful eyes. Upon his aching and swelling head the cold cloth was like a tender woman's hand.

"Yeh don't holler ner say nothin'," remarked his friend approvingly. "I know I'm a blacksmith at takin' keer 'a sick folks, an' yeh never squeaked. Yer a good un, Henry. Most 'a men would a' been in th' hospital long ago. A shot in th' head ain't foolin' business."

The youth made no reply, but began to fumble with the buttons of his jacket.

"Well, come, now," continued his friend, "come on. I must put yeh t' bed an' see that yeh git a good night's rest."

The other got carefully erect, and the loud young soldier led him among the sleeping forms lying in groups and rows. Presently he stooped and picked up his blankets. He spread the rubber one upon the ground and placed the woolen one about the youth's shoulders.

"There now," he said, "lie down an' git some sleep."

The youth, with his manner of doglike obedience, got carefully down like a crone stooping. He stretched out with a murmur of relief and comfort. The ground felt like the softest couch.

But of a sudden he ejaculated: "Hol' on a minnit! Where you goin' t' sleep?"

His friend waved his hand impatiently. "Right down there by yeh."

"Well, but hol' on a minnit," continued the youth. "What yeh goin' t' sleep in? I've got your——"

The loud young soldier snarled: "Shet up an' go on t' sleep. Don't be makin' a damn' fool 'a yerself," he said severely.

After the reproof the youth said no more. An exquisite drowsiness had spread through him. The warm comfort of the blanket enveloped him and made a gentle languor. His head fell forward on his crooked arm and his weighted lids went softly down over his eyes. Hearing a splatter of musketry from the distance, he wondered indifferently if those men sometimes slept. He gave a long sigh, snuggled down into his blanket, and in a moment was like his comrades.

Chapter XIV

When the youth awoke it seemed to him that he had been asleep for a thousand years, and he felt sure that he opened his eyes upon an unexpected world. Gray mists were slowly shifting before the first efforts of the sun rays. An impending splendor could be seen in the eastern sky. An icy dew had chilled his face, and immediately upon arousing he curled farther down into his blanket. He stared for a while at the leaves overhead, moving in a heraldic wind of the day.

The distance was splintering and blaring with the noise of fighting. There was in the sound an expression of a deadly persistency, as if it had not begun and was not to cease.

About him were the rows and groups of men that he had dimly seen the previous night. They were getting a last draught of sleep before the awakening. The gaunt, careworn features and dusty figures were made plain by this quaint light at the dawning, but it dressed the skin of the men in corpselike hues and made the tangled limbs appear pulseless and dead. The youth started up with a little cry when his eyes first swept over this motionless mass of men, thick-spread upon the ground, pallid, and in strange postures. His disordered mind interpreted the hall of the forest as a charnel place. He believed for an instant that he was in the house of the dead, and he did not dare to move lest these corpses start up, squalling and squawking. In a second, however, he achieved his proper mind. He swore a complicated oath at himself. He saw that this somber picture was not a fact of the present, but a mere prophecy.

He heard then the noise of a fire crackling briskly in the cold air, and, turning his head, he saw his friend pottering busily about a small blaze. A few other figures moved in the fog, and he heard the hard cracking of axe blows.

Suddenly there was a hollow rumble of drums. A distant bugle sang faintly. Similar sounds, varying in strength, came from near and far over the forest. The bugles called to each other like brazen gamecocks. The near thunder of the regimental drums rolled.

The body of men in the woods rustled. There was a general uplifting of heads. A murmuring of voices broke upon the air. In it there was much bass of grumbling oaths. Strange gods were addressed in condemnation of the early hours necessary to correct war. An officer's peremptory tenor rang out and quickened the stiffened movement of the men. The tangled limbs unraveled. The corpse-hued faces were hidden behind fists that twisted slowly in the eye sockets.

The youth sat up and gave vent to an enormous yawn. "Thunder!" he remarked petulantly. He rubbed his eyes, and then putting up his hand felt carefully of the bandage over his wound. His friend, perceiving him to be awake, came from the fire. "Well, Henry, ol' man, how do yeh feel this mornin'?" he demanded.

The youth yawned again. Then he puckered his mouth to a little pucker. His head, in truth, felt precisely like a melon, and there was an unpleasant sensation at his stomach.

"Oh, Lord, I feel pretty bad," he said.

"Thunder!" exclaimed the other. "I hoped ye'd feel all right this mornin'. Let's see th' bandage—I guess it's slipped." He began to tinker at the wound in rather a clumsy way until the youth exploded.

"Gosh-dern it!" he said in sharp irritation; "you're the hangdest man I ever saw! You wear muffs on your hands. Why in good thunderation can't you be more easy? I'd rather you'd stand off an' throw guns at it. Now, go slow, an' don't act as if you was nailing down carpet."

He glared with insolent command at his friend, but the latter answered soothingly. "Well, well, come now, an' git some grub," he said. "Then, maybe, yeh'll feel better."

At the fireside the loud young soldier watched over his comrade's wants with tenderness and care. He was very busy marshaling the little black vagabonds of tin cups and pouring into them the streaming, iron colored mixture from a small and sooty tin pail. He had some fresh meat, which he roasted hurriedly upon a stick. He sat down then and contemplated the youth's appetite with glee.

The youth took note of a remarkable change in his comrade since those days of camp life upon the river bank. He seemed no more to be continually regarding the proportions of his personal prowess. He was not furious at small words that pricked his conceits. He was no more a loud young soldier. There was about him now a fine reliance. He showed a quiet belief in his purposes and his abilities. And this inward confidence evidently enabled him to be indifferent to little words of other men aimed at him.

The youth reflected. He had been used to regarding his comrade as a blatant child with an audacity grown from his inexperience, thoughtless, headstrong, jealous, and filled with a tinsel courage. A swaggering babe accustomed to strut in his own dooryard. The youth wondered where had been born these new eyes; when his comrade had made the great discovery that there were many men who would refuse to be subjected by him. Apparently, the other had now climbed a peak of wisdom from which he could perceive himself as a very wee thing. And the youth saw that ever after it would be easier to live in his friend's neighborhood.[9]

His comrade balanced his ebony coffee-cup on his knee. "Well Henry," he said, "what d'yeh think th' chances are? D'yeh think we'll wallop 'em?"

The youth considered for a moment. "Day-b'fore-yesterday," he finally replied, with boldness, "you would 'a' bet you'd lick the hull kit-an'-boodle all by yourself."

His friend looked a trifle amazed. "Would I?" he asked. He pondered. "Well, perhaps I would," he decided at last. He stared humbly at the fire.

The youth was quite disconcerted at this surprising reception of his remarks. "Oh, no, you wouldn't either," he said, hastily trying to retrace.

But the other made a deprecating gesture. "Oh, yeh needn't mind, Henry," he said. "I believe I was a pretty big fool in those days." He spoke as after a lapse of years.

There was a little pause.

9. In the action that follows, both soldiers, emotionally immature at their enlistment, have won stature in the ordeal of reality, which is regarded as the indispensable access to wisdom.

"All th' officers say we've got th' rebs in a pretty tight box," said the friend, clearing his throat in a commonplace way. "They all seem t' think we've got 'em jest where we want 'em."

"I don't know about that," the youth replied. "What I seen over on th' right makes me think it was th' other way about. From where I was, it looked as if we was gettin' a good poundin' yestir-day."

"D'yeh think so?" inquired the friend. "I thought we handled 'em pretty rough yestirday."

"Not a bit," said the youth. "Why, lord, man, you didn't see nothing of the fight. Why!" Then a sudden thought came to him. "Oh! Jim Conklin's dead."

His friend started. "What? Is he? Jim Conklin?"

The youth spoke slowly. "Yes. He's dead. Shot in th' side."

"Yeh don't say so. Jim Conklin. . . . poor cuss!"

All about them were other small fires surrounded by men with their little black utensils. From one of these near came sudden sharp voices in a row. It appeared that two light-footed soldiers had been teasing a huge, bearded man, causing him to spill coffee upon his blue knees. The man had gone into a rage and had sworn comprehensively. Stung by his language, his tormentors had im-mediately bristled at him with a great show of resenting unjust oaths. Possibly there was going to be a fight.

The friend arose and went over to them, making pacific motions with his arms. "Oh, here, now, boys, what's th' use?" he said. "We'll be at th' rebs in less'n an hour. What's th' good fightin' 'mong ourselves?"

One of the light-footed soldiers turned upon him red-faced and violent. "Yeh needn't come around here with yer preachin'. I s'pose yeh don't approve 'a fightin' since Charley Morgan licked yeh; but I don't see what business this here is 'a yours or anybody else."

"Well, it ain't," said the friend mildly. "Still I hate t' see——"

There was a tangled argument.

"Well, he——," said the two, indicating their opponent with accusative forefingers.

The huge soldier was quite purple with rage. He pointed at the two soldiers with his great hand, extended clawlike. "Well, they——"

But during this argumentative time the desire to deal blows seemed to pass, although they said much to each other. Finally the friend returned to his old seat. In a short while the three antagonists could be seen together in an amiable bunch.

"Jimmie Rogers ses I'll have t' fight him after th' battle t'-day," announced the friend as he again seated himself. "He ses he don't allow no interferin' in his business. I hate t' see th' boys fightin' 'mong themselves."

The youth laughed. "Yer changed a good bit. Yeh ain't at all like yeh was. I remember when you an' that Irish feller——" He stopped and laughed again.

"No, I didn't use t' be that way," said his friend thoughtfully "That's true 'nough."

"Well, I didn't mean——" began the youth.

The friend made another deprecatory gesture. "Oh, yeh needn't mind, Henry."

There was another little pause.

"Th' reg'ment lost over half th' men yestirday," remarked the friend eventually. "I thought a course they was all dead, but, laws, they kep' a-comin' back last night until it seems, after all, we didn't lose but a few. They'd been scattered allover, wanderin' around in th' woods, fightin' with other reg'ments, an' everything. Jest like you done."

"So?" said the youth.

Chapter XV

The regiment was standing at order arms at the side of a lane, waiting for the command to march, when suddenly the youth remembered the little packet enwrapped in a faded yellow envelope which the loud young soldier with lugubrious words had intrusted to him. It made him start. He uttered an exclamation and turned toward his comrade.

"Wilson!"

"What?"

His friend, at his side in the ranks, was thoughtfully staring down the road. From some cause his expression was at that moment very meek. The youth, regarding him with sidelong glances, felt impelled to change his purpose. "Oh, nothing," he said.

His friend turned his head in some surprise, "Why, what was yeh goin' t' say?"

"Oh, nothing," repeated the youth.

He resolved not to deal the little blow. It was sufficient that the fact made him glad. It was not necessary to knock his friend on the head with the misguided packet.

He had been possessed of much fear of his friend, for he saw how easily questionings could make holes in his feelings. Lately, he had assured himself that the altered comrade would not tantalize him with a persistent curiosity, but he felt certain that during the first period of leisure his friend would ask him to relate his adventures of the previous day.

He now rejoiced in the possession of a small weapon with which he could prostrate his comrade at the first signs of a cross-examination. He was master. It would now be he who could laugh and shoot the shafts of derision.

The friend had, in a weak hour, spoken with sobs of his own death. He had delivered a melancholy oration previous to his funeral, and had doubtless in the packet of letters, presented various keepsakes to relatives. But he had not died, and thus he had delivered himself into the hands of the youth.

The latter felt immensely superior to his friend, but he inclined to condescension. He adopted toward him an air of patronizing good humor.

His self-pride was now entirely restored. In the shade of its flourishing growth he stood with braced and self-confident legs, and since nothing could now be discovered he did not shrink from an encounter with the eyes of judges, and allowed no thoughts of his own to keep him from an attitude of manfulness. He had performed his mistakes in the dark, so he was still a man.

Indeed, when he remembered his fortunes of yesterday, and looked at them from a distance he began to see something fine there. He had license to be pompous and veteranlike.

His panting agonies of the past he put out of his sight.

In the present, he declared to himself that it was only the doomed and the damned who roared with sincerity at circumstance. Few but they ever did it. A man with a full stomach and the respect of his fellows had no business to scold about anything that he might think to be wrong in the ways of the universe, or even with the ways of society. Let the unfortunates rail; the others may play marbles.

He did not give a great deal of thought to these battles that lay directly before him. It was not essential that he should plan his ways in regard to them. He had been taught that many obligations of a life were easily avoided. The lessons of yesterday had been that retribution was a laggard and blind. With these facts before him he did not deem it necessary that he should become feverish over the possibilities of the ensuing twenty-four hours. He could leave much to chance. Besides, a faith in himself had secretly blossomed. There was a little flower of confidence growing within him. He was now a man of experience. He had been out among the dragons, he said, and he assured himself that they were not so hideous as he had imagined them. Also, they were inaccurate; they did not sting with precision. A stout heart often defied, and defying, escaped.

And, furthermore, how could they kill him who was the chosen of gods and doomed to greatness?

He remembered how some of the men had run from the battle. As he recalled their terror-struck faces he felt a scorn for them. They had surely been more fleet and more wild than was absolutely necessary. They were weak mortals. As for himself, he had fled with discretion and dignity.

He was roused from this reverie by his friend, who, having hitched about nervously and blinked at the trees for a time, suddenly coughed in an introductory way, and spoke.

"Fleming!"

"What?"

The friend put his hand up to his mouth and coughed again. He fidgeted in his jacket.

"Well," he gulped, at last, "I guess yeh might as well give me back them letters." Dark, prickling blood had flushed into his cheeks and brow.

"All right, Wilson," said the youth. He loosened two buttons of his coat, thrust in his hand, and brought forth the packet. As he extended it to his friend the latter's face was turned from him.

He had been slow in the act of producing the packet because during it he had been trying to invent a remarkable comment upon the affair. He could conjure nothing of sufficient point. He was compelled to allow his friend to escape unmolested with his packet. And for this he took unto himself considerable credit. It was a generous thing.

His friend at his side seemed suffering great shame. As he contemplated him, the youth felt his heart grow more strong and stout. He had never been compelled to blush in such manner for his acts; he was an individual of extraordinary virtues.

He reflected, with condescending pity: "Too bad! Too bad! The poor devil, it makes him feel tough!"

After this incident, and as he reviewed the battle pictures he had seen, he felt quite competent to return home and make the hearts of the people glow with stories of war. He could see himself in a room of warm tints telling tales to listeners. He could exhibit laurels. They were insignificant; still, in a district where laurels were infrequent, they might shine.

He saw his gaping audience picturing him as the central figure in blazing scenes. And he imagined the consternation and the ejaculations of his mother and the young lady at the seminary as they drank his recitals. Their vague feminine formula for beloved ones doing brave deeds on the field of battle without risk of life would be destroyed.

Chapter XVI

A sputtering of musketry was always to be heard. Later, the cannon had entered the dispute. In the fog-filled air their voices made a thudding sound. The reverberations were continued. This part of the world led a strange, battleful existence.

The youth's regiment was marched to relieve a command that had lain long in some damp trenches. The men took positions behind a curving line of rifle pits that had been turned up, like a large furrow, along the line of woods. Before them was a level stretch, peopled with short, deformed stumps. From the woods beyond came the dull popping of the skirmishers and pickets, firing in the fog. From the right came the noise of a terrific fracas.

The men cuddled behind the small embankment and sat in easy attitudes awaiting their turn. Many had their backs to the firing. The youth's friend lay down, buried his face in his arms, and almost instantly, it seemed, he was in a deep sleep.

The youth leaned his breast against the brown dirt and peered over at the woods and up and down the line. Curtains of trees interfered with his ways of vision. He could see the low line of trenches but for a short distance. A few idle flags were perched on the dirt hills. Behind them were rows of dark bodies with a few heads sticking curiously over the top.

Always the noise of skirmishers came from the woods on the front and left, and the din on the right had grown to frightful proportions. The guns were roaring without an instant's pause for breath. It seemed that the cannon had come from all parts and were engaged in a stupendous wrangle. It became impossible to make a sentence heard.

The youth wished to launch a joke—a quotation from newspapers. He desired to say, "All quiet on the Rappahannock,"[10] but the guns refused to permit even a comment upon their uproar. He never successfully concluded the sentence. But at last the guns stopped, and among the men in the rifle pits rumors again flew, like birds, but they were now for the most part black creatures who flapped their wings drearily near to the ground and refused to rise on any wings of hope. The men's faces grew doleful

10. "All quiet along the Potomac" was a phrase satirically reiterated the previous year in newspapers critical of the inaction of McClellan and this army, now again facing defeat under Burnside along the Rappahannock.

from the interpreting of omens. Tales of hesitation and uncertainty on the part of those high in place and responsibility came to their ears. Stories of disaster were borne into their minds with many proofs. This din of musketry on the right, growing like a released genie of sound, expressed and emphasized the army's plight.

The men were disheartened and began to mutter. They made gestures expressive of the sentence: "Ah, what more can we do?" And it could always be seen that they were bewildered by the alleged news and could not fully comprehend a defeat.

Before the gray mists had been totally obliterated by the sun rays, the regiment was marching in a spread column that was retiring carefully through the woods. The disordered, hurrying lines of the enemy could sometimes be seen down through the groves and little fields. They were yelling, shrill and exultant.

At this sight the youth forgot many personal matters and became greatly enraged. He exploded in loud sentences. "B'jiminey, we're generaled by a lot 'a lunkheads."

"More than one feller has said that t'-day," observed a man.

His friend, recently aroused, was still very drowsy. He looked behind him until his mind took in the meaning of the movement. Then he sighed. "Oh, well, I s'pose we got licked," he remarked sadly.

The youth had a thought that it would not be handsome for him to freely condemn other men. He made an attempt to restrain himself, but the words upon his tongue were too bitter. He presently began a long and intricate denunciation of the commander of the forces.

"Mebbe, it wa'n't all his fault—not all together. He did th' best he knowed. It's our luck t' git licked often," said his friend in a weary tone. He was trudging along with stooped shoulders and shifting eyes like a man who has been caned and kicked.

"Well, don't we fight like the devil? Don't we do all that men can?" demanded the youth loudly.

He was secretly dumfounded at this sentiment when it came from his lips. For a moment his face lost its valor and he looked guiltily about him. But no one questioned his right to deal in such words, and presently he recovered his air of courage. He went on to repeat a statement he had heard going from group to group at the camp that morning. "The brigadier said he never saw a new reg'-ment fight the way we fought yesterday, didn't he? And we didn't do better than many another reg'ment, did we? Well, then, you can't say it's th' army's fault, can you?"

In his reply, the friend's voice was stern, "'A course not," he said. "No man dare say we don't fight like th' devil. No man will ever dare say it. Th' boys fight like hell-roosters. But still—still, we don't have no luck."

"Well, then, if we fight like the devil an' don't ever whip, it must be the general's fault," said the youth grandly and decisively. "And I don't see any sense in fighting and fighting and fighting, yet always losing through some derned old lunkhead of a general."

A sarcastic man who was tramping at the youth's side, then spoke lazily. "Mebbe yeh think yeh fit th' hull battle yestirday, Fleming," he remarked.

The speech pierced the youth. Inwardly he was reduced to an abject pulp by these chance words. His legs quaked privately. He cast a frightened glance at the sarcastic man.

"Why, no," he hastened to say in a conciliating voice, "I don't think I fought the whole battle yesterday."

But the other seemed innocent of any deeper meaning. Apparently, he had no information. It was merely his habit. "Oh!" he replied in the same tone of calm derision.

The youth, nevertheless, felt a threat. His mind shrank from going near to the danger, and thereafter he was silent. The significance of the sarcastic man's words took from him all loud moods that would make him appear prominent. He became suddenly a modest person.

There was low-toned talk among the troops. The officers were impatient and snappy, their countenances clouded with the tales of misfortune. The troops, sifting through the forest, were sullen. In the youth's company once a man's laugh rang out. A dozen soldiers turned their faces quickly toward him and frowned with vague displeasure.

The noise of firing dogged their footsteps. Sometimes, it seemed to be driven a little way, but it always returned again with increased insolence. The men muttered and cursed, throwing black looks in its direction.

In a clear space the troops were at last halted. Regiments and brigades, broken and detached through their encounters with thickets, grew together again and lines were faced toward the pursuing bark of the enemy's infantry.

This noise, following like the yellings of eager, metallic hounds, increased to a loud and joyous burst, and then, as the sun went serenely up the sky, throwing illuminating rays into the gloomy thickets, it broke forth into prolonged pealings. The woods began to crackle as if afire.

"Whoop-a-dadee," said a man, "here we are! Everybody fightin'. Blood an' destruction."

"I was willin' t' bet they'd attack as soon as th' sun got fairly up," savagely asserted the lieutenant who commanded the youth's company. He jerked without mercy at his little mustache. He strode to and fro with dark dignity in the rear of his men, who were lying down behind whatever protection they had collected.

A battery had trundled into position in the rear and was thoughtfully shelling the distance. The regiment, unmolested as yet, awaited the moment when the gray shadows of the woods before them should be slashed by the lines of flame. There was much growling and swearing.

"Good Gawd," the youth grumbled, "we're always being chased around like rats! It makes me sick. Nobody seems to know where we go or why we go. We just get fired around from pillar to post and get licked here and get licked there, and nobody knows what it's done for. It makes a man feel like a damn' kitten in a bag. Now, I'd like to know what the eternal thunders we was marched into these woods for anyhow, unless it was to give the rebs a regular pot shot at us. We came in here and got our legs all tangled up in these cussed briers, and then we begin to fight and the rebs had an easy time of it. Don't tell me it's just luck! I know better. It's this derned old——"

The friend seemed jaded, but he interrupted his comrade with a voice of calm confidence. "It'll turn out all right in th' end," he said.

"Oh, the devil it will! You always talk like a dog-hanged parson. Don't tell me! I know——"

At this time there was an interposition by the savage-minded lieutenant, who was obliged to vent some of his inward dissatisfaction upon his men. "You boys shut right up! There no need 'a your wastin' your breath in long-winded arguments about this an' that an' th' other. You've been jawin' like a lot 'a old hens. All you've got t' do is to fight, an' you'll get plenty 'a that t' do in about ten minutes. Less talkin' an' more fightin' is what's best for you boys. I never saw sech gabbling jackasses."

He paused, ready to pounce upon any man who might have the temerity to reply. No words being said, he resumed his dignified pacing.

"There's too much chin music an' too little fightin' in this war, anyhow," he said to them, turning his head for a final remark.

The day had grown more white, until the sun shed his full radiance upon the thronged forest. A sort of a gust of battle came sweeping toward that part of the line where lay the youth's regiment. The front shifted a trifle to meet it squarely. There was a wait. In this part of the field there passed slowly the intense moments that precede the tempest.

A single rifle flashed in a thicket before the regiment. In an instant it was joined by many others. There was a mighty song of clashes and crashes that went sweeping through the woods. The guns in the rear, aroused and enraged by shells that had been thrown burlike[1] at them, suddenly involved themselves in a hideous altercation with another band of guns. The battle roar settled to a rolling thunder, which was a single, long explosion.

In the regiment there was a peculiar kind of hesitation denoted in the attitudes of the men. They were worn, exhausted, having slept but little and labored much. They rolled their eyes toward the advancing battle as they stood awaiting the shock. Some shrank and flinched. They stood as men tied to stakes.

Chapter XVII

This advance of the enemy had seemed to the youth like a ruthless hunting. He began to fume with rage and exasperation. He beat his foot upon the ground, and scowled with hate at the swirling smoke that was approaching like a phantom flood. There was a maddening quality in this seeming resolution of the foe to give him no rest, to give him no time to sit down and think. Yesterday he had fought and had fled rapidly. There had been many adventures. For to-day he felt that he had earned opportunities for contemplative repose. He could have enjoyed portraying to uninitiated listeners various scenes at which he had been a witness or ably discussing the processes of war with other proved men. Too it was important that he should have time for physical recuperation. He was sore and stiff from his experiences. He had received his fill of all exertions, and he wished to rest.

But those other men seemed never to grow weary; they were fighting with their old speed. He had a wild hate for the relentless foe. Yesterday, when he had imagined the universe to be against him, he had hated it, little gods and big gods; to-day he hated the army of the foe with the same great hatred. He was not going to be badgered of his life, like a kitten chased by boys, he said. It was not well to drive men into final corners; at those moments they could all develop teeth and claws.

He leaned and spoke into his friend's ear. He menaced the words with a gesture. "If they keep on chasing us, by Gawd, they'd better watch out. Can't stand *too* much."

The friend twisted his head and made a calm reply. "If they keep on a-chasin' us they'll drive us all inteh th' river."

The youth cried out savagely at this statement. He crouched

1. So printed in 1895, perhaps for "burr-like."

behind a little tree, with his eyes burning hatefully and his teeth set in a cur-like snarl. The awkward bandage was still about his head, and upon it, over his wound, there was a spot of dry blood. His hair was wondrously tousled, and some straggling, moving locks hung over the cloth of the bandage down toward his forehead. His jacket and shirt were open at the throat, and exposed his young bronzed neck. There could be seen spasmodic gulpings at his throat.

His fingers twined nervously about his rifle. He wished that it was an engine of annihilating power. He felt that he and his companions were being taunted and derided from sincere convictions that they were poor and puny. His knowledge of his inability to take vengeance for it made his rage into a dark and stormy specter, that possessed him and made him dream of abominable cruelties. The tormentors were flies sucking insolently at his blood, and he thought that he would have given his life for a revenge of seeing their faces in pitiful plights.

The winds of battle had swept all about the regiment, until the one rifle, instantly followed by others, flashed in its front. A moment later the regiment roared forth its sudden and valiant retort. A dense wall of smoke settled slowly down. It was furiously slit and slashed by the knifelike fire from the rifles.

To the youth the fighters resembled animals tossed for a death struggle into a dark pit. There was a sensation that he and his fellows, at bay, were pushing back, always pushing fierce onslaughts of creatures who were slippery. Their beams of crimson seemed to get no purchase upon the bodies of their foes; the latter seemed to evade them with ease, and come through, between, around, and about with unopposed skill.

When, in a dream, it occurred to the youth that his rifle was an impotent stick, he lost sense of everything but his hate, his desire to smash into pulp the glittering smile of victory which he could feel upon the faces of his enemies.

The blue smoke-swallowed line curled and writhed like a snake stepped upon. It swung its ends to and fro in an agony of fear and rage.

The youth was not conscious that he was erect upon his feet. He did not know the direction of the ground. Indeed, once he even lost the habit of balance and fell heavily. He was up again immediately. One thought went through the chaos of his brain at the time. He wondered if he had fallen because he had been shot. But the suspicion flew away at once. He did not think more of it.

He had taken up a first position behind the little tree, with a direct determination to hold it against the world. He had not deemed it possible that his army could that day succeed, and from this he felt the ability to fight harder. But the throng had surged in all ways, until he lost directions and locations, save that he knew where lay the enemy.

The flames bit him, and the hot smoke broiled his skin. His rifle barrel grew so hot that ordinarily he could not have borne it upon his palms; but he kept on stuffing cartridges into it, and pounding them with his clanking, bending ramrod. If he aimed at some changing form through the smoke, he pulled his trigger with a fierce grunt, as if he were dealing a blow of the fist with all his strength.

When the enemy seemed falling back before him and his fellows, he went instantly forward, like a dog who, seeing his foes lagging, turns and insists upon being pursued. And when he was compelled to retire again, he did it slowly, sullenly, taking steps of wrathful despair.

Once he, in his intent hate, was almost alone, and was firing, when all those near him ceased. He was so engrossed in his occupation that he was not aware of a lull.

He was recalled by a hoarse laugh and a sentence that came to his ears in a voice of contempt and amazement. "Yeh infernal fool, don't yeh know enough t' quit when there ain't anything t' shoot at? Good Gawd!"

He turned then and, pausing with his rifle thrown half into position, looked at the blue line of his comrades. During this moment of leisure they seemed all to be engaged in staring with astonishment at him. They had become spectators. Turning to the front again he saw, under the lifted smoke, a deserted ground.

He looked bewildered for a moment. Then there appeared upon the glazed vacancy of his eyes a diamond point of intelligence. "Oh," he said, comprehending.

He returned to his comrades and threw himself upon the ground. He sprawled like a man who had been thrashed. His flesh seemed strangely on fire, and the sounds of the battle continued in his ears. He groped blindly for his canteen.

The lieutenant was crowing. He seemed drunk with fighting. He called out to the youth: "By heavens, if I had ten thousand wild cats like you I could tear th' stomach outa this war in less'n a week!" He puffed out his chest with large dignity as he said it.

Some of the men muttered and looked at the youth in awe-struck ways. It was plain that as he had gone on loading and firing and cursing without the proper intermission, they had found time to regard him. And they now looked upon him as a war devil.

The friend came staggering to him. There was some fright and dismay in his voice. "Are yeh all right, Fleming? Do yeh feel all right? There ain't nothin' th' matter with yeh, Henry, is there?"

"No," said the youth with difficulty. His throat seemed full of knobs and burs.[2]

These incidents made the youth ponder. It was revealed to him that he had been a barbarian, a beast. He had fought like a pagan who defends his religion. Regarding it, he saw that it was fine, wild, and, in some ways, easy. He had been a tremendous figure, no doubt. By this struggle he had overcome obstacles which he had admitted to be mountains. They had fallen like paper peaks, and he was now what he called a hero. And he had not been aware of the process. He had slept and, awakening, found himself a knight.[3]

He lay and basked in the occasional stares of his comrades. Their faces were varied in degrees of blackness from the burned powder. Some were utterly smudged. They were reeking with perspiration, and their breaths came hard and wheezing. And from these soiled expanses they peered at him.

"Hot work! Hot work!" cried the lieutenant deliriously. He walked up and down, restless and eager. Sometimes his voice could be heard in a wild, incomprehensible laugh.

When he had a particularly profound thought upon the science of war he always unconsciously addressed himself to the youth.

There was some grim rejoicing by the men. "By thunder, I bet this army'll never see another new reg'ment like us!"

"You bet!"

"A dog, a woman, an' a walnut tree,
Th' more yeh beat 'em, th' better they be!

That's like us."

"Lost a piler men, they did. If an' ol' woman swep' up th' woods she'd git a dustpanful."

"Yes, an' if she'll come around ag'in in'bout an' hour she'll git a pile more."

The forest still bore its burden of clamor. From off under the trees came the rolling clatter of the musketry. Each distant thicket seemed a strange porcupine with quills of flame. A cloud of dark smoke, as from smoldering ruins, went up toward the sun now bright and gay in the blue, enameled sky.

2. So printed in 1895.
3. *Cf.* Henry's earlier romantic abstraction of the hero; the present contrast is satirically heightened by Crane's portrayal of this "hero" driven only by instinct, fighting blind, with the "intent hate" of a ravening beast. Note the climax of animal images in the language describing this battle.

Chapter XVIII

The ragged line had respite for some minutes, but during its pause the struggle in the forest became magnified until the trees seemed to quiver from the firing and the ground to shake from the rushing of the men. The voices of the cannon were mingled in a long and interminable row. It seemed difficult to live in such an atmosphere. The chests of the men strained for a bit of freshness, and their throats craved water.

There was one shot through the body, who raised a cry of bitter lamentation when came this lull. Perhaps he had been calling out during the fighting also, but at that time no one had heard him. But now the men turned at the woeful complaints of him upon the ground.

"Who is it? Who is it?"

"It's Jimmie Rogers. Jimmie Rogers."

When their eyes first encountered him there was a sudden halt, as if they feared to go near. He was thrashing about in the grass, twisting his shuddering body into many strange postures. He was screaming loudly. This instant's hesitation seemed to fill him with a tremendous, fantastic contempt, and he damned them in shrieked sentences.

The youth's friend had a geographical illusion concerning a stream, and he obtained permission to go for some water. Immediately canteens were showered upon him. "Fill mine, will yeh?" "Bring me some, too." "And me, too." He departed, ladened. The youth went with his friend, feeling a desire to throw his heated body onto the stream and, soaking there, drink quarts.

They made a hurried search for the supposed stream, but did not find it. "No water here," said the youth. They turned without delay and began to retrace their steps.

From their position as they again faced toward the place of the fighting, they could of course comprehend a greater amount of the battle than when their visions had been blurred by the hurling smoke of the line. They could see dark stretches winding along the land, and on one cleared space there was a row of guns making gray clouds, which were filled with large flashes of orange-colored flame. Over some foliage they could see the roof of a house. One window, glowing a deep murder red, shone squarely through the leaves. From the edifice a tall leaning tower of smoke went far into the sky.

Looking over their own troops, they saw mixed masses slowly getting into regular form. The sunlight made twinkling points of

the bright steel. To the rear there was a glimpse of a distant roadway as it curved over a slope. It was crowded with retreating infantry. From all the interwoven forest arose the smoke and bluster
of the battle. The air was always occupied by a blaring.

Near where they stood shells were flip-flapping and hooting. Occasional bullets buzzed in the air and spanged into tree trunks.
Wounded men and other stragglers were slinking through the
woods.

Looking down an aisle of the grove, the youth and his companion saw a jangling general and his staff almost ride upon a
wounded man, who was crawling on his hands and knees. The
general reined strongly at his charger's opened and foamy mouth
and guided it with dexterous horsemanship past the man. The latter
scrambled in wild and torturing haste. His strength evidently failed
him as he reached a place of safety. One of his arms suddenly
weakened, and he fell, sliding over upon his back. He lay stretched
out, breathing gently.

A moment later the small, creaking cavalcade was directly in
front of the two soldiers. Another officer, riding with the skillful
abandon of a cowboy, galloped his horse to a position directly
before the general. The two unnoticed foot soldiers made a little
show of going on, but they lingered near in the desire to overhear
the conversation. Perhaps, they thought, some great inner historical
things would be said.

The general, whom the boys knew as the commander of their
division, looked at the other officer and spoke coolly, as if he were
criticising his clothes. "Th' enemy's formin' over there for another
charge," he said. "It'll be directed against Whiterside, an' I fear
they'll break through there unless we work like thunder t' stop
them."

The other swore at his restive horse, and then cleared his throat.
He made a gesture toward his cap. "It'll be hell t' pay stoppin'
them," he said shortly.

"I presume so," remarked the general. Then he began to talk
rapidly and in a lower tone. He frequently illustrated his words
with a pointing finger. The two infantrymen could hear nothing
until finally he asked: "What troops can you spare?"

The officer who rode like a cowboy reflected for an instant.
"Well," he said, "I had to order in th' 12th to help th' 76th, an'
I haven't really got any. But there's th' 304th. They fight like a lot
'a mule drivers. I can spare them best of any."

The youth and his friend exchanged glances of astonishment.

The general spoke sharply. "Get 'em ready, then. I'll watch de-
velopments from here, an' send you word when t' start them. It'll

happen in five minutes."

As the other officer tossed his fingers toward his cap and wheel-ing his horse, started away, the general called out to him in a sober voice: "I don't believe many of your mule drivers will get back."

The other shouted something in reply. He smiled.

With scared faces, the youth and his companion hurried back to the line.

These happenings had occupied an incredibly short time, yet the youth felt that in them he had been made aged. New eyes were given to him. And the most startling thing was to learn suddenly that he was very insignificant. The officer spoke of the regiment as if he referred to a broom. Some part of the woods needed sweeping, perhaps, and he merely indicated a broom in a tone properly indif-ferent to its fate. It was war, no doubt, but it appeared strange.

As the two boys approached the line, the lieutenant perceived them and swelled with wrath. "Fleming—Wilson—how long does its take yeh to git water, anyhow—where yeh been to."

But his oration ceased as he saw their eyes, which were large with great tales. "We're goin' t' charge—we're goin' t' charge!" cried the youth's friend, hastening with his news.

"Charge?" said the lieutenant. "Charge? Well, b'Gawd! Now, this is real fightin'." Over his soiled countenance there went a boastful smile. "Charge? Well, b'Gawd!"

A little group of soldiers surrounded the two youths. "Are we, sure 'nough? Well, I'll be derned! Charge? What fer? What at? Wilson, you're lyin'."

"I hope to die," said the youth, pitching his tones to the key of angry remonstrance. "Sure as shooting, I tell you."

And his friend spoke in re-enforcement. "Not by a blame sight, he ain't lyin'. We heard 'em talkin'."

They caught sight of two mounted figures a short distance from them. One was the colonel of the regiment and the other was the officer who had received orders from the commander of the division. They were gesticulating at each other. The soldier, pointing at them, interpreted the scene.

One man had a final objection: "How could yeh hear 'em talkin'?" But the men, for a large part, nodded, admitting that pre-viously the two friends had spoken truth.

They settled back into reposeful attitudes with airs of having accepted the matter. And they mused upon it, with a hundred vari-eties of expression. It was an engrossing thing to think about. Many tightened their belts carefully and hitched at their trousers.

A moment later the officers began to bustle among the men,

pushing them into a more compact mass and into a better alignment. They chased those that straggled and fumed at a few men
who seemed to show by their attitudes that they had decided to
remain at that spot. They were like critical shepherds struggling
with sheep.

Presently, the regiment seemed to draw itself up and heave a
deep breath. None of the men's faces were mirrors of large
thoughts. The soldiers were bended and stooped like sprinters
before a signal. Many pairs of glinting eyes peered from the grimy
faces toward the curtains of the deeper woods. They seemed to be
engaged in deep calculations of time and distance.

They were surrounded by the noises of the monstrous altercation
between the two armies. The world was fully interested in other
matters. Apparently, the regiment had its small affair to itself.

The youth, turning, shot a quick, inquiring glance at his friend.
The latter returned to him the same manner of look. They were
the only ones who possessed an inner knowledge. "Mule drivers—
hell t' pay—don't believe many will get back." It was an ironical
secret. Still, they saw no hesitation in each other's faces, and they
nodded a mute and unprotesting assent when a shaggy man near
them said in a meek voice: "We'll git swallowed."

Chapter XIX

The youth stared at the land in front of him. Its foliages now
seemed to veil powers and horrors. He was unaware of the machinery of orders that started the charge, although from the corners
of his eyes he saw an officer, who looked like a boy a-horseback,
come galloping, waving his hat. Suddenly he felt a straining and
heaving among the men. The line fell slowly forward like a toppling
wall, and, with a convulsive gasp that was intended for a cheer, the
regiment began its journey. The youth was pushed and jostled for
a moment before he understood the movement at all, but directly
he lunged ahead and began to run.

He fixed his eye upon a distant and prominent clump of trees
where he had concluded the enemy were to be met, and he ran toward it as toward a goal. He had believed throughout that it was a
mere question of getting over an unpleasant matter as quickly as
possible, and he ran desperately, as if pursued for a murder. His
face was drawn hard and tight with the stress of his endeavor. His
eyes were fixed in a lurid glare. And with his soiled and disordered
dress, his red and inflamed features surmounted by the dingy rag
with its spot of blood, his wildly swinging rifle and banging accou-
terments, he looked to be an insane soldier.

As the regiment swung from its position out into a cleared space
the woods and thickets before it awakened. Yellow flames leaped
toward it from many directions. The forest made a tremendous objection.

The line lurched straight for a moment. Then the right wing
swung forward; it in turn was surpassed by the left. Afterward the
center careered to the front until the regiment was a wedge-shaped
mass, but an instant later the opposition of the bushes, trees, and
uneven places on the ground split the command and scattered it
into detached clusters.

The youth, light-footed, was unconsciously in advance. His eyes
still kept note of the clump of trees. From all places near it the
clannish yell of the enemy could be heard. The little flames of
rifles leaped from it. The song of the bullets was in the air and
shells snarled among the treetops. One tumbled directly into the
middle of a hurrying group and exploded in crimson fury. There
was an instant's spectacle of a man, almost over it, throwing up his
hands to shield his eyes.

Other men, punched by bullets, fell in grotesque agonies. The
regiment left a coherent trail of bodies.

They had passed into a clearer atmosphere. There was an effect
like a revelation in the new appearance of the landscape. Some men
working madly at a battery were plain to them, and the opposing
infantry's lines were defined by the gray walls and fringes of smoke.

It seemed to the youth that he saw everything. Each blade of the
green grass was bold and clear. He thought that he was aware of
every change in the thin, transparent vapor that floated idly in
sheets. The brown or gray trunks of the trees showed each rough-
ness of their surfaces. And the men of the regiment, with their
starting eyes and sweating faces, running madly, or falling, as if
thrown headlong, to queer, heaped-up corpses—all were comprehended. His mind took a mechanical but firm impression, so that
afterward everything was pictured and explained to him, save why
he himself was there.

But there was a frenzy made from this furious rush. The men,
pitching forward insanely, had burst into cheerings, moblike and
barbaric, but tuned in strange keys that can arouse the dullard
and the stoic. It made a mad enthusiasm that, it seemed, would be
incapable of checking itself before granite and brass. There was the
delirium that encounters despair and death, and is heedless and
blind to the odds. It is a temporary but sublime absence of selfishness. And because it was of this order was the reason, perhaps, why
the youth wondered, afterward, what reasons he could have had for
being there.

Presently the straining pace ate up the energies of the men. As if by agreement, the leaders began to slacken their speed. The volleys directed against them had had a seeming windlike effect. The regiment snorted and blew. Among some stolid trees it began to falter and hesitate. The men, staring intently, began to wait for some of the distant walls of smoke to move and disclose to them the scene. Since much of their strength and their breath had vanished, they returned to caution. They were become men again.

The youth had a vague belief that he had run miles, and he thought, in a way, that he was now in some new and unknown land.

The moment the regiment ceased its advance the protesting splutter of musketry became a steadied roar. Long and accurate fringes of smoke spread out. From the top of a small hill came level belchings of yellow flame that caused an inhuman whistling in the air.

The men, halted, had opportunity to see some of their comrades dropping with moans and shrieks. A few lay under foot, still or wailing. And now for an instant the men stood, their rifles slack in their hands, and watched the regiment dwindle. They appeared dazed and stupid. This spectacle seemed to paralyze them, overcome them with a fatal fascination. They stared woodenly at the sights, and, lowering their eyes, looked from face to face. It was a strange pause, and a strange silence.

Then, above the sounds of the outside commotion, arose the roar of the lieutenant. He strode suddenly forth, his infantile features black with rage.

"Come on, yeh fools!" he bellowed. "Come on! Yeh can't stay here. Yeh must come on." He said more, but much of it could not be understood.

He started rapidly forward, with his head turned toward the men. "Come on," he was shouting. The men stared with blank and yokel-like eyes at him. He was obliged to halt and retrace his steps. He stood then with his back to the enemy and delivered gigantic curses into the faces of the men. His body vibrated from the weight and force of his imprecations. And he could string oaths with the facility of a maiden who strings beads.

The friend of the youth aroused. Lurching suddenly forward and dropping to his knees, he fired an angry shot at the persistent woods. This action awakened the men. They huddled no more like sheep. They seemed suddenly to bethink them of their weapons, and at once commenced firing. Belabored by their officers, they began to move forward. The regiment, involved like a cart involved in mud and muddle, started unevenly with many jolts and jerks. The men stopped now every few paces to fire and load, and in this manner moved slowly on from trees to trees.

The flaming opposition in their front grew with their advance until it seemed that all forward ways were barred by the thin leaping tongues, and off to the right an ominous demonstration could sometimes be dimly discerned. The smoke lately generated was in confusing clouds that made it difficult for the regiment to proceed with intelligence. As he passed through each curling mass the youth wondered what would confront him on the farther side.

The command went painfully forward until an open space interposed between them and the lurid lines. Here, crouching and cowering behind some trees, the men clung with desperation, as if threatened by a wave. They looked wild-eyed, and as if amazed at this furious disturbance they had stirred. In the storm there was an ironical expression of their importance. The faces of the men, too, showed a lack of a certain feeling of responsibility for being there. It was as if they had been driven. It was the dominant animal failing to remember in the supreme moments the forceful causes of various superficial qualities. The whole affair seemed incomprehensible to many of them.

As they halted thus the lieutenant again began to bellow profanely. Regardless of the vindictive threats of the bullets, he went about coaxing, berating, and bedamning. His lips, that were habitually in a soft and childlike curve, were now writhed into unholy contortions. He swore by all possible deities.

Once he grabbed the youth by the arm. "Come on, yeh lunkhead!" he roared. "Come on! We'll all git killed if we stay here. We've on'y got t' go across that lot. An' then"—the remainder of his idea disappeared in a blue haze of curses.

The youth stretched forth his arm. "Cross there?" His mouth was puckered in doubt and awe.

"Certainly. Jest 'cross th' lot! We can't stay here," screamed the lieutenant. He poked his face close to the youth and waved his bandaged hand. "Come on!" Presently he grappled with him as if for a wrestling bout. It was as if he planned to drag the youth by the ear on to the assault.

The private felt a sudden unspeakable indignation against his officer. He wrenched fiercely and shook him off.

"Come on yerself, then," he yelled. There was a bitter challenge in his voice.

They galloped together down the regimental front. The friend scrambled after them. In front of the colors the three men began to bawl: "Come on! come on!" They danced and gyrated like tortured savages.

The flag, obedient to these appeals, bended its glittering form and swept toward them. The men wavered in indecision for a moment, and then with a long, wailful cry the dilapidated regiment surged forward and began its new journey.

Over the field went the scurrying mass. It was a handful of men splattered into the faces of the enemy. Toward it instantly sprang the yellow tongues. A vast quantity of blue smoke hung before them. A mighty banging made ears valueless.

The youth ran like a madman to reach the woods before a bullet could discover him. He ducked his head low, like a football player. In his haste his eyes almost closed, and the scene was a wild blur. Pulsating saliva stood at the corners of his mouth.

Within him, as he hurled himself forward, was born a love, a despairing fondness for this flag which was near him. It was a creation of beauty and invulnerability. It was a goddess, radiant, that bended its form with an imperious gesture to him. It was a woman, red and white, hating and loving, that called him with the voice of his hopes. Because no harm could come to it he endowed it with power. He kept near, as if it could be a saver of lives, and an imploring cry went from his mind.

In the mad scramble he was aware that the color sergeant flinched suddenly, as if struck by a bludgeon. He faltered, and then became motionless, save for his quivering knees.

He made a spring and a clutch at the pole. At the same instant his friend grabbed it from the other side. They jerked at it, stout and furious, but the color sergeant was dead, and the corpse would not relinquish its trust. For a moment there was a grim encounter. The dead man, swinging with bended back, seemed to be obstinately tugging, in ludicrous and awful ways, for the possession of the flag.

It was past in an instant of time. They wrenched the flag furiously from the dead man, and, as they turned again, the corpse swayed forward with bowed head. One arm swung high, and the curved hand fell with heavy protest on the friend's unheeding shoulder.

Chapter XX

When the two youths turned with the flag they saw that much of the regiment had crumbled away, and the dejected remnant was coming slowly back. The men, having hurled themselves in projectile fashion, had presently expended their forces. They slowly retreated, with their faces still toward the spluttering woods, and their hot rifles still replying to the din. Several officers were giving orders, their voices keyed to screams.

"Where in hell yeh goin'?" the lieutenant was asking in a sarcastic howl. And a red-bearded officer, whose voice of triple brass could plainly be heard, was commanding: "Shoot into 'em! Shoot into 'em, Gawd damn their souls!" There was a *melée* of screeches, in which the men were ordered to do conflicting and impossible things.

The youth and his friend had a small scuffle over the flag. "Give it t' me!" "No, let me keep it!" Each felt satisfied with the other's possession of it, but each felt bound to declare, by an offer to carry the emblem, his willingness to further risk himself. The youth roughly pushed his friend away.

The regiment fell back to the stolid trees. There it halted for a moment to blaze at some dark forms that had begun to steal upon its track. Presently it resumed its march again, curving among the tree trunks. By the time the depleted regiment had again reached the first open space they were receiving a fast and merciless fire. There seemed to be mobs all about them.

The greater part of the men, discouraged, their spirits worn by the turmoil, acted as if stunned. They accepted the pelting of the bullets with bowed and weary heads. It was of no purpose to strive against walls. It was of no use to batter themselves against granite. And from this consciousness that they had attempted to conquer an unconquerable thing there seemed to arise a feeling that they had been betrayed. They glowered with bent brows, but dangerously, upon some of the officers, more particularly upon the red-bearded one with the voice of triple brass.

However, the rear of the regiment was fringed with men, who continued to shoot irritably at the advancing foes. They seemed resolved to make every trouble. The youthful lieutenant was perhaps the last man in the disordered mass. His forgotten back was toward the enemy. He had been shot in the arm. It hung straight and rigid. Occasionally he would cease to remember it, and be about to emphasize an oath with a sweeping gesture. The multiplied pain caused him to swear with incredible power.

The youth went along with slipping, uncertain feet. He kept watchful eyes rearward. A scowl of mortification and rage was upon his face. He had thought of a fine revenge upon the officer who had referred to him and his fellows as mule drivers. But he saw that it could not come to pass. His dreams had collapsed when the mule drivers, dwindling rapidly, had wavered and hesitated on the little clearing, and then had recoiled. And now the retreat of the mule drivers was a march of shame to him.

A dagger-pointed gaze from without his blackened face was held toward the enemy, but his greater hatred was riveted upon the man, who, not knowing him, had called him a mule driver.

When he knew that he and his comrades had failed to do anything in successful ways that might bring the little pangs of a kind of remorse upon the officer, the youth allowed the rage of the baffled to possess him. This cold officer upon a monument, who dropped epithets unconcernedly down, would be finer as a dead man, he thought. So grievous did he think it that he could never possess the secret right to taunt truly in answer.

He had pictured red letters of curious revenge. "We *are* mule drivers, are we?" And now he was compelled to throw them away.

He presently wrapped his heart in the cloak of his pride and kept the flag erect. He harangued his fellows, pushing against their chests with his free hand. To those he knew well he made frantic appeals, beseeching them by name. Between him and the lieutenant, scolding and near to losing his mind with rage, there was felt a subtle fellowship and equality. They supported each other in all manner of hoarse, howling protests.

But the regiment was a machine run down. The two men babbled at a forceless thing. The soldiers who had heart to go slowly were continually shaken in their resolves by a knowledge that comrades were slipping with speed back to the lines. It was difficult to think of reputations when others were thinking of skins. Wounded men were left crying on this black journey.

The smoke fringes and flames blustered always. The youth, peering once through a sudden rift in a cloud, saw a brown mass of troops, interwoven and magnified until they appeared to be thousands. A fierce-hued flag flashed before his vision.

Immediately, as if the uplifting of the smoke had been prearranged, the discovered troops burst into a rasping yell, and a hundred flames jetted toward the retreating band. A rolling gray cloud again interposed as the regiment doggedly replied. The youth had to depend again upon his misused ears, which were trembling and buzzing from the *melée* of musketry and yells.

The way seemed eternal. In the clouded haze men became panicstricken with the thought that the regiment had lost its path, and was proceeding in a perilous direction. Once the men who headed the wild procession turned and came pushing back against their comrades, screaming that they were being fired upon from points which they had considered to be toward their own lines. At this cry a hysterical fear and dismay beset the troops. A soldier, who heretofore had been ambitious to make the regiment into a wise little band that would proceed calmly amid the huge-appearing difficulties, suddenly sank down and buried his face in his arms with an air of bowing to a doom. From another a shrill lamentation rang out filled with profane allusions[4] to a general. Men ran hither and thither, seeking with their eyes roads of escape. With serene regularity, as if controlled by a schedule, bullets buffed into men.

The youth walked stolidly into the midst of the mob, and with his flag in his hands took a stand as if he expected an attempt to push him to the ground. He unconsciously assumed the attitude of the color bearer in the fight of the preceding day. He passed over his brow a hand that trembled. His breath did not come freely. He was choking during this small wait for the crisis.

His friend came to him. "Well, Henry, I guess this is good-by— John."

"Oh, shut up, you damned fool!" replied the youth, and he would not look at the other.

The officers labored like politicians to beat the mass into a proper circle to face the menaces. The ground was uneven and torn. The men curled into depressions and fitted themselves snugly behind whatever would frustrate a bullet.

The youth noted with vague surprise that the lieutenant was standing mutely with his legs far apart and his sword held in the manner of a cane. The youth wondered what had happened to his vocal organs that he no more cursed.

There was something curious in this little intent pause of the lieutenant. He was like a babe which, having wept its fill, raises its eyes and fixes upon a distant joy. He was engrossed in this contemplation, and the soft under lip quivered from self-whispered words.

Some lazy and ignorant smoke curled slowly. The men, hiding from the bullets, waited anxiously for it to lift and disclose the plight of the regiment.

The silent ranks were suddenly thrilled by the eager voice of the youthful lieutenant bawling out: "Here they come! Right onto us, b'Gawd!" His further words were lost in a roar of wicked thunder from the men's rifles.

The youth's eyes had instantly turned in the direction indicated by the awakened and agitated lieutenant, and he had seen the haze of treachery disclosing a body of soldiers of the enemy. They were so near that he could see their features. There was a recognition as he looked at the types of faces. Also he perceived with dim amazement that their uniforms were rather gay in effect, being light gray, accented with a brilliant-hued facing. Too, the clothes seemed new.

These troops had apparently been going forward with caution, their rifles held in readiness, when the youthful lieutenant had discovered them and their movement had been interrupted by the volley from the blue regiment. From the moment's glimpse, it was

4. Misprinted as "illusions" in 1895.

derived that they had been unaware of the proximity of their dark-suited foes or had mistaken the direction. Almost instantly they were shut utterly from the youth's sight by the smoke from the energetic rifles of his companions. He strained his vision to learn the accomplishment of the volley, but the smoke hung before him.

The two bodies of troops exchanged blows in the manner of a pair of boxers. The fast angry firings went back and forth. The men in blue were intent with the despair of their circumstances and they seized upon the revenge to be had at close range. Their thunder swelled loud and valiant. Their curving front bristled with flashes and the place resounded with the clangor of their ramrods. The youth ducked and dodged for a time and achieved a few unsatisfactory views of the enemy. There appeared to be many of them and they were replying swiftly. They seemed moving toward the blue regiment, step by step. He seated himself gloomily on the ground with his flag between his knees.

As he noted the vicious, wolflike temper of his comrades he had a sweet thought that if the enemy was about to swallow the regimental broom as a large prisoner, it could at least have the consolation of going down with bristles forward.

But the blows of the antagonist began to grow more weak. Fewer bullets ripped the air, and finally, when the men slackened to learn of the fight, they could see only dark, floating smoke. The regiment lay still and gazed. Presently some chance whim came to the pestering blur, and it began to coil heavily away. The men saw a ground vacant of fighters. It would have been an empty stage if it were not for a few corpses that lay thrown and twisted into fantastic shapes upon the sward.

At sight of this tableau, many of the men in blue sprang from behind their covers and made an ungainly dance of joy. Their eyes burned and a hoarse cheer of elation broke from their dry lips.

It had begun to seem to them that events were trying to prove that they were impotent. These little battles had evidently endeavored to demonstrate that the men could not fight well. When on the verge of submission to these opinions, the small duel had showed them that the proportions were not impossible, and by it they had revenged themselves upon their misgivings and upon the foe.

The impetus of enthusiasm was theirs again. They gazed about them with looks of uplifted pride, feeling new trust in the grim, always confident weapons in their hands. And they were men.

Chapter XXI

Presently they knew that no firing threatened them. All ways seemed once more opened to them. ' .e dusty blue lines of their friends were disclosed a short distance away. In the distance there were many colossal noises, but in all this part of the field there was a sudden stillness.

They perceived that they were free. The depleted band drew a long breath of relief and gathered itself into a bunch to complete its trip.

In this last length of journey the men began to show strange emotions. They hurried with nervous fear. Some who had been dark and unfaltering in the grimmest moments now could not conceal an anxiety that made them frantic. It was perhaps that they dreaded to be killed in insignificant ways after the times for proper military deaths had passed. Or, perhaps, they thought it would be too ironical to get killed at the portals of safety. With backward looks of perturbation, they hastened.

As they approached their own lines there was some sarcasm exhibited on the part of a gaunt and bronzed regiment that lay resting in the shade of trees. Questions were wafted to them.

"Where th' hell yeh been?"

"What yeh comin' back fer?"

"Why didn't yeh stay there?"

"Was it warm out there, sonny?"

"Goin' home now, boys?"

One shouted in taunting mimicry: "Oh, mother, come quick an' look at th' sojers!"

There was no reply from the bruised and battered regiment, save that one man made broadcast challenges to fist fights and the red-bearded officer walked rather near and glared in great swashbuckler style at a tall captain in the other regiment. But the lieutenant suppressed the man who wished to fist fight, and the tall captain, flushing at the little fanfare of the red-bearded one, was obliged to look intently at some trees.

The youth's tender flesh was deeply stung by these remarks. From under his creased brows he glowered with hate at the mockers. He meditated upon a few revenges. Still, many in the regiment hung their heads in criminal fashion, so that it came to pass that the men trudged with sudden heaviness, as if they bore upon their bended shoulders the coffin of their honor. And the youthful lieutenant, recollecting himself, began to mutter softly in black curses.

They turned when they arrived at their old position to regard the ground over which they had charged.

The youth in this contemplation was smitten with a large astonishment. He discovered that the distances, as compared with the brilliant measurings of his mind, were trivial and ridiculous. The stolid trees, where much had taken place, seemed incredibly near. The time, too, now that he reflected, he saw to have been short. He wondered at the number of emotions and events that had been crowded into such little spaces. Elfin thoughts must have exaggerated and enlarged everything, he said.

It seemed, then, that there was bitter justice in the speeches of the gaunt and bronzed veterans. He veiled a glance of disdain at his fellows who strewed the ground, choking with dust, red from perspiration, misty-eyed, disheveled.

They were gulping at their canteens, fierce to wring every mite of water from them, and they polished at their swollen and watery features with coat sleeves and bunches of grass.

However, to the youth there was a considerable joy in musing upon his performance during the charge. He had had very little time previously in which to appreciate himself, so that there was now much satisfaction in quietly thinking of his actions. He recalled bits of color that in the flurry had stamped themselves unawares upon his engaged senses.

As the regiment lay heaving from its hot exertions the officer who had named them as mule drivers came galloping along the line. He had lost his cap. His tousled hair streamed wildly, and his face was dark with vexation and wrath. His temper was displayed with more clearness by the way in which he managed his horse. He jerked and wrenched savagely at his bridle, stopping the hard-breathing animal with a furious pull near the colonel of the regiment. He immediately exploded in reproaches which came unbidden to the ears of the men. They were suddenly alert, being always curious about black words between officers.

"Oh, thunder, MacChesnay, what an awful bull you made of this thing!" began the officer. He attempted low tones, but his indignation caused certain of the men to learn the sense of his words. "What an awful mess you made! Good Lord, man, you stopped about a hundred feet this side of a very pretty success! If your men had gone a hundred feet farther you would have made a great charge, but as it is—what a lot of mud diggers you've got anyway!"

The men, listening with bated breath, now turned their curious eyes upon the colonel. They had a ragamuffin interest in this affair.

The colonel was seen to straighten his form and put one hand forth in oratorical fashion. He wore an injured air; it was as if a deacon had been accused of stealing. The men were wiggling in an ecstasy of excitement.

But of a sudden the colonel's manner changed from that of a deacon to that of a Frenchman. He shrugged his shoulders. "Oh, well, general, we went as far as we could," he said calmly.

"As far as you could? Did you, b'Gawd?" snorted the other. "Well, that wasn't very far, was it?" he added, with a glance of cold contempt into the other's eyes. "Not very far, I think. You were intended to make a diversion in favor of Whiterside. How well you succeeded your own ears can now tell you." He wheeled his horse and rode stiffly away.

The colonel, bidden to hear the jarring noises of an engagement in the woods to the left, broke out in vague damnations.

The lieutenant, who had listened with an air of impotent rage to the interview, spoke suddenly in firm and undaunted tones. "I don't care what a man is—whether he is a general or what—if he says th' boys didn't put up a good fight out there he's a damned fool."

"Lieutenant," began the colonel, severely, "this is my own affair, and I'll trouble you——"

The lieutenant made an obedient gesture. "All right, colonel, all right," he said. He sat down with an air of being content with himself.

The news that the regiment had been reproached went along the line. For a time the men were bewildered by it. "Good thunder!" they ejaculated, staring at the vanishing form of the general. They conceived it to be a huge mistake.

Presently, however, they began to believe that in truth their efforts had been called light. The youth could see this conviction weigh upon the entire regiment until the men were liked cuffed and cursed animals, but withal rebellious.

The friend, with a grievance in his eye, went to the youth. "I wonder what he does want," he said. "He must think we went out there an' played marbles! I never see sech a man!"

The youth developed a tranquil philosophy for these moments of irritation. "Oh, well," he rejoined, "he probably didn't see nothing of it at all and got mad as blazes, and concluded we were a lot of sheep, just because we didn't do what he wanted done. It's a pity old Grandpa Henderson got killed yestirday—he'd have known that we did our best and fought good. It's just our awful luck, that's what."

"I should say so," replied the friend. He seemed to be deeply wounded at an injustice. "I should say we did have awful luck! There's no fun in fightin' fer people when everything yeh do—no matter what—ain't done right. I have a notion t' stay behind next time an' let 'em take their ol' charge an' go t' th' devil with it."

The youth spoke soothingly to his comrade. "Well, we both did good. I'd like to see the fool what'd say we both didn't do as good as we could!"

"Of course we did," declared the friend stoutly. "An' I'd break th' feller's neck if he was as big as a church. But we're all right, anyhow, for I heard one feller say that we two fit th' best in th' reg'ment, an' they had a great argument 'bout it. Another feller, 'a course, he had t' up an' say it was a lie—he seen all what was goin' on an' he never seen us from th' beginnin' t' th' end. An' a lot more struck in an' ses it wasn't a lie—we did fight like thunder, an' they give us quite a send-off. But this is what I can't stand—these everlastin' ol' soldiers, titterin' an' laughin', an' then that general, he's crazy."

The youth exclaimed with sudden exasperation: "He's a lunk-head! He makes me mad. I wish he'd come along next time. We'd show 'im what——"

He ceased because several men had come hurrying up. Their faces expressed a bringing of great news.

"O Flem, yeh jest oughta heard!" cried one, eagerly.

"Heard what?" said the youth.

"Yeh jest oughta heard!" repeated the other, and he arranged himself to tell his tidings. The others made an excited circle. "Well, sir, th' colonel met your lieutenant right by us—it was damnedest thing I ever heard—an' he ses: 'Ahem! ahem!' he ses. 'Mr. Hasbrouck!' he ses, 'by th' way, who was that lad what carried th' flag?' he ses. There, Flemin', what d' yeh think 'a that? 'Who was th' lad what carried th' flag?' he ses, an' th' lieutenant, he speaks up right away: 'That's Flemin', an' he's a jimhickey,' he ses, right away. What? I say he did. 'A jimhickey,' he ses—those 'r his words. He did, too. I say he did. If you kin tell this story better than I kin, go ahead an' tell it. Well, then, keep yer mouth shet. Th' lieutenant, he ses: 'He's a jimhickey,' an' th' colonel, he ses: 'Ahem! ahem! he is, indeed, a very good man t' have, ahem! He kep' th' flag 'way t' th' front. I saw 'im. He's a good un,' ses th' colonel. 'You bet,' ses th' lieutenant, 'he an' a feller named Wilson was at th' head 'a th' charge, an' howlin' like Indians all th' time,' he ses. 'Head 'a th' charge all th' time,' he ses. 'A feller named Wilson,' he ses. There, Wilson, m'boy, put that in a letter an' send it hum t' yer mother, hay? 'A feller named Wilson,' he ses. An' the colonel, he ses: 'Were they, indeed? Ahem! ahem! My sakes!' he ses. 'At th' head 'a th' reg'ment?' he ses. 'They were,' ses th' lieutenant. 'My sakes!' ses th' colonel. He ses: 'Well, well, well,' he ses, 'those two babies?' 'They were,' ses th' lieutenant.

'Well, well,' ses th' colonel, 'they deserve t' be major generals,' he ses. 'They deserve t' be major-generals.'

The youth and his friend had said: "Huh!" "Yer lyin', Thompson." "Oh, go t' blazes!" "He never sed it." "Oh, what a lie!" "Huh!" But despite these youthful scoffings and embarrassments, they knew that their faces were deeply flushing from thrills of pleasure. They exchanged a secret glance of joy and congratulation.

They speedily forgot many things. The past held no pictures of error and disappointment. They were very happy, and their hearts swelled with grateful affection for the colonel and the youthful lieutenant.

Chapter XXII

When the woods again began to pour forth the dark-hued masses of the enemy the youth felt serene self-confidence. He smiled briefly when he saw men dodge and duck at the long screechings of shells that were thrown in giant handfuls over them. He stood, erect and tranquil, watching the attack begin against a part of the line that made a blue curve along the side of an adjacent hill. His vision being unmolested by smoke from the rifles of his companions, he had opportunities to see parts of the hard fight. It was a relief to perceive at last from whence came some of these noises which had been roared into his ears.

Off a short way he saw two regiments fighting a little separate battle with two other regiments. It was in a cleared space, wearing a set-apart look. They were blazing as if upon a wager, giving and taking tremendous blows. The firings were incredibly fierce and rapid. These intent regiments apparently were oblivious of all larger purposes of war, and were slugging each other as if at a matched game.

In another direction he saw a magnificent brigade going with the evident intention of driving the enemy from a wood. They passed in out of sight and presently there was a most awe-inspiring racket in the wood. The noise was unspeakable. Having stirred this prodigious uproar, and, apparently, finding it too prodigious, the brigade, after a little time, came marching airily out again with its fine formation in nowise disturbed. There were no traces of speed in its movements. The brigade was jaunty and seemed to point a proud thumb at the yelling wood.

On a slope to the left there was a long row of guns, gruff and maddened, denouncing the enemy, who, down through the woods, were forming for another attack in the pitiless monotony of conflicts. The round red discharges from the guns made a crimson flare and a high, thick smoke. Occasional glimpses could be caught of groups of the toiling artillerymen. In the rear of this row of guns stood a house, calm and white, amid bursting shells. A congregation of horses, tied to a long railing, were tugging frenziedly at their bridles. Men were running hither and thither.

The detached battle between the four regiments lasted for some time. There chanced to be no interference, and they settled their dispute by themselves. They struck savagely and powerfully at each other for a period of minutes, and then the lighter-hued regiments faltered and drew back, leaving the dark-blue lines shouting. The youth could see the two flags shaking with laughter amid the smoke remnants.

Presently there was a stillness, pregnant with meaning. The blue lines shifted and changed a trifle and stared expectantly at the silent woods and fields before them. The hush was solemn and churchlike, save for a distant battery that, evidently unable to remain quiet, sent a faint rolling thunder over the ground. It irritated, like the noises of unimpressed[5] boys. The men imagined that it would prevent their perched ears from hearing the first words of the new battle.

Of a sudden the guns on the slope roared out a message of warning. A spluttering sound had begun in the woods. It swelled with amazing speed to a profound clamor that involved the earth in noises. The splitting crashes swept along the lines until an interminable roar was developed. To those in the midst of it it became a din fitted to the universe. It was the whirring and thumping of gigantic machinery, complications among the smaller stars. The youth's ears were filled up. They were incapable of hearing more.

On an incline over which a road wound he saw wild and desperate rushes of men perpetually backward and forward in riotous surges. These parts of the opposing armies were two long waves that pitched upon each other madly at dictated points. To and fro they swelled. Sometimes, one side by its yells and cheers would proclaim decisive blows, but a moment later the other side would be all yells and cheers. Once the youth saw a spray of light forms go in houndlike leaps toward the wavering blue lines. There was much howling, and presently it went away with a vast mouthful of prisoners. Again, he saw a blue wave dash with such thunderous force against a gray obstruction that it seemed to clear the earth of it and leave nothing but trampled sod. And always in their swift and deadly rushes to and fro the men screamed and yelled like maniacs.

5. So printed in 1895, perhaps in error for "unrepressed."

Particular pieces of fence or secure positions behind collections of trees were wrangled over, as gold thrones or pearl bedsteads. There were desperate lunges at these chosen spots seemingly every instant, and most of them were bandied like light toys between the contending forces. The youth could not tell from the battle flags flying like crimson foam in many directions which color of cloth was winning.

His emaciated regiment bustled forth with undiminished fierceness when its time came. When assaulted again by bullets, the men burst out in a barbaric cry of rage and pain. They bent their heads in aims of intent hatred behind the projected hammers of their guns. Their ramrods clanged loud with fury as their eager arms pounded the cartridges into the rifle barrels. The front of the regiment was a smoke-wall penetrated by the flashing points of yellow and red.

Wallowing in the fight, they were in an astonishingly short time resmudged. They surpassed in stain and dirt all their previous appearances. Moving to and fro with strained exertion, jabbering the while, they were, with their swaying bodies, black faces, and glowing eyes, like strange and ugly fiends[6] jigging heavily in the smoke.

The lieutenant, returning from a tour after a bandage, produced from a hidden receptacle of his mind new and portentous oaths suited to the emergency. Strings of expletives he swung lashlike over the backs of his men, and it was evident that his previous efforts had in nowise impaired his resources.

The youth, still the bearer of the colors, did not feel his idleness. He was deeply absorbed as a spectator. The crash and swing of the great drama made him lean forward, intent-eyed, his face working in small contortions. Sometimes he prattled, words coming unconsciously from him in grotesque exclamations. He did not know that he breathed; that the flag hung silently over him, so absorbed was he.

A formidable line of the enemy came within dangerous range. They could be seen plainly—tall, gaunt men with excited faces running with long strides toward a wandering fence.

At sight of this danger the men suddenly ceased their cursing monotone. There was an instant of strained silence before they threw up their rifles and fired a plumping volley at the foes. There had been no order given; the men, upon recognizing the menace, had immediately let drive their flock of bullets without waiting for word of command.

But the enemy were quick to gain the protection of the wander-

6. Misprinted as "friends" in 1895.

ing line of fence. They slid down behind it with remarkable celerity, and from this position they began briskly to slice up the blue men.

These latter braced their energies for a great struggle. Often, white clinched teeth shone from the dusky faces. Many heads surged to and fro, floating upon a pale sea of smoke. Those behind the fence frequently shouted and yelped in taunts and gibe-like cries, but the regiment maintained a stressed silence. Perhaps, at this new assault the men recalled the fact they had been named mud diggers, and it made their situation thrice bitter. They were breathlessly intent upon keeping the ground and thrusting away the rejoicing body of the enemy. They fought swiftly and with a despairing savageness denoted in their expressions.

The youth had resolved not to budge whatever should happen. Some arrows of scorn that had buried themselves in his heart had generated strange and unspeakable hatred. It was clear to him that his final and absolute revenge was to be achieved by his dead body lying, torn and gluttering,[7] upon the field. This was to be a poignant retaliation upon the officer who had said "mule drivers," and later "mud diggers," for in all the wild graspings of his mind for a unit responsible for his sufferings and commotions he always seized upon the man who had dubbed him wrongly. And it was his idea, vaguely formulated, that his corpse would be for those eyes a great and salt reproach.

The regiment bled extravagantly. Grunting bundles of blue began to drop. The orderly sergeant of the youth's company was shot through the cheeks. Its supports being injured, his jaw hung afar down, disclosing in the wide cavern of his mouth a pulsing mass of blood and teeth. And with it all he made attempts to cry out. In his endeavor there was a dreadful earnestness, as if he conceived that one great shriek would make him well.

The youth saw him presently go rearward. His strength seemed in nowise impaired. He ran swiftly, casting wild glances for succor.

Others fell down about the feet of their companions. Some of the wounded crawled out and away, but many lay still, their bodies twisted into impossible shapes.

The youth looked once for his friend. He saw a vehement young man, powder-smeared and frowzled, whom he knew to be him.[8] The lieutenant, also, was unscathed in his position at the rear. He had continued to curse, but it was now with the air of a man who was using his last box of oaths.

For the fire of the regiment had begun to wane and drip. The

7. So printed in 1895, perhaps in error for "guttering," as when melting wax drips from a lighted candle.

8. So printed in 1895.

robust voice, that had come strangely from the thin ranks, was growing rapidly weak.

Chapter XXIII

The colonel came running along back of the line. There were other officers following him. "We must charge 'm!" they shouted. "We must charge 'm!" they cried with resentful voices, as if anticipating a rebellion against this plan by the men.

The youth, upon hearing the shouts, began to study the distance between him and the enemy. He made vague calculations. He saw that to be firm soldiers they must go forward. It would be death to stay in the present place, and with all the circumstances to go backward would exalt too many others. Their hope was to push the galling foes away from the fence.

He expected that his companions, weary and stiffened, would have to be driven to this assault, but as he turned toward them he perceived with a certain surprise that they were giving quick and unqualified expressions of assent. There was an ominous, clanging overture to the charge when the shafts of the bayonets rattled upon the rifle barrels. At the yelled words of command the soldiers sprang forward in eager leaps. There was new and unexpected force in the movement of the regiment. A knowledge of its faded and jaded condition made the charge appear like a paroxysm, a display of the strength that comes before a final feebleness. The men scampered in insane fever of haste, racing as if to achieve a sudden success before an exhilarating fluid should leave them. It was a blind and despairing rush by the collection of men in dusty and tattered blue, over a green sward and under a sapphire sky, toward a fence, dimly outlined in smoke, from behind which spluttered the fierce rifles of enemies.

The youth kept the bright colors to the front. He was waving his free arm in furious circles, the while shrieking mad calls and appeals, urging on those that did not need to be urged, for it seemed that the mob of blue men hurling themselves on the dangerous group of rifles were again grown suddenly wild with an enthusiasm of unselfishness. From the many firings starting toward them, it looked as if they would merely succeed in making a great sprinkling of corpses on the grass between their former position and the fence. But they were in a state of frenzy, perhaps because of forgotten vanities, and it made an exhibition of sublime recklessness. There was no obvious questioning, nor figurings, nor diagrams. There was, apparently, no considered loopholes. It appeared that the swift wings of their desires would have shattered against the iron gates of the impossible.

He himself felt the daring spirit of a savage, religion-mad.[9] He was capable of profound sacrifices, a tremendous death. He had no time for dissections, but he knew that he thought of the bullets only as things that could prevent him from reaching the place of his endeavor. There were subtle flashings of joy within him that thus should be his mind.

He strained all his strength. His eyesight was shaken and dazzled by the tension of thought and muscle. He did not see anything excepting the mist of smoke gashed by the little knives of fire, but he knew that in it lay the aged fence of a vanished farmer protecting the snuggled bodies of the gray men.

As he ran a thought of the shock of contact gleamed in his mind. He expected a great concussion when the two bodies of troops crashed together. This became a part of his wild battle madness. He could feel the onward swing of the regiment about him and he conceived of a thunderous, crushing blow that would prostrate the resistance and spread consternation and amazement for miles. The flying regiment was going to have a catapultian effect.[1] This dream made him run faster among his comrades, who were giving vent to hoarse and frantic cheers.

But presently he could see that many of the men in gray did not intend to abide the blow. The smoke, rolling, disclosed men who ran, their faces still turned. These grew to a crowd, who retired stubbornly. Individuals wheeled frequently to send a bullet at the blue wave.

But at one part of the line there was a grim and obdurate group that made no movement. They were settled firmly down behind posts and rails. A flag, ruffled and fierce, waved over them and their rifles dinned fiercely.

The blue whirl of men got very near, until it seemed that in truth there would be a close and frightful scuffle. There was an expressed disdain in the opposition of the little group, that changed the meaning of the cheers of the men in blue. They became yells of wrath, directed, personal. The cries of the two parties were now in sound an interchange of scathing insults.

They in blue showed their teeth; their eyes shone all white. They launched themselves as at the throats of those who stood resisting. The space between dwindled to an insignificant distance.

The youth had centered the gaze of his soul upon that other flag. Its possession would be high pride. It would express bloody minglings, near blows. He had a gigantic hatred for those who

---

9. Misprinted as "a savage religion mad" in 1895.

1. Like a catapult, an ancient military engine for hurling missiles.

made great difficulties and complications. They caused it to be as a craved treasure of mythology, hung amid tasks and contrivances of danger.

He plunged like a mad horse at it. He was resolved it should not escape if wild blows and darings of blows could seize it. His own emblem, quivering and aflare, was winging toward the other. It seemed there would shortly be an encounter of strange beaks and claws, as of eagles.

The swirling body of blue men came to a sudden halt at close and disastrous range and roared a swift volley. The group in gray was split and broken by this fire, but its riddled body still fought. The men in blue yelled again and rushed in upon it.

The youth, in his leapings, saw, as through a mist, a picture of four or five men stretched upon the ground or writhing upon their knees with bowed heads as if they had been stricken by bolts from the sky. Tottering among them was the rival color bearer, who[2] the youth saw had been bitten vitally by the bullets of the last formidable volley. He perceived this man fighting a last struggle, the struggle of one whose legs are grasped by demons. It was a ghastly battle. Over his face was the bleach of death, but set upon it were[3] the dark and hard lines of desperate purpose. With this terrible grin of resolution he hugged his precious flag to him and was stumbling and staggering in his design to go the way that led to safety for it.

But his wounds always made it seem that his feet were retarded, held, and he fought a grim fight, as with invisible ghouls fastened greedily upon his limbs. Those in advance of the scampering blue men, howling cheers, leaped at the fence. The despair of the lost was in his eyes as he glanced back at them.

The youth's friend went over the obstruction in a tumbling heap and sprang at the flag as a panther at prey. He pulled at it and, wrenching it free, swung up its red brilliancy with a mad cry of exultation even as the color bearer, gasping, lurched over in a final throe and, stiffening convulsively, turned his dead face to the ground. There was much blood upon the grass blades.

At the place of success there began more wild clamorings of cheers. The men gesticulated and bellowed in an ecstasy. When they spoke it was as if they considered their listener to be a mile away. What hats and caps were left to them they often slung high in the air.

At one part of the line four men had been swooped upon, and they now sat as prisoners. Some blue men were about them in an eager and curious circle. The soldiers had trapped strange birds, and

2. Misprinted as "whom" in 1895.   3. The 1895 text reads "was."

there was an examination. A flurry of fast questions was in the air.

One of the prisoners was nursing a superficial wound in the foot. He cuddled it, baby-wise, but he looked up from it often to curse with an astonishing utter abandon straight at the noses of his captors. He consigned them to red regions; he called upon the pestilential wrath of strange gods. And with it all he was singularly free from recognition of the finer points of the conduct of prisoners of war. It was as if a clumsy clod had trod upon his toe and he conceived it to be his privilege, his duty, to use deep, resentful oaths.

Another, who was a boy in years, took his plight with great calmness and apparent good nature. He conversed with the men in blue, studying their faces with his bright and keen eyes. They spoke of battles and conditions. There was an acute interest in all their faces during this exchange of view points. It seemed a great satisfaction to hear voices from where all had been darkness and speculation.

The third captive sat with a morose countenance. He preserved a stoical and cold attitude. To all advances he made one reply without variation, "Ah, go t' hell!"

The last of the four was always silent and, for the most part, kept his face turned in unmolested directions. From the views the youth received he seemed to be in a state of absolute dejection. Shame was upon him, and with it profound regret that he was, perhaps, no more to be counted in the ranks of his fellows. The youth could detect no expression that would allow him to believe that the other was giving a thought to his narrowed future, the pictured dungeons, perhaps, and starvations and brutalities, liable to the imagination. All to be seen was shame for captivity and regret for the right to antagonize.

After the men had celebrated sufficiently they settled down behind the old rail fence, on the opposite side to the one from which their foes had been driven. A few shot perfunctorily at distant marks.

There was some long grass. The youth nestled in it and rested, making a convenient rail support the flag. His friend, jubilant and glorified, holding his treasure with vanity, came to him there. They sat side by side and congratulated each other.

Chapter XXIV

The roarings that had stretched in a long line of sound across the face of the forest began to grow intermittent and weaker. The stentorian speeches of the artillery continued in some distant encounter, but the crashes of the musketry had almost ceased. The youth and his friend of a sudden looked up, feeling a deadened form of distress at the waning of these noises, which had become a part of life. They could see changes going on among the troops. There were marchings this way and that. A battery wheeled leisurely. On the crest of a small hill was the thick gleam of many departing muskets.

The youth arose. "Well, what now, I wonder?" he said. By his tone he seemed to be preparing to resent some new monstrosity in the way of dins and smashes. He shaded his eyes with his grimy hand and gazed over the field.

His friend also arose and stared. "I bet we're goin' t' git along out of this an' back over th' river," said he.

"Well, I swan!" said the youth.

They waited, watching. Within a little while the regiment received orders to retrace its way. The men got up grunting from the grass, regretting the soft repose. They jerked their stiffened legs, and stretched their arms over their heads. One man swore as he rubbed his eyes. They all groaned "O Lord!" They had as many objections to this change as they would have had to a proposal for a new battle.

They trampled slowly back over the field across which they had run in a mad scamper.

The regiment marched until it had joined its fellows. The re-formed brigade, in column, aimed through a wood at the road. Directly they were in a mass of dust-covered troops, and were trudging along in a way parallel to the enemy's lines as these had been defined by the previous turmoil.

They passed within view of a stolid white house, and saw in front of it groups of their comrades lying in wait beneath a neat breastwork. A row of guns were booming at a distant enemy. Shells thrown in reply were raising clouds of dust and splinters. Horsemen dashed along the line of intrenchments.

At this point of its march the division curved away from the field and went winding off in the direction of the river. When the significance of this movement had impressed itself upon the youth he turned his head and looked over his shoulder toward the trampled and *débris*-strewed ground. He breathed a breath of new satisfaction. He finally nudged his friend. "Well, it's all over," he said to him.

His friend gazed backward. "B'Gawd, it is," he assented. They mused.

For a time the youth was obliged to reflect in a puzzled and uncertain way. His mind was undergoing a subtle change. It took moments for it to cast off its battleful ways and resume its accustomed course of thought. Gradually his brain emerged from the clogged clouds, and at last he was enabled to more closely comprehend himself and circumstance.

He understood then that the existence of shot and counter-shot was in the past. He had dwelt in a land of strange, squalling upheavals and had come forth. He had been where there was red of blood and black of passion, and he was escaped. His first thoughts were given to rejoicings at this fact.

Later he began to study his deeds, his failures, and his achievements. Thus, fresh from scenes where many of his usual machines of reflection had been idle, from where he had proceeded sheeplike, he struggled to marshal all his acts.

At last they marched before him clearly. From this present viewpoint he was enabled to look upon them in spectator fashion and to criticise them with some correctness, for his new condition had already defeated certain sympathies.

Regarding his procession of memory he felt gleeful and unregretting, for in it his public deeds were paraded in great and shining prominence. Those performances which had been witnessed by his fellows marched now in wide purple and gold, having various deflections. They went gayly with music. It was pleasure to watch these things. He spent delightful minutes viewing the gilded images of memory.

He saw that he was good. He recalled with a thrill of joy the respectful comments of his fellows upon his conduct.

Nevertheless, the ghost of his flight from the first engagement appeared to him and danced. There were small shoutings in his brain about these matters. For a moment he blushed, and the light of his soul flickered with shame.

A specter of reproach came to him. There loomed the dogging memory of the tattered soldier—he who, gored by bullets and faint for blood, had fretted concerning an imagined wound in another; he who had loaned his last of strength and intellect for the tall soldier; he who, blind with weariness and pain, had been deserted in the field.

For an instant a wretched chill of sweat was upon him at the thought that he might be detected in the thing. As he stood persistently before his vision, he gave vent to a cry of sharp irritation and agony.

His friend turned. "What's the matter, Henry?" he demanded. The youth's reply was an outburst of crimson oaths.

As he marched along the little branch-hung roadway among his prattling companions this vision of cruelty brooded over him.

It clung near him always and darkened his view of these deeds in purple and gold. Whichever way his thoughts turned they were followed by the somber phantom of the desertion in the fields. He looked stealthily at his companions, feeling sure that they must discern in his face evidences of this pursuit. But they were plodding in ragged array, discussing with quick tongues the accomplishments of the late battle.

"Oh, if a man should come up an' ask me, I'd say we got a dum good lickin'."

"Lickin'—in yer eye! We ain't licked, sonny. We're goin' down here aways, swing aroun', an' come in behint 'em."

"Oh, hush, with your comin' in behint 'em. I've seen all 'a that I wanta. Don't tell me about comin' in behint——"

"Bill Smithers, he ses he'd rather been in ten hundred battles than been in that heluva hospital. He ses they got shootin' in the nighttime, an' shells dropped plum among 'em in th' hospital. He ses sech hollerin' he never see."

"Hasbrouck? He's th' best off'cer in this here reg'ment. He's a whale."

"Didn't I tell yeh we'd come aroun' in behint 'em? Didn't I tell yeh so? We——"

"Oh, shet yer mouth!"

For a time this pursuing recollection of the tattered man took all elation from the youth's veins. He saw his vivid error, and he was afraid that it would stand before him all his life. He took no share in the chatter of his comrades, nor did he look at them or know them, save when he felt sudden suspicion that they were seeing his thoughts and scrutinizing each detail of the scene with the tattered soldier.

Yet gradually he mustered force to put the sin at a distance. And at last his eyes seemed to open to some new ways. He found that he could look back upon the brass and bombast of his earlier gospels and see them truly. He was gleeful when he discovered that he now despised them.

With this conviction came a store of assurance. He felt a quiet manhood, nonassertive but of sturdy and strong blood. He knew that he would no more quail before his guides wherever they should point. He had been to touch the great death, and found that, after all, it was but the great death. He was a man.[4]

So it came to pass that as he trudged from the place of blood

4. *Cf.* references above to the "Question," especially in Chapters III, X, and XV; also the conclusion of Crane's story "The Open Boat," in which survivors of the shipwreck wade ashore feeling "that they could then be interpreters." Thus the themes of Henry's struggle for manhood and the search for the meaning of human existence are united. Critics debate the extent to which this conclusion is consistent with Crane's naturalistic premises.

and wrath his soul changed. He came from hot plowshares[5] to prospects of clover tranquilly, and it was as if hot plowshares were not. Scars faded as flowers.

It rained. The procession of weary soldiers became a bedraggled train, despondent and muttering, marching with churning effort in a trough of liquid brown mud under a low, wretched sky. Yet the youth smiled, for he saw that the world was a world for him, though many discovered it to be made of oaths and walking sticks. He had rid himself of the red sickness of battle. The sultry nightmare was in the past. He had been an animal blistered and sweating in the heat and pain of war. He turned now with a lover's thirst to images of tranquil skies, fresh meadows, cool brooks—an existence of soft and eternal peace.

Over the river a golden ray of sun came through the hosts of leaden rain clouds.[6]

1894, 1895

5. *I.e.*, swords, or weapons in general. *Cf.* "they shall beat their swords into plowshares * * *" (Isaiah ii:4).
6. According to R. W. Stallman (*Stephen Crane: An Omnibus*, p. 370, note 3), this last sentence, not present in the manuscript, was deliberately added before printing, thus showing that Crane was conscious of plotting a pattern of various persistent images, here the sun.

Backgrounds and Sources

The Manuscript: Unpublished Passages

For discussion of these passages see "A Note on the Text," preceding *The Red Badge of Courage*, above. Passages not excluded in the original manuscript but not present in the first edition of 1895 were first shown in the edition of *The Red Badge of Courage* published by The Folio Society, London, 1951. Amplified from the manuscript source they were restored in brackets in the text of *The Red Badge* appearing in *Stephen Crane: An Omnibus*, edited by R. W. Stallman (1952), from which the present list has been assembled. By following the page and line numbers in the present text, as shown below, the reader can readily study the effect of any omitted passage on the meaning and value of the passage from which it was excluded; and more importantly, assuming that Crane intended the exclusion, we can sometimes see something of the creative process as it affected this novel. In each entry below, the numbers in boldface type show the page and the line of the present text with which the excluded passage is associated; the key word or phrase, also in boldface type, shows the word at which the interpolation should be read into the present text.

6.22–23   care a hang.
I tell yeh what I know an' yeh kin take it er leave it. Suit yourselves. It don't make no difference t' me.

9.6   about right.
"Young fellers in the army get awful careless in their ways, Henry. They're away f'm home and they don't have nobody to look after 'em. I'm 'feared fer yeh about that. Yeh ain't never been used to doing for yerself. So yeh must keep writing to me how yer clothes are lasting.

9.15   us all.
Don't fergit to send yer socks to me the minute they git holes in 'em, and here's a little bible I want yeh to take along with yeh, Henry. I don't presume yeh'll be a-setting reading it all day long, child, ner nothin' like that. Many a time, yeh'll fergit yeh got it, I don't doubt. But there'll be many a time, too, Henry, when yeh'll

113

be wanting advice, boy, and all like that, and there'll be nobody round, perhaps, to tell yeh things. Then if yeh take it out, boy, yeh'll find wisdom in it—wisdom in it, Henry—with little or no searching.

16.23   perception.
"I told you so, didn't I?"

20.26–27   arms and ammunition.
In manuscript, the following speech reads "Yuh kin now eat, drink, sleep and shoot," said the tall soldier to the youth. "That's all you need. What do you want to do—carry a hotel?"

26.3   The skirmish
The manuscript reads The unceasing skirmish

27.29   a funny feller."
"Hear that what the ol' colonel ses, boys. He ses he'll shoot th' first man what'll turn an' run."
"He'd better try it. I'd like t' see him shoot at *me*."
"He wants t' look fer his *own* self. *He* don't wanta go 'round talkin' big."
"They say Perry's division's a-givin' 'em thunder."
"Ed Williams over in Company A, he ses the rebs'll all drop their guns an' run an' holler if we onct give 'em one good lickin'."

40.35   no words
who, through his suffering, thinks that he peers into the core of things and sees that the judgment of man is thistledown in wind.

47.10   had a wound,
In the manuscript, the succeeding phrase read, a little warm red badge of courage; *but* warm *was canceled in the manuscript and* little *was not finally printed.*

50.4   bone-crushing.
They could not understand.

51.9   like a wafer.
The final manuscript reads, like a [fierce] wafer; *an earlier manuscript reads* The [fierce] red sun * * * like a fierce wafer. *Crane canceled* fierce *in both positions before printing.*

52.39   blamed infernal
tooty-tooty-tooty-too

59.28   of the damned.
Manuscript reads doomed *followed immediately by the canceled sentence*, He lost concern for himself.

69.24–25   eye sockets.
It was the soldier's bath.

73.25   his sight.
The long tirades against nature he now believed to be foolish compositions born of his condition. He did not altogether repudiate them because he did not remember all that he had said. He was inclined to regard his past rebellions with an indulgent smile. They were all right in their hour, perhaps.

73.32   play marbles.
Since he was comfortable and contented, he had no desire to set things straight. Indeed, he no more contended that they were not straight. How could they be crooked when he was restored to a requisite amount of happiness. There was a slowly developeing [*sic*] conviction that in all his red speeches he had been ridiculously mistaken. Nature was a fine thing moving with a magnificent justice. The world was fair and wide and glorious. The sky was kind, and smiled tenderly, full of encouragement, upon him.

Some poets now received his scorn. Yesterday, in his misery, he had thought of certain persons who had written. Their remembered words, broken and detached, had come piece-meal to him. For these people he had then felt a glowing, brotherly regard. They had wandered in paths of pain and they had made pictures of the black landscape that others might enjoy it with them. He had, at that time, been sure that their wise, contemplating spirits had been in sympathy with him, had shed tears from the clouds. He had walked alone, but there had been pity, made before a reason for it.

But he was now, in a measure, a successful man and he could no longer tolerate in himself a spirit of fellowship for poets. He abandoned them. Their songs about black landscapes were of no importance to him since his new eyes said that his landscape was not black. People who called landscapes black were idiots.

He achieved a mighty scorn for such a snivelling race.

He felt that he was the child of the powers. Through the peace of his heart, he saw the earth to be a garden in which grew no weeds of agony. Or, perhaps, if there did grow a few, it was in obscure corners where no one was obliged to encounter them unless a ridiculous search was made. And, at any rate, they were tiny ones.

He returned to his old belief in the ultimate, astounding success of his life. He, as usual, did not trouble about processes. It was ordained, because he was a fine creation. He saw plainly that he was the chosen of some gods. By fearful and wonderful roads he was to be led to a crown. He was, of course, satisfied that he deserved it.

107.23 a mad scamper.
The fence, deserted, resumed with its careening posts and disjointed bars, an air of quiet and rural depravity. Beyond it, there lay spread a few corpses. Conspicuous was the contorted body of the color-bearer in grey whose flag the youth's friend was now bearing away.

107.33 line of intrenchments.
As they passed near other commands, men of the delapidated [*sic*] regiment procured the captured flag from Wilson and, tossing it high into the air cheered tumultuously as it turned, with apparent reluctance, slowly over and over.

108.17 certain sympathies.
His friend, too, seemed engaged with some retrospection, for he suddenly gestured and said: "Good Lord!"
"What?" asked the youth.
"Good Lord!" repeated his friend. "Yeh know Jimmie Rogers? Well, he—gosh, when he was hurt I started t' git some water fer 'im an', thunder, I aint seen 'im from that time 'til this. I clean forgot what I—say, has anybody seen Jimmie Rogers?"
"Seen 'im? No! He's dead," they told him.
His friend swore.
But the youth, regarding his procession of memory, felt * * *

108.26 his conduct.
He said to himself again the sentence of the insane lieutenant: "If I had ten thousand wild-cats like you, I could tear th' stomach outa this war in less'n a week." It was a little coronation. [*Cf. p.* 81. *The lieutenant was* fearless, *not* insane.]

108.28 danced.
Echoes of his terrible combat with the arrayed forces of the universe came to his ears.

108.30 with shame.
However, he presently procured an explanation and an apology. He said that those tempestuous moments were of the wild mistakes and ravings of a novice who did not comprehend. He had been a mere man railing at a condition, but now he was out of it and could see that it had been very proper and just. It had been necessary for him to swallow swords that he might have a better throat for grapes. Fate had in truth been kind to him; she had stabbed him with benign purpose and diligently cudgeled him for his own sake. In his rebellion, he had been very portentious, no doubt, and sincere, and anxious for humanity, but now that he stood safe,

with no lack of blood, it was suddenly clear to him that he had been wrong not to kiss the knife and bow to the cudgel. He had foolishly squirmed.

But the sky would forget. It was true, he admitted, that in the world it was the habit to cry devil at persons who refused to trust what they could not trust, but he thought that perhaps the stars dealt differently. The imperturbable sun shines on insult and worship.

As he was thus fraternizing again with nature, a spectre * * *

109.22   yer mouth!"
"You make me sick."
"G' home, yeh fool."

109.30   at a distance.
And then he regarded it with what he thought to be great calmness. At last, he concluded that he saw in it quaint uses. He exclaimed that its importance in the aftertime would be great to him if it even succeeded in hindering the workings of his egotism. It would make a sobering balance. It would become a good part of him. He would have upon him often the consciousness of a great mistake. And he would be taught to deal gently and with care. He would be a man.

This plan for the utilization of a sin did not give him complete joy but it was the best sentiment he could formulate under the circumstances, and when it was combined with his success, or public deeds, he knew that he was quite contented.

109.34   despised them.
He was emerged from his struggles, with a large sympathy for the machinery of the universe. With his new eyes, he could see that the secret and open blows which were being dealt about the world with such heavenly lavishness were in truth blessings. It was a diety [sic] laying about him with the bludgeon of correction.

His loud mouth against these things had been lost as the storm ceased. He would no more stand upon places high and false, and denounce the distant planets. He beheld that he was tiny but not inconsequent to the sun. In the space-wide whirl of events no grain like him would be lost.

109.39   it was but the great death.
and was for others.

Biographical and Documentary Sources

HAMLIN GARLAND
Stephen Crane: A Soldier of Fortune†

The death of Stephen Crane, far away in the mountains of Bavaria, seems to me at this moment a very sorrowful thing. He should have continued to be one of our most distinctive literary workers for many years to come. And yet I cannot say I am surprised. His was not the physical organization that runs to old age. He was old at twenty.

It happened that I knew Crane when he was a boy and have had some years exceptional opportunities for studying him. In the summer of 1888 or 1889 I was lecturing for a seaside assembly at Avon, New Jersey. The report of my first lecture (on "The Local Novelists," by the way) was exceedingly well done in the "Tribune," and I asked for the name of the reporter. "He is a mere boy," was the reply of Mr. Albert, the manager of the assembly, "and his name is Stephen Crane."

Crane came to see me the following evening, and turned out to be a reticent young fellow, with a big German pipe in his mouth. He was small, sallow and inclined to stoop, but sinewy and athletic for all that—for we fell to talk of sports, and he consented to practice baseball pitching with me. I considered him at this time a very good reporter, and a capital catcher of curved balls—no more, and I said goodby to him two weeks later with no expectation of ever seeing him again.

In the summer of '91, if I do not mistake, I was visiting Mr. and Mrs. Albert at their school in New York City, when a curious book came to me by mail.‡ It was a small yellow-covered volume, hardly

---

† First published in *The Saturday Evening Post*, CLXXIII (July 28, 1900), 16–17; reprinted in *Booklover* II, Autumn, 1900; and with various discrepancies in *Yale Review*, "Stephen Crane as I Knew Him," April, 1914; and in Garland's reminiscent *Roadside Meetings* (1930). By permission of Isabel Garland Lord and Constance Garland Doyle.

‡ *Maggie*, the "curious book," was first privately printed in 1893, not 1891 [Editors].

more than a pamphlet, without a publisher's imprint. The author's name was Johnston Smith. The story was called "Maggie, a Girl of the Streets," and the first paragraph described the battle of some street urchins with so much insight and with such unusual and vivid use of English that I became very much excited about it. Next day I mailed the book to Mr. Howells, in order that he might share the discovery with me. The author had the genius which makes an old world new.

On that very afternoon Crane called upon me and confessed that he had written the book and had not been able to get any one to publish it. Even the firm of printers that put it together refused to place their imprint upon it. He said that the bulk of the edition remained unsold, and that he had sent the book to a number of critics and also to several ministers. On the cover of each copy (as on mine) was written, in diagonal lines, these words or their substance in Crane's beautiful script: "The reader of this story must inevitably be shocked, but let him persist, and in the end he will find this story to be moral." I cannot remember exactly the quaint terms of this admonition, but these words give the idea.

I said to him: "I hardly dare tell you how good that story is. I have sent it to Mr. Howells as a 'find.' Go and see him when he has read it. I am sure he will like it."

He then told me that he had been discharged from the staff of the "Tribune." He seemed to be greatly encouraged by our conversation, and when he went away I talked with his friends about the book, which appealed to me with great power. I have it still. This desperate attempt of a young author to get a hearing is amusing to an outsider, but it was serious business with Crane then.

I did not see him again until the autumn of 1892, when I went to New York to spend the winter. He wrote occasionally, saying, "Things go pretty slow with me, but I manage to live."

My brother Franklin was in Mr. Herne's Shore Acres Company in those days, and as they were playing an all-season engagement at Daly's theater we decided to take a little flat and camp together for the winter. Our flat was on One Hundred and Fifth street, and there Crane visited us two or three times a week. He was always hungry and a little gloomy when he came, but my brother made a point of having an extra chop or steak ready for a visitor and Crane often chirped like a bird when he had finished dinner. We often smiled over it then, but it is a pleasure to us now to think we were able to cheer him when he needed it most.

He was living at this time with a group of artists—"Indians," he called them—in the old studio building on East Twenty-third street. I never called to see him there, but he often set forth their doings with grim humor. Most of them slept on the floor and painted on towels, according to his report. Sometimes they ate, but they all smoked most villainous tobacco, for Crane smelled so powerfully of their "smoke-talks" that he filled our rooms with the odor. His fingers were yellow with cigarette reek, and he looked like a man badly nourished.

This crowd of artists, according to his story, spent their days in sleep and their nights in "pow-wows" around a big table where they beat and clamored and assaulted each other under a canopy of tobacco smoke. They hated the world. They were infuriated with all hanging committees and art editors, and each man believed religiously in his own genius. Linson was one of those Crane mentioned, and Vosburg[h] and Green. Together they covenanted to go out some bleak day and slay all the editors and art critics of the city.

Crane at this time wore a light check suit and over it a long gray ulster which had seen much service. His habitual expression was a grim sort of smile. One day he appeared in my study with his outside pockets bulging with two rolls of manuscript. As he entered he turned ostentatiously to put down his hat, and so managed to convey to my mind an impression that he was concealing something. His manner was embarrassed, as if he had come to do a thing and was sorry about it.

"Come now, out with it," I said. "What is the roll I see in your pocket?"

With a sheepish look he took out a fat roll of legal cap paper and handed it to me with a careless, boyish gesture.

"There's another," I insisted, and he still more abruptly delivered himself of another but smaller parcel.

I unrolled the first package, and found it to be a sheaf of poems. I can see the initial poem now, exactly as it was then written, without a blot or erasure—almost without punctuation—in blue ink. It was beautifully legible and clean of outline.

It was the poem which begins thus:

"God fashioned the ship of the world carefully."

I read this with delight and amazement. I rushed through the others, some thirty in all, with growing wonder. I could not believe they were the work of the pale, reticent boy moving restlessly about the room.

"Have you any more?" I asked.

"I've got five or six all in a little row up here," he quaintly replied, pointing to his temple. "That's the way they come—in little rows, all made up, ready to be put down on paper."

"When did you write these?"

"Oh! I've been writing five or six every day. I wrote nine yester-day. I wanted to write some more last night, but those 'Indians' wouldn't let me do it. They howled over the other verses so loud they nearly cracked my ears. You see, we all live in a box together, and I've no place to write, except in the general squabble. They think my lines are funny. They make a circus of me." All this with a note of exaggeration, of course.

"Never you mind," I replied; "don't you do a thing till you put all these verses down on paper."

"I've got to eat," he said, and his smile was not pleasant.

"Well, let's consider. Can't we get some work for you to do? Some of these press syndicate men have just been after me to do short stories for them. Can't you do something there?"

"I'll try," he said, without much resolution. "I don't seem to be the kind of writer they want. The newspapers can't see me at all."

"Well, now, let's see what can be done. I'll give you a letter to Mr. Flower, of the 'Arena,' and one to Mr. Howells. And I want to take these poems to Mr. Howells to-morrow; I'm sure he'll help you. He's kind to all who struggle."

Later in the meal I said: "Why don't you go down and do a study of this midnight bread distribution which the papers are making so much of? Mr. Howells suggested it to me, but it isn't my field. It is yours. You could do it beyond anybody."

"I might do that," he said; "it interests me."

"Come to-morrow to luncheon," I said, as he went away visibly happier. "Perhaps I'll have something to report."

I must confess I took the lines seriously. If they were direct out-put of this unaccountable boy, then America had produced another genius, singular as Poe. I went with them at once to Mr. Howells, whose wide reading I knew and relied upon. He read them with great interest, and immediately said:

"They do not seem to relate directly to the work of any other writer. They seem to be the work of a singularly creative mind. Of course they reflect the author's reading and sympathies, but they are not imitations."

When Crane came next day he brought the first part of a war story which was at that time without a name. The first page of this was as original as the verses, and it passed at once to the description of a great battle. Such mastery of details of war was sufficiently startling in a youth of twenty-one who had never smelled any more carnage than a firecracker holds, but the seeing was so keen, the phrases so graphic, so fresh, so newly coined, that I dared not ex-press to the boy's face my admiration. I asked him to leave the story with me. I said:

"Did you do any more 'lines'?"

He looked away bashfully.

"Only six."

"Let me see them."

As he handed them to me he said: "Got three more waiting in line. I could do one now."

"Sit down and try," I said, glad of his offer, for I could not relate the man to his work.

He took a seat and began to write steadily, composedly, without hesitation or blot or interlineation, and so produced in my presence one of his most powerful verses. It flowed from his pen as smooth as oil.

The next day I asked for the other half of the novel. "We must get it published at once," I said. "It is a wonderful study. A mysterious product for you to have in hand. Where is the other part?"

He looked very much embarrassed. "It's in 'hock,'" he said.

"To whom?"

"To the typewriter."

We all laughed, but it was serious business to him. He could see the humor of the situation, but there was a bitter rebellion in his voice.

"How much is it 'hung up' for?"

"Fifteen dollars."

I looked at my brother. "I guess we can spare that, don't you think?"

So Crane went away joyously and brought the last half of "The Red Badge of Courage," still unnamed at the time. He told us that the coming of that story was just as mysterious as in the case of the verses, and I can believe it. It literally came of its own accord like sap flowing from a tree.

I gave him such words of encouragement as I could. "Your future is secure. A man who can write 'The Red Badge of Courage' can not be forever a lodger in a bare studio."

He replied: "That may be, but if I had some money to buy a new suit of clothes I'd feel my grip tighten on the future."

"You'll laugh at all this—we all go through it," said I.

"It's ridiculous, but it doesn't make me laugh," he said, soberly.

My predictions of his immediate success did not come true. "The Red Badge of Courage" and "Maggie" were put through the Syndicate with very slight success. They left Crane almost as poor as before.

In one of his letters, in April, he wrote: "I have not been up to see you because of various strange conditions—notably my toes coming through one shoe, and I have not been going out into society as much as I might. I mail you last Sunday's 'Press.' I've moved now—live in a flat. People can come to see me now. They come in shoals, and say I am a great writer. Counting five that are sold, four that are unsold and six that are mapped out, I have fifteen short stories in my head and out of it. They'll make a book. The 'Press' people pied some of 'Maggie,' as you will note."

I saw little of him during '93 and '94, but a letter written in May, '94, revealed his condition:

"I have not written you because there has been little to tell of late. I am plodding along on the 'Press' in a quiet and effective way. We now eat with charming regularity at least two times a day. I am content and am now writing another novel which is a bird. . . . I am getting lots of free advertising. Everything is coming along nicely now. I have got the poetic spout so that I can turn it on and off. I wrote a Decoration Day thing for the 'Press' which aroused them to enthusiasm. They said in about a minute, though, that I was firing over the heads of the soldiers."

His allusion to free advertising means that the critics were wrangling over "The Black Riders" and "Maggie." But the public was not interested. I had given him a letter to a Syndicate Press Company, and with them he had left the manuscript of his war novel. In a letter written in November, 1894, he makes sad mention of his lack of success:

"My Dear Friend: So much of my row with the world has to be silence and endurance that sometimes I wear the appearance of having forgotten my best friends, those to whom I am indebted for everything. As a matter of fact, I have just crawled out of the fifty-third ditch into which I have been cast, and now I feel that I can write you a letter which will not make you ill. ——— put me in one of the ditches. He kept 'The Red Badge' six months until I was near mad. Oh, yes—he was going to use it but— Finally I took it to B. They used it in January in a shortened form. I have just completed a New York book that leaves 'Maggie' at the post. It is my best thing. Since you are not here I am going to see if Mr. Howells will not read it. I am still working for the 'Press.' "

At this point his affairs took a sudden turn, and he was made the figure I had hoped to see him two years before. The English critics spoke in highest praise of "The Red Badge," and the book became the critical bone of contention between military objectors and literary enthusiasts here at home, and Crane became the talk of the day. He was accepted as a very remarkable literary man of genius.

He was too brilliant, too fickle, too erratic to last. Men cannot go on doing stories like "The Red Badge of Courage." The danger with such highly individual work lies in this—the words which astonish, the phrases which excite wonder and admiration, come eventually to seem like tricks. They lose force with repetition, and come at last to be absolutely distasteful. "The Red Badge of Courage" was marvelous, but manifestly Crane could not go on doing such work. If he wrote in conventional phrase, his power lessened. If he continued to write in his own phrases he came under the charge of repeating himself.

It seems now that he was destined from the first to be a sort of present-day Poe. His was a singular and daring soul, as irresponsible as the wind. He was a man to be called a genius, for we call that power genius which we do not easily understand or measure. I have never known a man whose source of power was so unaccounted for.

The fact of the matter seems to be this. Crane's mind was more largely subconscious in its workings than that of most men. He did not understand his own mental processes or resources. When he put pen to paper he found marvelous words, images, sentences, pictures already [*sic*] to be drawn off and fixed upon paper. His pen was "a spout," as he says. The farther he got from his own field, his own inborn tendency, the weaker he became. Such a man cannot afford to enter the white-hot public thoroughfare, for his genius is of the lonely and the solitary shadow-land.

STEPHEN CRANE

Letters: A Selection†

4. *To Odell Hathaway*

[Lafayette College, September or October, 1890]
Dear Boys,/ I send you a piece of the banner we took away from the Sophemores [*sic*] last week. It dont look like much does it? Only an old rag, ain't it? But just remember I got a *black and blue nose*, a barked shin, skin off my hands and a lame shoulder, in the row you can appreciate it.[5] So, keep it, and when you look at it think of me scraping [*sic*] about twice a week over some old rag that says "Fresh '94" on it.

Stephen Crane

† From *Stephen Crane: Letters*, edited by R. W. Stallman and Lillian Gilkes, New York, 1960; pp. 7–159, *passim*.

5. This tug of war for the flag probably became the inspirational source of the contest between the enemy flag-bearers in *The Red Badge of Courage*.

5. *To a Claverack College Schoolmate*

#170 East Hall Lafayette College/[November ? 1890]
My dear boy,/ Your letter gladly recd. So you are not having a hell
of a time at C.C.,[6] eh? Well, you had better have it now because,
mark my words, you will always regret the day you leave old C.C.
The fellows here raise more hell than any college in the country,
yet I have still left a big slice of my heart up among the pumpkin
seeds and farmers of Columbia Co. You asked me if I thought as
much of Pete as ever. Well, I should think so, and a great deal
more besides, and don't you forget it. We both may possibly come
up on Thanksgiving and you fellows whom I still love as of old,
must give us a jolly time. So long, old man, don't forget me even if
I can't be at C.C. Yours, as ever

Stephen Crane

25. *To Mrs. Armstrong*

[April 2, 1893]
Thank you very much for letting me keep these so long.[29] I have
spent ten nights writing a story of the war on my own responsibility
but I am not sure that my facts are real and the books won't tell
me what I want to know so I must do it all over again, I guess.

30. *Hamlin Garland To S. S. McClure*

January 2, 1894
Dear Mr. McClure: I send here by Mr. Crane the mss. you let me
read. They are good and nothing like what I looked for. If you
have any work for Mr. Crane, talk things over with him and for
mercy's sake! don't keep him *standing* for an hour as he did before
out in your pen for *culp*rits. Yours sincerely,   *Hamlin Garland*

31. *To Holmes Bassett*

[February 24, 1894]
. . . I have just sold another book and my friends think it is pretty
good and that some publisher ought to bring it out when it has
been shown as a serial. It is a war-story and the syndicate people
think that several papers could use it.[5]

6. Claverack College and Hudson River
Institute.
29. The Century's *Battles and Leaders
of the Civil War*. This note to Mrs.
Armstrong, says Beer (p. 231), is "the
birth notice" of *The Red Badge of
Courage*. What Crane had then written was the first draft; the story as yet
had no name. When Crane did give a

title to the revised and expanded manuscript, he first called it "Private Flem-
ing/His Various Battles." Later he
wrote above this title (on MS LV) the
final and symbolic title: "The Red
Badge of Courage./An Episode of the
American Civil War."
5. According to Beer (p. 288), Crane
had sold *The Red Badge* to Irving

32. To John Henry Dick

[Late February, 1894]

Dear Dicon: Beg, borrow or steal fifteen dollars. [McClure's] like the Red Badge and want to make a contract for it. It is in pawn at the typewriter's for fifteen. Thine,

Steve

46. To Hamlin Garland

143 East 23d St, NYC/Thursday Nov 15th. [1894]

My dear friend: So much of my row with the world has to be silence and endurance that sometimes I wear the appearance of having forgotten my best friends, those to whom I am indebted for everything. As a matter of fact, I have just crawled out of the fifty-third ditch into which I have been cast and I now feel that I can write you a letter that wont make you ill. McClure was a Beast about the war-novel and that has been the thing that put me in one of the ditches. He kept it for six months until I was near mad. Oh, yes, he was going to use it, but— Finally I took it to Bacheller's. They use it in January in a shortened form.[31] I have just completed a New Year book† that leaves Maggie at the post. It is my best thing. Since you are not here, I am going to see if Mr. Howells will not read it. I am still working for the *Press*. Yours as ever

Stephen Crane

92. To Willis Brooks Hawkins

Hartwood, Sul. Co., N.Y./Nov. 1st, 1895

My dear Willis: My correspondence—incoming—has reached mighty proportions and if I answered them all I would make Hartwood a better class office and my brother a better class postmaster for you know he is a postmaster, justice-of-the-peace, iceman, farmer, mill-wright, blue stone man, lumberman, station agent on the P.J.M. and N.Y.R.R. and many other things which I now forget. He and his tribe can swing the majority in the township of Lumberland. By that reference to my correspondents I meant the fellows before the war.‡ They're turning up. Heaven send them somebody to appreciate them more although it is true

---

Bacheller, whose syndicate was then in the planning stage. The facts, as subsequent letters show, contradict Beer, for the manuscript of *The Red Badge* was out with McClure's for several months.
31. *The Red Badge* was syndicated by Bacheller's agency in newspapers during early December, one month sooner than

Crane here expected. It appeared, in much shortened form, first in the Philadelphia *Press*, December 3–8, and then in the New York *Press*, December 9, as well as in several other unidentified newspapers.
† Probably *George's Mother* [Editors].
‡ Veterans of the Civil War [Editors].

I write two or three perfunctory little notes each day.

There has been an enormous raft of R. B. of C. reviews and Appleton and Co. have written me quite a contented letter about the sale of the book. Copeland and Day have written for my New York sketches and Appleton and Co. wish to put my new story in the Zeit-Geist series. Which I leave you alone to pronounce. Devil take me if I give you any assistance.

That's enough about books.

On the bicycle question, I refuse to listen to you. In the old days at military school I once rode a wheel—a high one—about three miles high, I think. An unsmiling young cadet brought one into the armory one morning and as I was his senior officer I took it away from him. I mounted by means of a friend and rode around and around the armory. It was very simple.

When I wished to dismount however I found I couldn't. So I rode around and around the armory. Shafer, who was champion of Pennsylvania in those old high-wheel days, watched me and said I did some things on that wheel which were impossible to him. A group of cadets gathered in a corner and yelled whenever I passed them. I adjured them at intervals to let me off that wheel but they only hollered. At last, I ran into a bench and fell neatly on my head. It broke the machine, too, praise God. Some days later I whipped the boy who had loaned it me. Not for that mind you, but for something else. . . .

111. *To an Editor of* Leslie's Weekly

[About November, 1895]

. . . I can't do any sort of work that I don't like or don't feel like doing and I've given up trying to do it. When I was at school few of my studies interested me, and as a result I was a bad scholar. They used to say at Syracuse University, where, by the way, I didn't finish the course, that I was cut out to be a professional base-ball player. And the truth of the matter is that I went there more to play base-ball than to study. I was always very fond of literature, though. I remember when I was eight years old I became very much interested in a child character called, I think, Little Goodie Bright-eyes, and I wrote a story then which I called after this fascinating little person. When I was about sixteen I began to write for the New York newspapers, doing correspondence from Asbury Park and other places. Then I began to write special articles and short stories for the Sunday papers and one of the literary syndicates, reading a great deal in the meantime and gradually acquiring a style. I decided that the nearer a writer gets to life the greater he becomes as an artist, and most of my prose writings have been toward the goal partially described by that misunderstood and abused word, realism. Tolstoi is the writer I admire most of all. I've been a free lance during most of the time I have been doing literary work, writing stories and articles about anything under heaven that seemed to possess interest, and selling them wherever I could. It was hopeless work. Of all human lots for a person of sensibility that of an obscure free lance in literature or journalism is, I think, the most discouraging. It was during this period that I wrote "The Red Badge of Courage." It was an effort born of pain —despair, almost; and I believe that this made it a better piece of literature than it otherwise would have been. It seems a pity that art should be a child of pain, and yet I think it is. Of course we have fine writers who are prosperous and contented, but in my opinion their work would be greater if this were not so. It lacks the sting it would have if written under the spur of a great need.

But, personally, I was unhappy only at times during the period of my struggles. I was always looking forward to success. My first great disappointment was in the reception of "Maggie, a Girl of the Streets." I remember how I looked forward to its publication, and pictured the sensation I thought it would make. It fell flat. Nobody seemed to notice it or care for it. I am going to introduce Maggie again to the world some time, but not for a good while.†
Poor Maggie! she was one of my first loves.

I suppose I ought to be thankful to "The Red Badge," but I am much fonder of my little book of poems, "The Black Riders." The reason, perhaps, is that it was a more ambitious effort. My aim was to comprehend in it the thoughts I have had about life in general, while "The Red Badge" is a mere episode in life, an amplification. A rather interesting fact about the story is that it lay for eight months in a New York magazine office waiting to receive attention. I called on the editor‡ time and again and couldn't find out whether he intended to publish it or not, so at last I took it away. Now that it is published and the people seem to like it I suppose I ought to be satisfied, but somehow I am not as happy as I was in the uncertain, happy-go-lucky newspaper writing days. I used to dream continually of success then. Now that I have achieved it in some measure it seems like mere flimsy paper.

123. *To Curtis Brown*[121]

Hartwood, N.Y./Dec. 31st, 1896 [for 1895]
My Dear Curtis, Thank you for your kind words and for *Sketch*

---

† Actually he found a publisher for the revised *Maggie* soon afterward, in 1896 [Editors].

‡ See comment on McClure, Letter 46 [Editors].
121. Literary agent; at this time Sunday editor of the New York *Press*.

clipping.[122] I hear the damned book ["The Red Badge of Courage"] is doing very well in England. In the meantime I am plodding along. I have finished my new novel— "The Third Violet"—and sent it to Appleton and Co., as per request, but I've an idea it won't be accepted.[123] It's pretty rotten work. I used myself up in the accursed "Red Badge." Yours as ever,

Stephen Crane

125. *To John Northern Hilliard*

Hartwood, N.Y./January 2ᵈ [1896]

Dear Mr. Hilliard: If you will pardon this kind of paper,[3] I think I will be able to [tell?] you more easily what you wish to know. However even then I am not sure that I will succeed as I am not much versed in talking about myself. As to the picture I am sorry I cannot give you one but I haven't had a picture taken since early boyhood.

Occasionally, interested acquintances [sic] have asked me if "Stephen Crane" was a nom de guerre; but it is my own name. In childhood, I was bitterly ashamed of it and now, when I sometimes see it in print, it strikes me as being the homliest [sic] name in created things. The first Stephen Crane to appear in America, arrived in Massachusetts from England in 1635. His son Stephen Crane settled in Connecticut and the Stephen Crane of the third American generation settled in New Jersey on lands that now hold the cities of Newark and Elizabeth. When the troubles with England came, he was president of both Colonial Assemblies that met in New York. Then he was sent by New Jersey to the Continental Congress and he served in that body until just about a week before the Declaration was signed, when the Tories made such trouble in New Jersey that he was obliged to return and serve as speaker in the colony's assembly. He died in the old homestead at Elizabeth when the British troops were marching past to what pappened [sic] to be the defeat at Trenton. His eldest son commanded the 6th New Jersey infantry during the Revolution and ultimately died the ranking Major-general in the regular army from an old wound recieved [sic] in the expedition to Quebec. The second son became the ranking commodore in the navy at a time when the title of Admiral was unknown. The youngest son, while proceeding to his father's bedside, was captured by some Hessians and upon his refusing to tell the road by which they intended to surprise a certain American out-post, they beat him with their muskets and then having stabbed him with their bayonets,

---

122. This item has not been traced.
123. Appleton's published *The Third Violet* in 1897.
3. Written on blue-lined paper (8 by 12½ inches) with red-lined margin, almost like the legal cap used for writing *The Red Badge*.

they left him dead in the road. In those old times the family did it's duty.

Upon my mother's side, everybody as soon as he could walk, became a Methodist clergyman—of the old ambling-nag, saddle-bag, exhorting kind. My uncle, Jesse T. Peck, D.D., L.L.D., was a bishop in the Methodist Church. My father was also a clergyman of that church, author of numerous works of theology, an editor of various periodicals of the church. He graduated at Princeton. He was a great, fine, simple mind.

As for myself, I went to Lafayette College but did not graduate. I found mining-engineering not at all to my taste. I preferred baseball. Later I attended Syracuse University where I attempted to study literature but found base ball again much more to my taste. At Lafayette I joined the Delta Upsilon fraternity.

My first work in fiction was for the *New York Tribune* when I was about eighteen years old. During this time, one story of the series went into the *Cosmopolitan*.[5] Previous to this I had written many articles of many kinds for many newspapers. I began when I was sixteen. At age of twenty I wrote my first novel—*Maggie*. It never really got on the market but it made for me the friendships of W. D. Howells and Hamlin Garland and since that time I have never been conscious for an instant that those friendships have at all diminished. After completing *Maggie* I wrote mainly for the *New York Press* and for the *Arena* magazine. The latter part of my twenty-first year I began *The Red Badge of Courage* and completed it early in my twenty-second year. In my twenty-third year, I wrote *The Black Riders*.[7] On the 1st day of November, 1895, I was precisely 24 years old. Last week I finished my new novel: "The Third Violet." It is a story of life among the younger and poorer artists in New York.

I have only one pride and that is that the English edition of *The Red Badge of Courage* has been recieved [sic] with great praise by the English reviewers. I am proud of this simply because the remoter people would seem more just and harder to win.

I live in Hartwood, Sullivan Co., N.Y., on an estate of 3500 acres belonging to my brother and am distinguished for corduroy trousers and briar-wood pipes. My idea of happiness is the saddle of a good-riding horse. . . .

I am not so sure that the above is what you want but I am sure that it is the most complete I have ever written. I hope you will like [it] and if you find that you need enlightenment on certain points, let

5. "A Tent in Agony," in the series of Sullivan County sketches, was published in *Cosmopolitan*, December, 1892. Crane was then twenty-one (not eighteen, as he has it).
7. Elsewhere Crane claimed "I wrote the things in February of 1893" (see Beer, p. 297), but he did not write them until after hearing Emily Dickinson's poetry read to him by Howells, and this inspirational meeting did not occur until the first week of April, 1893.

me know. Please remember me to Mr. Bragdon. With assurances of my regard I am Very sincerely

Stephen Crane

My father died when I was seven y'rs old. My mother when I was nineteen.

216. *To John Northern Hilliard*

[Ravensbrook, 1897?]

* * * Mr. George Wyndham, Under Secretary for War in the British Government, says, in an essay, that the [Red Badge] challenges comparison with the most vivid scenes of Tolstoi's "War and Peace" or of Zola's "Downfall"; and the big reviews here praise it for just what I intended it to be, a psychological portrayal of fear.[140] They all insist that I am a veteran of the civil war, whereas the fact is, as you know, I never smelled even the powder of a sham battle. I know what the psychologists say, that a fellow can't comprehend a condition that he has never experienced, and I argued that many times with the Professor. Of course, I have never been in a battle, but I believe that I got my sense of the rage of conflict on the football field, or else fighting is a hereditary instinct, and I wrote intuitively; for the Cranes were a family of fighters in the old days, and in the Revolution every member did his duty. But be that as it may, I endeavored to express myself in the simplest and most concise way. If I failed, the fault is not mine. I have been very careful not to let any theories or pet ideas of my own creep into my work. Preaching is fatal to art in literature. I try to give to readers a slice out of life; and if there is any moral or lesson in it, I do not try to point it out. I let the reader find it for himself. The result is more satisfactory to both the reader and myself. As Emerson said, "There should be a long logic beneath the story, but it should be kept carefully out of sight." Before "The Red Badge of Courage" was published, I found it difficult to make both ends meet. The book was written during this period. It was an effort born of pain, and I believe that it was beneficial to it as a piece of literature. It seems a pity that this should be so—that art should be a child of suffering; and yet such seems to be the case. Of course there are fine writers who have good incomes and live comfortably and contentedly; but if the conditions of their lives were harder, I believe that their work would be better. Bret Harte is an example. He has not done any work in recent years to compare with those early California sketches.

* * *

140. In *The New Review*, January, 1896, Wyndham called Crane a great artist and *The Red Badge* "a remark-able book." "Mr. Crane's picture of war is more complete than Tolstoi's, more true than Zola's."

Source Studies

LYNDON UPSON PRATT
A Possible Source of *The Red Badge of Courage*†

Before entering upon a discussion of new material concerning *The Red Badge of Courage*, it is necessary to review the old. Information relating to sources and origins of the novel has always been meager. It is commonly said that the book was undertaken because of a dare which Crane accepted to surpass Zola's depiction of war, *Le Débâcle*, which he read one afternoon during the winter of 1892–1893.[1] Shortly thereafter, he is known to have spent some time searching through old magazines and poring over the stiffly pictured heroics of the *Century's* "Battles and Leaders of the Civil War."[2] Mr. Beer has also shown that, during Crane's boyhood, realistic war reminiscences had impressed him, such as the fatuousness of burying the regimental dead with canteens of whiskey still upon them.[3] Other Crane authorities, notably Mr. Follett, have mentioned the existence of a relative whose war stories Crane listened to during the years at Port Jervis.[4] Finally there is the statement that Stephen's older brother William was considered an expert in the strategy of Chancellorsville and Gettysburg.[5] But fragments as scarce as these are suggestive rather than illuminating.

Mr. Beer was apparently led to believe that, while at Claverack, Crane sensed much the same irony in the presence of military pomp that he later wrote into "War Is Kind."[6] Evidence that this view is inadequate has already been offered.[7] The record of Crane's activity in the school battalion as shown by his repeated promotions can hardly be construed as evincing either lack of interest or deficiency of skill. When one considers that military drill was com-

† From *American Literature*, XI (March, 1939), 1–10. By permission of *American Literature*.

1. Thomas Beer, *Stephen Crane: A Study in American Letters* (New York, 1924), p. 97.
2. *Ibid.*, p. 98.
3. *Ibid.*, p. 46.
4. Wilson Follett, "The Second Twenty-Eight Years," *Bookman*, LXVIII, 532–537 (Jan., 1929).
5. Beer *op. cit.*, p. 47.
6. *The Collected Poems of Stephen Crane*, ed. Wilson Follett (New York, 1930), pp. 77–78.
7. Lyndon U. Pratt, "The Formal Education of Stephen Crane," *American Literature*, X, 460–471. (Jan., 1939).

pulsory for the boys at Claverack, and that the masculine part of the school's enrollment stood in 1890 at about one hundred,[8] Crane's acting as the Colonel's adjutant seems no less remarkable than his being singled out in June for one of the next year's captaincies.[9] Finally it should not be forgotten that the company of which he was then lieutenant won the Washington's Birthday "prize-drill," earning by the precision of its manoeuvres the praise of the judges and the smiles of the young ladies.[10] It seems probable, in fact, that Crane's success in the school battalion would, in itself, have tended toward keeping pleasantly alive his boyish interest in war. There is little reason to doubt that Crane's memories of Claverack were in his mind as he drew the picture of Henry Fleming's farewell to his schoolmates at the "seminary."[11]

But there is another possible connection between Claverack and *The Red Badge of Courage* of considerably greater potential importance. One of the judges of the "prize-drill" which Crane's company won was General John Bullock Van Petten, professor of history and elocution at Claverack.[12] It seems altogether possible that *The Red Badge of Courage* owes more to General Van Petten than to any other single source of influence.

While at Claverack Crane had ample opportunity to become acquainted with the General. The relatively small size of the institution meant, in fact, that everyone knew everyone else, and the custom of commemorating the various holidays throughout the year brought students and faculty together in assemblies as well. The more elaborate of such exercises took the form of banquets, after which toasts and speeches were given.[13] At the conclusion of the dinner on Thanksgiving, 1889, one of the toasts, delivered by Captain Puzey of Company D of the battalion, was reprinted in the *Vidette* as follows:

"I would today present to you a member of the Grand Army of the Republic; an organization whose name implies patriotism, bravery, and indomitable energy. . . . The member whom I would toast is one of its most honored and respected. One who has bravely endured the hardships of war as well as enjoyed the pleasures of peace. One who, in the service of his country, has stood before the cannon's mouth, and in the service of his God appeared in the pulpit to instruct and enlighten his fellow-men, and now in his old age is imparting to the young, knowledge of incalculable worth,—a brave

8. *Claverack Catalog* (1890), p. 25. Of course, some of the boys would have been too young to serve as officers.
9. Pratt, *op. cit.*, p. 465.
10. *Ibid.*
11. "The Red Badge of Courage," *The Work of Stephen Crane* (hereinafter referred to as *Work*) (New York, 1925–1926), I, 28.
12. *Claverack Catalog* (1890), p. 2. See also Pratt, *op. cit.*, p. 464.
13. *Vidette* (the Claverack school magazine), I, 4 (Dec., 1890).

soldier, a true Christian, and an enlightened scholar. The Rev. General Van Petten, Ph. D., LL. D."[14]

The *Vidette's* next sentence reads: "This toast was received in a manner showing the estimation in which the worthy General is held, alike by pupils and teachers."

On the same occasion the General himself was called upon to speak. The *Vidette* further reports that "Prof. McAfee next introduced General Van Petten, from whom we are always glad to hear." From this and other references equally cordial in tenor, the inference is clear that the General was a genuinely popular as well as a prominent figure in school life. At the Washington's Birthday devotions, he "very appropriately had charge of the Service" and chose the hymns.[15] Later in the year, when spring came, the condition of his garden received attention by the *Vidette*.[16] And before the summer vacation, his plans were announced as follows: "Gen. and Mrs. Van Petten will attend the National Grand Army Encampment at Boston. The General's class will also meet at Wesleyan [Conn.] for the 40th Anniversary, with which he will meet."[17]

In the natural course of Crane's schoolwork, contact with the General was inevitable. Declamation was required of each student during his stay at the institution,[18] and the *Vidette* for the month following the occasion reported that the exercises preceding the Christmas, 1889, recess included orations by the members of the fourth form, "under the tutorship of Gen'l Van Petten." As has been indicated, the General also taught classes in Roman, English, and American history, although the first two were optional. In addition, the General's wife, listed in the catalog as Mrs. M. B. Van Petten, A.M., taught French, and Crane, by his own admission, studied French while at Claverack.[19]

Since General Van Petten's career forms a considerable basis of what follows, a biographical summary[20] is here inserted for convenience:

"Van Petten, John B., educator; *b.* in Sterling, N. Y., June 19, 1827; *s.* Peter and Lydia (Bullock) V.; grad. Wesleyan Univ., Conn., 1850; completed conf. course in divinity, 1856 (Ph.D., Syracuse Univ., 1888); *m.* Aug. 10, 1850, Mary B. Mason. Prin. Fairfield (N. Y.) Sem., 1855–61 and 1866–9. Was clergyman, M. E. Ch., chaplain 34th N. Y. inf., June 15, 1861, to Sept. 22, 1862; lt.-col.

14. *Ibid.*, p. 8. Mr. Beer (*op. cit.*, p. 162) notes Crane's fondness for elderly people.
15. *Ibid.*, I, 2 (March, 1890).
16. *Ibid.*, I, 10 (April, 1890).
17. *Ibid.*, I, 13 (June, 1890).
18. *Claverack Catalog* (1890), p. 16. The curriculum is reprinted by Pratt, *op. cit.*, pp. 462–463.
19. *Claverack Catalog* (1890), p. 2. See also Beer, *op. cit.*, p. 53.
20. *Who's Who in America*, 1903–1909.

160th N. Y. inf., Sept. 25, 1862, to Jan. 20, 1865; in permanent command of regiment over 2 yrs.; comd. 2d brigade of 1st div., 19th corps, at Pt. Hudson, June 14, 1863; severely wounded at battle of Opequan, Sept. 19, 1864; complimented in gen. orders by Gen. Sheridan for conspicuous gallantry; col. 193d N. Y. inf. and bvt. brig.-gen. U. S. V., comdg. dist. of Cumberland in W. Va., June, 1865, to Jan., 1866; State senator, 1868-9. Prin. Sedalia, Mo., Sem., 1877-82; prof. Latin and history, Claverack Coll., N. Y., 1885-1900."

Doubtless the reader will have noted one singularity in Van Petten's war record: his commission as lieutenant-colonel of the 160th infantry followed with peculiar suddenness his discharge as chaplain of the 34th regiment. Attention is thus naturally directed to the circumstances surrounding such an immediate change in his status, and the search for a possible explanation leads to the history of his regiment during the latter part of September, 1862.

The 34th New York Volunteers, or Herkimer regiment,[21] had served in the Peninsular campaign during 1862, participating in the battles of Williamsburg, Fair Oaks, Allen's Farm, White Oak Swamp, Malvern Hill, and the Second Bull Run.[22] At the beginning of September, Pope's unsuccessful army of Virginia being amalgamated with the army of the Potomac, and the whole command reverting to McClellan, the 34th New York constituted one of the many regimental units of the Second Corps under General Sumner. Within the Second Corps, Sedgwick commanded the Second Division, in the first brigade of which, that of General Gorman, was the 34th New York regiment under Colonel Suiter.[23]

After Lee's invasion of Maryland had been partly checked at South Mountain, the two armies faced each other on September 16 along a line extending north from the village of Sharpsburg, Maryland. That evening McClellan advanced his right wing to the attack, Hooker and Mansfield crossing Antietam Creek and occupying a position to the north of the Confederate left wing. The next morning they advanced southward to the attack, and fought a severe but indecisive engagement until they were in need of reinforcements. General Sumner's Second Corps marched to their relief late in the forenoon of the seventeenth, the General himself accompanying Sedgwick's 2nd Division which led the attack. "Shortly after nine, Sedgwick's three brigades in three columns emerged from the belt of woods east of the Hagerstown turnpike, deployed, and in three lines, facing west, crossed the cornfield and

21. Frederick H. Dyer, *Compendium of the War of the Rebellion* (Des Moines, 1908), p. 1416.
22. Louis N. Chapin, *A Brief History of the Thirty-fourth Regiment N. Y. S. V.* (New York, 1903), *passim.*
23. Frederick Phisterer (comp.), *New York in the War of the Rebellion, 1861-1865* (3d ed., Albany, 1912), III, 2125-2137, *passim.*

the turnpike, passing Greene's troops who heartily cheered them, and, leaving the Dunker Church on their left, entered the woods which lay west of the turnpike."[24] The line of Gorman's leading brigade, however, somehow became over-extended, and the regiment on the extreme left, while under severe enemy fire, lost touch with the other regiments of its brigade.[25] This unfortunate regiment was the 34th New York Volunteers.[26] The Confederates, sensing their advantage, advanced at this time, and were thus in a position to deliver a fire upon the flank of the 34th as well as in front.[27]

At this difficult juncture of events, an attempt was made by the 34th New York to extend its own front perhaps in order to reestablish contact with Union forces next to it.[28]

". . . The manoeuvre was attempted under a fire of the greatest intensity, and the regiment broke. At the same moment the enemy perceiving their advantage, came round on that flank. Crawford was obliged to give way on the right, and his troops pouring in confusion through the ranks of Sedgwick's advance brigade, threw it into disorder and back on the second and third lines. The enemy advanced their fire increasing.

General Sedgwick was three times wounded, in the shoulder, leg, and wrist, but he persisted in remaining in the field as long as there was a chance of saving it. . . . Lieutenant Howe, of General Sedgwick's staff, endeavored to rally the Thirty-Fourth New York. They were badly cut up and would not stand. Half their officers were killed or wounded, their colors shot to pieces, the color-sergeant killed, every one of the color-guard wounded."[29]

Other less hysterical sources, while varying in detail, corroborate the essential features. The brigade-commander, General Gorman, reported:

"The Thirty-fourth New York, being upon the extreme left in the front line of battle, after having withstood a most terrific fire, and having lost nearly one-half of the entire regiment in killed and wounded, was ordered by Major General Sedgwick, as will be seen

24. John C. Ropes, *The Story of the Civil War* (New York, 1898), Pt. II, p. 363.
25. Colonel Suiter, in his official report, says: "From some cause to me unknown, I had become detached from my brigade, the One Hundred and Twenty-fifth Regiment Pennsylvania Volunteers being on my right . . ." (*The War of the Rebellion: A Compilation of the Official Records of the Union and Confederate Armies*, Washington, 1901, XIX, Pt. I, p. 316. Hereinafter called *War Records*.)
26. *War Records*, XIX, Pt. I, p. 312.

27. William A. Crafts, *The Southern Rebellion* (Boston, 1870), II, 243.
28. The (New York) *Tribune*, Sept. 20, 1862, p. 5. The account was written by George N. Smalley, the *Tribune's* special correspondent, from the "battlefield, near Sharpsburg," Wednesday evening, Sept. 17, 1862. This *Tribune* account is also printed in *Rebellion Records*, ed. Frank Moore (New York, 1863), V, 469.
29. *Ibid.* There seems to be disagreement among the sources as to the origin of the order.

by Colonel Suiter's official report, to retire and take up a new position behind a battery to the right and rear. Immediately ordered them to reform on the left of the brigade, which they did."[30]

Colonel Suiter's report, naturally, pays less attention to the details of his regiment's rout than to the bravery of certain individuals under the galling circumstances of the battle.

"Of my color-sergeant [Colonel Suiter writes] I cannot speak in too high terms. He had carried the banner through all of the battles in which we have been engaged while on the Peninsular without receiving a wound. Here it was his fate to be struck five times, and when he was compelled to drop his colors he called upon his comrades to seize them and not to let them fall into the hands of the enemy. This was done by Corporal G. S. Haskins, who nobly bore them from the field."[31]

The casualties suffered by the unfortunate 34th, while actually less than the *Tribune* account would lead one to expect, were however considerable. The regiment lost in all 4 officers and 150 men, or about forty per cent of its total strength, although of this aggregate only ten were ultimately reported missing.[32] In other words, despite the heavy casualties suffered, and the probability that during the flight many of the men became separated from the regiment, these men sought out their command and returned to it, until all but ten were accounted for. Of these ten it is likely that several were among the unknown dead on the battlefield.[33]

Such was the course of events that so closely preceded Van Petten's transfer and promotion, although it is not the purpose of this study to infer any causal relationship between these happenings. The significance for the present purpose surely lies in the fact that Van Petten's regiment was forced into flight at the Battle of Antietam, and that he in all probability was an eyewitness to the scenes described. If this was indeed the case, it is unlikely that even his subsequent responsibilities and honors would have wholly obliterated from his mind the memory of his regiment's rout.[34]

30. *War Records*, XIX, Pt. I, p. 312.
31. *Ibid.*, XIX, Pt. I, p. 316.
32. *Ibid.*, XIX, Pt. I, p. 192.
33. The 34th Regiment enjoyed an excellent record throughout the war. Except for the disaster at Antietam, no regiment of Sumner's corps lost a gun or a flag up until May 10, 1864, and was, in fact, "the only corps in the army which could make that proud claim" (Francis W. Palfrey, *The Antietam and Fredericksburg*, New York, 1897, pp. 81–82).
34. It should be here admitted that no specific mention of Van Petten's presence at Antietam has been found. There are even discrepancies in the sources concerning the date of his discharge. However, besides the entry in *Who's Who in America* already cited, the records of the 34th regiment filed with the Adjutant General of the State of New York specify September 20. (This information was furnished by Mr. William A. Saxton, Chief, Bureau of War Records, State of New York, in a letter dated Feb. 19, 1937, to the present writer.) September 20 is also given by Frederick Phisterer, *op. cit.*, III, 2136. Finally in Van Petten's Declaration for Original Invalid Pension, dated Nov. 17, 1888, now on file in the office

It is reasonable to expect that General Van Petten's public utterances would have contained no mention of the 34th at Antietam. Certainly his Thanksgiving speech at Claverack in 1889 is filled with conventional patriotic fervor.[35] But not all of his contacts with the students were formal, and the tone of the *Vidette's* paragraphs concerning him surely indicates that he possessed a compelling, human side. He even used to lend his choice sword to a favored student to wear on dress parades.[36]

At Claverack the custom obtained of having faculty members preside over the tables in the dining hall. General Van Petten had charge of one such table, and thus, three times a day, a small group of students would be gathered around him under circumstances which, while assuredly polite, were to a certain degree informal. Under such conditions as these it is not impossible to conceive of the General remembering Antietam. A feminine student of the time was able to recall the following: "While at Claverack I was at General Van Petten's table for one year and he often recounted some of his war experiences. I can not now recall them, of course, but he became much excited as he lived over the old days."[37]

The aim of the foregoing pages has been to establish a sequence of likelihood, not to claim a factual necessity. It has already been shown that Crane, fond of war from boyhood, became while at Claverack still more interested in military matters. Furthermore, it seems certain that the elderly Van Petten, who had real war anecdotes to tell, was exactly the sort of man to whom Crane would have been responsive. Under these circumstances, then, Crane would surely have disregarded no opportunity to absorb further the lore of the battlefield from this veteran whose eyes had witnessed the scenes he so eloquently described.

It would be useless, of course, for anyone to seek in *The Red Badge of Courage* a transliteration of the Battle of Antietam. Numerous details of the story, such as the references to the pontoon-

of the Adjutant General of the War Department in Washington, he himself states that he served as Chaplain of the 34th "to about 25 Sept. 1862." (This information is taken from a letter dated April 30, 1937, written by Mr. Nelson Vance Russell, Chief, Division of Reference, The National Archives.)

It is in the statements Van Petten made during later years that discrepancies occur which are quite irreconcilable. But the earlier mentions seem reasonably consistent, and a New York State Senator who was also a Brevet Brigadier General, and had been cited for gallantry in action, certainly cannot be considered remiss, because of a slight inexactitude in dates. Finally, probability of Van Petten's presence at Antietam becomes almost a certainty when the fact is noted that he was a trustee of the National Cemetery at Antietam (*Who's Who in New York City and State*, rev. ed., New York, 1905, p. 914).

35. *Vidette*, I, 5 (Dec., 1889).
36. Letter of Aug. 10, 1936, to the writer from the late Rev. Robert W. Courtney, who attended Claverack between 1891 and 1894.
37. Letter to the writer dated Feb. 5, 1937, written by Mrs. Bertha Holmes Courtney.

bridges,[38] the plank road,[39] and the Rappahannock,[40] obviously support the traditional view that Crane had Chancellorsville in mind.[41] But in other respects the story more closely resembles certain aspects of Antietam than coincidence would seem to dictate.[42] As a result, the novel may rather be regarded as a synthesis of more than one battle than an historical portrayal of a single engagement. In all probability, some elements were drawn from one source, and some from another. If this principle is accepted, the higher reality of the story is made more credible by broadening the basis in fact even from one battle to two. Thus, if Chancellorsville contributed the general setting and rough plan of the novel, Antietam may well have provided at least two additional elements: the idea of Henry's panic and flight,[43] and the heroism of the wounded color-bearer.[44]

Of these two elements, the latter is admittedly the sort of incident that is traditional in war, and Crane might have found his inspiration in a score of other sources as well. But the former element, that of Henry's flight, seems clearly otherwise, for honest treatments of such disasters do not abound either in pictures or in writings dealing with the Civil War. It should be especially recalled, moreover, that Crane's unheroic treatment of the panic-

38. *Work*, I, 46; and Abner Doubleday, *Chancellorsville and Gettysburg* (New York, 1912), p. 9.
39. *Work*, I, 113; and Doubleday, *op. cit.*, pp. 44 ff.
40. *Work*, I, 140; and Doubleday, *op. cit.*, *passim*.
41. Ripley Hitchcock, in his introduction to the second edition of *The Red Badge of Courage* (New York, 1900) has written: ". . . the battle which he [Crane] had in mind more than any other was that of Chancellorsville." But the very phrase "more than any other" clearly implies plurality, and, since Hitchcock had himself been the book's purchaser for Appleton's in 1894, his information should have been correct. See also Beer, *op. cit.*, p. 125.
42. Note, for example, the number assigned to Fleming's mythical regiment, the 304th New York (*Work*, I, 57). Since there was no actual 304th regiment among the New York contingent ("Bibliography of State Participation in the Civil War," *United States War Department Library*, 3d ed., Washington, 1913, p. 546), it seems, to say the least, uncanny that Crane should have happened by chance upon a fictitious number so similar to that of Van Petten's 34th New York Volunteers. Other details in the novel are worth noting. When the 304th is sent into the line as a relief regiment (p. 52;

this and the following page numbers refer to the *Work*, Vol. I), the men march westward to their assignment (p. 39). The battle itself is commenced by the brigade on their right (p. 56), and their division occupies a position in the center of the line of battle (p. 59). After the first day's fighting, the number of men "missing" gradually dwindles from half the enrollment of the regiment to a mere handful as the stragglers make their way back (p. 133). When the 304th is itself relieved, the men are marched to the rear, past a battery of artillery, and across the same stream over which they had come to the battle field (p. 196). Although these details are by no means uniquely true of the Battle of Antietam, they more nearly describe the rout of Sedgwick's brigade in that engagement than they do the destruction of Howard's corps at Chancellorsville, for example (Palfrey, *op. cit.*, pp. 81–88, and Doubleday, *op. cit.*, pp. 25–40; also Ropes, *op. cit.*, pp. 363–365, and Pt. III, Book I, pp. 161–165). In opposition, however, such statements cannot be ignored as that the 304th was an inexperienced regiment (p. 33), and that it awaited an attack instead of delivering one (p. 62).
43. *Work*, I, 74 ff.
44. *Ibid.*, pp. 164–165.

stricken youth has been largely responsible for the notable position of *The Red Badge of Courage* among war novels.

From this viewpoint, a corresponding importance accrues to the various possible springs of Crane's thinking. Realisms of war remembered since boyhood, as well as unrecorded presumptive conversations with William Crane, are in this sense consequential, since their reflection at least is to be found in *The Red Badge of Courage*. But the weakness of attaching an exclusive momentousness to such origins as the war tales of Crane's "grandfather," for example, as Mr. Follett appears to do, seems apparent in the fact that to annotate *The Red Badge of Courage* Mr. Follett offers only "The Veteran."[45] The latter tale, it should be noted, first appeared in August, 1896,[46] and thus might conceivably have been even a fictitious, though convincing, completion of the story of Henry Fleming, perhaps deriving its very existence from the success of Fleming's earlier appearance. The fact remains, however, that in the rout of Van Petten's 34th New York regiment, one finds for the first time a definite episode basically analogous to the story of Henry Fleming's 304th New York regiment, and one which in all probability Crane had heard told. If this be so, Crane had only to invest the characters of the actual drama with his own thoughts and emotions, which has always been the way of the creative artist.

H. T. WEBSTER

Wilbur F. Hinman's *Corporal Si Klegg* and Stephen Crane's *The Red Badge of Courage*†

In 1887, Wilbur F. Hinman, late lieutenant colonel of the 65th regiment, Ohio volunteer infantry, published a volume of Civil War reminiscences entitled *Corporal Si Klegg and His "Pard."* *Corporal Si Klegg* is written in a manner which is often engaging, and evidently it enjoyed a fair popularity, for the second edition of 1890 carried it through twenty-six thousand copies and another was forthcoming in 1898. Probably the sale was largely confined to Civil War veterans. In his preface Colonel Hinman has the following to say of the nature of his book:

45. Follett, *loc. cit.*
46. Claude E. Jones, "Stephen Crane: A Bibliography of His Short Stories and Essays," *Bulletin of Bibliography*, XV, 170 (Jan.–April, 1936).
† From *American Literature*, XI (November, 1939), 285–93. By permission of *American Literature*.

"There is no end of histories—of campaigns and battles and regiments—and lives of prominent generals; but these do not portray the everyday life of the soldier. To do this, and this only, has been the aim of the author in *Corporal Si Klegg and his 'Pard.'* "

"This volume is not a history, nor is it a 'story,' in the usual acceptation of the word. 'Si Klegg' and 'Shorty,' his 'Pard,' are imaginary characters—though their prototypes were in every regiment—and Company Q, 200th Indiana, to which they belonged, is of course, fictitious. Their haps and mishaps while undergoing the process of transformation that made them soldiers . . . were those that entered directly into the daily life or observation of all the soldiers. . . . The author has made no attempt at literary embroidery, but has rather chosen the 'free and easy' form of language that marked the intercourse of the soldiers, and therefore seemed most appropriate to the theme."

Colonel Hinman's seven-hundred-odd pages of text were supplemented by the pencil of George Y. Coffin, who gave the book one hundred and ninety-three illustrations which are not without a grotesque realism.

Unless chance violates probability, Stephen Crane was much more intimately indebted to both the text and illustrations of *Corporal Si Klegg* for his *Red Badge of Courage* than he was to *Battles and Leaders of the Civil War* or to the conversations with veterans such as General Petten.[1] Indeed, Crane's extreme youth at the time he wrote *The Red Badge of Courage* supports the belief that there is a single written source to which the work is mainly indebted; for youth does not have a multitude of impressions to fuse together. The following pages, then, attempt to demonstrate that nearly everything that makes up *The Red Badge of Courage* exists at least in germ in *Corporal Si Klegg*.

Colonel Hinman's preface alone very pointedly suggests two familiar ingredients of *The Red Badge of Courage*: the hero who has his "prototype in every regiment," and the extensive use of American dialect. And if we recognize a general coincidence of aim in the separate works, their parallelism of general imaginative conception is even more striking. Each story tells of the development of a raw recruit into an experienced soldier, constantly emphasizing the thesis and investing it with a quasi-philosophical significance. It is impossible to read very far in either text without becoming aware of this basic similarity in the interpretation of the characters and their adventures. The protagonists who embody the "development" theme, Hinman's Si Klegg and Crane's Henry Fleming, are both farm boys much given to self-dramatization. Moved by patriotism

---

1. Mr. Lyndon Upson Pratt suggests this possibility in *American Literature,* XI, 1–10 (March, 1939).

and romantic imaginings of military glory, they enlist in the Union army against the wishes of their parents,[2] and each boy comes home to a touching domestic scene. There is some description in both books of the kit that the mother gives to the departing soldier. After joining his regiment, each boy goes through a period of training and delay which very largely dispels his romantic notions of war. When the first battle finally impends, Si and Henry each lies awake at night and doubts his courage,[3] but each later distinguishes himself in the conflict, seizing the flag from the falling standard bearer to lead a charge,[4] and learning from hearsay afterwards that he has been noticed and praised by the colonel.[5]

In addition, it should be remarked that both Stephen Crane and Colonel Hinman tend to see their characters symbolically in the moment of battle. On Hinman's part, this symbolism is quite explicit. Si Klegg "pictured what it was that conquered the great rebellion. See in those flashing eyes and firmly-set lips the spirit of courage, of unyielding determination, and of patriotic devotion, even to the supreme sacrifice if need be, of life itself."[6] That is the way Colonel Hinman is likely to put things in moments of fervor, which are fortunately rare. Stephen Crane, on the other hand, lets the reader guess for himself what Henry Fleming represents, but the task is not difficult, though the description is less formal and stylized. Henry Fleming, like Si Klegg before him, loads and fires his musket with a blind intensity, but his lips instead of being "firmly set" are contorted into a "cur-like snarl," and when the enemy seemed to give way, "he went instantly forward, like a dog who, seeing his foes lagging, turns and insists on being pursued."[7] Pretty clearly, Henry here symbolizes the spirit of conflict, and a slightly Kiplingesque reversion to the latent savagery in civilized man.

In addition to these parallels of imaginative conception, many details confirm the impression that Stephen Crane had *Corporal Si Klegg* in mind when he wrote *The Red Badge of Courage*. When Henry Fleming comes home after enlisting, he finds his mother "milking the brindle cow."[8] It is Si's sister, not his mother, who is milking. She drops the pail in surprise at seeing Si in uniform

2. Wilbur F. Hinman, *Corporal Si Klegg and His "Pard"* (Cleveland: N. G. Hamilton and Co., 1890), pp. 4, 15. This edition is not listed in the Library of Congress catalogue, but two other editions are, one printed by the Williams Publishing Company, Cleveland, 1887, and the other issued by N. G. Hamilton and Company, 1898. *The Red Badge of Courage*, ed. Max J. Herzberg (New York: D. Appleton and Co., 1926), pp. 6–8.

3. *Corporal Si Klegg*, pp. 394–395. *The Red Badge of Courage*, pp. 30–31.
4. *Corporal Si Klegg*, pp. 483–484; also illustration facing p. 484. *The Red Badge of Courage*, p. 182.
5. *Corporal Si Klegg*, pp. 494–495. *The Red Badge of Courage*, pp. 206–207.
6. *Corporal Si Klegg*, p. 407.
7. *The Red Badge of Courage*, pp. 164, 167.
8. *The Red Badge of Courage*, p. 7.

and Si himself takes over the chore patting the cow and calling her "old brindle."[9] Henry Fleming is given eight pairs of socks and some blackberry jam when he leaves for the army;[10] for Si Klegg, the jam is cranberry; the socks number only three pairs![11] When Henry and Si join their regiments, they each meet a tall soldier of considerable sang-froid: Jim Conklin in *The Red Badge of Courage*, and Si's "pard," Shorty, in the Hinman book. A good deal is made of the way Si gets rid of his superfluous kit during the first long march.[12] Henry Fleming and his companions simply throw their knapsacks away completely in the same circumstances.[13] When, in his first battle, Si feels "a smart rap on his head," and says to his pard: "Did ye bump me with yer gun, Shorty?"[14] he finds that he has been grazed by a bullet. It will be remembered that during his panic Henry Fleming is hit over the head by the gun of another fleeing soldier, and is thus enabled to tell his comrades that he has been shot during the battle. "Yeh've been grazed by a ball. It's raised a queer lump jest as if some feller had lammed yeh on the head with a club,"[15] says the companion who examines him. Incidentally, a procession of wounded like that which Henry Fleming joins during his flight[16] is seen by Si as he goes into action, and is also represented for the reader by Coffin's pencil.[17]

It is possible to cite other incidents of this sort which these two books have in common, but those already mentioned are the least open to question, and perhaps they are sufficient. They illustrate the fact that Stephen Crane frequently parallels details which are found in *Corporal Si Klegg*. There are, in addition, some passages which are remarkably similar in content. Four examples of these are here cited:

1. From *Corporal Si Klegg*:
    As we have seen in the experience of the 200th Indiana, full regiments on taking the field were rapidly decimated by the ravages of disease and bullets. Scarcely more than half of the men enlisted proved to be physically able to "stand the service," and battles fast thinned the ranks. New organizations were constantly going to the front, but a "veteran" regiment having three hundred men was a large one. . . .[18]
    From *The Red Badge of Courage*:
    But the regiment was not yet veteranlike in appearance. Veteran regiments in the army were likely to be very small aggregations

9. *Corporal Si Klegg*, pp. 20–21.
10. *The Red Badge of Courage*, pp. 8–9.
11. *Corporal Si Klegg*, pp. 31–32.
12. *Corporal Si Klegg*, pp. 156–161.
13. *The Red Badge of Courage*, p. 33.
14. *Corporal Si Klegg*, p. 410.
15. *The Red Badge of Courage*, p. 133.
16. *The Red Badge of Courage*, p. 85.
17. *Corporal Si Klegg*, p. 402.
18. *Corporal Si Klegg*, p. 696.

of men. Once, when the command had first come to the field, some perambulating veterans, noting the length of their column, had accosted them thus: "Hey, fellers, what brigade is that?" And when the men had replied that they formed a regiment and not a brigade, the older soldiers had laughed, and said, "O Gawd!"[19]

2. From *Corporal Si Klegg*:

The single hour's experience on the road had served to remove the scales from the eyes of a goodly number of the members of Company Q. They began to foresee the inevitable, and at the first halt they made a small beginning in the labor of getting themselves down to light marching orders—a process of sacrifice which a year later had accomplished its perfect work, when each man took nothing in the way of baggage save what he could roll up in a blanket and toss over his shoulder.[20]

From *The Red Badge of Courage*:

The men had begun to count the miles upon their fingers, and they grew tired. "Sorefeet an' damned short rations, that's all," said the loud soldier. There was perspiration and grumblings. After a time they began to shed their knapsacks. Some tossed them unconcernedly down; others hid them carefully, asserting their plans to return for them at some convenient time. Men extricated themselves from thick shirts. Presently few carried anything but their necessary clothing, blankets, haversacks, canteens, and arms and ammunition. . . .[21]

3. From *Corporal Si Klegg*:

The officers had ordered the men to lie down, that they might be less exposed to the enemy's fire. But Si will not lie down. . . . This feeling was common to new troops in their first flight. In their minds there was an odium connected with the idea of seeking cover. It was too much like showing the white feather. But in the fullness of time they all got over this foolish notion.[22]

From *The Red Badge of Courage*:

During this halt many men in the regiment began erecting tiny hills in front of them. . . . This procedure caused a discussion among the men. Some wished to fight like duelists, believing it to be correct to stand erect and be, from their feet to their foreheads, a mark. They said they scorned the devices of the cautious. But the others scoffed in reply, and pointed to the veterans on the flanks who were digging at the ground like terriers.[23]

4. From *Corporal Si Klegg*:

Pretty soon he struck a veteran regiment from Illinois, the members of which were sitting and lying in all the picturesque and indescribable attitudes which the old soldiers found gave them the greatest comfort during a "rest." Then the fun com-

19. *The Red Badge of Courage*, pp. 33–34.
20. *Corporal Si Klegg*, p. 153.
21. *The Red Badge of Courage*, p. 33.
22. *Corporal Si Klegg*, p. 409.
23. *The Red Badge of Courage*, p. 41.

menced. . . .

"What rijiment is this?" asked Si, timidly.

"Same old rijiment!" was the answer from half a dozen at once. A single glance told the swarthy veterans that the fresh-looking youth who asked this conundrum belonged to one of the new regiments, and they immediately opened their batteries upon him:

"Left—Left—Left!" . . .

"Ye'd better shed that knapsack, or it'll be the death of ye!"

"I say, there, how's all the folks to home?"

"How d'ye like it's fur's ye've got, anyway?"

Si had never been under so hot a fire before. He stood it as long as he could, and then stopped.

"Halt!" shouted a chorus of voices. "Shoulder—Arms! Order—Arms!"

By this time Si's wrath was at the boiling point. Casting around him a look of defiance, he exclaimed:

"Ye cowardly blaggards. I kin jest lick any two of ye, an' I'll dare ye to come on. Ef the 200th Injianny was here we'd clean out the hull pack of ye quicker'n ye kin say scat!"[24]

From *The Red Badge of Courage:*

As they approached their own lines there was some sarcasm exhibited on the part of a gaunt and bronzed regiment that lay resting in the shade of trees. Questions were wafted to them.

"Where th' hell yeh been?"

"What yeh comin' back fer?"

"Why didn't yeh stay there?"

"Was it warm out there, sonny?"

"Goin' home now, boys?"

One shouted in taunting mimicry: "Oh, mother, come quick an' look at th' sojers!"

There was no reply from the bruised and battered regiment, save that one man made broadcast challenges to fist fights. . . .[25]

The writer believes that the repetition of matter and essential situation in the preceding passages establishes beyond serious doubt that Stephen Crane drew extensively from *Corporal Si Klegg* for his own war novel. This belief raises the question of the precise use he made of his source. Clearly Crane's narrative style is quite unaffected by that of Hinman. This, one would take for granted. Three of the parallel passages, moreover, occur in totally different contexts, though in the passages where the new recruits show reluctance to shelter themselves from the bullets, the context is the same in each text. This juxtaposition of material is characteristic of the way in which Crane handles his source. While most of the

24. *Corporal Si Klegg,* pp. 192–193.   25. *The Red Badge of Courage,* p. 200.

detail in *The Red Badge of Courage* can be paralleled in *Corporal Si Klegg*, little of it is given exactly the same application. The much withered condition of example four as it appears in *The Red Badge of Courage* is interesting and illustrative. Hinman revels in incident and authorial comment for its own sake. In no sense an imitator of Dickens, he nevertheless gives the impression that he knew his Dickens intimately, and that he almost intuitively followed the rambling Dickensian pattern in his war book. Crane, on the other hand, subordinates detail to the whole of his conception, and passages which cover pages in *Corporal Si Klegg* offer merely a minor suggestion to the author of *The Red Badge of Courage*. Thus, for example, Henry Fleming's conversation with a Confederate picket[26] recalls to the present writer a much longer passage of the sort in the Hinman book,[27] while the veteran's comment to Henry on the conversation suggests several similar remarks in *Corporal Si Klegg*.[28] The only material which Crane duplicates and greatly expands is the theme of the hero's fright before and during battle. Si Klegg runs away in momentary panic several times in his career, but these incidents are brief and comic. For the most part Hinman keeps his hero hyperconventionally heroic.

In conclusion, it seems appropriate to attempt a summary of what Stephen Crane does and does not owe to Colonel Hinman, if the likelihood of the debt is accepted by the reader. It should be emphasized at once that the total effects of the two books are dissimilar, in spite of their many common details. Hinman's book is much longer than *The Red Badge of Courage*, and a substantial part of the difference in length is taken up with comic incident and comment. The author, indeed, has a flair for drollery, while in passages of purported seriousness he is likely to pull out all the stops on the organ of Victorian rhetoric with results which have already been illustrated. Thus *Corporal Si Klegg* by the intention and talent of its creator, remains a comic book. *The Red Badge of Courage* is hardly that. But evidently, Crane got his conception of a commonplace, unromantic hero from Hinman, together with the theme of this raw recruit's development into the capable veteran. The development theme is much emphasized in both stories, and if Crane looked into a copy of *Corporal Si Klegg*, he could hardly have remained unaware of its existence there, for Coffin's pencil assists the reader with a double frontispiece delineating how Si went away to war, and how he came back. In addition to this, Crane apparently adapted a good deal of the essential structure of

26. *The Red Badge of Courage*, pp. 11–12.

27. *Corporal Si Klegg*, pp. 466–469.

28. *Corporal Si Klegg*, p. 133.

his narrative from Hinman, as well as many incidents and details of army life.

It is difficult to say how far Crane may have been influenced by Hinman in his use of dialect. Very probably, the influence is slight. The flavor of the speech is noticeably different, and certainly indicates an attempt on the part of each author to capture the regionalisms familiar to him.[29] Hinman's dialect has a certain raciness which hardly belongs in the scope of Crane's book, and it is set in a less mannered narrative style which gives it a certain advantage as far as naturalness is concerned, but Crane impresses the present writer as being the more accurate transcriber of actual speech. It would seem plausible to believe that Hinman was the source of Crane's army slang, but the correspondence between the expressions actually used is not great. One then gets the impression that Crane was relying mainly on his ear in his reproduction of the soldiers' speech, for certainly army slang and dialect were available to him from many sources.

Crane's narrative style and his descriptive passages are, of course, not suggested by Hinman, and his psychologizing is developed from his model's barest hints. To be sure, Si Klegg, like Henry Fleming, is endowed with a considerable degree of self-consciousness, and a tendency to self-dramatization, but what he thinks and feels is entirely conventional and obvious. Hinman shows no desire to deal with more than the externals of army life. He mitigates the serious and seamy side of war with bursts of Victorian rhetoric, on the one hand, and comedy on the other. Thus, Crane is entirely original when he reconciles meanness and self-sacrifice, panic and heroism in Henry Fleming and his comrades.

29. Perhaps examples will be of interest here. The writer submits for comparison two dialect passages of similar content:

The Red Badge of Courage, pp. 206–207: "Yeh jest oughta hear!" repeated the other, and he arranged himself to tell his tidings. The others made an excited circle. "Well, sir, th' colonel met your lieutenant right by us—it was the damnedest thing I ever heard—an' he ses: 'Ahem! ahem!' he ses. 'Mr. Hasbrouck!' he ses, 'by th' way, who was that lad what carried th' flag?' he ses, an' th' lieutenant, he speaks up right away: 'That's Flemin', an' he's a jimhickey,' he ses, right away. What? I say he did. 'A jimhickey,' he ses—those'r his words. He did, too. I say he did. If you kin tell this story better than I kin, go ahead an' tell it. Well, then, keep yer mouth shet. Th' lieutenant, he ses: 'He's a jimhickey,' an' th' colonel, he ses: 'Ahem! ahem! he is, indeed, a very good man t' have, ahem! He kep' th' flag 'way t' th' front. I saw 'im. He's a good un,' ses th' colonel. . . ."

Corporal Si Klegg, pp. 494–495: "I axed the cap'n 'f I mout hunt ye up, 'n' he said he didn't have no 'bjections pervidin' the colonel was willin'. I made bold to ax him 'cause I knowed he allus had a warm side fer ye, 'n' I didn't b'lieve he'd think any less on ye fer carryin' the flag o' the old 200th Injianny up to the top o' that blazin' ridge. Jest' soon' I told him what I wanted he said right away, the colonel did: 'Certingly, my man, 'n' when ye git back' says he, 'come straight ter my tent 'n' tell me how badly Corp'ral Klegg's wounded. He's a brave fellow, is Klegg.' . . ."

LARS ÅHNEBRINK

[Naturalism: Zola, Tolstoy, and Crane]†

* * *

In the eighties and nineties the American writers whose aim was a faithful reproduction of everyday life commonly referred to themselves as "*realists*." At the same time American writers and critics were generally employing the terms "realism" or "new realism" for French naturalism as it entered the United States. This led to a confusion of terminology, which, not limited to those two decades, has, to some extent, persisted to this day. A definition of the terms "realism" and "naturalism" . . . therefore is necessary. *Realism* is a manner and method of composition by which the author describes *normal, average life* in an accurate and truthful way (exemplified in Howells' *The Rise of Silas Lapham*). *Naturalism*, on the other hand, is a manner and method of composition by which the author portrays *life as it is in accordance with the philosophic theory of determinism* (exemplified in Zola's *L'Assommoir*). In contrast to a realist, a naturalist believes that man is fundamentally an animal without free will. To a naturalist man can be explained in terms of the forces, usually heredity and environment, which operate upon him.

* * *

The theme of war, occasionally used in *The Black Riders*, was to be the motif of most of Crane's subsequent books. In 1895 appeared *The Red Badge of Courage*, his most important war narrative and perhaps his greatest achievement. In spite of the shift of background from the New York slums of *Maggie* to the imagined battlefields of Chancellorsville in this war story, Crane did not change his focus of interest: the individual in his relationship to society and the group. Since he wrote the novel without any personal experience of war, it may be worth while investigating what books he read or may have had access to at this period. Beer has it that *The Red Badge of Courage* was written on a dare after Crane had dipped into a translation of *La Débâcle*. No doubt even before the composition of *Maggie*, he was familiar with some of Zola's work. Once he wrote of *Nana*:

† From *The Beginnings of Naturalism in American Fiction*, Upsala and Cambridge, 1950; pp. 96–357, *passim*. Reprinted by permission.

148

". . . this girl in Zola is a real streetwalker. I mean, she does not fool around making excuses for her career. You must pardon me if I cannot agree that every painted woman on the streets of New York was brought there by some evil man. Nana, in the story, is honest."

Crane admired Zola's sincerity and honesty, but he ranked Tolstoy as "the supreme living writer of our time . . ."[1] He liked both *Anna Karenina*[2] and *War and Peace*,[3] although he resented their length and didacticism. Crane may also have read Bierce's *Tales of Soldiers and Civilians* (1891) and *Can Such Things Be?* (1893), or looked into Frank Wilkeson's *Recollections of a Private Soldier in the Army of the Potomac* (1887), or Warren Goss's *Recollections of a Private* (1891). He may also have seen some of the numerous Civil War articles with illustrations that were running in *Harper's Weekly* in the eighties and early nineties. He possibly read *Corporal Si Klegg and His Pard* (1887) by Wilbur F. Hinman.[4] On April 2 (1894?) he sent back *Battles and Leaders of the Civil War* to one Mrs. Armstrong with the following note:

"Thank you very much for letting me keep these so long. I have spent ten nights writing a story of the war on my own responsibility but I am not sure that my facts are real and the books won't tell me what I want to know so I must do it all over again, I guess."[5]

Moreover, Crane had talked with many veterans of the Civil War, and his brother William was an expert on the strategy of the battle of Chancellorsville—the protracted battle of *The Red Badge of Courage*. From these and other sources Crane created a war story which revealed his extraordinary power of probing the mind of a raw recruit. The novel told of the reactions of an unexperienced youth in his first battle, of his dreams, his deadly terror, and final victory over himself. The boy's soul was dissected with an anatomist's care for details, and the inner causes of his behavior were sought for with a scientist's zeal for truth. He was viewed against a background of war: the vibration and roar of booming guns, the choking smell of gunpowder, the red flames of cracking rifles, the sound of whistling bullets, the whirling clouds of smoke, explosions and cries, dead horses and soldiers in agony, men and animals

1. Introduction by Thomas Beer to Vol. VII, xiii, of *The Work of Stephen Crane*, ed. by Wilson Follett (12 vols., New York, 1925–27). This edition will hereafter be referred to as *Work*.
2. Beer, *Stephen Crane*, p. 157.
3. *Ibid.*, p. 143.
4. See H. T. Webster's article "Wilbur F. Hinman's *Corporal Si Klegg*, and Stephen Crane's *The Red Badge of Courage*," *American Literature*, XI (November, 1939), 285–93. Crane may

also have glanced at Abner Doubleday, *Chancellorsville and Gettysburg* (New York, 1882) in *Campaigns of the Civil War*, VI.
5. Beer, *op. cit.*, p. 98. Between 1884 and 1887 the *Century Magazine* published a series of articles on the Civil War, written by both Confederate and Federate men who had taken part in it. Those articles were afterward published in four volumes as *Battles and Leaders of the Civil War* (New York, 1887–9).

drawn helplessly into a maelstrom of desperate confusion. The book is a sample of naturalism because of its candor, its treatment of men as dominated by instincts, its pictures of masses, and its pessimistic outlook.

* * *

Crane[6] revolted not only against the social conditions of his time, but also against the smug complacency of the genteel tradition and the conventional standard of American literature. Sentimentalism, melodrama, and romanticism were alien to his conception of life. He wanted "art straight," nearness to life, and personal honesty. Like Keats, he voiced the belief that a work of art was not born without pain. Of *The Red Badge of Courage* he once wrote:

"It was an effort born of pain—despair, almost; and I believe that this made it a better piece of literature than it otherwise would have been. It seems a pity that art should be a child of pain, and yet I think it is. Of course, we have fine writers who are prosperous and contented, but in my opinion their work would be greater if this were not so. It lacks the sting it would have if written under the spur of a great need."[7]

In an undated letter to a friend of his, written about 1896, he told how he came to join the realistic forces in American literature. Crane wrote:

"You know, when I left you, I renounced the clever school in literature. It seemed to me that there must be something more in life than to sit and cudgel one's brains for clever and witty expedients. So I developed all alone a little creed of art which I thought was a good one. Later I discovered that my creed was identical with the one of Howells and Garland and in this way I became involved in the beautiful war between those who say that art is man's substitute for nature and we are the most successful in art when we approach the nearest to nature and truth and those who say—well, I don't know what they say . . . they can't say much but they fight villainously and keep Garland and I out of the big magazines. Howells, of course, is too powerful for them.

If I had kept to my clever Rudyard Kipling style the road might have been shorter but, oh, it wouldn't be the true road. The two years of fighting have been well spent. And now I am almost at the end of it. This winter fixes me firmly. We have proved too formidable for them, confound them."[8]

6. Material for a discussion of Crane's literary theories is scarce. Besides hints in his works, there exist a few letters and at least one article which give some information on his credo.

7. *The Red Badge of Courage* (Mod. lib. ed., New York, n. d.), pp. xvi–xvii.
8. Unpublished letter of Crane to Miss Lily Brandon. Reproduced by the permission of Ames W. Williams.

This letter shows that Crane helped to fight the battle for realism in America together with his admired leaders, Howells and Garland, and his literary theories, too, conform in many respects to those advanced by the two writers. Above all he considered truthfulness the most important principle. The author should be true to himself and true to the life that surrounded him. "I decided," wrote Crane once, "that the nearer a writer gets to life the greater he becomes as an artist . . ." And he summed up his aim in writing as follows: ". . . most of my prose writings have been towards the goal partially described by that misunderstood and abused word, realism." In his work he aimed at accuracy and truth and requested "personal honesty" of himself and other writers. His purpose was to achieve nearness to life, but life can evade us and Crane realized his inability to record it truthfully. In his "War Memories" he wrote: " 'But to get the real thing!' . . . 'It seems impossible! It is because war is neither magnificent nor squalid; it is simply life, and an expression of life can always evade us. We can never tell life, one to another, although sometimes we think we can.' "

Some time after the publication of *The Red Badge of Courage* Crane wrote the following letter which demonstrates what a conscientious artist he was:

"The one thing that deeply pleases me in my literary life—brief and inglorious as it is—is the fact that men of sense believe me to be sincere. *Maggie,* published in paper covers, made me the friendship of Hamlin Garland and W. D. Howells; and the one thing that makes my life worth living in the midst of all this abuse and ridicule is the consciousness that never for an instant have those friendships at all diminished. Personally I am aware that my work does not amount to a string of dried beans—I always calmly admit it. But I also know that I do the best that is in me, without regard to cheers or damnation. When I was the mark for every humorist in the country, I went ahead; and now, when I am the mark for only 50 per cent of the humorists of the country, I go ahead, for I understand that a man is born into the world with his own pair of eyes, and he is not at all responsible for his quality of personal honesty. To keep close to my honesty is my supreme ambition. There is a sublime egotism in talking of honesty. I, however, do not say that I am honest. I merely say that I am as nearly honest as a weak mental machinery will allow. This aim in life struck me as being the only thing worth while. A man is sure to fail at it, but there is something in the failure."[9]

Howells, Garland, Crane, and Norris, all working for the liberation of American literature, are linked together in their demand for

9. "Some Letters of Stephen Crane," *Academy,* LIX (August 11, 1900), 116.

truth and sincerity in the writer. * * * Howells maintained that the novel should have an intention, but it should never preach. Crane held the same idea in a letter to a friend written immediately after the success of his first war novel:

"I have been very careful not to let any theories or pet ideas of my own creep into my work. Preaching is fatal to art in literature. I try to give to readers a slice out of life; and, if there is any moral or lesson in it, I do not try to point it out. I let the reader find it for himself. The result is more satisfactory to both the reader and myself. As Emerson said: 'There should be a long logic beneath the story, but it should be kept carefully out of sight.' "[10]

On these grounds he objected to the preaching of Tolstoy, although, otherwise, he was a warm admirer of his art. "I confess," wrote Crane in 1897, "that the conclusions of some of his novels, and the lectures he sticks in, leave me feeling that he regards his genius as the means to an end." *Anna Karenina* was "too long because he has to stop and preach but it's a bully book."[11] He also considered the didacticism of *War and Peace* and *Sebastopol* out of place in a work of art. He even advanced the opinion that *McTeague* was too moral.[12]

As has been said Crane, like Garland, advocated the short novel and he demonstrated it in such works as *Maggie* and *George's Mother*. After a reading of *Nana* he wrote: "Zola is a sincere writer but—is he much good? He hangs one thing to another and his story goes along but I find him pretty tiresome."[13] Crane acknowledged the sincerity of Zola's work, but found his scope in the novel too broad. He also turned against the unwieldy bulk of *War and Peace* and remarked that Tolstoy "could have done the whole business in one third of the time and made it just as wonderful. It goes on and on like Texas."[14] Crane even considered *The Red Badge of Courage* too long.

* * *

It is difficult to ascertain Crane's attitude toward and understanding of French naturalism, since he did not advance any opinion on the subject, as far as I have been able to make out. He spoke, however, as has been said, with qualified praise of Zola whose sincerity he admired.

Crane's literary credo, although expressed only in occasional fragments, has points in common with that of James, Howells, and Garland and demonstrates that, in theory, he was a *realist*—not a

10. *Ibid.*
11. Beer, *Stephen Crane*, p. 157.
12. *Ibid.*, p. 226.
13. *Ibid.*, p. 148.
14. *Ibid.*, p. 143.

naturalist. In practice, however, he went beyond the realism of James and Howells and the veritism of Garland in such naturalistic stories as *Maggie* and *George's Mother*.

* * *

We know that Crane had read *Sebastopol* and *War and Peace*, and that he ranked Tolstoy as "the supreme living writer of our time." The effects of Crane's reading of Tolstoy are evident, it seems, in many of the American writer's tales of war, notably in *The Red Badge of Courage*, which has many points in common with Tolstoy's war narratives. Some of these, however, grow essentially out of the similarity of theme, and others represent incidental details; yet there are elements in Crane's war stories that suggest Tolstoy in the first place as a possible source of inspiration.

Let us first examine Crane's concept of war. It has been noted earlier that it deviated from Zola's, who looked upon war as a necessity, and that it was more closely related to the Russian's. Tolstoy was a pacifist, and to him, as to Crane, war was meaningless slaughter. Neither Tolstoy nor Crane had any illusions about the glory of war. In Tolstoy's stories as well as in those of Crane, war was painted "without the brilliant and accurate alignment of troops, without music, without the drum-roll, without standards flying in the wind, without galloping generals."[15] Both authors depicted it as it was, "in blood, in suffering, and in death." To Tolstoy and Crane the pain and bloodshed of war were even more horrible, because they believed that war was not only unnecessary, but completely meaningless. Frequently Tolstoy asked the questions: "What's the use? What's the meaning?" "For what, then, had those legs and arms been torn off, those men been killed?"[16] There was no answer, however. Crane asked himself similar questions, but found no reply.

"Lying near one of the enemy's trenches was a red-headed Spanish corpse. I wonder how many hundreds were cognizant of this red-headed Spanish corpse? It arose to the dignity of a landmark. There were many corpses, but only one with a red head. This red-head. He was always there. Each time I approached that part of the field I prayed that I might find that he had been buried. But he was always there—red-headed. His strong simple countenance was a malignant sneer at the system which was for ever killing the credulous peasants in a sort of black night of politics, where the peasants merely followed whatever somebody had told them was lofty and

15. *Sebastopol* (New York, 1887), p. 27. Cf. in Crane's *War Memories:* "War is death, and a plague of the lack of small things, and toil." *Work,* IX, 219. See also *ibid.,* I, 87.
16. *War and Peace* (Mod. Lib. ed., New York, n. d.), p. 382.

good. But, nevertheless, the red-headed Spaniard was dead. He was irrevocably dead. And to what purpose? The honour of Spain? Surely the honour of Spain could have existed without the violent death of this poor red-headed peasant? . . . You came to another hemisphere to fight because—because you were told to, I suppose. Well, there you are, buried in your trench on San Juan Hill. That is the end of it, your life has been taken—that is a flat, frank fact."[17]

Despite the fact that war was horrible and without purpose, men went to war and were killed. Why? Neither Tolstoy nor Crane could give an answer. The soldiers "went because they went."[18] That was all.

Moreover, Tolstoy and Crane shared the concept that the actual happenings on the battlefield were not the logical results of careful planning on behalf of the generals; on the contrary, victories were "accidents, the outcome of a blind dash of unintelligent forces, rather than due to strategy and generalship."[19] Thus, what occurred on the battlefield had no connection with any previously determined plan. Things happened because incomprehensible forces were at work over which man had no control.

In order to illustrate the meaningless cruelty of war, Tolstoy did not hesitate to depict in detail the sordidness and brutality of the soldier's life. In hospitals and on battlefields the reader witnessed the terror and the bloodshed, the intense pain of war, in a number of heart-rending scenes, the vivid realism of which was perhaps only equaled by similar scenes in *La Débâcle*. Tolstoy recorded minutely and accurately the hissing of the bullets, the roar of the mortars, the piercing cries of the dying and the wounded, the nauseating smell of corpses, etc. It is probable that the Russian writer served to some extent as a model for the intense realism of Crane's tales of war. To exemplify this, it may perhaps suffice to compare the following two passages. The scene below is taken from *War and Peace*:

"Some crows, scenting blood, flitted to and fro among the birches, cawing impatiently. For more than five acres round the tents there were sitting or lying men stained with blood, and variously attired. They were surrounded by crowds of dejected-looking and intently observant soldiers, who had come with stretchers. Officers, trying to keep order, kept driving them away from the place; but it was of no use. The soldiers, heedless of the officers, stood leaning against the stretchers, gazing intently at what was passing before their eyes, as though trying to solve some difficult problem in this spectacle. From the tents came the sound of loud, angry wailing, and

17. *Work*, IX, 238–9.
18. *Ibid.*, II, 241.

19. Parrington, *Main Currents in American Thought*, III, 328.

piteous moans. At intervals a doctor's assistant ran out for water, or to point out those who were to be taken in next. The wounded, awaiting their turn at the tent, uttered hoarse groans and moans, wept, shouted, swore, or begged for vodka. Several were raving in delirium."[20]

Here is a similar scene taken from **Wounds in the Rain**:

"The low white tents of the hospital were grouped around an old schoolhouse. There was here a singular commotion. In the foreground two ambulances interlocked wheels in the deep mud. The drivers were tossing the blame of it back and forth, gesticulating and berating, while from the ambulances, both crammed with wounded, there came an occasional groan. An interminable crowd of bandaged men were coming and going. Great numbers sat under trees nursing heads or arms or legs. There was a dispute of some kind raging on the steps of the schoolhouse. Sitting with his back against a tree a man with a face as grey as a new army blanket was serenely smoking a corncob pipe. The lieutenant wished to rush forward and inform him that he was dying."[21]

In both passages, which present an objective picture of how the wounded were taken care of, we note the same stress laid upon the horror of war. Each writer depicted its bloodshed, its futility, its absence of glamour and heroic postures.

Another feature of Tolstoy's war stories was his new type of soldier, an ordinary individual[22] possessed of the usual shortcomings of the average man, whose sensations and emotions under fire were carefully analyzed. Turning to Crane, we observe that he, too, created a type of soldier that in some respects resembles Tolstoy's. To illustrate this, let us compare Volodia in *Sebastopol* with Henry in *The Red Badge of Courage*. In a burst of enthusiasm both Volodia, a second-ensign, and Henry enlisted as volunteers, dreaming happy dreams of bold deeds on the battlefield. However, their imaginary romance of warfare contrasted sharply with the stern reality of war itself. Since both were of a sensitive, impressionable, and meditative disposition, they began to reflect whether they would be able to fulfil the demands required of them or not. This was the main problem in both stories. When attempting to solve this problem by way of persuading themselves that they would not run away; their fear of being cowards[23] only augmented. The idea

20. *War and Peace*, p. 758.
21. *Work*, IX, 133. Cf. also *ibid.*, pp. 207, 234 and *ibid.*, pp. 88, 113.
22. Occasionally Tolstoy has a tendency, it seems, to idealize the common soldier. See, for instance, *Sebastopol*, pp. 41–2. There is no such tendency in Crane.
23. Cf. Maurice, whose fear was less a psychological problem than a normal reaction in the face of danger. When first under fire Maurice wanted to run away like a frightened animal. Zola, *L'Assommoir*.

of failure tortured them constantly and would not leave their harassed minds. This is Volodia:

"The feeling of this desertion in the presence of danger, of death, as
he believed, oppressed his heart with the glacial weight of a stone.
Halting in the middle of the place, he looked all about him to see if
he was observed, and taking his head in both hands, he murmured,
with a voice broken by terror, "My God! am I really a despicable poltroon, a coward? I who have lately dreamed of dying for my country,
for my Czar, and that with joy! Yes, I am an unfortunate and despicable being!" he cried, in profound despair, and quite undeceived
about himself."[24]

And this is Henry:

"He felt alone in space when his injured comrade had disappeared.
His failure to discover any mite of resemblance in their view-points
made him more miserable than before. No one seemed to be wrestling with such a terrific personal problem. He was a mental outcast."

Both Volodia and Henry were kept awake at night, brooding, trying
to persuade themselves that they would not be cowards when under
fire. This is Volodia:

"Left alone with his thoughts, Volodia at first felt a return of
the terror caused by the trouble which agitated his soul. Counting
upon sleep to be able to cease thinking of his surroundings and to
forget himself, he blew out his candle and lay down, covering himself all up with his overcoat, even his head, for he had kept his fear
of darkness since his childhood. But suddenly the idea came to him
that a shell might fall through the roof and kill him. . . .
"He rose and walked the room. The fear of the real danger had
stifled the mysterious terror of darkness. He hunted and found to
hand only a saddle and a samovar. 'I am a coward, a poltroon, a
wretch,' he thought again, filled with disgust and scorn of himself.
He lay down and tried to stop thinking; but then the impressions of
the day passed again through his mind, and the continual sounds
which shook the panes of his single window recalled to him the danger he was in. Visions followed. Now he saw the wounded covered
with blood; now bursting shells, pieces of which flew into his room;
now the pretty Sister of Charity who dressed his wounds weeping
over his agony, or his mother, who, carrying him back to the pro-
vincial town, praying to God for him before a miraculous image, shed
hot tears. Sleep eluded him; but suddenly the thought of an all-
powerful Deity who sees everything and who hears every prayer
flashed upon him distinct and clear in the midst of his reveries. He
fell upon his knees, making the sign of the cross, and clasping his
hands as he had been taught in his childhood. This simple gesture

24. *Sebastopol*, pp. 174–5.

aroused in him a feeling of infinite, long-forgotten calm.

" 'If I am to die, it is because I am useless! Then, may Thy will be done, O Lord! and may it be done quickly. But if the courage and firmness which I lack are necessary to me, spare me the shame and the dishonor, which I cannot endure, and teach me what I must do to accomplish Thy will.'

"His weak, childish, and terrified soul was fortified, was calmed at once, and entered new, broad, and luminous regions. He thought of a thousand things; he experienced a thousand sensations in the short duration of this feeling; then he quietly went to sleep, heedless of the dull roar of the bombardment and of the shaking windows."[25]

And Henry:

"He went slowly to his tent and stretched himself on a blanket by the side of the snoring tall soldier. In the darkness he saw visions of a thousand-tongued fear that would babble at his back and cause him to flee, while others were going coolly about their country's business. He admitted that he would not be able to cope with this monster. He felt that every nerve in his body would be an ear to hear the voices, while other men would remain stolid and deaf.

"And as he sweated with the pain of these thoughts, he could hear low, serene sentences. 'I'll bid five.' 'Make it six.' 'Seven.' 'Seven goes.'

"He stared at the red, shivering reflection of a fire on the white wall of his tent until, exhausted and ill from the monotony of his suffering, he fell asleep."

Whereas Volodia freed himself temporarily from his fear by means of a prayer, Henry found no relief until sleep finally came.

When eventually under fire, they overcame their panic and emerged from the trial as victors, thus proving to be true heroes. This is Volodia's transformation:

"Once at work, there remained no trace of that terror which the evening before showed itself so plainly. . . . As to Volodia, stirred by an enthusiastic satisfaction, he thought no more of the danger. The joy he felt at doing his duty well, at being no longer a coward, at feeling himself, on the contrary, full of courage, the feeling of commanding and the presence of twenty men, who he knew were watching him with curiosity, had made a real hero of him."[26]

And Henry's:

"These incidents made the youth ponder. It was revealed to him that he had been a barbarian, a beast. He had fought like a pagan who defends his religion. Regarding it, he saw that it was fine, wild, and, in some ways, easy. He had been a tremendous figure, no doubt. By this struggle he had overcome obstacles which he had admitted

25. *Sebastopol*, pp. 179–82.   26. *Sebastopol*, p. 223.

to be mountains. They had fallen like paper peaks, and he was now what he called a hero. And he had not been aware of the process. He had slept and, awakening, found himself a knight.

"He saw that he was good. He recalled with a thrill of joy the re-spectful comments of his fellows upon his conduct."

* * *

Thus, the problem which had tortured the young soldiers' minds was solved in the same positive way, a problem which was vital because it was in the authors' own hearts.

There are dissimilarities, however, which deserve to be noted. As hinted, Henry gave way to his fright and ran away in the midst of the battle. Volodia, on the other hand, controlled his fear, stayed, and fought gallantly till the end. There is also a divergence in Tolstoy's and Crane's treatment of the fear motif, which may originate from the difference in scope between Tolstoy's short story and Crane's novel. If Tolstoy suggested the motif, which is prob-able, Crane expanded and deepened the problem of fear to com-prehend various phases of Henry's mind, ranging from sheer nerv-ousness to absolute panic and bottomless shame. Furthermore, Crane's portrayal of Henry was more intense, the feeling of frustra-tion more marked, than in the case of Volodia. With Tolstoy the idea was to illustrate how a good soldier overcame his terror,[27] and

27. The idea of flight caused by panic was a recurrent motif in *War and Peace*, where Nikolay Rostov was seized by a sudden fear and ran away. He soon overcame his weakness, however, and like Volodia proved a real hero in the moment of danger. *War and Peace*, pp. 244, 608. Crane, too, utilized this motif several times. The loud soldier in *The Red Badge of Courage* also conquered his battle fright and emerged a victor: "He was no more a loud young soldier. There was about him now a fine reli-ance. He showed a quiet belief in his purposes and his abilities." *Work*, I, 129.

Two American scholars [Lyndon Up-son Pratt, "A Possible Source of *The Red Badge of Courage*," *American Literature*, XI (March, 1939), 1–10 and H. T. Webster, "Wilbur F. Hin-man's *Corporal Si Klegg* and Stephen Crane's *The Red Badge of Courage*," *American Literature*, XI (November, 1939), 285–93] have made attempts to trace some of Crane's sources for his chief war novel. Pratt remarked that "if Chancellorsville contributed the gen-eral setting and rough plan of the novel, Antietam may well have provided at least two additional elements: the idea of Henry's panic and flight, and the heroism of the wounded color-bearer."

P. 9. This statement is open to objec-tion, since Pratt has not taken into con-sideration any literary sources which Crane may have used, such as *Sebas-topol* and *War and Peace*. Webster is more convincing than Pratt, but his conclusion seems questionable: "But evidently, Crane got his conception of a commonplace, unromantic hero from Hinman, together with the theme of this raw recruit's development into the ca-pable veteran. . . . In addition to this, Crane apparently adapted a good deal of the essential structure of his narra-tive from Hinman, as well as many in-cidents and details of army life." Pp. 291–2.

A close examination of *The Red Badge of Courage* on the one hand, and of *La Débâcle*, *Sebastopol*, and *War and Peace* on the other—neither Pratt nor Webster mentioned these books in their articles—makes it clear that the majority of the parallels adduced by the above-mentioned scholars can ac-tually be found in the three novels just referred to, books which we know Crane was familiar with. If Crane ever read *Si Klegg*, which we do not know, he prob-ably borrowed only external details, for it is not convincingly proved that Crane got his conception of the unromantic hero type from Hinman's portrayal of

with Crane this was also the central problem; in addition, however, he wanted to analyze all the various emotions felt in the process of conquering fear.

Since Tolstoy and Crane regarded war as a result of a series of events caused by uncontrollable forces, they looked upon the role played by the leaders, generals, etc. as of little consequence. "In historical events," asserted Tolstoy, "great men [Napoleon and Alexander]—so called—are but the labels that serve to give a name to an event, and like labels, they have the least possible connection with the event itself."[28] * * * Zola, as we remember, also formed a low estimate of the qualifications of the generals, and blamed them ruthlessly for their mismanagement of the army. Crane had a similarly critical attitude to the war leaders. If referred to at all, they were made to seem stupid or ineffective with few exceptions. As a rule, he neglected to mention them, which once made Joseph Hergesheimer write of *The Red Badge of Courage*: "Where was Lincoln bearing his benevolence like a tendered pardon to fault? Where was Grant with his half-consumed cigar? Where, above everything, was General Lee?"

If Tolstoy and Crane looked upon the actions of the generals in a critical way, their attitude toward the enemy was far more positive.[29] Both regarded the enemies above all as human beings, frightened and like their own troops, at heart averse to killing, only doing their duty because they had to. This attitude was illustrated by Tolstoy in his description of the truce in *Sebastopol,* where French and Russian soldiers fraternized, talking and joking and exchanging souvenirs. The Russian officers even complimented the French officers on the bravery of their soldiers and *vice versa*, and deplored the tragedy of war. The following quotation from *The Red Badge of Courage* indicates Crane's attitude:

"The only foes he had seen were some pickets along the river bank. They were a sun-tanned, philosophical lot, who sometimes shot re-

---

the common soldier, nor yet the theme of Henry's development into a real war hero. Webster, it seems to me, has ignored the psychological aspects of Crane's novel. He has not taken into consideration Crane's careful and intimate analysis of the emotions of his hero, but has paid too much attention to exterior details. This has led him to overemphasize Crane's possible debt to Hinman. Although Webster admits that *Si Klegg* and *The Red Badge of Courage* were basically different in tone, that the effects of the two books were "dissimilar"—*Si Klegg* being "a comic book"—he did not moderate the conclusion quoted above.

28. *War and Peace*, p. 566. Cf. the following passage taken from *The Red Badge of Courage*: "They had taken themselves and the enemy very seriously and had imagined that they were deciding the war. Individuals must have supposed that they were cutting the letters of their names deep into everlasting tablets of brass, or enshrining their reputations for ever in the hearts of their countrymen, while, as to fact, the affair would appear in printed reports under a meek and immaterial title." *Work*, I, 86.

29. Zola, however, was hostile in his attitude toward the enemy in *La Débâcle*.

flectively at the blue pickets. When reproached for this afterward, they usually expressed sorrow, and swore by their gods that the guns had exploded without their permission. The youth, on guard duty one night, conversed across the stream with one of them. He was a slightly ragged man, who spat skilfully between his shoes and possessed a great fund of bland and infantile assurance. The youth liked him personally.

" 'Yank,' the other had informed him, 'yer a right dum good feller.' This sentiment, floating to him upon the still air, had made him temporarily regret war." * * *

The problem of free will came particularly to the fore in the war narratives of Tolstoy and Crane. On the whole, both writers looked upon man as devoid of free will. Tolstoy said of the Russian generals that they "were but the blind instruments of the most melancholy law of necessity."[30] Moreover: "Every action of theirs, that seems to them an act of their own free-will, is in an historical sense not free at all, but in bondage to the whole course of previous history, and predestined from all eternity."[31]

* * *

In *The Red Badge of Courage* Crane made it clear that the soldiers had little free will, and were pawns in the hands of forces they could not control. Henry Fleming was aware of the fact that his enlistment, for example, was no action determined by his own will:

"But he instantly saw that it would be impossible for him to escape from the regiment. It enclosed him. And there were iron bars of tradition and law on four sides. He was in a moving box.

"As he perceived this fact it occurred to him that he had never wished to come to the war. He had not enlisted of his free will. He had been dragged by the merciless government. And now they were taking him out to be slaughtered."

Moreover, the disorder on the battlefield served to emphasize the lack of free will on the part of the human mites fighting blindly and desperately:

" 'Good Gawd,' the youth grumbled, 'we're always being chased around like rats! It makes me sick. Nobody seems to know where we go or why we go. We just get fired around from pillar to post and get licked here and get licked there, and nobody knows what it's done for. It makes a man feel like a damn' kitten in a bag. Now, I'd like to know what the eternal thunders we was marched into these woods for anyhow, unless it was to give the rebs a regular pot-shot at us. We came in here and got our legs all tangled up in these cussed

30. *War and Peace*, p. 1011. See also   31. *Ibid.*, p. 566.
ibid., p. 988.

briers, and then we begin to fight and the rebs had an easy time of it. Don't tell me it's just luck! I know better. It's this derned old—' "

Premonition of death is a recurrent theme in the works of Tolstoy and Crane. Take, for instance, Mikhailoff's strange presentiment of death in *Sebastopol* before he went out on the bastion for the thirteenth time. " 'I shall be killed, I'm sure,' he said to himself; 'I feel it. . . .' " Similarly, the loud one in *The Red Badge of Courage* felt that he was to die when the battle began. " 'It's my first and last battle, old boy.' " The scene was made even more dramatic by the package of letters which the soldier handed over to Henry before going under fire. In Tolstoy's tale Mikhaïloff wrote a farewell letter to his father and gave it to his valet to keep and deliver after his death. In both stories, neither of the men was killed in the ensuing action.

* * *

There is also the incident of the flag. In *War and Peace* Prince Andrey stood forth as a true hero when, seizing the staff of the falling flag, he bravely led his retreating comrades back into battle, most of whom were killed when following the flag. The scene is reminiscent of a similar one in *The Red Badge of Courage*. Henry grabbed the battered flag from the dying colorbearer and led his wavering fellow soldiers back to the fight.

Both Tolstoy and Crane attempted to analyze the concept of heroism. The kind of false heroism or foolish bravery that Crane described in his short story "A Mystery of Heroism" recalls Tolstoy's endeavor to investigate the nature of heroism in *War and Peace*. Both authors were baffled, and could give no definite answer. Heroism sprang perhaps from man's vanity, from his desire to make an impression on other individuals at any cost. Rostov, feeling discomfort and vague remorse after his gallant but silly exploit, inquired: " 'Why, is this all that's meant by heroism? And did I do it for the sake of my country?' " And Collins, the hero of Crane's story, reflected after a similar gallant feat: "He was, then, a hero. He suffered that disappointment which we would all have if we discovered that we were ourselves capable of those deeds which we most admire in history and legend. This, then, was a hero. After all, heroes were not much."

R. W. STALLMAN

[The Question of Influences]†

The whole question of Crane influences is very difficult to pin down. It cannot be denied, however, that he drew his material for *The Red Badge of Courage* from contemporary accounts of the Civil War and very considerably, I think, from Matthew Brady's remarkable photographs. He took his sources from books, such as Century's *Battles and Leaders* and Harper's *History*, and from the conversation of veterans—*i.e.*, war reminiscences of his brother William, who was an expert in the strategy of Chancellorsville; from the tactical accounts of General Van Petten, who was Crane's teacher at Claverack Academy; but above all from Colonel Wilbur F. Hinman's account of *Corporal Si Klegg and his "Pards"*—from which Crane drew for *The Red Badge* the conception of the new recruit who develops into a veteran. Hinman's book was, I think, almost certainly Crane's primary literary source.‡ He created his own war novel out of all this material, but we are still left wondering where he learned *how* to write. The answer to that question is given, I think, in Hemingway's remark: "I learned to write looking at paintings at the Luxembourg Museum in Paris."

Crane had Brady's poignant photographs to brood over, Coffin's illustrations to Hinman's *Si Klegg*, the Monet paintings which he knew, and the apprenticeship paintings of his fellow lodgers at the Art Students' League in New York City, where he lived in 1891–1892.§ It was during this same period that he was composing the impressionistic painting of *Maggie*.** He had used color imagery,

† Reprinted from the Introduction by Robert Wooster Stallman to the Modern Library Edition of *The Red Badge of Courage*. Copyright © 1951 by Random House, Inc. Reprinted by permission. Pp. xv–xvii, xix.

Our extract is from the second part, "Influences and Parallelisms," of Stallman's Introduction (the third part will be found in our Critical Essay section, entitled "Notes Toward an Analysis of *The Red Badge of Courage*"). In the section from which this excerpt comes, Stallman reviews a number of influences that have been suggested; he states, "It is debatable whether Crane took over anything out of his French and Russian readings. Most of these so-called influences are, in fact, I think, nothing more than parallelisms."

Mr. Stallman has asked the editors of the present volume to represent his 1961 revisions, which are substantive corrections and do not alter his expression of critical opinion. These revisions appear as footnotes in italics, and are identified by the date, "1961." ‡ Author's note (1961): *See H. T. Webster in* American Literature, *XII (1939).* § Author's substitution (1961): *1893–1894.* ** Author's note (1961): Maggie: A Girl of the Streets *is a Bowery version of Flaubert's* Madame Bovary, *which it echoes in several parallel scenes and in its overall structural design of double mood (contrasted moods contradictory one to the other). See "Stephen Crane's Primrose Path" in* New Republic, *CXXXIII (1955),*

162

however, in his early *Sullivan County Sketches*, and his very manner of speech was quite as colorful as his prose or poetry. Here again little proof of influence can be established one way or the other, but whether he borrowed something of his technique from the studio or nothing at all, the fact remains (as H. G. Wells concluded) "there is Whistler even more than there is Tolstoy in *The Red Badge of Courage*."†

* * *

Crane anticipated the French post-impressionist painters. His style is, in brief, prose pointillism. It is composed of disconnected images which, like the blobs of color in a French impressionist painting, coalesce one with another, every word-group having a cross-reference relationship, every seemingly disconnected detail having interrelationship to the configurated pattern of the whole. The intensity of a Crane tale is due to this patterned coalescence of disconnected things, everything at once fluid and precise.‡

* * *

THE RED WAFER OF CONTROVERSY: KIPLING AND CRANE

SCOTT C. OSBORN

Stephen Crane's Imagery: "Pasted Like a Wafer"†

Probably the most famous of Stephen Crane's "revolutionary" impressionistic images concludes Chapter IX of *The Red Badge of Courage* (1895): "The red sun was pasted in the sky like a wafer."[1] Such images, critics have said, marked the beginning of

and the expanded version of this study of Maggie in Modern Fiction Studies, V (1959), reprinted in my Houses That James Built (1961).
† Author's note (1961): *I do not think it can be doubted that Crane borrowed something of his prose technique from the studio.*
‡ Author's note (1961): *As I point out in my* Stephen Crane: An Omnibus (*Knopf, 1952; Heinemann, 1954*): *"A striking analogy is established between Crane's use of colors and the method employed by the impressionists and the neo-impressionists or divisionists, and it is as if he had known*

about their theory of contrasts and had composed his own prose paintings by the same principle." For a collation of those principles of contrast employed by the French impressionists and Crane's prose pointillism see Omnibus, pages 185–187.
† From *American Literature*, XXIII (December, 1951), 362. Reprinted by permission. This comment may be compared with those of Robert W. Stallman and James R. Colvert, following.
1. Wilson Follett (ed.), *The Work of Stephen Crane*, 12 vols. (New York, 1925–1926), I, 98.

"modernism" in American prose fiction. Yet no one, so far as I know, has pointed out the resemblance of Crane's image to one in Kipling's *The Light That Failed* (1891): "The fog was driven apart for a moment, and the sun shone, a blood-red wafer, on the water."[2] The images seem nearly identical, and in both the sun seems compared to a red wafer of wax used to seal an envelope.[3] Kipling's figure is as "impressionistic" as Crane's, but no one, so far as I have found, has called Kipling an impressionist or a "colorist."

In view of Crane's known enthusiasm for Kipling in the early nineties[4] and his interest early and late in war, it seems altogether probable that he read *The Light That Failed* before writing *The Red Badge of Courage*. He was not plagiarizing Kipling, but perhaps unconsciously using a figure or an impression (though impressed by a literary evocation instead of by a direct observation) which he had felt to be striking and apt when he first saw it. Simple coincidence seems incredible in this case. In any event, Kipling, not Crane, should be credited with first using the "revolutionary" wafer image.

R. W. STALLMAN

[Kipling's Wafer—and Crane's]†

"If I had kept to my clever Rudyard-Kipling style, the road might have been shorter but ah, it wouldn't be the true road."[1] That Stephen Crane studied Kipling and emulated his style some of his early stories are evidence enough, and also some of his later pieces. That Kipling influenced Crane need not be questioned. What needs to be questioned, however, is what is meant by claiming the "influence" of one author on another?

By "influence" is meant, I take it, that the influenced author evidences in his works points of resemblance, correspondences ranging

2. *The Writings in Prose and Verse of Rudyard Kipling*, 14 vols. (New York, 1897), IX, 63; first published in the United States in *Lippincott's Magazine*, Jan., 1891, as a complete novel, with the "wafer" image on p. 29.

3. Robert W. Stallman thinks Crane's metaphorical wafer to be that used in the communion, by which Crane symbolizes Henry Fleming's absolution and salvation; see The Modern Library edition of *The Red Badge of Courage*, (New York, 1951), Introduction, pp. xxxiv–xxxv. More likely the wafer or seal—both "red" and "pasted"—indicates the ironically enigmatic indifference of heaven to the youth's blasphemy against war.

4. John Berryman, *Stephen Crane* (New York, 1951), pp. 24, 97, 248.

† From "The Scholar's Net: Literary Sources," *College English*, XVII (October, 1955), 20–22. Reprinted by permission. *Cf.* the comments by Osborn, above, and by Colvert, following.

1. *Stephen Crane: An Omnibus*, ed. R. W. Stallman (1952), p. xxxix.

from more or less remote echoes to parallelisms having more or less closeness of identity—as in (a) their style (their word-way of thinking things through); (b) their philosophical or literary outlook; or (c) their technique of rendering plot-situation, point of view, theme, symbol, or imagery.

Thus Crane's famous image of the red sun "pasted in the sky like a wafer" is said to resemble Kipling's image in *The Light That Failed* (1891): "The fog was driven apart for a moment, and the sun shone, a blood-red wafer, on the water." Discovery of this Crane source was made by Professor Scott C. Osborn (*AL*, 23, Nov. 1951, 362). Mr. Osborn overlooked, however, what is rather obvious about this literary source: the fact that the first part of Kipling's image suggests the very opening image of Crane's *Red Badge of Courage*: "The cold passed reluctantly from the earth, and the retiring fogs revealed an army stretched out on the hills, resting." The evidence for claiming that Crane drew inspirational source from Kipling's image is reinforced by this additional correspondence. The correspondence is two-fold. However, the resemblance involves a difference: Crane's novel is patterned from beginning to end with imagery of fog and rain *versus* sun, whereas Kipling's novel makes only incidental use of the fog image.

Mr. Osborn tells us that these images "seem nearly identical," but I would underscore the word *seem* and inquire into the basis of their supposed identity. They seem nearly identical, but what this claim of resemblance overlooks is the difference of what they mean and how they are used. Examine their metaphoric intent and you will find that they bear only a surface resemblance. At their metaphoric or symbolic level there is no resemblance whatsoever. Mr. Osborn failed to explore the related images for what they mean and how they are used. The resemblance is strictly literal and extrinsic; nor is there any other point of correspondence between *The Light That Failed* and *The Red Badge of Courage*—only this single image.

The images, says Mr. Osborn, "seem nearly identical, and in both the sun seems compared to a red wafer of wax used to seal an envelope." Now this possible notion is commonly accepted, I believe, amongst interpreters of Crane's notorious image, namely that the literal referent for the image is "a red wafer of wax used to seal an envelope." But the fact is that what was used for sealing envelopes and affixing legal documents during the 19th Century was a red wafer devoid of wax. The specimen I have at hand is a sticker of glue, not wax; a small, round, orange-red, stickable sealing-wafer. Kipling fashions it "blood-red," and Crane has it properly "pasted."

Mr. Osborn's discovery stirred my curiosity to know how Kipling used his wafer image, whether simply as image or rather as symbol, and if as symbol then what meaning and purpose it served the whole novel. Here, then, is a study of the relevant passages.

Dick Heldar has attained notoriety as a painter, and his friends whiplash him for selling out his talent for commercial success with "a public who think with their boots and read with their elbows! . . . Hasn't he been praised and cockered up too much?" (*Collected Works*, Doubleday, 1941, XV, 45). Like Henry Fleming, Dick Heldar is "suffering from swelled head" (p. 29). He turns his back upon his friends and walks in the London fog to take counsel with himself. At Westminster Bridge he leans over the Embankment wall and watching the passersby he speculates what he can use in his paintings from the faces he observes. He is literally looking down on his public.

"The poor at least should suffer that he might learn, and the rich should pay for the output of his learning. Thus his credit in the world and his cash balance at the bank would be increased. So much the better for him. He had suffered. Now he would take toll of the ills of others.

"*The fog was driven apart for a moment, and the sun shone, a blood-red wafer*, on the water. Dick watched the spot till he heard the voice of the tide between the piers die down like the wash of the sea at low tide. A girl hard pressed by her lover shouted shamelessly, 'Ah, get away, you beast!' and a shift of the same wind that had opened the fog drove across Dick's face the black smoke of a river-steamer at her berth below the wall. He was blinded for a moment, then spun round and found himself face to face with—Maisie." (p. 47)

The fog lifts at the moment of his insight, and the blood-red sun mirrors his own mood of defiance. "Dick had instinctively sought running water for a comfort to his mood of mind" (p. 47). According to his friends, he's working for cash: "Dick's soul is in the bank" (p. 46). And now on the bank of the river here is Dick, having sold himself for success in the stream. (There is, as it were, some *currency* in the current!) The sun shining on the water "a blood-red wafer" is a forewarning to the painter of the death of the artist in him. What the water reflects—the blood-red sun—is the bloody truth: money is the shining thing. But it is also a death. Listening to the Thames, Dick hears the voice of the sea (the sea of life), and what it tells him is that human nature—like the blood-red sun—is bestial and destructive, greedy and competitive. But success, the cheap success Dick's soul is fired for, is as temporary as the appearance of the sun that shines one moment between drifts of fog and black smoke. Dick as artist isn't going to get anywhere. The fact is, he doesn't cross the bridge.

The blood-red sun is like the red daub appearing in one of Dick's paintings. Torpenhow had singled it out for criticism: "that red daub isn't going anywhere—unless you take precious good care, you will fall under the damnation of the check-book, and that's worse than death" (p. 43).

Incidentally, Henry Fleming in *The Red Badge*, in the final manuscript version for Chapter X, vents his fury upon the sky and would throw at it if he could a pot of paint. "He would have like[d] to have splashed it with derisive paint" (*Omnibus*, p. 292). Kipling's red daub is only identified with money, and in the scene at the Embankment wall the blood-red wafer-sun shining on the water signifies the same thing as in Dick's painting. *Wafer*, by cross-reference to the red daub, suggests a flat round disk of money—a coin. As a curious footnote, *not* to be taken as Kipling's source, there is a passage in Blake where the sun is compared with a coin: " 'What,' it will be Question'd, 'When the Sun rises, do you not see a round disk of fire somewhat like a Guinea?' O no, no, I see an Innumerable company of the Heavenly host crying, 'Holy, Holy, Holy, is the Lord God Almighty.' "[2]

In Kipling's *Letters of Marque*, I might add, there is an image of the sun as blood-red—"a blood-red glare shot up from the horizon and, inky black against the intense red, a giant crane floated out towards the sun. . . ." What slight resemblance this has with the blood-red sun as wafer in *The Light That Failed* is scarcely worth noticing except that the image is here linked with Biblical allusion. "While he watched, it seemed to the Englishman that some voices on the hills were intoning the first verses of Genesis" (*Collected Works*, I, pp. 236–237). In *The Light That Failed* there is nothing in the way of Biblical allusion or religious symbolism.

In both novels the sun-wafer images appear at a moment of recognition. Crane's image is used at a crucial point in the narrative and with symbolic import (as I see it), the wafer of the sun

2. "A Vision of the Last Judgment," *Poetry and Prose of William Blake*, ed. Geoffrey Keynes (1948), p. 652. Kipling's sun-wafer image was anticipated by Dante Gabriel Rossetti in a letter to William Allingham, Rossetti describing the sun as dead and wafer-like and red: "The thick sky has a thin red sun stuck in the middle of it, like the specimen wafer stuck outside the box of them. Even if you turned back the lid, there would be nothing behind it, be sure, but a jumble of such flat dead suns." *Letters of Dante Gabriel Rossetti to William Allingham: 1854–1870*, ed. George Birkbeck Hill (London, 1897), p. 206. (I am indebted to Mrs. Ann Winston for this information.) So Kipling was not the first to coin that wafer image of the red sun, though he was the first (so far as I know) to put it to any literary use. The latest use of it is Faulkner's wafer-sun in *The Wild Palms*: "the hazy wafer of the intolerable sun . . ." (*The Wild Palms*, 1939, p. 273).

representing the wafer of the Mass. "More likely the wafer or seal —both 'red' and 'pasted'—indicates," as Mr. Osborn reads it, "the ironically enigmatic indifference of heaven to youth's blasphemy against war." But heaven at this conjunction of events is anything but indifferent. The sun appears, in the final handwritten manuscript of *The Red Badge*, as "pasted in the sky like a fierce wafer," and in the earlier manuscript draft: "The fierce [canceled] red sun was pasted in the sky like a fierce wafer." The conjectured indifference of heaven to the youth's blasphemy against war seems to me repudiated by Crane's emphatic *fierce*.

Among skeptics of the symbolic interpretation of the wafer-image is the anonymous critic in *The New Yorker* (29, 2 May 1953, 124) who contends that Crane could not possibly employ the symbolism of Catholic ritual because Crane's parents were Methodists, not Catholics! But consider the converse of this proposition: if an author uses Catholic ritual then he or his parents subscribe to the Catholic faith, and conversely if an author employs Catholic symbolism then you thereby know what church denomination he or his parents subscribed to!

Another skeptic of the symbolic interpretation contends, in echo of *The New Yorker*, that "the word 'pasted' clearly shows that the wafer is not the Host but the seal affixed to a document attesting its having been completed" (CE, 16, Apr. 1955, 427). He dismisses the symbolic interpretation of the wafer image as "unjustifiable," but he produces no evidence to justify his dismissal of it. I am curious to know how the epithet *fierce* is justified if the wafer image exemplifies nothing more than a sealing-wafer? And what is the purpose of Henry's cursing the sun if it is nothing more than the sun as sealing-wafer that he curses? A sealing-wafer seals a document, but what has this to do with Henry's plight at the moment of Conklin's death? If it signifies nothing more than a sealing-wafer, what then does it signify in the patterned relationship or configuration of the whole?‡

Mr. Osborn's Crane-Kipling source-note is an example of the source-hunter's risk in neglecting analysis of the related works. The pursuit of sources tends to become an end in itself, as though it sufficed for scholarship to bring to light an echo. Influences and source-identifications constitute what scholarship is largely all about, and meanwhile the purpose and value of this branch of scholarship is taken for granted without the question as to what precisely *is* its purpose and value.

‡ Author's note (1961): *For further discussion of Crane's image see "Fiction and Its Critics" in my* Houses That James Built And Other Literary Studies *(1961), pp. 247 ff. The short version of this essay appeared in* Kenyon Review, *Spring, 1957.*

JAMES B. COLVERT

[Crane's Debt to Kipling]†

Literary source hunters have experienced little difficulty in suggesting influences upon Stephen Crane's early novels and stories. But where such study should ideally throw light upon the genesis and processes of Crane's art, too often the claims and surmises about his literary origins are so general or so tenuous that they serve more to endarken than enlighten. Spiller, in the *Literary History of the United States*, fairly states the whole case:

"The appearance of an original artist, springing without antecedent into life, is always illusion, but the sources of Crane's philosophy and art are as yet undeciphered. Neither the cold-blooded determinism of his belief nor the sensuous awareness of his writing can be without source, but nowhere in the scant record he has left is there evidence that he, like Garland, read widely in the current books on biological science. A direct influence of Darwin, Spencer, Haeckel, or their American popularizers cannot be established. Rather he seems to have absorbed these influences at second hand through Russian and French writers."[1]

* * *

There is good reason to believe that Crane was unusually ill-read. John Barry, the editor of *The Forum* who read Crane's *The Black Riders* in manuscript in 1894, referred to the young poet as "woefully ignorant of books,"[9] and Berryman, who thinks Crane's reading has been underestimated, can nevertheless assert that "it is not easy to think of another important prose-writer or poet so ignorant of traditional literature in English as Stephen Crane was and remained."[10] All his life he denied, sometimes with considerable irritation, any connection with the naturalists. "They stand me against walls," he complained about his English acquaintances to James Huneker in 1897, "with a teacup in my hand and tell me how I have stolen all my things from de Maupassant, Zola, Loti, and the bloke who wrote—I forget the name."[11] Except for a refer-

† Published as "The Origins of Crane's Literary Creed," *University of Texas Studies in English*, XXXIV (1955), 179–88. *Cf.* comments above by Osborn and by Stallman, and *cf.* Mr. Colvert's concluding footnote.

1. Robert E. Spiller and others, eds., *Literary History of the United States* (3 vols., New York, 1948), II, 1021.

9. John D. Barry, "A Note on Stephen Crane," *The Bookman*, XIII (1901), 148.
10. John Berryman, *Stephen Crane* (New York, 1950), 24.
11. Robert W. Stallman, ed., *Stephen Crane: An Omnibus* (New York, 1952), 674. All references to Crane's letters are to this source.

ence to the brief period in 1891 when, as a student at Syracuse, he was studying intensely with a view to forming his style, there is little evidence that he ever read much at all, an omission he once defended on the ground that in this way he avoided the risk of unconscious imitation.[12] Unlike Frank Norris, who once referred to himself as "Mr. Norris, Esq. (The Boy Zola)!" Crane seems to owe little, if anything, to nineteenth-century French and Russian naturalism.[13]

How, then, can the literary beginnings of this precocious (but, one supposes, hardly supernatural) young writer be accounted for? "Here came a boy," Beer wrote of the twenty-year-old ex-college student who went into the East Side slums in the spring of 1891 for material for *Maggie*, "whose visual sense was unique in American writing and whose mind by some inner process had stripped itself of all respect for these prevalent theories which have cursed the national fiction. He was already an ironist, already able to plant his impressions with force and reckless of the consequent shock to a public softened by long nursing at the hands of limited men."[14] But what had stimulated to action his natural rebelliousness and what were the "inner processes" that turned him to slums for the subject of his painfully realistic *Maggie*? From whom had he learned the use of irony, and to whom was he indebted for his interest in painting and his characteristic use of color imagery? What was the origin of his belief that direct personal experience is the only valid material for the writer, and what led him to emphasize so strongly his belief that absolute honesty is a prime virtue of the artist? These questions, it would seem, define the problem of Crane's literary origins, and the answers are to be found in the period of his almost incredibly brief apprenticeship to the craft of fiction in the years 1891–92.

Crane left one of the most important clues to his artistic origins in a letter of 1896 to Lily Brandon Munro, a lady he was once in love with in his Syracuse student days. "You know," he wrote, "when I left you [in the fall of 1892] I renounced the clever school in literature. It seemed to me that there must be something more in life than to sit and cudgel one's brains for clever and witty expedients. So I developed all alone a little creed of art which I thought was a good one. . . . If I had kept to my clever Rudyard-

12. Barry, "A Note on Stephen Crane," 148.

13. This view is in harmony with that of Albert J. Salvan, a student of Zola who concludes in his study of the naturalist's influence in the United States: "Dans la question toujours délicate d'établir un rapport d'influence définie entre Zola et Stephen Crane, nous sommes forcés de rester sur une note évasive. Il n'est guère douteux que l'auteur de Maggie manquait d'une connaissance très entendue de la littérature française du XIX⁰ siecle en général." *Zola aux Etats-Unis* (Providence, 1943), 163.

14. Beer, *Stephen Crane: A Study in American Letters*, 77.

Kipling style, the road might have been shorter, but, ah, it wouldn't be the true road."[15] The significant point here is not so much Crane's rejection of Kipling as a literary mentor as his implicit admission that the Englishman had served him as a model sometime between 1891 and 1892. It seems more than likely that the young American owed to Kipling the basic principles of his artistic beliefs, for Crane's theory of literature matches precisely the esthetic credo of Dick Heldar, the young artist-hero of Kipling's *The Light That Failed*, a novel Crane read sometime before 1892, probably during the spring semester of 1891 at Syracuse University.

Few young writers in a rebellious mood were likely to escape the attraction of Kipling in the first years of the nineties. At the time *The Light That Failed* was appearing in *Lippincott's Magazine* in January of 1891, Kipling was already a best-selling author whose fiction was considered new and unorthodox. His amazing popularity had in fact become a subject for reviewer's verse:

> No matter where I go, I hear
> The same old tale of wonder;
> It's some delusion wild, I fear,
> The world is laboring under.
> Why every friend I've met today
> (I couldn't help but note it)
> Has asked me "Have you read 'Mulvaney'
> Rudyard Kipling wrote it."[16]

Immediately following this is a review of *The Light That Failed* which emphasizes the unorthodoxy of his realistic tale of an artist's adventures as a war correspondent and suggests something of the appeal it must have had for the youthful Crane, then a cub reporter for his brother Townley's Asbury Park news agency: "Bohemian and unconventional as the characters are," the reviewer states, "no one who has seen much of the two classes whence they are chiefly drawn—newspaper correspondents and lady art students—can say they are grossly exaggerated."[17]

There is convincing evidence that Crane not only knew this novel before 1892, but that it indeed made a profound impression upon him. S. C. Osborn notes that Crane's famous image at the end of Chapter IX in *The Red Badge of Courage*, "The sun was pasted against the sky like a wafer," occurs in Kipling's *The Light That Failed* and concludes that the younger writer unconsciously incorporated the idea into *The Red Badge*.[18] There are strong re-

15. Stallman, *Stephen Crane: An Omnibus*, 648.
16. "The Light That Failed," *The Literary News*, XII (1891), 29.
17. *Ibid.*, 19.

18. Scott C. Osborn, "Stephen Crane's Imagery: 'Pasted Like a Wafer,'" *AL*, XXIII (1951), 363. Osborn notes only one occurrence: "The fog was driven apart for a moment, and the sun shone,

flections, moreover, of Kipling's early manner—the impressionistic "modern" imagery, the sententious, often flippant, dialogue, and a keen sense of the ironic—in Crane's earliest fiction, *The Sullivan County Sketches*, written in the summers of 1891 and 1892. In these pieces, which comprise all that may be properly called apprentice work, if the first drafts of *Maggie* and a story published in the Syracuse school paper are excepted, Crane put into practice the basic theories of Dick Heldar, the rebellious and unorthodox artist in *The Light That Failed*.

Dick Heldar must have been the apotheosis of all that the nineteen-year-old Crane hoped to become. Dick is an Impressionist painter in revolt against the canons of nineteenth-century respectability. He chooses Bohemian life for the freedom it gives him in his enthusiastic pursuit of fame, and with great determination he seeks the truth about life in the slums of London and on the battlegrounds of remote deserts. He is proud, independent, and free in the expression of iconoclastic opinions.

Crane's orientation was remarkably similar. As a boy he was in perpetual revolt against the respectability of his conventional, middle-class Methodist home life, and at Claverack College, Lafayette, and Syracuse, an indifferent student at all three places, he incurred the displeasure of the faculty for expressing "angular" opinions. He was asked to withdraw from Lafayette at the end of his first semester for refusing to conform to academic regimen. "Away with literary fads and canons," he exclaimed to a friend in the late spring of 1891,[19] and about the same time he began making trips to New York to study life on the Bowery and in the slums. In the fall of 1892, after he was dismissed from the *Tribune* for writing an ironic account of an Asbury Park labor parade, Crane moved into the East Side more or less permanently, where he remained, observing and writing in wretched poverty, for more than two years.

This way of life he led by choice like Kipling's Dick Heldar, from whom he probably got the idea that this privation was valuable, perhaps even indispensable, to his development as an artist. "There are few things more edifying unto Art than the actual bellypinch of hunger," Kipling explains when he puts Dick into the London slums to starve and paint within walking distance of an affluent friend. "I never knew," Dick says in explaining the value

a blood-red wafer, on the water." *The Writings in Prose and Verse of Rudyard Kipling* (New York, 1897), IX, 63. The image occurs in variations twice more: "A puddle far across the mud caught the last rays of the sun and turned it into a wrathful red disc" (p. 13), and again: "The sun caught the steel and turned it into a savage red disc" (p. 31). See n. 37.
19. Arthur Oliver, "Jersey Memories—Stephen Crane," *New Jersey Historical Society Proceedings*, n.s., XVI (1931), 454–55.

of his experience with poverty, "what I had to learn about the human face before."[20] When he is at last paid for some art work, Dick calls upon his friend and explains that he could not have asked for help because "I had a sort of superstition that this temporary starvation—that's what it was—and it hurt—would bring me more luck later."[21] Crane, as his way of life during this period shows, was of the same belief. One of his nieces, recalling her uncle's misery in the New York slums, was puzzled by his conduct: "We still wonder why he went through such experiences when he was always so very welcome at both our house and Uncle Edmund's. Perhaps he was seeking his own 'Experience in Misery' . . . altho doubtless it came also through his desire to make his own way independently."[22] To these views Crane himself assented, but a more significant explanation lies in his persistent notion that great art is born of the "belly-pinch of hunger":

"It was during this period [he wrote to the editor of Leslie's Weekly about November, 1895] that I wrote 'The Red Badge of Courage.' It was an effort born of pain—despair, almost; and I believe that this made it a better piece of literature than it otherwise would have been. It seems a pity that art should be a child of pain, and yet I think it is. Of course we have fine writers who are prosperous and contented, but in my opinion their work would be greater if this were not so. It lacks the sting it would have if written under the spur of a great need."[23]

The remarkable kinship in temperament and attitude between Kipling's protagonist and Crane strongly suggests that Dick's ideas about art deeply impressed the young writer. Dick may have inspired Crane in the use of color images for special effects, a stylistic feature which blazes forth in the Sullivan County tales of 1892. For *The Light That Failed* bristles with artist talk about color. Heldar exclaims with sensuous enthusiasm about the scenery of Sudan: "What color that was! Opal and amber and claret and brick-red and sulphur—cockatoo-crest sulphur—against brown, with a nigger black rock sticking up in the middle of it all, and a decorative frieze of camels festooning in front of a pure pale turquoise sky."[24] Crane's interest in painting, it is true, probably originated in his associations with his sister, Mary Helen, who taught art in Asbury Park in the late eighties and early nineties, and with Phebe English, a young art student with whom he fell in love when he was a stu-

20. Rudyard Kipling, *The Light That Failed*, in *The Writings in Prose and Verse of Rudyard Kipling* (New York, 1897), IX, 41.
21. *Loc. cit.*
22. Edna Crane Sidbury, "My Uncle, Stephen Crane, As I Knew Him," *Literary Digest International Book Review*, IV (1926), 249.
23. Stallman, *Stephen Crane: An Omnibus*, 591.
24. *The Light That Failed*, 53.

dent at Claverack College.[25] But in *The Light That Failed* he had before him not only an enthusiastic appreciation of the expressive potentialities of color, but also a striking example, in Kipling's "wrathful red disk" images, of how color could be used by the writer to evoke mood and emotional atmosphere.

More important in Crane's literary credo, though, are the principles governing the selection of materials, their treatment, and the attitude of the artist toward them. In *The Light That Failed* Kipling advances and defends the position that real life furnishes the only valid materials for art. "How can you do anything," his hero exclaims, "until you have seen everything, or as much as you can?"[26] Like the blind and ruined Heldar, who met his death following wars to the far corners of the earth, Crane, ill with tuberculosis, wandered away his energies—in the West, Mexico, the Florida swamps, Greece, and Cuba—in quest of experience in the world of action. "I decided," he wrote once in reference to his literary creed of 1892, "that the nearer a writer gets to life the greater he becomes as an artist,"[27] and in 1897, when his career was drawing to a close, he wrote from England to his brother William: "I am a wanderer now and I must see enough."[28] Both Crane and Kipling's hero expressed and acted upon the firm belief that the artist's material is necessarily drawn from personal experience.

Important corollaries for the realist are the convictions that all experience, ugly and unpleasant though it may be, must be faithfully and truthfully reported if the artist is to maintain his integrity. Around this idea Kipling builds one of the key scenes in *The Light That Failed*. Heldar, disappointed because one of his realistic war sketches has been rejected by all the magazines, decides to alter it to conform to the conventional idea of what the soldier is like:

"I lured my model, a beautiful rifleman, up here with drink. . . . I made him a flushed dishevelled, bedevilled scallawag, with his helmet at the back of his head, and the living fear of death in his eye, and the blood oozing out of a cut over his ankle-bone. He wasn't pretty, but he was all soldier and very much man. . . . The artmanager of that abandoned paper said that his subscribers wouldn't like it. It was brutal and coarse and violent. . . . I took my 'Last Shot' back. . . . I put him into a lovely red coat without a speck on it. That is Art. I cleaned his rifle—rifles are always clean on service—because that is Art. . . . I shaved his chin, I washed his hands, and gave him an air of fatted peace. . . . Price, thank Heaven! twice as much as for the first sketch."[29]

25. Joseph J. Kwiat, "Stephen Crane and Painting," *The American Quarterly*, IV (1952), 331.
26. *The Light That Failed*, 105.
27. Stallman, *Stephen Crane: An Omnibus*, 627.
28. *Ibid.*, 663.
29. *The Light That Failed*, 55–56.

"If you try to give these people the thing as God gave it," Dick argues when his friend Torpenhow reprimands him for this practice, "keyed down to their comprehension and according to the powers he has given you . . . half a dozen epicene young pagans who haven't even been to Algiers will tell you, first that your notion is borrowed and, secondly, that it isn't Art!"[30] But Torpenhow destroys the repainted picture and delivers Dick an impassioned lecture on truth and integrity in the practice of art, after which the penitent Heldar concludes, "You're so abominably reasonable!"[31]

This idea Crane was expounding as early as the spring of 1891, about the time he read Kipling's novel. "I became involved," he wrote again in reference to his creed of 1892, "in the beautiful war between those who say that art is man's substitute for nature and we are the most successful in art when we approach the nearest to nature and truth, and those who say—well, I don't know what they say. Then they can't say much but they fight villainously."[32] On another occasion he stated Dick's idea more explicitly: "I cannot see why people hate ugliness in art. Ugliness is just a matter of treatment. The scene of Hamlet and his mother and old Polonius behind the curtain is ugly, if you heard it in a police court. Hamlet treats his mother like a drunken carter and his words when he has killed Polonius are disgusting. But who cares?"[33]

Writing in 1898 about his literary aims, Crane reasserted his belief in this principle and showed how largely it had figured in his career: "The one thing that deeply pleases me in my literary life —brief and inglorious as it is—is the fact that men of sense believe me to be sincere. . . . I do the best that is in me, without regard to cheers or damnation."[34] This echoes the principle oratorically preached to Dick upon the occasion of his moral lapse: "For work done without conviction, for power wasted in trivialities, for labor expended with levity for the deliberate purpose of winning the easy applause of a fashion-driven public, there remains but one end,—the oblivion that is preceded by toleration and cenotaphed with contempt."[35]

These striking parallels in the artistic aims and attitudes of Dick Heldar and Crane strongly suggest that Kipling's novel provided the young American with his basic conception of the art of fiction. Since the evidence for the influence of the naturalists upon Crane's literary theory is unconvincing, and since he knew neither Howells nor Garland's theories of realism and veritism until after 1892, be

30. *Ibid.*, 49.
31. *Ibid.*, 56.
32. Stallman, *Stephen Crane: An Omnibus*, 648.
33. Berryman, *Stephen Crane*, 21.
34. Stallman, *Stephen Crane: An Omnibus*, 679–80.
35. *The Light That Failed*, 67.

fore which time he had read *The Light That Failed*, it seems likely indeed that Kipling is Crane's chief literary ancestor. This belief is further strengthened by the fact that Crane read Kipling's book at the most impressionable period of his literary life. As a rank novice, rebellious against social and literary conventions and searching for a rationale for a new fiction, Crane must have found Kipling's ideas immensely stimulating. "For short, scattered periods Crane read curiously," Berryman states, "and instinct or luck or fate led him early to what mattered."[36] Later, it is true, he found support for his creed in the ideas of Howells, Garland, and the Impressionist painters with whom he was in constant association during his Bohemian New York period. But the book which laid the basic principle was *The Light That Failed*. Here is developed explicitly a whole literary credo which exactly parallels Crane's. In advocating and following closely the principles that art is grounded in actual experience, that absolute honesty in the artist is an indispensable virtue, that all experience, including the ugly and the unpleasant, is material for the artist, Crane, through Kipling, anticipated the "cult of experience" in American fiction which reached its full development in the literary renaissance of the twenties.[37]

THOMAS A. GULLASON

New Sources for Stephen Crane's War Motif†

In the effort to find European models for *The Red Badge of Courage* (1895) in the works of Zola[1] and Tolstoi,[2] critics have overlooked the possible influences of Stephen Crane's rich family heritage, particularly the martial exploits of his ancestors and his

36. Berryman, *Stephen Crane*, 24.
37. When this article was in page proof, I saw R. W. Stallman's "The Scholar's Net: Literary Sources," *College English*, XVII (1955), 20–27, in which Mr. Stallman states that Scott C. Osborn, who first pointed out the similarity between Kipling and Crane's wafer image, "failed to explore the related images for what they mean and how they are used. . . . Nor is there any other point of correspondence between *The Light That Failed* and *The Red Badge of Courage*—only this single image (p. 20)."
† Reprinted from *Modern Language Notes*, LXXII (December, 1957), 572–75. By permission of The Johns Hopkins Press.
1. Critics who stress the influence of

Zola's *La Débâcle* include: Russell Blankenship, *American Literature* (New York: Henry Holt, 1931), p. 523; Oscar Cargill, *Intellectual America* (New York: Macmillan, 1941), pp. 85–86; James B. Colvert, "*The Red Badge of Courage* and a Review of Zola's *La Débâcle*," *Modern Language Notes*, LXXI (February, 1956), 98–100; and *Literary History of the United States*, II, ed. Spiller, Thorp, *et al.* (New York: Macmillan, 1949), p. 1022.
2. Critics who stress the influence of Tolstoi's *War and Peace* and *Sevastopol* include: V. S. Pritchett, *The Living Novel* (New York: Reynal & Hitchcock, 1947), p. 173; and Lars Ahnebrink, *The Beginnings of Naturalism in American Fiction* (Upsala: American Institute, 1950), p. 347.

father's obsession with war.[3] Willa Cather's interview with the ubiquitous Crane in Nebraska in 1895 suggests that earlier Cranes helped him to formulate his "imaginary" ideas on war: ". . . His ancestors had been soldiers, and he had been imagining war stories ever since he was out of knickerbockers, and in writing his first war story he had simply gone over his imaginary campaigns and selected his favorite imaginary experiences."[4] With intense pride, Crane continually marvelled over the military feats of his fore-fathers. Once he made a summary of their Revolutionary War record and concluded: "In those olden times the family did its duty."[5]

Stephen's father, the minister Jonathan Townley Crane, must have done his duty to these same ancestors by relating tales of their heroism and courage to his children.[6] Besides this, Jonathan Crane left behind (following his death in 1880 when Stephen was only eight) a number of his works, mostly theological, which reveal a deep interest in war. Stephen cherished his father's writings, and as late as 1900 in England, he kept a "shelf of books, for the most part the pious and theological works of various antecedent Stephen Cranes. He had been at some pains to gather together these alien products of his kin."[7]

There was more than enough in the father's books to inspire his son's war theme. Never having witnessed a battle, Jonathan Crane could still say to the readers of his pious works: "Let us again recur to military life for illustration."[8] Two of his volumes, *Arts of Intoxication*[9] and *Popular Amusements*,[10] begin with scenes of conflict. There are many other references to war in his volumes. A few point directly to *The Red Badge*. The following passage in *An Essay on Dancing* (1851), for example, foreshadows the way

3. Several critics mention other possible native American sources like *Corporal Si Klegg*, Ambrose Bierce, *Century's Battles and Leaders*, *Harper's History*, the drawings of Winslow Homer, and Walt Whitman's *Specimen Days*. See: H. T. Webster, "Wilbur F. Hinman's *Corporal Si Klegg* and Stephen Crane's *Red Badge of Courage*," *American Literature*, XI (1939), 285–293; Percy Boynton, *Literature and American Life* (New York: Ginn & Co., 1936), pp. 677–678; Thomas Beer, *Stephen Crane: A Study in American Letters* (New York: Alfred A. Knopf, 1923), pp. 47, 97; Van Wyck Brooks, *The Confident Years* (New York: E. P. Dutton, 1952), p. 137; *The Red Badge of Courage*, ed. Robert W. Stallman (New York: Random House, 1951), pp. xii–xvi.
4. Willa Cather, "When I Knew Stephen Crane," *The Prairie Schooner*, XXIII (1949), 235.
5. *Stephen Crane: An Omnibus*, ed. Robert W. Stallman (New York: Alfred A. Knopf, 1952), pp. 689–690.
6. For this reason, it is not surprising that one of the minister's sons, William, became an expert "in the strategy of Chancellorsville and Gettysburg" and that another son always selected appropriate gifts for the youngest child, Stephen—the romantic war tales for boys by Harry Castleman. See Beer, *op. cit.*, p. 47.
7. *The Shock of Recognition*, ed. Edmund Wilson (New York: Doubleday, 1943), p. 671.
8. *Methodism and its Methods* (New York: Nelson & Phillips, 1876), p. 390.
9. *Arts of Intoxication* (New York: Carlton & Lanahan, 1870), p. 15.
10. *Popular Amusements* (New York: Carlton & Lanahan, 1870), p. 2.

in which Henry Fleming dreams of the heroics associated with battle, and later, upon finding himself at the front, becomes disillusioned by the grim reality he has to face:

". . . Recruiting officers of the most plausible manners are sent into the large towns, their faces beaming with smiles, and their persons glittering in uniform. The banner of the Union floats over their abode; ever and anon, the stirring sounds of martial music are heard there; and those of the recruits already enlisted, who are least likely to run away, are seen reclining about the door of the rendezvous, clothed in very blue coats, and girded with very white belts, and apparently in the enjoyment of great peace of mind. And it is only when mustered into actual service, that the dreaming soldier wakes to all the bliss of hard fare, stern discipline, toilsome marches, battles, wounds, and death."[11]

Another scene, from *The Right Way* (1853), suggests the tragic ironies of battle, continually dealt with in *The Red Badge*:

"Hard is the lot of the youthful hero, battling for the right, who is struck down at the first onset of some great victory, and who, as the long columns of his comrades press past him in full pursuit of the flying foe, and their exultant shouts are borne backward on the wind, lies upon the field, far in the rear, bleeding and faint, with his sword still in his feeble grasp."[12]

Finally, like his son after him, Jonathan Crane imagines (in a passage from *Arts of Intoxication*, 1870) the psychological responses of a human being under the stress of battle:

". . . We are susceptible of excitement, a mounting tide of mental, emotional, and physical energy, which rises more or less gradually, and, when at its height, sweeps along with a power to which in our cooler moments we are strangers, and things at other times impossible are done with ease. The soldier, worn down by a long march, is so weary that he can hardly carry his weapons, but when the battle opens, with its exciting sights and sounds, its rapid evolutions, its fierce passions, his once languid frame becomes as steel for strength and endurance."[13]

One can even find some evidences of animal imagery, used so frequently in *The Red Badge*. Jonathan Crane wrote of the "panther-like yell of assault," of "the strangling coils of the gigantic serpent" which crushes out "the life of nations."[14]

11. *An Essay On Dancing* (New York: Lane & Scott, 1851), p. 38.
12. *The Right Way* (New York: Carlton & Phillips, 1853), p. 138.
13. *Arts of Intoxication, op. cit.*, p. 31.
14. *Ibid.*, p. 247. Also *An Essay On Dancing, op. cit.*, p. 39. For a further study of this imagery, see my unpublished dissertation, "Some Aspects of the Mind and Art of Stephen Crane" (Madison: Univ. of Wisconsin, 1953), pp. 120–122.

The above passages more than imply that Jonathan Crane was influenced by his vivid recollections of the recent Civil War and of the military achievements of earlier Cranes; later he supplied his son with the tensions and moods of battle, with theme, imagery, and psychology. Not foreign sources but native American materials such as these served Stephen Crane so well that he created masterpieces of fiction, beginning with *The Red Badge*.

EDWARD STONE

Crane's "Soldier of the Legion"†

The reader will recall the time in "The Open Boat" when the thought occurs to the correspondent that "nature does not regard him as important," that he—even he—may be drowned; and in the pathos of his situation "a verse mysteriously entered" his mind. It turns out to be a telescoped version of the opening lines of a poem by Caroline E. S. Norton (1808–1877) entitled "Bingen on the Rhine." This obscure, lachrymose ballad, still widely reprinted, is one that, we are told, has been dinned into the correspondent's ears in youth by a myriad of schoolroom declamations, until he knew it by rote[1] and to the point of boredom. It is therefore worth examining by anyone looking for the sources of Crane's art.

Various possibilities of influence appear. Several are mildly curious. First, both "Bingen" and *The Red Badge of Courage* concern themselves with a young man who is attracted to war by the romantic evocations of the word and who finds it anything but romantic. Although Henry Fleming, so far from having had a military tradition handed down to him by a father, has no father at all, the general situation of the young German soldier in several particular respects may be seen to correspond to that of the young American. Like his Rhenish precursor, Henry Fleming comes from a poor family, thinks his home a "cage" of sorts, and enlists against his mother's wishes; the German youth's sweetheart of the merry, sparkling eye but sincere and loving nature reappears as two girls

† From *American Literature*, XXX (May, 1958), 242–44. Reprinted by permission.

1. Note that one of the phrases in the original omitted in the correspondent's quotation ("while his lifeblood ebbed away") is a most vivid part of the extended reverie that follows the quotation: "The correspondent plainly saw the soldier. He lay on the sand with his feet out straight and still. While his pale left hand was upon his chest in an attempt to thwart the going of his life, the blood came between his fingers." Also, as will be noted below, the correspondent remembers that the time of the German soldier's dying speech is sunset.

in the American youth's experience—the one a tease, the other turning "sad and demure" at his approaching departure; in both stories a soldier, whether dying from wounds or from premonition of them asks a comrade to take "a message and a token" back to his family; and in both a comrade stands by solicitously while a soldier dies a bloody death.

But far more significant are the similarities in two other, larger respects. One is the abundant self-pity of both stories. Dying hero and unfledged recruit alike look sorrowfully about them and think or speak elaborately and self-consciously of the pitifulness of their plight—the German lamenting the untimeliness of his approaching death and the American frequently envisioning his immolation on the altar of the unfeeling god of war.

The other similarity is in a companion respect, that of the overwhelming, abiding impersonality and inexorability of the transactions of the universe, and of the infinitely small importance of the individual in these transactions. The "soft" moon rising slowly on the gory "red land" of the Algerian battlefield and shining as calmly on the "dreadful scene" of the dead and dying, young and old alike, "as it shone on distant Bingen"—this Ecclesiastes note rings through the *Red Badge* (and elsewhere through Crane's work). Thus Henry, after performing what he takes to be prodigies of conspicuous valor in battle, is chagrined to perceive how unimportant in the scale of battle was his particular fighting. Even more impressive is the fact that the symbolical denominator of this inscrutable impersonality almost matches Crane's. Thus, as Henry gazes about him in the passage in question (Chap. v) he "felt a flash of astonishment at the blue, pure sky and the sun gleaming on the trees and fields. It was surprising that Nature had gone tranquilly on with her golden process in the midst of so much devilment."[2] Further, we note that most memorable in the Algerian scene the correspondent's mind conjures up in "The Open Boat" is the part played by the sun: as the German youth lies bleeding to death, "In the far Algerian distance, a city of low square forms was set against a sky that was faint with the last sunset hues." To these parallels may be added the reactions of the correspondent: his feeling of spiritual annihilation at the thought that the heavens—in this instance, the star-studded sky—take no cognizance of his existence, much less of his resentment.

In terms of its most important ingredient,—the complex psychological metamorphosis of a young soldier,—to be sure, Crane's

2. And in a later-deleted passage at the end of the novel, even the battle-tried Henry speaks of the sun as shining "imperturbable" on both "insult and worship" (Rinehart ed., p. 372).

200-page modern novel fairly begins where Norton's 50-line Victorian tableau ends. And by the time he came to write "The Open Boat," Crane's own hazardous experiences could easily have evoked such naturalistic reflections in such terms. But the untried youth who wrote *The Red Badge* could have had recourse to literary example. Not "mysteriously" at all, then, need the Norton verse have entered Henry Fleming's mind: for him, as well as for the correspondent, the sentiment of its lines may have seemed perfectly to "chime the notes of his emotion."

ERIC SOLOMON

Another Analogue for *The Red Badge of Courage*†

The search for the source used by Stephen Crane in *The Red Badge of Courage* has fascinated literary researchers ever since it became known that Crane had never experienced the warfare he depicted so accurately in his novel. Despite his denials of any real source other than a knowledge of conflict drawn from the football field, the hunt for the novel's inspiration goes ever bravely on.

From such obvious precursors as Tolstoy, Stendhal, Zola, De Forest, and Bierce, scholars have extended their range to include Wilbur F. Hinman's *Corporal Si Klegg and His "Pard,"* Whitman's *Specimen Days*, Matthew Brady's photographs, Winslow Homer's paintings, the life of General Van Petten—Crane's teacher at Claverack College—and, most recently, a book review of *La Débâcle*.[1] Where all these offer certain correspondences in detail or tone to Crane's masterpiece, none provides quite so exciting a plot resemblance as Joseph Kirkland's *The Captain of Company K.*

This novel, which describes the triumphs and trials of a volunteer company in the Civil War, was published in book form in 1891; it had previously won the Detroit *Free Press* literary competition and was serialized in that newspaper in 1890. Although the novel is largely controlled by the evasions of the genteel tradition, his previous work had stamped Kirkland, a major in the U. S. Volunteers during the war, as a regional writer of some realistic pretensions (his *Zury* was a touchstone for Hamlin Garland's first

† Copyright © 1958, by The Regents of the University of California. Reprinted from *Nineteenth Century Fiction*, XIII, 63–67, by permission of The Regents.

1. J. B. Colvert, *"The Red Badge of Courage* and a Review of Zola's *La Débâcle,"* *MLN*, LXXI (February, 1956), 98–100.

fiction). Underneath the conventional love plot and the heightened diction appears a grim, bitter picture of combat. Kirkland brings out the horror which encompasses a body of men suddenly faced with the reality of bullets that maim and kill, destroying the romantic image of war the simple farm boys had carried into battle. The novel is full of realistic touches—veteran troops scoffing at new recruits moving up, the nervous rumors which afflict an army before action—and it provides many carefully worked out descriptions of infantry engagements. Like Crane, Kirkland handles war in ironic terms, appalled by the situation that erases men's individuality, making them "food for powder, the mere sport of fate."[2]

More directly apposite to the theme of *The Red Badge of Courage*, however, is the portrait of the hero, William Fargeon, the captain of Company K. Like Henry Fleming, Fargeon is an innocent who rapidly gains maturity and self-reliance in the crucible of war. Full of pride at the start, he goes through the successive stages of intellectual doubt as to his courage, acute fear just before the baptism of fire, unnoticed cowardice in combat, and final confidence and strength as he becomes a veteran—the same path of development that Crane's hero follows. This is not to assume for a moment that the two books are in any way comparable as works of art. Kirkland's novel is a piece of hack writing by a crude technician who was primarily interested in supplying a stylized love plot with an honest background of war. There is not a hint anywhere in *The Captain of Company K* of the symbolism, control of language, and architectonics displayed by Crane. Yet Kirkland, a veteran of combat, anticipated Crane in many aspects of war fiction by four years.

Whether or not Crane was familiar with the Chicagoan's work is open to question. Crane never mentioned having read Kirkland. However, Hamlin Garland, who was in contact with Crane as a friend and literary adviser during the period of *The Red Badge of Courage*'s conception and creation,[3] maintained a similar relationship with Kirkland. Garland reviewed Kirkland's novel of middle western life, *Zury*, for the Boston *Transcript* and in 1886 paid him a visit. "I found in Chicago a new friend whose sympathy was so stimulating, so helpful that I delayed my journey for two days in order that I might profit by his critical comment."[4] It was Kirkland who first insisted that the young writer should attempt a novel, and Garland was always grateful to the older man for his support. He talked with Kirkland again in 1889[5] when he must

2. Joseph Kirkland, *The Captain of Company K* (Chicago, 1891), p. 119.
3. John Berryman, *Stephen Crane* (New York, 1950), p. 66 *et passim*.
4. Hamlin Garland, *A Son of the Middle Border* (New York, 1917), p. 353.
5. *Ibid.*, p. 407. A copy of *The Captain of Company K*, inscribed by Kirkland

have been involved with the war novel.

But did Garland ever mention Kirkland to Crane? Here the evidence is more vague. Garland's statement that when he talked with Walt Whitman at this time they discussed Cable, Kirkland, Harris, and Wilkins,[6] points up the fact that Joseph Kirkland served as a literary reference for him. It is possible that Garland's address on "The Local Novel" given in New Jersey in July of 1891 and reported for the New York *Tribune* by Stephen Crane[7] would have made some mention of the author of *Zury*. We have no way of knowing whether Kirkland's work ever came up for discussion in the meetings between Crane and Garland from 1891 to 1893, when Crane wrote the first draft of his war novel. It was Crane's little joke to refuse to let Garland in on the secret of the background of *The Red Badge of Courage*. "It was as if this youth in some mystic way had secured the coöperation of the spirit of an officer in the Civil War. How else would one account for his knowledge of war?"[8]

There is no external evidence to prove that Crane, who deliberately set out to write a potboiler for the newspapers,[9] used as a source Kirkland's potboiler, which had been successful enough to win a newspaper competition. *The Captain of Company K* is of interest in connection with *The Red Badge of Courage* not because Crane *could* have read Kirkland's novel, nor because both books exhibit a similar approach to war; the startling fact is that both writers fix upon the same plot device to portray the hero's escape from the accusation of cowardice—an accidental wound. One of the major ironies of Crane's book develops from the circumstances under which Henry Fleming receives his wound, the badge which gains him the sympathy and admiration of his fellow soldiers. He is wounded by a blow on his head from the rifle of a fleeing comrade. The wound brings him honor, yet he was in a position to receive it because of his cowardice, having fled the battlefield in panic. Crane makes much of this irony; the appearance of courage and the reality of fear play an integral part in the development of his hero's character.

Nearly the same situation occurs in *The Captain of Company K*. As Fargeon advances on his first skirmish, he succumbs to a chill of terror at the sound of bullets whistling by and takes cover behind a tree. Emotionally unable to stir from this protection, he

to Garland in 1892, was included in the latter's library. See Lars Ahnebrink, *The Beginnings of Naturalism in American Fiction 1891–1903* (Upsala, 1950), p. 427.
6. Hamlin Garland, *Roadside Meetings*
(New York, 1930), p. 135.
7. Hamlin Garland, "Stephen Crane as I Knew Him," *Yale Review*, III (April, 1914), 494.
8. *Ibid.*, p. 498.
9. Garland, *Roadside Meetings*, p. 204.

berates himself for cowardice, anticipates the shame and disgrace his lack of action will cause, and prays for a good wound which will preserve his honor. " 'Oh, if I could take a bullet in my hand— my arm—anywhere but in my face!' " In his fearful state he momentarily loses control: "He brought back his hand against the tree trunk; and between his thumbs pressed his forehead hard against the flinty bark, and rolled it from side to side, as if to get a little bodily pain to assuage his mental agony."[10] He finally regains his senses and manages to take part in the attack. The dramatic irony of the situation is made explicit when the men are relaxing after the successful action and Fargeon's bloody brow is noticed. " 'Why, Captain, did you get hit? Your forehead looks as if it had been grazed by a ball.' "[11] Unlike Fleming, Kirkland's hero does not take credit for a combat wound, and he brushes it off as an accident. But he feels the same shame that makes Fleming later blush and grow silent in memory of his fear. In both novels the growth of the hero from cowardice to courage revolves around the incident of a wound received as a direct result of fear, unnoticed as such, and taken by others as a symbol of courage.

Rather than seek another "source" for Crane's work, it is better to define Kirkland's novel as an "analogue," a work employing some similar devices and, since it appeared before *The Red Badge of Courage* was started, providing a possible inspiration or suggestion. In any case, a study of *The Captain of Company K* with its inclusion of the same themes and contrivances as those of the greater novel, yet overlaid with the genteel absurdities of an unsure writer, helps to indicate the remarkable artistic achievement reached by Crane through his manipulation of these materials.

CECIL D. EBY, JR.

[General Philip Kearny's "Red Badge of Courage"]†

Although there seems no end to the speculations about the source of the Civil War framework upon which Stephen Crane based *The Red Badge of Courage*, the source of the central metaphor itself has drawn only a single guess by Abraham Feldman, who suggests that it may be derived from Shakespeare's "murder's

10. Kirkland, *The Captain of Company K*, p. 97.
11. *Ibid.*, p. 104.
† Published as "The Source of Crane's Metaphor, *Red Badge of Courage*," *American Literature*, XXXII (May, 1960), 204–7. Reprinted by permission.

crimson badge" in *Henry VI: Part III*.[1] Knowing something of Crane's impatient and often unsympathetic reading tastes, we find it difficult to imagine his laboring through that unwieldy drama, though it is not impossible that he struck upon the line by accident. Mr. Feldman is correct, however, in suspecting that Crane borrowed rather than originated his metaphor, but its source was a popular phrase in use during and after the Civil War.

For any Union veteran with service in Virginia, "red badge of courage" would have brought to mind both the New Jersey general, Philip Kearny, and his famous "red badge" (also called "red diamond" and "red patch") division of the Third Corps, Army of the Potomac. Kearny, whom General Winfield Scott called "the bravest man I ever knew and the most perfect soldier,"[2] was a resident of Newark and its most outstanding soldier of the war. The Kearny family home stood within the city limits of Newark during Stephen Crane's lifetime, and Philip Kearny's mansion, "Belle Grove," was a landmark on the Hudson County side of the Passaic River. Crane's brother William, we are told, was an authority on the Civil War;[3] he would have been a dull authority, indeed, had he not known something of Kearny and the "red badge" division.

Philip Kearny was, apparently, the first Union commander to order his men to wear a special badge so that he could distinguish them in battle.[4] Disgusted at what he considered the incompetence of Union command during the campaigns before Richmond in 1862, he directed his officers "to wear a red patch in shape of a diamond on the crown or left side of their cap, while enlisted men were to wear theirs in front of the cap."[5] From the first the patch was a "sign of good character and a badge of honor."[6] Moreover, the red diamond was recognized by the enemy as a special mark of valor; Kearny's biographers tell of a Union colonel buried with full military honors by the Confederates because of their respect for his red badge.[7] Although other generals soon adopted divisional patches, the red diamond became almost sacrosanct. It remained the badge of the original Kearny division even after his death at Chantilly in September, 1862, and after his command had been absorbed into the Second Corps (the official badge for which was the trefoil).[8]

---

1. "Crane's Title from Shakespeare," *American Notes & Queries*, VIII, 185–186 (March, 1950).
2. Quoted in John Watts DePeyster, *Personal and Military History of Philip Kearny* (New York, 1869), p. 495.
3. Thomas Beer, *Stephen Crane* (London, 1924), p. 40.

4. Thomas Kearny, *General Philip Kearny: Battle Soldier of Five Wars* (New York, 1937), p. 267.
5. DePeyster, p. 495.
6. *Ibid.*, p. 354.
7. *Ibid.*, p. 368, and Kearny, p. 268.
8. DePeyster, p. 367.

It might also be noted that in addition to the Kearny red badge, there was also a Kearny red medal designed by his successor, General David B. Birney. This was awarded to those soldiers who distinguished themselves by individual acts of heroism in battle; engraved on the cross below the ribbon was the Kearny motto, *"Dulce et decorum est pro patria mori."*[9] Both the red badge and the red medal were familiar to most Union soldiers serving in Virginia, just as both are now well known to Civil War historians.

The evidence linking Crane and Kearny in not entirely circumstantial. A Kearny family tradition credits Crane with visits to "Belle Grove" on several occasions for talks with Philip Kearny's son, John Watts Kearny. One of the General's biographers has this to say in a footnote:

"Crane, born in Newark, while resident in Asbury Park and later before he became famous visited "Kearny Castle" ["Belle Grove"]. When his fame was achieved he again visited General [John Watts] Kearny and told the General the symbolic meaning hidden under the title of his famous book."[10]

Unfortunately nothing more is said of this "symbolic meaning."

These fragments may be fitted together for a possible explanation of the meaning of Crane's title, "The Red Badge of Courage." We know that Crane's original title was the prosaic *Henry Fleming, His Various Battles,*[11] but at some point in his composition he struck upon the phrase "red badge of courage," which in Chapter ix he used as a synonym for "wound." Ironically, Henry's wound, inflicted by a fellow Union soldier, is a private badge of cowardice which passes as a public badge of courage. By changing his title, Crane underscored the irony of the novel, but he also had in mind another purpose. What better title could be chosen for a book that he had originally intended as a "pot-boiler" (his own designation)[12] than one which would echo a public and hallowed metaphor? Union veterans would, of course, associate his title with Kearny and the red badge division; therefore it is little wonder that the novel was bitterly criticized by former soldiers who resented the author's wholly unexpected and unflattering exploration of the nature of courage.[13]

9. For an illustration of the Kearny medal see *ibid.*, facing p. 368; for an illustration of the Kearny patch see the front cover of Gilbert A. Hayes, *Under the Red Patch* (Pittsburgh, 1908).

10. Kearny, p. 267.

11. Robert W. Stallman, *Stephen Crane: An Omnibus* (New York, 1952), p. 218.

12. *Ibid.*, p. 210.

13. Thomas Beer records a sample of the veteran's outrage (p. 133).

Essays in Criticism

GEORGE WYNDHAM

From A Remarkable Book†

* * *

Mr. Stephen Crane, the author of *The Red Badge of Courage* (London: Heinemann), is a great artist with something new to say, and consequently, with a new way of saying it. His theme, indeed, is an old one, but old themes re-handled anew in the light of novel experience, are the stuff out of which masterpieces are made, and in *The Red Badge of Courage* Mr. Crane has surely contrived a masterpiece. He writes of war—the ominous and alluring possibility for every man, since the heir of all the ages has won and must keep his inheritance by secular combat. The conditions of the age-long contention have changed and will change, but its certainty is coeval with progress: so long as there are things worth fighting for fighting will last, and the fashion of fighting will change under the reciprocal stresses of rival inventions. Hence its double interest of abiding necessity and ceaseless variation. Of all these variations the most marked has followed, within the memory of most of us, upon the adoption of long-range weapons of precision, and continues to develop, under our eyes, with the development of rapidity in firing. And yet, with the exception of Zola's *la Débâcle*, no considerable attempt has been made to portray war under its new conditions. The old stories are less trustworthy than ever as guides to the experiences which a man may expect in battle and to the emotions which those experiences are likely to arouse. No doubt the prime factors in the personal problem—the chances of death and mutilation—continue to be about the same. In these respects it matters little whether you are pierced by a bullet at two thousand yards or stabbed at hands' play with a dagger. We know that the most appalling death-rolls of recent campaigns have been more than equalled in ancient warfare; and, apart from history, it is clear that, unless one side runs away, neither can win save by the infliction of decisive losses. But although these personal risks continue to be essentially the same, the picturesque and emotional aspects of war are completely al-

† The London *New Review*, XIV (January, 1896), 30–40. In the present transcript the first two pages of generalization are omitted. Of the several early English reviews, Conrad especially praised this (see "[His War Book]" included in this collection). George Wyndham had experienced battle service in 1884 in the Anglo-Egyptian Sudan; after 1892 he engaged in periodical writing, criticism, editing, and translating, while continuing a political career which began with his support of Balfour in Parliament, and led to distinguished posts in government, including that of Chief Secretary for Ireland.

tered by every change in the shape and circumstance of imminent death. And these àre the fit materials for literature—the things which even dull men remember with the undying imagination of poets, but which, for lack of the writer's art, they cannot communicate. The sights flashed indelibly on the retina of the eye; the sounds that after long silences suddenly cypher; the stenches that sicken in after-life at any chance allusion to decay; or, stirred by these, the storms of passions that force yells of defiance out of inarticulate clowns; the winds of fear that sweep by night along prostrate ranks, with the acceleration of trains and the noise as of a whole town waking from nightmare with stertorous, indrawn gasps —these colossal facts of the senses and the soul are the only colours in which the very image of war can be painted. Mr. Crane has composed his palette with these colours, and has painted a picture that challenges comparison with the most vivid scenes of Tolstoï's *la Guerre et la Paix* or of Zola's *la Débâcle*. This is unstinted praise, but I feel bound to give it after reading the book twice and comparing it with Zola's Sédan and Tolstoï's account of Rostow's squadron for the first time under fire. Indeed, I think that Mr. Crane's picture of war is more complete than Tolstoï's, more true than Zola's. Rostow's sensations are conveyed by Tolstoï with touches more subtile than any to be found even in his *Sébastopol*, but they make but a brief passage in a long book, much else of which is devoted to the theory that Napoleon and his marshals were mere waifs on a tide of humanity or to the analysis of divers characters exposed to civilian experiences. Zola, on the other hand, compiles an accurate catalogue of almost all that is terrible and nauseating in war; but it is his own catalogue of facts made in cold blood, and not the procession of flashing images shot through the senses into one brain and fluctuating there with its rhythm of exaltation and fatigue. *La Débâcle* gives the whole truth, the truth of science, as it is observed by a shrewd intellect, but not the truth of experience as it is felt in fragments magnified or diminished in accordance with the patient's mood. The terrible things in war are not always terrible; the nauseating things do not always sicken. On the contrary, it is even these which sometimes lift the soul to heights from which they become invisible. And, again, at other times, it is the little miseries of most ignoble insignificance which fret through the last fibres of endurance.

Mr. Crane, for his distinction, has hit on a new device, or at least on one which has never been used before with such consistency and effect. In order to show the features of modern war, he takes a subject—a youth with a peculiar temperament, capable of exaltation and yet morbidly sensitive. Then he traces the successive impressions made on such a temperament, from minute to minute, during two days of heavy fighting. He stages the drama of war, so to speak, within the mind of one man, and then admits you as to a theatre. You may, if you please, object that this youth is unlike most other young men who serve in the ranks, and that the same events would have impressed the average man differently; but you are convinced that this man's soul is truly drawn, and that the impressions made in it are faithfully rendered. The youth's temperament is merely the medium which the artist has chosen: that it is exceptionally plastic makes but for the deeper incision of his work. It follows from Mr. Crane's method that he creates by his art even such a first-hand report of war as we seek in vain among the journals and letters of soldiers. But the book is not written in the form of an autobiography: the author narrates. He is therefore at liberty to give scenery and action, down to the slightest gestures and outward signs of inward elation or suffering, and he does this with the vigour and terseness of a master. Had he put his descriptions of scenery and his atmospheric effects, or his reports of overheard conversations, into the mouth of his youth, their very excellence would have belied all likelihood. Yet in all his descriptions and all his reports he confines himself only to such things as that youth heard and saw, and, of these, only to such as influenced his emotions. By this compromise he combines the strength and truth of a monodrama with the directness and colour of the best narrative prose. The monodrama suffices for the lyrical emotion of Tennyson's *Maud*; but in Browning's *Martin Relf* you feel the constraint of a form which in his *Ring and the Book* entails repetition often intolerable.

Mr. Crane discovers his youth, Henry Fleming, in a phase of disillusion. It is some monotonous months since boyish "visions of broken-bladed glory" impelled him to enlist in the Northern Army towards the middle of the American war. That impulse is admirably given:—"One night as he lay in bed, the winds had carried to him the clangouring of the church bells, as some enthusiast jerked the rope frantically to tell the twisted news of a great battle. This voice of the people rejoicing in the night had made him shiver in a prolonged ecstasy of excitement. Later he had gone down to his mother's room, and had spoken thus: 'Ma, I'm going to enlist.' 'Henry, don't you be a fool,' his mother had replied. She had then covered her face with the quilt. There was an end to the matter for that night." But the next morning he enlists. He is impatient of the homely injunctions given him in place of the heroic speech he expects in accordance with a tawdry convention, and so departs, with a "vague feeling of relief." But, looking back from the gate, he sees his mother "kneeling among the potato parings. Her brown face upraised and stained with tears, her spare form quivering." Since then the army has done "little but sit still and try to keep warm" till he has "grown to regard himself merely as a part of a vast blue demonstration." In the sick langour of this waiting, he begins to suspect his courage and lies awake by night through hours of morbid introspection. He tries "to prove to himself mathematically that he would not run from a battle"; he constantly leads the conversation round the problem of courage in order to gauge the confidence of his messmates.

" 'How do you know you won't run when the time comes?' asked the youth. 'Run?' said the loud one, 'run?—of course not!' He laughed. 'Well,' continued the youth, 'lots of good-a-'nough men have thought they was going to do great things before the fight, but when the time come they skedaddled.' 'Oh, that's all true, I s'pose,' replied the other, 'but I'm not going to skedaddle. The man that bets on my running will lose his money, that's all.' He nodded confidently."

The youth is a "mental outcast" among his comrades, "wrestling with his personal problem," and sweating as he listens to the muttered scoring of a card game, his eyes fixed on the "red, shivering reflection of a fire." Every day they drill; every night they watch the red campfires of the enemy on the far shore of a river, eating their hearts out. At last they march:—"In the gloom before the break of the day their uniforms glowed a deep purple blue. From across the river the red eyes were still peering. In the eastern sky there was a yellow patch, like a rug laid for the feet of the coming sun; and against it, black and pattern-like, loomed the gigantic figure of the colonel on a gigantic horse." The book is full of such vivid impressions, half of sense and half of imagination:—The columns as they marched "were like two serpents crawling from the cavern of night." But the march, which, in his boyish imagination, should have led forthwith into melodramatic action is but the precursor of other marches. After days of weariness and nights of discomfort at last, as in life, without preface, and in a lull of the mind's anxiety, the long-dreaded and long-expected is suddenly and smoothly in process of accomplishment:—"One grey morning he was kicked on the leg by the tall soldier, and then, before he was entirely awake, he found himself running down a wood road in the midst of men who were panting with the first effects of speed. His canteen banged rhythmically upon his thigh, and his haversack bobbed softly. His musket bounced a trifle from his shoulder at each stride and made his cap feel uncertain upon his head." From this moment, reached on the thirtieth page, the drama races through another hundred and sixty pages to the end of the book, and to read those pages is in itself an experience of breathless, lambent, detonating life. So brilliant and detached are the images evoked that, like illuminated bodies actually seen, they leave their fever-bright phantasms floating before the brain. You may shut the book, but you still see the battle-flags "jerked about madly in the smoke," or sinking with "dying gestures of despair," the men "dropping here and there like bundles"; the captain shot dead with "an astonished and sorrowful look as if he thought some friend had done him an ill-turn"; and the litter of corpses, "twisted in fantastic contortions," as if "they had fallen from some great height, dumped out upon the ground from the sky." The book is full of sensuous impressions that leap out from the picture: of gestures, attitudes, grimaces, that flash into portentous definition, like faces from the climbing clouds of nightmare. It leaves the imagination bounded with a "dense wall of smoke, furiously slit and slashed by the knife-like fire from the rifles." It leaves, in short, such indelible traces as are left by the actual experience of war. The picture shows grisly shadows and vermilion splashes, but, as in the vast drama it reflects so truly, these features, though insistent, are small in size, and are lost in the immensity of the theatre. The tranquil forest stands around; the "fairy-blue of the sky" is over it all. And, as in the actual experience of war, the impressions which these startling features inflict, though acute, are localised and not too deep: are as it were mere pin-pricks, or, at worst, clean cuts from a lancet in a body thrilled with currents of physical excitement and sopped with anæsthetics of emotion. Here is the author's description of a forlorn hope:—

"As the regiment swung from its position out into a cleared space the woods and thickets before it awakened. Yellow flames leaped toward it from many directions. The line swung straight for a moment. Then the right wing swung forward; it in turn was surpassed by the left. Afterward the centre careered to the front until the regiment was a wedge-shaped mass . . . . the men, pitching forward insanely, had burst into cheerings, mob-like and barbaric, but tuned in strange keys that can arouse the dullard and the stoic . . . . There was the delirium that encounters despair and death, and is heedless and blind to odds . . . . Presently the straining pace ate up the energies of the men. As if by agreement, the leaders began to slacken their speed. The volleys directed against them had a seeming wind-like effect. The regiment snorted and blew. Among some stolid trees it began to falter and hesitate . . . . The youth had a vague belief that he had run miles, and he thought, in a way, that he was now in some new and unknown land . . . ."

The charge withers away, and the lieutenant, the youth, and his friend run forward to rally the regiment.

"In front of the colours three men began to bawl, 'Come on! Come on!' They danced and gyrated like tortured savages. The flag, obedient to these appeals, bended its glittering form and swept toward them. The men wavered in indecision for a moment, and then with a long wailful cry the dilapidated regiment surged forward and began its new journey. Over the field went the scurrying mass. It was a handful of men splattered into the faces of the enemy. Toward it instantly sprang the yellow tongues. A vast quantity of blue smoke hung before them. A mighty banging made ears valueless. The youth ran like a madman to reach the woods before a bullet could discover him. He ducked his head low, like a football player. In his haste his eyes almost closed, and the scene was a wild blur. Pulsating saliva stood at the corner of his mouth. Within him, as he hurled forward, was born a love, a despairing fondness for this flag that was near him. It was a creation of beauty and invulnerability. It was a goddess radiant, that bended its form with an imperious gesture to him. It was a woman, red and white, hating and loving, that called him with the voice of his hopes. Because no harm could come to it he endowed it with power. He kept near, as if it could be a saver of lives, and an imploring cry went from his mind."

This passage directly challenges comparison with Zola's scene, in which the lieutenant and the old tradition, of an invincible Frenchman over-running the world "between his bottle and his girl," expire together among the morsels of a bullet-eaten flag. Mr. Crane has probably read *la Débâcle*, and wittingly threw down his glove. One can only say that he is justified of his courage.

Mr. Crane's method, when dealing with things seen and heard, is akin to Zola's: he omits nothing and extenuates nothing, save the actual blasphemy and obscenity of a soldier's oaths. These he indicates, sufficiently for any purpose of art, by brief allusions to their vigour and variety. Even Zola has rarely surpassed the appalling realism of Jim Conklin's death in Chapter X. Indeed, there is little to criticise in Mr. Crane's observation, except an undue subordination of the shrill cry of bullets to the sharp crashing of rifles. He omits the long chromatic whine defining its invisible arc in the air, and the fretful snatch a few feet from the listener's head. In addition to this gift of observation, Mr. Crane has at command the imaginative phrase. The firing follows a retreat as with "yellings of eager metallic hounds"; the men at their mechanic loading and firing are like "fiends jigging heavily in the smoke"; in a lull before the attack "there passed slowly the intense moments that precede the tempest"; then, after single shots, "the battle roar settled to a rolling thunder, which was a single long explosion." And, as I have said, when Mr. Crane deals with things felt he gives a truer report than Zola. He postulates his hero's temperament—a day-dreamer given over to morbid self-analysis who enlists, not from any deep-seated belief in the holiness of fighting for his country, but in hasty pursuit of a vanishing ambition. This choice enables Mr. Crane to double his picturesque advantage with an ethical advantage equally great. Not only is his youth, like the sufferer in *The Fall of the House of Usher*, super-sensitive to every pin-prick of sensation: he is also a delicate meter of emotion and fancy. In such a nature the waves of feeling take exaggerated curves, and hallucination haunts the brain. Thus, when awaiting the first attack, his mind is thronged with vivid images of a circus he had seen as a boy: it is there in definite detail, even as the Apothecary's shop usurps Romeo's mind at the crisis of his fate. And thus also, like Herodotus' Aristodemus, he vacillates between cowardice and heroism. Nothing could well be more subtle than his self-deception and that sudden enlightenment which leads him to "throw aside his mental pamphlets on the philosophy of the retreated and rules for the guidance of the damned." His soul is of that kind which, "sick with self-love," can only be saved "so as by fire"; and it is saved when the battle-bond of brotherhood is born within it, and is found plainly of deeper import than the cause for which he and his comrades fight, even as that cause is loftier than his personal ambition. By his choice of a hero Mr. Crane displays in the same work a pageant of the senses and a tragedy of the soul.

But he does not obtrude his moral. The "tall soldier" and the lieutenant are brave and content throughout, the one by custom as a veteran, the other by constitution as a hero. But the two boys, the youth and his friend, "the loud soldier," are at first querulous braggarts, but at the last they are transmuted by danger until either might truly say:—

> We have proved we have hearts in a cause, we are noble still,
> And myself have awaked, as it seems, to the better mind;
> It is better to fight for the good than to rail at the ill;
> I have felt with my native land, I am one with my kind,
> I embrace the purpose of God, and the doom assigned.

Let no man cast a stone of contempt at these two lads during their earlier weakness until he has fully gauged the jarring discordance of battle. To be jostled on a platform when you have lost your luggage and missed your train on an errand of vital importance gives a truer pre-taste of war than any field-day; yet many a well-disciplined man will denounce the universe upon slighter provocation. It is enough that these two were boys and that they became men.

Yet must it be said that this youth's emotional experience was singular. In a battle there are a few physical cowards, abjects born with defective circulations, who literally turn blue at the approach of danger, and a few on whom danger acts like the keen, rare atmosphere of snow-clad peaks. But between these extremes come many to whom danger is as strong wine, with the multitude which gladly accepts the "iron laws of tradition" and finds welcome support in "a moving box." To this youth, as the cool dawn of his first day's fighting changed by infinitesimal gradations to a feverish noon, the whole evolution pointed to "a trap"; but I have seen another youth under like circumstances toss a pumpkin into the air and spit it on his sword. To this youth the very landscape was filled with "the stealthy approach of death." You are convinced by the author's art that it was so to this man. But to others, as the clamour increases, it is as if the serenity of the morning had taken refuge in their brains. This man "stumbles over the stones as he runs breathlessly forward"; another realises for the first time how right it is to be adroit even in running. The movement of his body becomes an art, which is not self-conscious, since its whole intention is to impress others within the limits of a modest decorum. We know that both love and courage teach this mastery over the details of living. You can tell from the way one woman, out of all the myriads, walks down Piccadilly, that she is at last aware of love. And you can tell from the way a man enters a surgery or runs toward a firing-line that he, too, realises how wholly the justification of any one life lies in its perfect adjustment to others. The woman in love, the man in battle, may each say, for their moment, with the artist, "I was made perfect too." They also are of the few to whom "God whispers in the ear."

But had Mr. Crane taken an average man he would have written an ordinary story, whereas he has written one which is certain to last. It is glorious to see his youth discover courage in the bed-rock of primeval antagonism after the collapse of his tinsel bravado; it is something higher to see him raise upon that rock the temple of resignation. Mr. Crane, as an artist, achieves by his singleness of purpose a truer and completer picture of war than either Tolstoï, bent also upon proving the insignificance of heroes, or Zola, bent also upon prophesying the regeneration of France. That is much; but it is more that his work of art, when completed, chimes with the universal experience of mankind; that his heroes find in their extreme danger, if not confidence in their leaders and conviction in their cause, at least the conviction that most men do what they

can or, at most, what they must. We have few good accounts of
battles—many of shipwrecks; and we know that, just as the storm
rises, so does the commonplace captain show as a god, and the
hysterical passenger as a cheerful heroine.

It is but a further step to recognise all life for a battle and this
earth for a vessel lost in space. We may then infer that virtues easy
in moments of distress may be useful also in everyday experience.

EDWARD GARNETT

[Stephen Crane: an Appreciation]†

A short time ago I picked up on a London book-stall, the first
edition of *The Red Badge of Courage*. Its price was six-pence.
Obviously the bookseller lay no store by it, for the book had been
thrown on the top of a parcel of paper-covered novels among the
waifs and strays of literature. Chancing to meet a young American
poet I asked him, curiously, how his countrymen esteemed today
that intensely original genius, Crane, the creator of "The Open
Boat," "George's Mother," "Maggie," *The Black Riders*. He answered, "One rarely hears Crane's name mentioned in America.
His work is almost forgotten, but I believe it has a small, select
circle of admirers." I confess I was amused, especially when a little
later a first edition of *Almayer's Folly*, the first Conrad, was sold at
auction for five hundred times the amount of the early Crane. And
Conrad was also amused when I told him, and we suggested a title
for an allegorical picture yet to be painted—the Apotheosis of an
Author crowned by Fashion, Merit and Midas. For we both had in
mind the years when the critics hailed *The Nigger of the Narcissus*
as a worthy pendent to the battle-pictures presented in *The Red
Badge of Courage*, and when Sir, then Mr. Arthur Quiller-Couch
spoke of *The Nigger*, as "having something of Crane's insistence."

We talked together over Crane and his work and cast our memories back over twenty years when we were both in touch with "poor
Steve," he more than I. And we agreed that within its peculiar
limited compass Crane's genius was unique. Crane, when living

† "Mr Stephen Crane, an Appreciation," published in the *London Academy*, December 17, 1898, was one of
the early reviews praised by Conrad
(*cf.* the note on Wyndham's article
above). Garnett incorporated it in the
retrospective "Stephen Crane and His
Work," a chapter in his volume *Friday Nights* (1922). As a publisher's
editor, Garnett "discovered" such authors as Conrad, Galsworthy, and D. H.
Lawrence; as essayist and man of letters he was prolific and respected.

at Oxted, was a neighbour of mine, and one day, on my happening to describe to him an ancient Sussex house, noble and grey with the passage of five hundred years, nothing would satisfy him but that he must become the tenant of Brede Place. It was the lure of romance that always thrilled Crane's blood, and Brede Place had had indeed, an unlucky, chequered history. I saw Crane last, when he lay dying there, the day before his wife was transporting him, on a stretcher bed, to a health resort in the Black Forest, in a vain effort to arrest the fatal disease, and I see again his bloodless face and the burning intensity of his eyes. He had lived at too high pressure and his consumptive physique was ravaged by the exhausting strain of his passionate life, and sapped by the hardships of the Cuban campaign, which he suffered as a war-correspondent. Crane's strange eyes, with their intensely concentrated gaze, were those of a genius. * * * Crane, as Conrad reminded me, never knew how good his best work was. He simply never knew. He never recognized that in the volume "The Open Boat," he had achieved the perfection of his method. If he had comprehended that in "The Bride Comes to Yellow Sky" and in "Death and the Child" he had attained then, his high water mark, he might perhaps have worked forward along the lines of patient, ascending effort; but after "The Open Boat," 1898, his work dropped to lower levels. * * * My view of Crane as a born impressionist and master of the short story, I emphasized in an Appreciation in 1898, and since it is germane to my purpose here, I reprint the criticism:—

Mr. Stephen Crane
an Appreciation

"What Mr. Crane has got to do is very simple: he must not mix reporting with his writing. To other artists the word must often be passed: rest, work at your art, live more; but Mr. Crane has no need of cultivating his technique, no need of resting, no need of searching wide for experiences. In his art he is unique. Its certainty, its justness, its peculiar perfection of power arrived at its birth, or at least at that precise moment in its life when other artists—and great artists too—were preparing themselves for the long and difficult conquest of their art. I cannot remember a parallel case in the literary history of fiction. Maupassant, Meredith, Mr. James, Mr. Howells, Tolstoy, all were learning their expression at the age where Mr. Crane had achieved his, achieved it triumphantly. Mr. Crane has no need to learn anything. His technique is absolutely his own, and by its innate laws of being has arrived at a perfect fulness of power. What he has not got he has no power of acquiring. He has no need to acquire it. * * * We would define him by saying he is the perfect artist and interpreter of the surfaces of life. And that explains why he so swiftly attained his peculiar power, and what is the realm his art commands, and his limitations.

"Take 'George's Mother,' for example—a tale which I believe he wrote at the ridiculous age of twenty-one. In *method* it is a masterpiece. It is a story dealing simply with the relations between an old woman and her son, who live together in a New York tenement block. An ordinary artist would seek to dive into the mind of the old woman, to follow its workings hidden under the deceitful appearances of things, under the pressure of her surroundings. A great artist would so recreate her life that its griefs and joys became significant of the griefs and joys of all motherhood on earth. But Mr. Crane does neither. He simply reproduces the surfaces of the individual life in so marvellous a way that the manner in which the old woman washes up the crockery, for example, gives us the essentials. * * * But, of course, the written word in the hands of the greatest artist often deals directly with the depths, plunges us into the rich depths of consciousness that cannot be more than hinted at by the surface; and it is precisely here that Mr. Crane's natural limitation must come in. At the supreme height of art the great masters so plough up the depths of life that the astonished spectator loses sight of the individual life altogether, and has the entrancing sense that all life is really one and the same thing, and is there manifesting itself before him. He feels that, for example, when he watches Duse at her best, or when he stands before Leonardo da Vinci's 'La Joconda' in the Louvre and is absorbed by it. I do not think that Mr. Crane is ever great in the sense of so fusing all the riches of the consciousness into a whole, that the reader is struck dumb as by an inevitable revelation; but he is undoubtedly such an interpreter of the significant surface of things that in a few strokes he gives us an amazing insight into what the individual life is. And he does it all straight from the surface; a few oaths, a genius for slang, an exquisite and unique faculty of exposing an individual scene by an odd simile, a power of interpreting a face or an action, a keen realizing of the primitive emotions—that is Mr. Crane's talent. In 'The Bride Comes to Yellow Sky,' for example, the art is simply immense. There is a page and a half of conversation at the end of this short story of seventeen pages which, as a dialogue revealing the whole inside of the situation, is a lesson to any artist living. And the last line of this story, by the gift peculiar to the author of using some odd simile which cunningly condenses the feeling of the situation, defies analysis altogether. Foolish people may call Mr. Crane a reporter of genius; but nothing could be more untrue. He is thrown away as a picturesque reporter: a secondary style of art, of which, let us say, Mr. G. W. Steevens is, perhaps, the ablest exponent of today, and which is the heavy clay of Mr. Kipling's talent. Mr. Crane's technique is far superior to Mr. Kipling's, but he does not experiment ambitiously in various styles and develop in new directions as Mr. Kipling has done. I do not think that Mr. Crane will or can develop further. Again, I do not think he has the building faculty, or that he will ever do better in constructing a perfect whole out of many parts than he has arrived at in *The Red Badge of Courage*. That book was a series of episodic scenes, all melting naturally into one another and forming a just whole; but it was not constructed, in any sense of the word. And further, Mr. Crane does not show any faculty of taking his characters and revealing in them deep mysterious worlds of human nature, of developing fresh riches in them, acting under the pressure of circumstance. * * * He is the chief impressionist of our day as Sterne was the great impressionist, in a different manner, of his day. If he fails in anything he undertakes, it will be through abandoning the style he has invented. He may, perhaps, fail by and by, through using up the picturesque phases of the environment that nurtured him, as Swinburne came to a stop directly he had rung the changes a certain number of times on the fresh rhythms and phrases he had created. But that time is not yet, and every artist of a special unique faculty has that prospect before him. Mr. Crane's talent is unique; nobody can question that. America may well be proud of him, for he has just that perfect mastery of form which artists of the Latin races often produce, but the Teutonic and Anglo-Saxon races very rarely. And undoubtedly of the young school of American artists Mr. Crane is the genius—the others have their talents."

On the above criticism Conrad wrote me at the time, "The Crane thing is just—precisely just a ray of light flashed in and showing all there is."

But when I wrote that criticism, that journalistic novel *On Active Service* was yet to be published, and I did not fully comprehend Crane's training and his circumstances. I sounded a warning not against "reporting," but though he had emerged from journalism, he was still haunted by journalism and was encircled by a— well! by a crew of journalists. I remarked, "I do not think Mr. Crane can or will develop further," but pressing him were duns and debts and beckoning him was the glamour of the war-correspondent's life, and before him were editors ready for ephemeral stuff, while they shook their heads sadly over such perfect gems as *The Pace of Youth*.

* * *

We must therefore be thankful that his instinct for style emerged when his psychological genius broke out and so often possessed him in the teeth of the great stucco gods and the chinking of brass in the market place. * * * Was that genius ever appreciated by America? I doubt it, though Americans were forced to accept him, first because of the fame which *The Red Badge of Courage* brought Crane in England, and secondary because his subject was the American Civil War, a subject that could not be disregarded. On re-reading *The Red Badge of Courage* I am more than ever struck by the genius with which Crane, in imagination, pierced to the essentials of War. Without any experience of war at the time, Crane was essentially true to the psychological core of war—if not to actualities. He naturally underestimated the checks placed by physical strain and fatigue on the faculties, as well as war's malignant, cold ironies, its prosaic dreadfulness, its dreary, deadening tedium. But as Goethe has pointed out, the artist has a license to ignore actualities, if he is obeying inner, æsthetic laws. And Crane's subject was the passions, the passions of destruction, fear, pride, rage, shame and exaltation in the heat of action. The deep artistic unity of *The Red Badge of Courage,* is fused in its flaming, spiritual intensity, in the fiery ardour with which the shock of the Federal and Confederate armies is imaged. The torrential force and impetus, the check, sullen recoil and reforming of shattered regiments, and the renewed onslaught and obstinate resistance of brigades and divisions are visualized with extraordinary force and colour. If the sordid grimness of carnage, is partially screened, the feeling of War's cumulative rapacity, of its breaking pressure and fluctuating tension is caught with wonderful fervour and freshness of style. It is of course, the work of ardent youth, but when Crane returned from the Graeco-Turkish war he said to Conrad, "My picture of war was all right! I have found it as I imagined it." * * *

And here I must enlarge and amend my criticism of 1898 by saying that two qualities in especial, combined to form Crane's unique quality, viz his wonderful insight into, and mastery of the primary passions, and his irony deriding the swelling emotions of the self. It is his irony that checks the emotional intensity of his delineation, and suddenly reveals passion at high tension in the clutch of the implacable tides of life. It is the perfect fusion of these two forces of passion and irony that creates Crane's spiritual background, and raises his work, at its finest, into the higher zone of man's tragic conflict with the universe. His irony is seen in its purest form in *Black Riders*, 1896, a tiny collection of *vers libres*, as sharp in their naked questioning as sword blades. These verses pierce with dreadful simplicity certain illusions of unregarding sages, whose earnest commentaries pour, and will continue to pour from the groaning press. * * * Crane holds a peculiar niche in American literature. Where it is weak, viz in the æsthetic and psychologically truthful delineation of passion, Stephen Crane is a master. And masters are rare, yes how rare are masters, let the men of Crane's generation, looking back on the twenty years since his death, decide.

H. G. WELLS

From Stephen Crane from an English Standpoint†

The untimely death at thirty of Stephen Crane robs English literature of an interesting and significant figure, and the little world of those who write, of a stout friend and a pleasant comrade. For a year and more he had been ailing. The bitter hardships of his Cuban expedition had set its mark upon mind and body alike, and the slow darkling of the shadow upon him must have been evident to all who were not blinded by their confidence in what he was yet to do. Altogether, I knew Crane for less than a year, and I saw him for the last time hardly more than seven weeks ago. He was then in a hotel at Dover, lying still and comfortably wrapped about, before an open window and the calm and spacious sea. If you would figure him as I saw him, you must think of him as a face of a type very typically American, long and spare, with very straight hair and straight features and long, quiet hands and hollow eyes, moving slowly, smiling and speaking slowly, with that deliberate New Jersey manner he had, and lapsing from speech again into a quiet contemplation of his ancient enemy. For it was the sea that had taken his strength, the same sea that now shone, level waters beyond level waters, with here and there a minute, shining ship, warm and tranquil beneath the tranquil evening sky. Yet I felt

† The *North American Review*, CLXXI (August, 1900), 233–42. Wells (1866–1946), who became the most successful "journalist" among serious English authors of Crane's generation, perceptively analyzes the journalistic hazards which contributed to the tragedy of Crane's last four years.

scarcely a suspicion then that this was a last meeting. One might have seen it all, perhaps. He was thin and gaunt and wasted, too weak for more than a remembered jest and a greeting and good wishes. It did not seem to me in any way credible that he would reach his refuge in the Black Forest only to die at the journey's end. It will be a long time yet before I can fully realize that he is no longer a contemporary of mine; that the last I saw of him was, indeed, final and complete.

Though my personal acquaintance with Crane was so soon truncated, I have followed his work for all the four years it has been known in England. I have always been proud, and now I am glad, that, however obscurely, I also was in the first chorus of welcome that met his coming. It is, perhaps, no great distinction for me; he was abundantly praised; but, at least, I was early and willing to praise him when I was wont to be youthfully jealous of my praises. His success in England began with the *Red Badge of Courage,* which did, indeed, more completely than any other book has done for many years, take the reading public by storm. Its freshness of method, its vigor of imagination, its force of color and its essential freedom from many traditions that dominate this side of the Atlantic, came—in spite of the previous shock of Mr. Kipling—with a positive effect of impact. It was a new thing, in a new school. When one looked for sources, one thought at once of Tolstoy; but, though it was clear that Tolstoy had exerted a powerful influence upon the conception, if not the actual writing, of the book, there still remained something entirely original and novel. To a certain extent, of course, that was the new man as an individual; but, to at least an equal extent, it was the new man as a typical young American, free at last, as no generation of Americans have been before, of any regard for English criticism, comment, or tradition, and applying to literary work the conception and theories of the cosmopolitan studio with a quite American directness and vigor. For the great influence of the studio on Crane cannot be ignored; in the persistent selection of the essential elements of an impression, in the ruthless exclusion of mere information, in the direct vigor with which the selected points are made, there is Whistler even more than there is Tolstoy in the *Red Badge of Courage.* And witness this, taken almost haphazard:

"At nightfall the column broke into regimental pieces, and the fragments went into the fields to camp. Tents sprang up like strange plants. Camp fires, like red, peculiar blossoms, dotted the night. . . . From this little distance the many fires, with the black forms of men passing to and fro before the crimson rays, made weird and satanic effects."

And here again; consider the daring departure from all academic requirements in this void countenance:

"A warm and strong hand clasped the youth's languid fingers for an instant, and then he heard a cheerful and audacious whistling as the man strode away. As he who had so befriended him was thus passing out of his life, it suddenly occurred to the youth that he had not once seen his face."

I do not propose to add anything here to the mass of criticism upon this remarkable book. Like everything else which has been abundantly praised, it has occasionally been praised "all wrong"; and I suppose that it must have been said hundreds of times that this book is a subjective study of the typical soldier in war. But Mr. George Wyndham, himself a soldier of experience, has pointed out in an admirable preface to a reissue of this and other of Crane's war studies that the hero of the *Red Badge* is, and is intended to be, altogether a more sensitive and imaginative person than the ordinary man. He is the idealist, the dreamer of boastful things brought suddenly to the test of danger and swift occasions and the presence of death. To this theme Crane returned several times, and particularly in a story called *Death and the Child* that was written after the Greek war. That story is considered by very many of Crane's admirers as absolutely his best. I have carefully reread it in deference to opinions I am bound to respect, but I still find it inferior to the earlier work. The generalized application is, to my taste, a little too evidently underlined; there is just that touch of insistence that prevails so painfully at times in Victor Hugo's work, as of a writer not sure of his reader, not happy in his reader, and seeking to drive his implication (of which also he is not quite sure) home. The child is not a natural child; there is no happy touch to make it personally alive; it is THE CHILD, something unfalteringly big; a large, pink, generalized thing. I cannot help but see it, after the fashion of a Vatican cherub. The fugitive runs panting to where, all innocent of the battle about it, it plays; and he falls down breathless to be asked, "Are you a man?" One sees the intention clearly enough; but in the later story it seems to me there is a new ingredient that is absent from the earlier stories, an ingredient imposed on Crane's natural genius from without—a concession to the demands of a criticism it had been wiser, if less modest, in him to disregard—criticism that missed this quality of generalization and demanded it, even though it had to be artificially and deliberately introduced.

Following hard upon the appearance of the *Red Badge of Cour-*

age in England came reprints of two books, *Maggie* and *George's Mother*, that had already appeared in America six years earlier. Their reception gave Crane his first taste of the peculiarities of the new public he had come upon. These stories seem to me in no way inferior to the *Red Badge*; and at times there are passages, the lament of Maggie's mother at the end of *Maggie*, for example, that it would be hard to beat by any passage from the later book. But on all hands came discouragement or tepid praise. The fact of it is, there had been almost an orgy of praise—for England, that is; and ideas and adjectives and phrases were exhausted. To write further long reviews on works displaying the same qualities as had been already amply discussed in the notices of the *Red Badge* would be difficult and laborious; while to admit an equal excellence and deny an equal prominence would be absurd. * * *

And since Crane had demonstrated, beyond all cavil, that he could sit at home and, with nothing but his wonderful brain and his wonderful induction from recorded things, build up the truest and most convincing picture of war; since he was a fastidious and careful worker, intensely subjective in his mental habit; since he was a man of fragile physique and of that unreasonable courage that will wreck the strongest physique; and since, moreover, he was habitually a bad traveler, losing trains and luggage and missing connections even in the orderly circumstances of peace, it was clearly the most reasonable thing in the world to propose, it was received with the applause of two hemispheres as a most right and proper thing, that he should go as a war correspondent, first to Greece and then to Cuba. Thereby, and for nothing but disappointment and bitterness, he utterly wrecked his health. He came into comparison with men as entirely his masters in this work as he was the master of all men in his own; and I read even in the most punctual of his obituary notices the admission of his journalistic failure. I have read, too, that he brought back nothing from these expeditions. But, indeed, even not counting his death, he brought back much. On his way home from Cuba he was wrecked, and he wrote the story of the nights and days that followed the sinking of the ship with a simplicity and vigor that even he cannot rival elsewhere.

The Open Boat is to my mind, beyond all question, the crown of all his work. It has all the stark power of the earlier stories, with a new element of restraint; the color is as full and strong as ever, fuller and stronger, indeed; but those chromatic splashes that at times deafen and confuse in the *Red Badge*, those images that astonish rather than enlighten, are disciplined and controlled.

"That and *Flanagan*,"† he told me, with a philosophical laugh, "was all I got out of Cuba." I cannot say whether they were worth the price, but I am convinced that these two things are as immortal as any work of any living man. And the way *The Open Boat* begins, no stress, plain—even a little gray and flattish:

"None of them knew the color of the sky. Their eyes glanced level, and were fastened upon the waves that swept toward them. These waves were of the hue of slate, save for the tops, which were of foaming white, and all of the men knew the color of the sea. The horizon narrowed and widened, and dipped and rose, and at all times its edge was jagged with waves that seemed thrust up in points like rocks.

Many a man ought to have a bathtub larger than the boat which here rode upon the sea. These waves were most wrongfully and barbarously abrupt and tall, and each froth top was a problem in small-boat navigation."

From that beginning, the story mounts and mounts over the waves, wave frothing after wave, each wave a threat, and the men toil and toil and toil again; by insensible degrees the day lights the waves to green and olive, and the foam grows dazzling. . . .

The Open Boat gives its title to a volume containing, in addition to that and *Flanagan*, certain short pieces. One of these others, at least, is also to my mind a perfect thing, *The Wise Men*. It tells of the race between two bartenders in the city of Mexico, and I cannot imagine how it could possibly have been better told. And in this volume, too, is that other masterpiece—the one I deny—*Death and the Child*.

Now I do not know how Crane took the reception of this book, for he was not the man to babble of his wrongs; but I cannot conceive how it could have been anything but a grave disappointment to him. To use the silly phrase of the literary shopman, "the vogue of the short story" was already over; rubbish, pure rubbish, provided only it was lengthy, had resumed its former precedence again in the reviews, in the publishers' advertisements, and on the library and booksellers' counters. The book was taken as a trivial by-product, its author was exhorted to abandon this production of "brilliant fragments"—anything less than fifty thousand words is a fragment to the writer of literary columns—and to make that "sustained effort," that architectural undertaking, that alone impresses the commercial mind. * * * I think it is indisputable that the quality of this reception, which a more self-satisfied or less sensitive

---

† "Flanagan and His Short Filibustering Adventure" had appeared in *McClure's Magazine,* October, 1897, and was collected in *The Open Boat and Other Tales of Adventure* in 1898 [Eds.]

man than Crane might have ignored, did react very unfavorably upon his work. They put him out of conceit with these brief intense efforts in which his peculiar strength was displayed.

It was probably such influence that led him to write *The Third Violet*. I do not know certainly, but I imagine, that the book was to be a demonstration, and it is not a successful demonstration, that Crane could write a charming love story. It is the very simple affair of an art student and a summer boarder, with the more superficial incidents of their petty encounters set forth in a forcible, objective manner that is curiously hard and unsympathetic. The characters act, and on reflection one admits they act, *true*, but the play of their emotions goes on behind the curtain of the style, and all the enrichments of imaginative appeal that make love beautiful are omitted. Yet, though the story as a whole fails to satisfy, there are many isolated portions of altogether happy effectiveness, a certain ride behind an ox cart, for example. Much more surely is *On Active Service* an effort, and in places a painful effort, to fit his peculiar gift to the uncongenial conditions of popular acceptance. It is the least capable and least satisfactory of all Crane's work.

While these later books were appearing, and right up to his last fatal illness, Crane continued to produce fresh war pictures that show little or no falling off in vigor of imagination and handling; and, in addition, he was experimenting with verse. In that little stone-blue volume, *War Is Kind*, and in the earlier *Black Riders*, the reader will find a series of acute and vivid impressions and many of the finer qualities of Crane's descriptive prose, but he will not find any novel delights of melody or cadence or any fresh aspects of Crane's personality. There remain some children's stories to be published and an unfinished romance. With that the tale of his published work ends, and the career of one of the most brilliant, most significant, and most distinctively American of all English writers comes to its unanticipated *finis*.

It would be absurd, here and now, to attempt to apportion any relativity of importance to Crane, to say that he was greater than A or less important than B. That class-list business is, indeed, best left forever to the newspaper plebiscite and the library statistician; among artists, whose sole just claim to recognition and whose sole title to immortality must necessarily be the possession of unique qualities, that is to say, of unclassifiable factors, these gradations are absurd. Suffice it that, even before his death, Crane's right to be counted in the hierarchy of those who have made a permanent addition to the great and growing fabric of English letters was not only assured, but conceded. To define his position in time, however, and in relation to periods and modes of writing will be a more reasonable undertaking; and it seems to me that, when at last the true proportions can be seen, Crane will be found to occupy a position singularly cardinal. He was a New Englander† of Puritan lineage, and the son of a long tradition of literature. There had been many Cranes who wrote before him. He has shown me a shelf of books, for the most part the pious and theological works of various antecedent Stephen Cranes. He had been at some pains to gather together these alien products of his kin. For the most part they seemed little, insignificant books, and one opened them to read the beaten *clichés*, the battered, outworn phrases, of a movement that has ebbed. Their very size and binding suggested a dying impulse, that very same impulse that in its prime had carried the magnificence of Milton's imagery and the pomp and splendors of Milton's prose. In Crane that impulse was altogether dead. He began stark— I find all through this brief notice I have been repeating that in a dozen disguises, "freedom from tradition," "absolute directness," and the like—as though he came into the world of letters without ever a predecessor. In style, in method, and in all that is distinctively *not* found in his books, he is sharply defined, the expression in literary art of certain enormous repudiations. Was ever a man before who wrote of battles so abundantly as he has done, and never had a word, never a word from first to last, of the purpose and justification of the war? And of the God of Battles, no more than the battered name; "Hully Gee!"—the lingering trace of the Deity! And of the sensuousness and tenderness of love, so much as one can find in *The Third Violet!* Any richness of allusion, any melody or balance of phrase, the half quotation that refracts and softens and enriches the statement, the momentary digression that opens like a window upon beautiful or distant things, are not merely absent, but obviously and sedulously avoided. It is as if the racial thought and tradition had been razed from his mind and its site plowed and salted. He is more than himself in this; he is the first expression of the opening mind of a new period, or, at least, the early emphatic phase of a new initiative— beginning, as a growing mind must needs begin, with the record of impressions, a record of a vigor and intensity beyond all precedent.

† In the first paragraph of this essay, Wells referred to Crane's "deliberate New Jersey manner"; Crane was in fact born in Newark, New Jersey [Editors].

JOSEPH CONRAD

[Recollections of Crane and His War Book]†

* * *

My wife's recollection is that Crane and I met in London in October, 1897, and that he came to see us for the first time in our Essex home in the following November.

I have mentioned in a short paper written two years ago that it was Mr. S. S. Pawling, partner in the publishing firm of Mr. Heinemann, who brought us together. It was done at Stephen Crane's own desire.

* * *

I can safely say that I earned this precious friendship by something like ten months of strenuous work with my pen. It took me just that time to write *The Nigger of the "Narcissus,"* working at what I always considered a very high pressure. It was on the ground of the authorship of that book that Crane wanted to meet me. Nothing could have been more flattering than to discover that the author of *The Red Badge of Courage* appreciated my effort to present a group of men held together by a common loyalty and a common perplexity in a struggle not with human enemies, but with the hostile conditions testing their faithfulness to the conditions of their own calling.

Apart from the imaginative analysis of his own temperament tried by the emotions of a battlefield, Stephen Crane dealt in his book with the psychology of the mass—the army; while I—in mine —had been dealing with the same subject on a much smaller scale and in more specialized conditions—the crew of a merchant ship, brought to the test of what I may venture to call the moral problem of conduct. This may be thought a very remote connection between

† Reprinted by permission of the Joseph Conrad Estate and J. M. Dent & Sons Ltd. from *Last Essays*, New York, 1926; pp. 93–124, *passim*. Joseph Conrad (1857–1924) became Crane's intimate friend in England during his last three years. Conrad's first and famous novel, *Almayer's Folly*, and Crane's masterpiece both appeared in 1895. When the two writers first met in London in 1897, Conrad had published his third novel, *The Nigger of the Narcissus*, which he shrewdly likened to *The Red Badge* because Crane's book and his each portrayed "A group of men held together by a common loyalty and a common perplexity in a struggle not with human enemies but with hostile conditions testing their faithfulness." The excerpt from *Last Essays* in the present collection includes relevant passages from two consecutive essays by Conrad: "A Preface to Thomas Beer's *Stephen Crane*," New York, 1923; and "His War Book: A Preface to Stephen Crane's *The Red Badge of Courage*," London, 1925.

these two works and the idea may seem too far-fetched to be mentioned here; but that was my undoubted feeling at the time. It is a fact that I considered Crane, by virtue of his creative experience with *The Red Badge of Courage*, as eminently fit to pronounce a judgment on my first consciously planned attempt to render the truth of a phase of life in the terms of my own temperament with all the sincerity of which I was capable.

* * *

. . . this Introduction, which I am privileged to write, can only trace what is left on earth of our personal intercourse, which was even more short and fleeting than it may appear from the record of dates. October, 1897–May, 1900. And out of that beggarly tale of months must be deducted the time of his absence from England during the Spanish-American War, and of his visit to the United States shortly before the beginning of his last illness. Even when he was in England our intercourse was not so close and frequent as the warmth of our friendship would have wished it to be. We both lived in the country and, though not very far from each other, in different counties. I had my work to do, always in conditions which made it a matter of urgency. He had his own tasks and his own visions to attend to. * * * He had a quiet smile that charmed and frightened one. It made you pause by something revelatory it cast over his whole physiognomy, not like a ray but like a shadow. I often asked myself what it could be, that quality that checked one's care-free mood, and now I think I have had my answer. It was the smile of a man who knows that his time will not be long on this earth.

I would not for a moment wish to convey the impression of melancholy in connection with my memories of Stephen Crane. I saw his smile first over the tablecloth in a restaurant. We shook hands with intense gravity and a direct stare at each other, after the manner of two children told to make friends. It was under the encouraging gaze of Sydney Pawling, who, a much bigger man than either of us and possessed of a deep voice, looked like a grown-up person entertaining two strange small boys—protecting and slightly anxious as to the experiment. He knew very little of either of us. I was a new author and Crane was a new arrival. It was the meeting of *The Red Badge* and *The Nigger* in the presence of their publisher; but as far as our personalities went we were three strangers breaking bread together for the first time. Yet it was as pleasantly easy a meal as any I can remember. Crane talked in his characteristic deliberate manner about Greece at war. I had already sensed the man's intense earnestness underlying his quiet surface. Every time he raised his eyes, that secret quality (for his voice was careless) of his soul was betrayed in a clear flash. Most of the true Stephen Crane was in his eyes, most of his strength at any rate, though it was apparent also in his other features, as, for instance, in the structure of his forehead, the deep solid arches under the fair eyebrows.

Some people saw traces of weakness in the lower part of his face. What I could see there was a hint of the delicacy of sentiment, of the inborn fineness of nature which this man, whose life had been anything but a stroll through a rose-garden, had managed to preserve like a sacred heritage. I say heritage, not acquisition, for it was not and could not have been acquired. One could depend on it on all occasions; whereas the cultivated kind is apt to show ugly gaps under very slight provocation. The coarseness of the professedly delicate must be very amusing to the misanthrope. But Crane was no enemy of his kind. That sort of thing did not amuse him. As to his own temper, it was proof against anger and scorn, as I can testify, having seen him both angry and scornful, always quietly, on fitting occasions. Contempt and indignation never broke the surface of his moderation, simply because he had no surface. He was all through of the same material, incapable of affectation of any kind, of any pitiful failure of generosity for the sake of personal advantage, or even from sheer exasperation which must find its relief. * * * On a certain occasion (it was at Brede Place), after two amazingly conceited idiots had gone away, I said to him, "Stevie, you brood like a distant thundercloud." He had retired early to the other end of the room, and from there had sent out, now and then, a few words, more like the heavy drops of rain that precede the storm than growls of thunder. Poor Crane, if he could look black enough at times, never thundered; though I have no doubt he could have been dangerous if he had liked. There always seemed to be something (not timidity) which restrained him, not from within but, I could not help fancying, from outside, with an effect as of a whispered *memento mori* in the ear of a reveller not lost to the sense of grace. * * * Though the word is discredited now and may sound pretentious, I will say that there was in Crane a strain of chivalry which made him safe to trust with one's life.

* * *

What I discovered very early in our acquaintance was that Crane had not the face of a lucky man. That certitude came to me at our first meeting while I sat opposite him listening to his simple tales of Greece, while S. S. Pawling presided at the initiatory feast— friendly and debonair, looking solidly anchored in the stream of life, and very reassuring, like a big, prosperous ship to the sides of which we two in our tossing little barks could hook on for safety. He was interested in the tales too; and the best proof of it is that when he looked at his watch and jumped up, saying, "I must leave you two now," it was very near four o'clock. Nearly a whole afternoon wasted, for an English business man.

No such consideration of waste or duty agitated Crane and myself. The sympathy that, even in regard of the very few years allotted to our friendship, may be said to have sprung up instantaneously between us, was the most undemonstrative case of that sort in the last century. We not only did not tell each other of it (which would have been missish), but even without entering formally into a previous agreement to remain together, we went out and began to walk side by side in the manner of two tramps without home, occupation, or care for the next night's shelter. We certainly paid no heed to direction. The first thing I noticed were the Green Park railings, when to my remark that he had seen no war before he went to Greece, Crane made answer: "No. But *The Red Badge* is all right." I assured him that I never had doubted it; and, since the title of the work had been pronounced for the first time, feeling I must do something to show I had read it, I said shyly: "I like your General." He knew at once what I was alluding to, but said not a word. Nothing could have been more tramp-like than our silent pacing, elbow to elbow, till, after we had left Hyde Park Corner behind us, Crane uttered with his quiet earnestness the words: "I like your young man—I can just see him." Nothing could have been more characteristic of the depth of our three-hour-old intimacy than that each of us should have selected for praise the merest by-the-way vignette of a minor character. This was positively the only allusion we made that afternoon to our immortal works. Indeed we talked very little of them at any time, and then always selecting some minor point for particular mention; which, after all, is not a bad way of showing an affectionate appreciation of a piece of work done by a friend.

* * *

The articulate literary conscience at our elbow was Edward Garnett. He, of course, was worth listening to. His analytical appreciation (or appreciative analysis) of Crane's art, in the London *Academy* of 17th December, 1898,[1] goes to the root of the matter with Edward's almost uncanny insight, and a well-balanced sympathy with the blind, pathetic striving of the artist towards a complete realization of his individual gift. How highly Edward Garnett rated

1. Extended and republished in the volume *Friday Nights*.

Crane's gift is recorded in the conclusions of that admirable and, within the limits of its space, masterly article of some two columns, where at the end are set down such affirmative phrases as: "The chief impressionist of the age." . . . "Mr. Crane's talent is unique" . . . and where he hails him as "the creator of fresh rhythms and phrases," while the very last words state confidently that: "Undoubtedly, of the young school it is Mr. Crane who is the genius—the others have their talents."

My part here being not that of critic but of private friend, all I will say is that I agreed warmly at the time with that article, which from the quoted phrases might be supposed a merely enthusiastic pronouncement, but on reading will be found to be based on that calm sagacity which Edward Garnett, for all his fiery zeal in the cause of letters, could always summon for the judgment of matters emotional—as all response to the various forms of art must be in the main. I had occasion to re-read it last year in its expanded form in a collection of literary essays of great, now almost historical, interest in the record of American and English imaginative literature. I found there a passage or two, not bearing precisely on Crane's work but giving a view of his temperament, on which of course his art was based; and of the conditions, moral and material, under which he had to put forth his creative faculties and his power of steady composition.

* * *

His greatest extravagance was hospitality, of which I, too, had my share; often in the company, I am sorry to say, of men who after sitting at his board chose to speak of him and of his wife slightingly. Having some rudimentary sense of decency, their behaviour while actually under the Cranes' roof often produced on me a disagreeable impression. Once I ventured to say to him, "You are too good-natured, Stephen." He gave me one of his quiet smiles, that seemed to hint so poignantly at the vanity of all things, and after a period of silence remarked: "I am glad those Indians are gone." He was surrounded by men who, secretly envious, hostile to the real quality of his genius (and a little afraid of it), were also in antagonism with the essential fineness of his nature. But enough of them. *Pulvis et umbra sunt.* I mean even those that may be alive yet. * * * I have heard one of these "friends" hint before several other Philistines that Crane could not write his tales without getting drunk!

Putting aside the gross palpable stupidity of such a statement—which the creature gave out as an instance of the artistic temperament—I am in a position to disclose what may have been the foundation of this piece of gossip. I have seen repeatedly Crane at work. A small jug of still smaller ale would be brought into the study at about ten o'clock; Crane would pour out some of it into a glass and settle himself at the long table at which he used to write in Brede Place. I would take a book and settle myself at the other end of the same table, with my back to him; and for two hours or so not a sound would be heard in that room. At the end of that time Crane would say suddenly: "I won't do any more now, Joseph." He would have covered three of his large sheets with his regular, legible, perfectly controlled handwriting, with no more than a half-a-dozen erasures—mostly single words—in the whole lot. It seemed to me always a perfect miracle in the way of mastery over material and expression. Most of the ale would be still in the glass, and how flat by that time I don't like to think! The most amusing part was to see Crane, as if moved by some obscure sense of duty, drain the last drop of that untempting remnant before we left the room to stroll to and fro in front of the house while waiting for lunch. Such is the origin of some of these gleeful whispers making up the Crane legend of "unrestrained temperament." I have known various sorts of temperaments—some perfidious and some lying—but "unrestrained temperament" is mere parrot talk. It has no meaning. But it was suggestive. It was founded on Crane's visits to town, during which I more than once met him there. We used to spend afternoons and evenings together, and I did not see any of his supposed revels in progress; nor yet have I ever detected any after effects of them on any occasion. Neither have I ever seen anybody who would own to having been a partner in those excesses—if only to the extent of standing by charitably—which would have been a noble part to play. I daresay all those "excesses" amounted to very little more than the one in which he asked me to join him in the following letter. It is the only note I have kept from the very few which we exchanged. The reader will see why it is one of my most carefully preserved possessions.

RAVENSBROOK, OXTED,
March 17 (1899).

MY DEAR CONRAD:
I am enclosing you a bit of MS. under the supposition that you might like to keep it in remembrance of my warm and endless friendship for you. I am still hoping that you will consent to Stokes' invitation to come to the Savage† on Saturday night. Can-

† The Savage Club [Editors].

not you endure it? Give my affectionate remembrances to Mrs. Conrad and my love to the boy.

Yours always,
STEPHEN CRANE.

P. S. You must accept says Cora—and I—our invitation to come home with me on Sat. night.

I joined him. We had a very amusing time with the Savages. Afterwards Crane refused to go home till the last train. Evidence of what somebody has called his "unrestrained temperament," no doubt. So we went and sat at Gatti's, I believe—unless it was in a Bodega which existed then in that neighbourhood—and talked. I have a vivid memory of this awful debauch because it was on that evening that Crane told me of a subject for a story—a very exceptional thing for him to do. He called it "The Predecessor." I could not recall now by what capricious turns and odd associations of thought he reached the enthusiastic conclusion that it would make a good play, and that we must do it together. He wanted me to share in a certain success—"a dead sure thing," he said. His was an unrestrainedly generous temperament. But let that pass. I must have been specially predisposed, because I caught the infection at once. There and then we began to build up the masterpiece, interrupting each other eagerly, for, I don't know how it was, the air around us had suddenly grown thick with felicitous suggestions. We carried on this collaboration as far as the railway time-table would let us, and then made a break for the last train.

* * *

Thirteen years afterwards I made use, half consciously, of the shadow of the primary idea of "The Predecessor" in one of my short tales which were serialized in the *Metropolitan Magazine* * * * this the mere distorted shadow of what we two used to talk about in a fantastic mood; but now and then, as I wrote, I had the feeling that he had the right to come and look over my shoulder. But he never came. I received no suggestions from him, subtly conveyed without words. There will never be any collaboration for us now. But I wonder, were he alive, whether he would be pleased with the tale. I don't know. Perhaps not. Or, perhaps, after picking up the volume with that detached air I remember so well and turning over page after page in silence, he would suddenly read aloud a line or two and then, looking straight into my eyes as was his wont on such occasions, say with all the intense earnestness of affection that was in him: "I—like—that, Joseph."

One † of the most enduring memories of my literary life is the sensation produced by the appearance in 1895 of Crane's *Red Badge of Courage* in a small volume belonging to Mr. Heinemann's Pioneer Series of Modern Fiction. * * * Crane's work detonated on the mild din of that attack on our literary sensibilities with the impact and force of a twelve-inch shell charged with a very high explosive. Unexpected it fell amongst us; and its fall was followed by a great outcry.

Not of consternation, however. The energy of that projectile hurt nothing and no one (such was its good fortune), and delighted a good many. It delighted soldiers, men of letters, men in the street; it was welcomed by all lovers of personal expression as a genuine revelation, satisfying the curiosity of a world in which war and love have been subjects of song and story ever since the beginning of articulate speech.

Here we had an artist, a man not of experience but a man inspired, a seer with a gift for rendering the significant on the surface of things and with an incomparable insight into primitive emotions, who, in order to give us the image of war, had looked profoundly into his own breast. We welcomed him. As if the whole vocabulary of praise had been blown up sky-high by this missile from across the Atlantic, a rain of words descended on our heads, words well or ill chosen, chunks of pedantic praise and warm appreciation, clever words, and words of real understanding, platitudes, and felicities of criticism, but all as sincere in their response as the striking piece of work which set so many critical pens scurrying over the paper.

One of the most interesting, if not the most valuable, of printed criticisms was perhaps that of Mr. George Wyndham, soldier, man of the world, and in a sense a man of letters. He went into the whole question of war literature, at any rate during the nineteenth century * * * He rendered justice to the interest of what soldiers themselves could tell us, but confessed that to gratify the curiosity of the potential combatant who lurks in most men as to the picturesque aspects and emotional reactions of a battle we must go to the artist with his Heaven-given faculty of words at the service of his divination as to what the truth of things is and must be. He comes to the conclusion that:

"Mr. Crane has contrived a masterpiece."

"Contrived"—that word of disparaging sound is the last word I would have used in connection with any piece of work by Stephen

† Conrad's second essay, entitled "His War Book," begins here; it was published two years later than the preceding reminiscences. See bibliographical citation at the beginning of this selection [Editors].

Crane, who in his art (as indeed in his private life) was the least "contriving" of men. But as to "masterpiece," there is no doubt that *The Red Badge of Courage* is that, if only because of the marvellous accord of the vivid impressionistic description of action on that woodland battlefield, and the imaged style of the analysis of the emotions in the inward moral struggle going on in the breast of one individual—the Young Soldier of the book, the protagonist of the monodrama presented to us in an effortless succession of graphic and coloured phrases.

Stephen Crane places his Young Soldier in an untried regiment. And this is well contrived—if any contrivance there be in a spontaneous piece of work which seems to spurt and flow like a tapped stream from the depths of the writer's being. In order that the revelation should be complete, the Young Soldier has to be deprived of the moral support which he would have found in a tried body of men matured in achievement to the consciousness of its worth. His regiment had been tried by nothing but days of waiting for the order to move; so many days that it and the Youth within it have come to think of themselves as merely "a part of a vast blue demonstration." The army had been lying camped near a river, idle and fretting, till the moment when Stephen Crane lays hold of it at dawn with masterly simplicity: "The cold passed reluctantly from the earth. . . ." These are the first words of the war book which was to give him his crumb of fame.

The whole of that opening paragraph is wonderful in the homely dignity of the indicated lines of the landscape, and the shivering awakening of the army at the break of the day before the battle. In the next, with a most effective change to racy colloquialism of narrative, the action which motivates, sustains and feeds the inner drama forming the subject of the book, begins with the Tall Soldier going down to the river to wash his shirt. He returns waving his garment above his head. He had heard at fifth-hand from somebody that the army is going to move to-morrow. The only immediate effect of this piece of news is that a Negro teamster, who had been dancing a jig on a wooden box in a ring of laughing soldiers, finds himself suddenly deserted. He sits down mournfully. For the rest, the Tall Soldier's excitement is met by blank disbelief, profane grumbling, an invincible incredulity. But the regiment is somehow sobered. One feels it, though no symptoms can be noticed. It does not know what a battle is, neither does the Young Soldier. He retires from the babbling throng into what seems a rather comfortable dugout and lies down with his hands over his eyes to think. Thus the drama begins.

He perceives suddenly that he had looked upon wars as historical phenomenons of the past. He had never believed in war in his own country. It had been a sort of play affair. He had been drilled, inspected, marched for months, till he has despaired "of ever seeing a Greek-like struggle. Such were no more. Men were better or more timid. Secular and religious education had effaced the throat-grappling instinct, or else firm finance held in check the passions."

Very modern this touch. We can remember thoughts like these round about the year 1914. That Young Soldier is representative of mankind in more ways than one, and first of all in his ignorance. His regiment had listened to the tales of veterans, "tales of gray bewhiskered hordes chewing tobacco with unspeakable valour and sweeping along like the Huns." Still, he cannot put his faith in veterans' tales. Recruits were their prey. They talked of blood, fire, and sudden death, but much of it might have been lies. They were in no wise to be trusted. And the question arises before him whether he will or will not "run from a battle"? He does not know. He cannot know. A little panic fear enters his mind. He jumps up and asks himself aloud, "Good Lord, what's the matter with me?" This is the first time his words are quoted, on this day before the battle. He dreads not danger, but fear itself. He stands before the unknown. He would like to prove to himself by some reasoning process that he will not "run from the battle." And in his unblooded regiment he can find no help. He is alone with the problem of courage.

In this he stands for the symbol of all untried men.

Some critics have estimated him a morbid case. I cannot agree to that. The abnormal cases are of the extremes; of those who crumple up at the first sight of danger, and of those of whom their fellows say "He doesn't know what fear is." Neither will I forget the rare favourites of the gods whose fiery spirit is only soothed by the fury and clamour of a battle. Of such was General Picton of Peninsular fame. But the lot of the mass of mankind is to know fear, the decent fear of disgrace. Of such is the Young Soldier of *The Red Badge of Courage*. He only seems exceptional because he has got inside of him Stephen Crane's imagination, and is presented to us with the insight and the power of expression of an artist whom a just and severe critic, on a review of all his work, has called the foremost impressionist of his time; as Sterne was the greatest impressionist, but in a different way, of his age.

This is a generalized, fundamental judgment. More superficially both Zola's *La Débâcle* and Tolstoi's *War and Peace* were mentioned by critics in connection with Crane's war book. But Zola's main concern was with the downfall of the imperial régime he fancied he was portraying; and in Tolstoi's book the subtle presentation of Rostov's squadron under fire for the first time is a mere episode lost in a mass of other matter, like a handful of pebbles in a heap of sand. I could not see the relevancy. Crane was concerned with elemental truth only; and in any case I think that as an artist he is non-comparable. He dealt with what is enduring, and was the most detached of men.

That is why his book is short. Not quite two hundred pages. Gems are small. This monodrama, which happy inspiration or unerring instinct has led him to put before us in narrative form, is contained between the opening words I have already quoted and a phrase on page 194 of the English edition, which runs: "He had been to touch the great death, and found that, after all, it was but the great death. He was a man."

On these words the action ends. We are only given one glimpse of the victorious army at dusk, under the falling rain, "a procession of weary soldiers became a bedraggled train, despondent and muttering, marching with churning effort in a trough of liquid brown mud under a low wretched sky . . .", while the last ray of the sun falls on the river through a break in the leaden clouds.

This war book, so virile and so full of gentle sympathy, in which not a single declamatory sentiment defaces the genuine verbal felicity, welding analysis and description in a continuous fascination of individual style, had been hailed by the critics as the herald of a brilliant career. Crane himself very seldom alluded to it, and always with a wistful smile. Perhaps he was conscious that, like the mortally wounded Tall Soldier of his book, who, snatching at the air, staggers out into a field to meet his appointed death on the first day of battle—while the terrified Youth and the kind Tattered Soldier stand by silent, watching with awe "these ceremonies at the place of meeting"—it was his fate, too, to fall early in the fray.

HARRY HARTWICK

[The Red Badge of Nature]†

* * *

Naturalism (the philosophy of *laissez faire*) "implies that Nature considers man just another of her creatures and ignores his claim to be akin to the angels. Our strongest animal impulses are

† From *The Foreground of American Fiction*, Copyright 1934 by American Book Company. Reprinted by permission. Pp. 17–44, *passim.* Cf., below, the comparable article by C. C. Walcutt, twenty-two years later.

most fundamental to life's continuance and are therefore most to be trusted."[25] The naturalist lets Nature take its course, accepts the universe of science, and cares only for things "as they are," rather than for things "as they have been," or "should be." "What is," he agrees with Pope, "is right." Nature is a vast contrivance of wheels within wheels; man is a "piece of fate" caught in the machinery of Nature; and love is ultimately a product of the same forces that control gravitation. The world is a jungle, where men grapple with one another for life and its accessories, murder (and are in turn murdered), fly after pleasure, and resign themselves with stoic calm to whatever pain they cannot elude. Man's only duty is to discharge his energies and die, at the same time expressing his individuality as best he can. Naturalism deserts conventional ethics (which magnetize people into the strict patterns of popular opinion and social health) to espouse the neuter tempests of Nature and the winds of impulse. It regards men, not as divided into good and evil, but into strong and weak; conceives everything to be "true in its own time, place, circumstance, and untrue outside of its own place, time, circumstance";[26] and has no moral axe to grind. People, insists the naturalist, "always deceive themselves by abandoning experience to follow imaginary systems. Man is the work of Nature: he exists in Nature: he is submitted to her laws: he cannot deliver himself from them."[27] He is a poor instrument "for converting stimuli into reactions."[28]

Life is "a perpetual gushing forth of novelties," as Bergson has said. Nothing is good or bad; it is only unique. The naturalist is convinced that man is an animal, governed by his visceral impulses and desires; that his mind is a slavish echo of these bodily tropisms, and his soul an empty legend; that he is shaped and limited by factors beyond his jurisdiction; that only Nature, with its blind spasms of caprice, is real; and that men should court the simple atavistic behavior of children and savages, who have not yet been corrupted by ideas. Things, from his point of view, never progress; they merely change. "Life is a horizontal fall," and humanity always has the same quantum of folly to squander. The prime thing is to avoid ethical bookkeeping; for man is a ledger that will not balance, and "Morality is a cerebral weakness." Of pity, reason, self-control, and human sympathy, the naturalist is very skeptical. Such abstractions hold no meaning for him. He has decided to enjoy each thing for its own sake, and not for the sake of future or spiritual rewards. He has come to prefer the earth to heaven, to

25. Parrott, Thomas Marc, and Willard Thorp, *Poetry of the Transition* (1932), p. xxviii.
26. Lawrence, D. H., "Morality and the Novel," *The Golden Book* (February, 1926), III, 249.
27. Holbach, Paul H. T., *The System of Nature* (1868), I, 11.
28. London, Jack, *John Barleycorn* (1913), p. 327.

desire art for art's sake and passion for the sake of passion. With Jack London he says, "The ultimate word is I LIKE."

Nothing remains for him, save Nature and its "struggle for existence." A helpless bundle of molecules, nerves, and glands, he must take his chances with the rest of matter, live minute by minute, and capitulate to every prompting (good or bad), without attempting or being able to modify it. Frequently he leads a vegetable existence, founded upon pure intensity and the superlative. "The sin I impute to each frustrate ghost," he hears Browning intone, with approval,

> Is—the unlit lamp and the ungirt loin,
> Though the end in sight was a vice, I say.[29]

* * *

Crane's fiction plainly reflects the naturalistic concept of man as a helpless animal, driven by instinct and imprisoned in a web of forces entirely deaf to the hopes or purposes of humanity. Nowhere do we find this more clearly indicated than in "The Open Boat," his story of four shipwrecked men trying to beach their dinghy upon a rocky strip of Florida coast. On the shore there was a windmill, "a giant, standing with its back to the plight of the ants. It represented in a degree, to the correspondent, the serenity of nature amid the struggles of the individual—nature in the wind, and nature in the vision of men. She did not seem cruel to him then, nor beneficent, nor treacherous, nor wise. But she was indifferent, flatly indifferent."[5]

The Red Badge of Courage embodies this same theme. Its tumbling clouds of smoke and gunfire blow Henry Fleming, the youthful private, up and down the battle field, first in blind panic and then in wild bravery, like some tortured beast, divorced from intelligence and free will.

"He saw instantly that it would be impossible for him to escape from the regiment. It enclosed him. And there were iron laws of tradition and law on four sides. He was in a moving box."[6]

Crazed with fear, he runs away during a Confederate attack, loses his regiment, and finally discovers that it has met the charge and held the line. He wanders over the field, stricken with shame, meets a wounded friend, and sees him die in a ghastly "rendezvous with death" (which may have inspired Alan Seeger's poem). "A dull, animal-like rebellion against his fellows, war in the abstract,

29. Browning, Robert, *The Complete Poetic and Dramatic Works of Robert Browning* (1895), p. 286.
5. Follett, Wilson (ed.), *The Work of Stephen Crane* (1925–1926), XII, 55–56.
6. Follett, Wilson (ed.), *op. cit.*, I, 48.

and fate grew within him."[7] Yet a moment later he finds, as an excuse for his cowardice, that everything in Nature operates upon the principle of self-preservation.

"He threw a pine cone at a jovial squirrel, and he ran with chattering fear. High in a tree-top he stopped and, poking his head cautiously from behind a branch, looked down with an air of trepidation.

The youth felt triumphant at this exhibition. There was the law, he said. Nature had given him a sign. The squirrel, immediately upon recognizing danger, had taken to his legs without ado. He did not stand stolidly baring his furry belly to the missile, and die with an upward glance at the sympathetic heavens. On the contrary, he had fled as fast as his legs could carry him; and he was but an ordinary squirrel, too—doubtless no philosopher of his race. The youth wended, feeling that Nature was of his mind. She reinforced his argument with proofs that lived where the sun shone."[8]

Hours pass, and the private roves on, afraid to return to his brigade, until after he is struck on the head in a chance skirmish with another frightened member of his own troop. Then he picks his way back to camp in the dark, and allows his comrades to suppose that his injury has been caused by a bullet. But in succeeding encounters with the enemy he proves himself a man of maniacal valor, and reaches the conclusion that the chief thing is to resign himself to his fate, to participate in Darwin's "survival of the fittest," to play "follow the leader" with Nature, and to confront this mad, implacable world with "intestinal fortitude" and a brave smile; in one word, to become a stoic.

"He felt a quiet manhood, non-assertive but of sturdy and strong blood. He knew that he would no more quail before his guides, wherever they should point. He had been to touch the great death, and found that, after all, it was but the great death. He was a man."[9]

Armed with this new code of *laissez faire*, Henry Fleming moves on. Crane does not slay him during the war, for we meet him again in "The Lynx" and "The Veteran," where he dies trying to save a cow from a burning barn, a fighter to the end. Like Frank Norris and Jack London, Crane admired the man of action, the brawler, the trail-maker, and "men with the bark on." Hence these are the types he chose for his heroes.

* * *

From a military point of view, *The Red Badge of Courage* represents the change that has come over warfare since knights engaged

7. *Ibid.*, I, 81.
8. *Ibid.*, I, 82–83.
9. *Ibid.*, I, 199.

in strife with opponents they could see and touch. No whistling death came arching down upon King Richard the Lion-Hearted from guns sixty miles away. Man was a free creature (or so he placidly imagined), not bound to take part in a "struggle for existence," whether he wanted to or not. He had not yet decided to adopt the doctrine of *laissez faire* and "let Nature take its course" with him; in his scheme of things, there were no such arbitrary currents, no such blind forces as those that swept Crane's luckless recruit up and down the field in impotent bewilderment, at the complete mercy of Nature.

Yet the comparison becomes even more significant if, for this theater of war, we substitute the theater of life, which in medieval times housed grand opera. Men in that period looked upon the universe as a small theater, built in one stroke by God about the year 4004 B.C., and never changed. The properties, curtains, backdrops, wings, furniture, and costumes on the stage meant nothing. In fact the play itself mattered little; it was not a drama to be enjoyed in the acting. What counted was its sequel in heaven, for which it was only a prologue. * * * Naturalism, with its emphasis upon the physiological forces that rule this modern and scientific world of the twentieth century, has reduced the hero in fiction to an animal, to a savage dwarf, to nil.[13]

Crane's treatment of children is also enlightening, as a further index to the modern mind. His affection for them led him to include children in almost every one of his sketches, and even to write an entire book about them, which he entitled *Whilomville Stories* (1900). During his stay in England he became very fond of Conrad's son, and used to sit by the hour, studying him in silence; for he tended to sympathize with the naturalistic argument that children, animals, and savages (because they are untainted by civilization) must be nearer to the secrets of Nature. This is the idea of "the noble savage" which, ever since Jean Jacques Rousseau enunciated it in the eighteenth century, has governed a wide section of our thought, and buttressed with emotion the scientific foundations of *laissez faire*. It is the same thing that Havelock Ellis had in mind when he said, "Animals living in nature are everywhere beautiful; it is only among men that ugliness flourishes. Savages, nearly everywhere, are gracious and harmonious; it is only among the civilised that harshness and discord are permitted to prevail."[14]

* * *

13. *Cf.* Thompson, Alan Reynolds, "Farewell to Achilles," *The Bookman* (January, 1930), LXX, 465–471.

14. Ellis, Havelock, *Fountain of Life* (1930), p. 11.

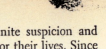

His [Crane's] poems speak of God with definite suspicion and view the world as a place where men must fight for their lives. Since God's departure before the new broom of science, no "friend behind phenomena" remains. No motive lingers in the gyrations of Nature.

> A man said to the universe:
> "Sir, I exist!"
> "However," replied the universe,
> "The fact has not created in me
> A sense of obligation."[17]

The world itself is depicted in Crane's poetry as a ship, built for no ethical reason by the hand of chance.

> So that, forever rudderless, it went upon the seas
> Going ridiculous voyages,
> Making quaint progress,
> Turning as with serious purpose
> Before stupid winds.[18]

In 1874 the French painter, Monet, labeled one of his canvases "Sunrise—An Impression," and provoked a controversy that has not yet subsided. Many artists, in his wake, discarded the old practice of "telling a story" in their pictures, and began producing those compositions "that show you in one corner a pair of stays, in another a bit of the foyer of a music hall, in another a fragment of early morning landscape, and in the middle a pair of eyes, the whole bearing the title of 'A Night Out.'"[19]

Novelists like Crane and Conrad, as well as poets like Mallarmé, were beginning to do the same thing in literature, where the technique consisted of reducing prose or verse to a procession of images. In Crane, for instance, we discover these examples:

"The guns squatted in a row like savage chiefs. They argued with abrupt violence. It was a grim pow-wow."

"The red sun was pasted in the sky like a wafer."

"Canton-flannel gulls flew near and far. Sometimes they sat down on the sea, near patches of brown seaweed that rolled over the waves with a movement like carpets on a line in a gale."

"The swing doors, snapping to and fro like ravenous lips, made gratified smacks as the saloon gorged itself with plump men."

* * *

17. Follett, Wilson (ed.), *op. cit.*, VI, 131.
18. *Ibid.*, VI, 38.

19. Hueffer, Ford Madox, "On Impressionism," *Poetry and Drama* (December, 1914), II, 175.

What we call "Impressionism as a technique is a means of recording the transitory nature of phenomena and the fluidity of motion. As a principle it is based on a philosophy of change. As painters, as writers, as musicians, impressionists are not so much men of strong convictions and deep words as they are craftsmen recording the flitting sensations of an ever changing world. The chief interest of impressionism is the ephemeral."[34] It stands for anarchy and the erasure of emphasis from life, and bears to older styles in prose and morals the same relation that "free verse" does to poetry with established rhythms and meters. It represents the collapse of consistency in thought and literature, and abolishes every form of tradition or precedence. It sees the universe, with Bertrand Russell, as "all spots and jumps, without unity, without continuity, without coherence or orderliness or any of the other properties that governesses love."[35] "*Life*," it contends, "*does not proceed by the association and addition of elements, but by dissociation and division.*"[36] Borrowing the words of a prominent contemporary philosopher, we might define it as an attempt "to solidify into discontinuous images the fluid continuity of the real."[37] * * *

According to one English critic, Edward Garnett, *The Red Badge of Courage* is "a series of episodic scenes," and Crane "the chief impressionist" of his day. His sentences jerk themselves out breathlessly, and there is a conscious, almost smart, felicity of phrasing about them. Crane's pages bleed with exquisite miniatures and startling images (a comparison rendered apt by his taste for red). Over the surface of existence darts his eye, picking out details and whipping them up into welts of fire. But while he could lay the bricks, one by one, he lacked the architectonic touch, a larger sense of the whole; he did not know how to build up connective tissues. Consequently his work is a mass of fragments, sunshine dancing on the bayonet points of a marching regiment. * * * "His superlative skill lay in the handling of isolated situations; he knew exactly how to depict them with dazzling brilliance, and he knew, too, how to analyze them with penetrating insight, but beyond that he was rather at a loss: he lacked the pedestrian talent for linking one situation to another."[41]

How far Crane was influenced in his impressionism, it is hard to say. The spirit of his age, of course, must have guided him to some extent. He was probably not inspired by the French school

---

34. Weinberg, Louis, "Current Impressionism," *The New Republic* (March 6, 1915), II, 124.
35. Russell, Bertrand, *The Scientific Outlook* (1931), p. 95.
36. Bergson, Henri, *Creative Evolution* (1911), p. 89.
37. *Ibid.*, p. 302.
41. Mencken, H. L., in his Introduction to Follett, Wilson (ed.), *op. cit.*, X, xii.

of impressionistic poetry, whose leader, Mallarmé, he fondly imagined to be an Irishman!

* * *

Much less debatable is the part that he played in establishing naturalism as a branch of American literature. It is easier to chart in Norris, London, Dreiser, Anderson, Hemingway, or Faulkner the outlines of a scientific universe with its "struggle for existence." Yet Crane was plainly a preface to naturalism, with his gaunt "soldiers of fortune," Bowery toughs, cadavers, wars, morbid catastrophes, and mood of *laissez faire*. Action and atavism flavored his stories of lean, intrepid men, matching wits, muscle, and courage in pre-Adamic conflicts; and he ushered in a whole literature, devoted to cruelty, adventure, wayfaring, lechery, and "strong, silent men" who thirst for money, "life in the raw," or women, and run amok down the peaceful avenues of society. He lived in the "dime novel" days, when the public, feverish with prosperity and indifferent to the defects of this massive country, demanded fiction of a similar quality, in which "men were men," "shot at the drop of a hat," and "died in their boots." It was, significantly enough, the age of dawning pugilism, of Sullivan, Corbett, Fitzsimmons, Jefferies, and Johnson. The old frontier had gone, to be sure, but new ones were springing up in the Klondike, Mexico, the trenches of Cuba, the Bowery, the wheat pit in Chicago, and the open sea, where men still lived by craft and brute strength, where the strong devoured the puny, bravery counted for more than mercy, and reason chose Nature, amoral and impulsive, for its guide.

FORD MADOX FORD

[Crane's Life in England]†

If it were desired to prove that supernatural beings pay rare visits to this earth, there could be no apparition more suited to supporting the assertion than was Stephen Crane, whose eclipse is as fabulous as was his fabulous progress across this earth. . . . One awakened one morning in the nineties in England and *The Red Badge of Courage* was not; by noon of the same day it filled the universe. There was nothing you could talk of but that book. And, by tea-time, as it were, this hot blast of fame had swept back across

† From, "Stephen Crane," *The American Mercury*, XXXVII (January, 1936), as reprinted in Ford's *Portraits From Life*. Copyright 1937, Houghton Mifflin Company; pp. 21–27, *passim*. Reprinted by permission.

the Atlantic and there was nothing they could talk of in New York and its hinterlands but that book.

There was no doubt a non-literary reason for the phenomenon. The middle nineties and the twenty years that succeeded them formed together a period of war consciousness and war preparation such as the world has seldom seen, and it came after a quarter century of profoundly peaceful psychology. From the end of the Franco-Prussian War in 1871 to about 1895, no one thought of organized bloodshed as affording a solution for human problems— no one except perhaps Bismarck—and he regarded his army only as an instrument for policing the French. The strife of 1870–71 had for the moment exhausted the human appetite for blood in the gutters. Yet the next twenty years saw nothing, the world over, but preparations for conflict. The United States prepared and brought off a war against Spain after very nearly bringing off, over Venezuela, a war against Great Britain. Greece and Italy prepared several wars against Turkey, China against Japan, Japan against Russia. Great Britain, after equally preparing for war against this country, over Venezuela, brought off one of great difficulty against the South Africans. . . . And all the while, in every state of the globe, went on the sabre-rattling that ended in the late Armageddon. It was universal.

There was thus no man below a certain age who had not at one time or another to think of how he would behave in the case of his participation in a feast of bloodshed. For already it was manifest that in any considerable war all the manhood of the countries engaged must be called upon. And there was nothing to show him how he, the ordinary milkman or bank clerk, would probably behave when bullets were flying. There was nothing. No book; no memories; no pictures except those of poorly invented posturings. Bewhiskered major generals had written about campaigns; historians had dug accounts of strategy out of documents; dryly admirable staff officers had recorded the movings of wedges labelled 'infantry' or 'gunners' here and there on the escarpments of hills or against embrasures or redans. * * * But few had given any picture at all of post-medieval warfare, and absolutely none had introduced us behind the foreheads of the units who made up those moving wedges.

And suddenly there was *The Red Badge of Courage* showing us, to our absolute conviction, how the normal, absolutely undistinguished, essentially civilian man from the street had behaved in a terrible and prolonged war—without distinction, without military qualities, without special courage, without even any profound apprehension of, or passion as to, the causes of the struggle in which, almost without will, he was engaged. (And is it beside the mark to note that this was exactly how we all did take it twenty years later, from the English Channel to the frontiers of Italy?) The point was that, with *The Red Badge* in the nineties, we were provided with a map showing us our own hearts. If before that date we had been asked how we should behave in a war, we should no doubt have answered that we should behave like demigods, with all the marmoreal attributes of war memorials. But, a minute after peeping into *The Red Badge*, we knew that, at best, we should behave doggedly but with weary non-comprehension, flinging away our chassepot rifles, our haversacks, and fleeing into the swamps of Shiloh. We could not have any other conviction. The idea of falling like heroes on ceremonial battle-fields was gone forever; we knew that we should fall like street-sweepers subsiding ignobly into rivers of mud.

It was none the less convincing that those secrets of the heart in battle were revealed by a boy hardly out of his teens—and a boy who had never seen a war. The book was a revelation so miraculous that the more of the wonderful there was in its inception and preparation, the more profoundly convincing it seemed. * * * In any case Crane left on me an impression of supernaturalness that I still have. It was perhaps the aura of that youth that never deserted him—perhaps because of his aspect of frailty. He seemed to shine—and perhaps the November sun really did come out and cast on his figure, in the gloom of my entry, a ray of light.

* * *

In his life of Crane, which was written ten or a dozen years ago and which, for a man who did not know Crane, was a very difficult and creditable labor of love, Mr. Thomas Beer said that Crane did not have a very tumultuous reception in England. He was wrong, for that was exactly the type of reception that poor Crane did get once he was settled at first in Oxted and afterwards in Brede. Before that he had the reception that any serious man of letters should have wanted at that date to have in England. He was, that is to say, accepted at once, on his achievements and personality, as a serious and distinguished human being by practically all the serious people in England. Obviously the steamer in which he went over was not met in Gallions' Reach by tugboats full of interviewers, nor did the Queen in a drawing-room step two paces forward to clasp him by the hand. . . . But a young foreigner of twenty-five coming into a country as suspicious, reserved, and toughly conservative as was the England of that date, and being received at once as an equal into the intimacies of Conrad and

Henry James, and Mr. Edward Garnett and all the intensely high-brow Fabians of Limpsfield, and Mr. Shaw and Professor Hobson, and the more distinguished members of the Savile, the Devonshire, and the Savage Clubs, was done about as well as highbrow England could do him. And for the matter of that, he had what is called the entrée into aristocratic circles which would be closed as if against the breath of infection to the most brilliant young English writers. So that, at first, I found his reflections on England a little trying because of the titled qualifications of his informants. He seemed to have been received by half the Cabinet and a perfect galaxy of Irish peeresses. And his manners were so quiet and un-marked that there was no reason why he should not have climbed to Jamesian heights and have had Lady Maude Warrender to tea on his lawn every other afternoon. It might, really, have been better for him if he had.

For Crane was scarcely established in his Oxted villa before the tumultuous note began. Literary London of that day—I do not know how it may be now—was filled to about capacity by the most discreditable bums that any city can ever have seen. They pullu-lated mostly about the purlieus of the Savage Club, but you would find them in Bedford Park and you would find them in Limehouse. And no sooner did the word go round that there was in Oxted, and afterwards in Brede, a shining young American of genius, earning twenty pounds for every thousand words that he wrote, and ready to sit up all night dispensing endless hampers of caviar, *foie gras*, champagne, and oysters in season . . . ah, then there was tumult indeed in the twenty miles that separate Limehouse from Bedford Park.

The reverberations were terrific. London was at that time full of American reporters. It was the fat time for war correspondents and they all went through the Savage Club—to the Balkans, to Athens, to Vladivostok by the Trans-Siberian; and innumerable lame ducks, bad hats, *tristes sires*, and human detritus from New York to Tin Can, Nevada, were left by the tide between Fleet Street and Adelphi Terrace, which was the Mecca of the Bohemian out-at-elbows. And, merely to be reputed to have known that Fortunate Youth was to have parcels of that flotsam drift onto one's doorstep. * * * I had moved before that to Winchelsea, the next parish to Brede. I was naïve in those days, but not so naïve as to send them on to poor Steevie—but they bothered me a good deal. * * *

I avoided Brede Place during that period, but Crane used to ride over, perched on the top of one of his two enormous carriage horses which gave him the air of a frail eagle astride a gaunt elephant, and would talk with discouragement of the revival of medieval places of sanctuary. I didn't avoid Brede because I was afraid of the company there. Amongst a perfect wilderness of cats and monkeys there would always be at least one just soul who was really devoted to Steevie—Conrad, or occasionally the Old Man himself, or Mr. Garnett, or Harold Frederic, or Robert Barr, all strong and good men in their day. But I could not stand the sunlight there. It filtered down into those dank green places and was ghastly.

An Elizabethan manor's ground plan is that of an E—out of compliment to the Virgin Queen—and Brede Place conformed exactly to that plan. . . . Two longish wings, one at each end; in the centre a shorter wing which held the arched porch and the entrance hall. All the mass of the building of grey stone with mullioned, leaded windows, offering a proud and sinister front to sunlight coming through lowering clouds. On the bank which supported it played all the things in the world that nobody wanted—unwanted children, dogs, men, old maids—like beachcombers washed up on green sands. And behind the façade, a rabbit warren of passages with beer barrels set up at odd corners, and barons of beef for real tramps at the kitchen door, and troops of dogs and maids and butlers and sham tramps of the New York newspaper world and women who couldn't sell their manuscripts. . . .

And poor, frail Steevie, with all the organs of his body martyred to the waters of Cuba, the mosquitoes of the swamps around Athens, the cold Caribbean, the dusts of Wyoming or Nevada or Colorado, the stenches of Bowery slums, the squalor of New York hall-bedrooms . . . Heaven knows where he really had or hadn't been; he might, like Cyrano, have come sliding from the moon to the earth down a sunbeam. . . . Poor, frail Steevie, in the little room over the porch in the E, writing incessantly—like a spider that gave its entrails to nourish a wilderness of parasites. For, with his pen that moved so slowly in microscopic black trails over the immense sheets of paper that he affected, he had to support all that wilderness. That was the thought I could not bear.

I drove over several times, behind a pony that for some reason detested the Udimore highroad so that the driving was a weariness —several times from Winchelsea to Brede, and then turned back because I was unable to bear the prospect of seeing that little figure perched, as if at the foot of a mountain, before those great sheets, in that Elizabethan cave, with an untasted glass of very small beer, gone flat beside him.

The last time I drove that way was on the second day of January, 1900, and that time I did not see him in his workroom. I was led instead by an imposing maid to a hide-hole in a summer house up the bank behind that lugubrious place. It seemed a singular spot for a consumptive to choose on a January afternoon. But when I approached him, he sprang out, his face radiant, and exclaimed:

"Hueffer,† thank God, it's you! . . . I always say you bring me luck. . . ."

The luck I had brought him was that of not being the tax collector from whom he was hiding. He had the theory that if, in England, you did not pay your taxes on New Year's Day, you went to prison.

* * *

The main job of a writer is to write—to have circumstances favourable to his writing at the best. I suppose that if Crane had settled down in the cottage on Limpsfield Chart, he might have gone on writing till today—or if he had evolved all the hide-holes from contact with the life of Lamb House. . . . But perhaps his writing would have grown thinner.

* * *

I appear once to have offended one of his Canadian friends and, as I am never tired of repeating, in almost his last letter Crane wrote to him:

"You must not be offended by Mr. Hueffer's manner. He patronizes Mr. James. He patronizes Mr. Conrad. Of course he patronizes me and he will patronize Almighty God when they meet, but God will get used to it, for Hueffer is all right. . . ."

That is almost like having the Victoria Cross of the long sad battlefield that is a writer's life.

Crane's work is the most electric thing that ever happened in that struggle—it was and so remains. His influence on his time, and the short space of time that has succeeded his day, was so tremendous that if today you read *Maggie*, it is as if you heard a number of echoes, so many have his imitators been; and you can say as much of *The Red Badge*. That is simply because his methods have become the standard for dealing with war scenes or slum life. Until there comes a new Homer, we shall continue to see those things in that way.

His technique was amazing and extraordinarily contagious. How many stories since its day have not opened with a direct imitation of the marvellous first sentence of *The Open Boat*:

"None of them knew the colour of the sky."

† Ford changed his name from "Hueffer" in 1919, reportedly because of his anti-German feeling [Editors].

Haven't a thousand stories, since then, opened with just that cadence, like a machine-gun sounding just before stand-to at dawn and calling the whole world to attention? And of course there is more to it than just the cadence of the eight monosyllables to the one dissyllable. The statement is arresting because it is mysterious and yet perfectly clear. So your attention is grasped even before you realize that the men in the boat were pulling or watching the waves so desperately that they had no time to look up. That is skill, and when it comes, as it did with Crane, intuitively, out of the very nature of the narrator, it is the pledge of genius. It is the writing of somebody who cannot go wrong . . . who is authentic.

I have spoken of Crane as the first American writer. The claim is not new, though I do not know who made it first. I dare say I did because I must certainly have been one of the first to think it. It remains perhaps a little controversial. But all American writers who preceded him had their eyes on Europe. They may have aped Anglicism in their writings, like the Concord group; or, like Mark Twain—or even if you like, O. Henry—they were chronic protesters against Europeanism. At any rate, the Old World preoccupied them.

There was nothing of this about Crane. To say that he was completely ignorant of Zola or Maupassant would probably be untrue. He would state at one moment, with expletives, that he had never heard of those fellows and, at the next, display a considerable acquaintance with their work. Indeed, he said that it was after dipping into Zola's novel about the Franco-Prussian War that he determined to write a real war novel, and so sat down to *The Red Badge*.

No, he was the first American writer because he was the first to be passionately interested in the life that surrounded him—and the life that surrounded him was that of America. Don't believe that he was in the least changed by his residence at Brede. He paid, as it were, a courteous attention to Oxted or London or Brede, but he moved about in them an abstracted and solitary figure . . . and he footed the bills. I don't mean to say that he was homesick for a bench in Union Square. He didn't have to be; he was always there, surveying the world from that hard seat. He picked his way between dogs snarling over their bones in the rushes of the medieval hall, but he was thinking how to render the crash of dray horses' hooves and the rattle of the iron-bound wheels on the surface of Broadway where it crosses Fourteenth Street. Or he was lost in the Bowery. Or Havana. Or the Oranges. He had been shoved into Brede because his friends thought that he needed a little medievalizing to rub off the rough edges of his merciless thought—and because Mrs. Crane wanted to be a medieval lady of the castle with her long sleeves brushing with their tips those same rushes.

* * *

Before honourable congressmen claim that by their labours they are raising monuments such as the Age of Pericles alone could show, they might remember, a little shamefacedly, if congressmen can know shame, a certain stone in the cemetery of Elizabeth, New Jersey. I had occasion to go through that town a dozen times a month or so ago and I remember saying to one of my companions that I couldn't imagine any reason in the world why one should want to stop off in Elizabeth, New Jersey. That was before I knew that Crane was buried there, for, not taking much interest in necrologies, I did not know that Steevie lay there until I read again, the other day, Mr. Beer's painstaking biography. . . . Well, then, if America is to be saved—America of the typewriting machine, of the libraries, of the universities, of the paint brushes and music paper and plumb line, which is the only America that counts, *pace* Congress and its labours—that day will come when as many pious pilgrims go to Elizabeth as to Stratford itself.

V. S. PRITCHETT

[Crane's Gift for Raising the Veil]†

* * *

It is worth while turning at this point to an American novelist who is the child of the Tolstoy-Whitman movement, the child of the Crimea and Bull Run. I am thinking of Stephen Crane and his book *The Red Badge of Courage* which was published in the 'nineties. The achievement of Crane was individual and high, but in placing it we must now confess that it came in on the Tolstoy wave; and that but for Tolstoy, it would never have been written. There is an important difference of experience between Tolstoy and Crane. In writing respectively about the Napoleonic and the American Civil Wars, both writers were reconstructing wars they had not seen; but Tolstoy *had* seen the Crimea, he had been a soldier, whereas Crane had seen war only as an intrepid journalist

† From *The Living Novel*, London, 1946; New York, 1947; pp. 173–78. Reprinted by permission of the author and Chatto & Windus. Here is an "English standpoint" a half century later than those expressed above by Crane's British contemporaries.

will see it, and the journalist does not go through the mill of sol-
diering. However adventurous he may be, he is not fully-condi-
tioned. He does not, in the end, feel this is his inescapable fate.
He does not look mildly into the blank expressionless features of
death; but, dramatically, with face half-averted. One feels that
Crane stands apart from his scene and that a great skill has to
take the place of an inured contemplation of the subject. Crane
is simply the specialist and expert who has narrowed his interest to
the relation of a man with himself or a crowd's relation with other
crowds in the battle; whereas Tolstoy in his wide survey saw that
war was a continuation of peace. One curious common emotion
nevertheless unites the master and the disciple. They reject the
formal, the professional and rhetorical attitude to war; they reject
the illusions of the profession and the traditional litanies of patriotism; but they cannot quite conceal a certain sadness at the passing of these things. In Tolstoy one so often suspects the secret
longing of the repentant, the too-repentant soldier; in Crane the
faint harking back to romance expresses, I suppose, the reporter's
hidden regret that he has not a profound and comprehensive point
of view.

The Red Badge of Courage is a *tour de force*. Crane starts a
bugle call and sustains it without a falter to the end of the book.
The scene is a single battlefield in the American Civil War, and
the purpose of the novel is to show the phases by which a green
young recruit loses his romantic illusions and his innocence in
battle, and acquires a new identity, a hardened virtue. War has
ceased to be a bewraying and befogging dream in his mind; it has
become his world and he derives virtue from his unity with it.
There is a second element in the story. To Crane a battlefield is
like a wounded animal. The convulsions of its body, its shudders,
its cries and its occasional repose, are the spasmodic movements
and dumb respites of the groups of soldiers. There is not only the
individual mind in the battlefield, but there is the mass mind also.
Crane watches the merging of the individual with the herd. There
is no plot in this book; it is a collection of episodes. We do not
know which battle is being described or what are its objects. The
rights and wrongs of the war itself are not discussed. No civilian
and hardly a sight of the work of man, like a house or a cultivated
field, comes into the picture. Few of the characters are named; the
central figure is known simply as "the young man". The enemy
are just the enemy, something fabulous and generally invisible in
the blue smoke line of the engagement, terrifying and dragon-like
at the worst, and at the best a singularity to be mistrusted. Who
wins or loses is obscure. The whole thing is almost as anonymous

as a poem or a piece of music and has the same kind of tension and suspense. For we are not specially interested in the mortal fate of the boy. We do not specially fear that he will be killed, nor do we privately hope he will cover himself with glory. Our eyes are fixed on something different in him; on each adjustment in his character as it comes along. At the end of this book, we say to ourselves, we too shall know how we shall behave when we discard our illusions about war and meet the reality. Romantically we fear or hope for battle as a way of singling ourselves out and dying; but underneath this day-dream is the awe of knowing that battle is a way of living before it is a way of dying, and one in which we cannot calculate our behaviour in advance. It was one of the discoveries of the unrhetorical attitude to war in literature, that even the men on the right side and in the just cause are afraid; and to Crane—an adventurous man who died young from the effects of going to see trouble all over the earth—the deep fear of fear was a personal subject.

This comes out in the first chapter of *The Red Badge of Courage*, where the young man is seen in the camp listening to the rumours and torturing himself with questions. He feels courageous but will courage stand? Will he stay or will he run in panic? These are overmastering questions. The first dead do not scare him, nor does the early uproar. He can stand the first attack and face the fear hidden in the wall of forest where the enemy lie, and after the frenzy of the first onslaught he lies for a few moments in the trench overcome by a sense of fellowship with his companions and experiencing with astonishment "the joy of a man who at last finds leisure". But, fixed on their intense personal problem, his heart and mind have not yet understood that while the imagination expects decisive and single answers, reality does not deal in such simplicities. The attack, to everyone's despair, is renewed. The second phase has begun. It is too much. The youth throws down his rifle and runs. Here Crane shows his power as a novelist, for in this part of the story he writes those dramatic scenes and draws those portraits which have given the book its place in the literature of war. This is where the dying soldier, walking white and erect like a rejected prince among his broken court, goes stiffly towards his grave. Crane was an observer of the ways of dying, but this death is one of the most terrible, for it is a progress to death:

"The spectral soldier was at his side like a stalking reproach. The man's eyes were still fixed in a stare into the unknown. His grey, appalling face had attracted attention in the crowd, and men, slowing to his dreary pace, were walking with him. They were discussing his plight, questioning and giving him advice. In a dogged way he repelled them, signing to them to go on and leave him alone. The shadows of his face were deepening and his tight lips seemed holding in check the moan of great despair. There could be seen a certain stiffness in the movement of his body, as if he were taking infinite care not to arouse the passion of his wounds. As he went on he seemed always looking for a place like one who goes to choose a grave. Something in the gesture of the man as he waved the bloody and pitying soldiers away made the youth start as if bitten. He yelled in horror. Tottering forward he laid a quivering hand upon the man's arm. As the latter slowly turned his wax-like features toward him the youth screamed:

" 'Gawd! Jim Conklin!'

"The tall soldier made a little commonplace smile.

" 'Hello, Henry,' he said."

If the boy's horror and quivering seem conventionally overemphatic in that passage, the rest is not. Writers are always faced by two sets of words before they write; those which will draw a literary curtain over reality, and those which will raise the veil in our minds and lead us to see for the first time. Crane's gift for raising the veil is clear. The presence of "spectre" and "commonplace smile" in that portrait is imaginative observation at its best.

The book is filled with observation of this kind. Some is placed there by poetic intuition:

"The sun spread disclosing rays, and, one by one, regiments burst into view like armed men just born of the earth. The youth perceived that the time had come. He was about to be measured. For a moment he felt in the face of his great trial like a babe, and the flesh over his heart seemed but thin. He seized time to look about him calculatingly.

But he instantly saw that it would be impossible for him to escape from the regiment. It enclosed him. There were iron laws of tradition and law on four sides. He was in a moving box."

This inner sensation of the experience is matched by wonderful, small phrases of verisimilitude: "His *forgotten feet* were constantly knocking against stones or getting entangled in briars." Or there is this picture—how common it has become in modern realism, which Crane anticipates by thirty or forty years:

"Once the line encountered the body of a dead soldier. He lay upon his back staring at the sky. He was dressed in an awkward suit of yellowish brown. The youth could see that the soles of his shoes had been worn to the thinness of writing paper, and from a great rent in one the dead foot projected piteously. And it was as if fate had betrayed the soldier. In death it exposed to his enemies that poverty which in life he had perhaps concealed from his friends."

The only word a modern reporter would not have written in that passage is the word "piteously".

Toughness, that is to say fear of facing the whole subject, as Crane faced it, has intervened to make the modern writer's picture purely visual and inhumane—one remembers the turned-out pockets of the dead in Hemingway and his bravado about writing a natural history of the dead. The pathetic fallacy abounds in Crane's prose and we hear of "the remonstrance" and "arguments" of the guns; but for all the artiness—which belongs to the 'nineties—there is pity, there is human feeling. There is a background of value and not a backdrop gaudy with attitudes. There is a quest for virtue—what else is the meaning of the young boy's innocent odyssey among his fears, his rages and his shames?—and not as one sees in Kipling, the search for a gesture or some dramatic personal stand which avoids the issue and saves the face. Crane ignores the actor in human beings, the creature with the name on the personal playbill; he goes—at any rate in *The Red Badge of Courage*—for the anonymous voice in the heart.

JOHN BERRYMAN

[The Significance of Crane's English Reception]†

* * *

The difficulties with supposing Stephen Crane's "little creed of art" indebted to the views of Howells or Garland are two: it does not resemble theirs, and he already had Tolstoy before him. Tolstoy was Howells's great master also, but he did not learn from the Russian what Crane did. Crane learnt how an ironic mind takes expression in literary art, or learnt something about this; and since this is the dominant aspect of what is called Crane's "realism," it is not very easy to see how his creed could have been "identical" with Howells's and Garland's, neither of these men being really an ironist at all. Labels are slippery, of course. "I decided," Crane said on another occasion, "that the nearer a writer gets to life the greater he becomes as an artist, and most of my prose writings have been towards the goal partially described by that misunderstood and abused word, realism. Tolstoy is the writer I admire most of all." The term is so heavily qualified that we may hope to learn

† From *Stephen Crane* by John Berryman, copyright 1950 by William Sloane Associates, Inc. By permission of William Sloane Associates. Pp. 54–127, *passim.*

more from one of the phrases, "the nearer a writer gets to life," especially when we repeat in connection with it his formulation to Mrs. Munroe: "we are most successful in art when we approach the nearest to nature and truth." The question is what he meant by these statements: *how*, that is, one approaches life or nature or truth.

What he seems to have meant is impressionism. Well before any of these statements were made, late in the same year he finished *Maggie* (1893), Crane spoke his faith repeatedly to a friend who has recorded it. "Impressionism was his faith. Impressionism, he said, was truth, and no man could be great who was not an impressionist, for greatness consisted in knowing truth. He said that he did not expect to be great himself, but he hoped to get near the truth." This was to his fellow-lodgers on 23rd Street, and the book he was then writing is identical in method with *Maggie*. Impressionism must be the creed which he developed late in 1892 and in terms of which he rewrote his story of the slums. But literary impressionism had no status, and he could hardly announce "I believe in Irony," so he allied himself as best he could with the few men who seemed to be trying at any rate to get at the truth. If he came in *Crumbling Idols* (1894) on Garland's conviction that art was a question of "one man facing certain facts and telling his individual relations to them," Crane could feel less alone, and it was easy to ignore Garland's insistence that "The realist or veritist is really an optimist"; he knew better. So if he came (probably in 1895) on Henry James's "A novel is in its broadest definition a personal, a direct impression of life: that, to begin with, constitutes its value, which is greater or less according to the intensity of the impression," or the master's view that among the qualifications of the young aspirant in fiction "the first is a capacity for receiving straight impressions," or his dictum that the only condition attaching to the composition of the novel was "that it be sincere"—he could feel reassured and reinforced. These men, with Howells, were "realists," and so was he. Stephen Crane's program, however, was his own.

* * *

The Red Badge of Courage is the story of the mind of a new young Northern soldier as it accustoms itself to war during two days in and out of his first battle. There is a preliminary debate with himself as to whether he will run away or not. When his regiment is charged a second time, he does; and hides resentfully in a wood, where he meets a rotting corpse in a chapellike place. He joins the march of wounded away from the battle, and comes on a friend hurt horribly, a tall soldier, whom he accompanies to his extraordinary death. A tattered man has befriended him on the march; this man, whose plight is very bad, his mind wandering, the youth deserts in shame, on the question, reiterated, of *where* he is wounded. Then in a flight of the troops he is clubbed with a rifle when he tries to ask a panic-stricken man a question. An unseen man finally helps him back to his regiment. Since it has got scattered during the battle, his shame is unknown; he says he was shot and is cared for by a friend, a loud youth, who bandages his bloody head. He sleeps. Next morning he feels no remorse, and is full of "self-pride" even, when the loud youth reluctantly and shame-facedly has to ask for the return of a packet of papers given the youth, in fear, before the battle. "He had been possessed of much fear of his friend, for he saw how easily questionings could make holes in his feelings." Now "his heart grew more strong and stout. He had never been compelled to blush in such manner for his acts; he was an individual of extraordinary virtues." In the battle of this second day he is a war devil. During the charge, when the color-bearer is killed, he wrenches the flag free and bears it. In hard new fighting he and the loud youth are commended. The regiment takes a fence and a flag, and rests. "He had been to touch the great death, and found that, after all, it was but the great death. He was a man. . . . Scars faded as flowers.

"It rained. . . . Yet the youth smiled, for he saw that the world was a world for him, though many discovered it to be made of oaths and walking sticks. He had rid himself of the red sickness of battle. . . ."

Though the major circumstantial irony survives in this account, Crane's sympathy as he dances near and behind his hero's mind does not, nor does, of course, the imagination of fear and war in the book; together, these produced a thing that was new in literature. It is produced with awful simplicity. Henry Fleming, the meditative, panic-stricken farm boy, is the one character to whom we attend; the tall soldier Jim Conklin and the loud one Wilson are scarcely developed, and the others are mere vignettes, sometimes admirable. Critics have not failed to ask *how* it was produced. Garland, who read the manuscript with amazement, was the first: How did Crane know about war? and "in his succinct, self-derisive way, he candidly confessed that all his knowledge of battle had been gained on the football field! 'The psychology is the same. The opposite team is an enemy tribe!' "

Football was more instructive, probably, than Zola; and some other roots of *The Red Badge* [that have been] mentioned. * * * Perhaps the book took its origin really from Mark Twain's young pilot in *Life on the Mississippi*, who hid during his maiden engagement and then was acclaimed.* Who knows how many origins a deep work has? An advance is perceptible at any rate from the fully developed style of Crane's first book to a style much better capable of registering degrees of variation of feeling. The grotesquerie as well is better knitted into narrative, and when let loose, in the great ninth chapter, this gave him a scene decisively beyond anything he had done before, as well as one of the major scenes in American writing.†

Thomas Beer's account, however, which Crane could hardly give, would have answered Garland's question best. How did Crane know about war? "There had been a boy who went confidently off to make war on a world and a city. He had been beaten to shelter and had lurched up a lane in darkness on the arm of some stranger. He had been praised for his daring while his novel, like a retreating army, lay in unsold heaps and the maker of images was sure of his own clay."

* * *

The sensation of *The Red Badge of Courage* was made by the English critics. Crane's publisher Ripley Hitchcock, Thomas Beer, and others have denied this for fifty years, but the facts are simple. The book appeared in London two months later than here, and it was not until early in January that news of the British reviews came in: the *Pall Mall's*, George Wyndham's in the *New Review*, the *Saturday Review's*, others'. These were different from the American reviews. Wyndham, one of England's ablest critics, in a long article on "A Remarkable Book," said simply that "Mr. Stephen Crane, the author of *The Red Badge of Courage*, is a great artist," and "Mr. Crane's picture of war is more complete than Tolstoi's, more true than Zola's." The *Saturday Review* also thought Zola inferior to Crane, mentioned Tolstoy, Kipling, and Mérimée, thought Crane's irony Sophoclean, and in general seemed to lose its head: the book was "an inspired utterance that will reach the universal heart of man." "In the whole range of literature," said the *Daily Chronicle*, "we can call to mind nothing so searching in its analysis." They vied with each other. To *St. James's Gazette* it was "not merely a remarkable book: it is a revelation." "Most astonishing" —"no possibility of resistance"—and so on. But let us make sure of the dates. The issue in which the *Saturday Review* went over-

* Chapter xxvi. "I had often had a curiosity to know how a green hand might feel. . . . So to me his story was valuable—it filled a gap for me which all histories had left till that time empty. . . . 'All through that fight I was scared nearly to death . . . but you see, nobody knew that but me. Next day General Polk sent for me, and praised me. . . . I never said anything, I let it go at that. I judged it wasn't so, but it was not for me to contradict a general officer.' "
† *I.e.*, The death of Jim Conklin [Eds.].

board is dated January 11, 1896. Next day, Crane posted to a girl a clipping from the *Scranton Tribune*: "*The Red Badge of Courage* has fascinated England. The critics are wild over it and the English edition has been purchased with avidity. Mr. Crane has letters from the most prominent English publishers asking for the English rights to all of his future productions; but the young author refuses to be hurried. . . ." In mid-January, as Beer says, New York began to buy the book; and these were the reasons. The advertisements quoted the British reviews (until 1896 the book went unmentioned or just listed in Appleton ads), people talked of them, American critics fell resentfully or eagerly into line, and in ten months of 1896 *The Red Badge* went through thirteen editions in America.

The anomaly was pointed out repeatedly at the time, John D. Barry (the sponsor of Crane's "lines") being perhaps the first to do so. From New York for the Boston *Literary World*, also dated January 11th, he observed: "It is a satisfaction to note that the unique and promising work which Mr. Stephen Crane has done during the past three years has at last won distinguished recognition. I wish that this recognition came from Mr. Crane's own countrymen. . . . I cannot think of the case of another American writer who was accepted as a man of consequence in England before winning marked recognition in his own country, and I doubt if Mr. Crane's recent experience has a precedent. At any rate, now that the English critics are crying out his praises . . ." English fame had always helped, of course,—a few years later Ezra Pound and Robert Frost were to have similar experiences. In February the New York *Bookman* took up the refrain ("Why is it . . . that in America critics are less sure and readers slower to discover a good book in spite of the genius in it?"), and on March 14th the *Literary Digest*: "It is scarcely to the credit of America that this book . . . was first pronounced a work of genius in England, where its success is great and growing. The story has now caught the attention of the American public, and it is said that during the first week in February the publishers were unable to supply the demand." By April 11th it was "now pretty generally admitted that Stephen Crane is a 'genius.'" * * * The American press had praised the book more highly than soon either it or the English press was recognizing; but the essential features of the success are unmistakable. It was inevitable that the truth should have got mislaid here since. * * * Crane never forgot. Writing to an American editor shortly before his death, he came to the matter again, absolutely: "I have only one pride, and that is that the English edition of *The Red Badge of Courage* has been received with great praise."

JOHN W. SHROEDER

From Stephen Crane Embattled†

* * *

Crane, certainly, too often took his ease in the Naturalistic Zion; within the limits of Naturalism, he was moved but once to the creative effort of mastering, digesting, and evaluating his matter. Crane needed the stimulation of something more challenging, of one of those "problems that matter" that I left dangling on an earlier page.

Well, what does matter? What problems are of an intensity sufficient to call out a valid creative effort? I do not mean to be so foolish as to set down a list of eternals in art. But I can point to something that has mattered. *The Scarlet Letter*, *Moby-Dick*, *The Ambassadors*, *A Farewell to Arms*, and *The Waste Land*—and I trust that no one will object to my regarding these works as touchstones—are heterogeneous enough on their surfaces. But if we bother to peer beneath these surfaces, if, this is to say, we take the trouble to find out what is behind Hester's long penance, Ahab's God-insulting quest, Strether's growth into total awareness, Lieutenant Henry's separate peace, and the voice of the Thunder, we will find a common problem there. And we might define the problem, giving our definition not too much latitude, as that of salvation.

Here, at least, is something that has mattered to an eminent degree. And it is not a problem to which my archetypal Naturalist would normally address himself, since it implies a set of values outside of the physical universe and since it implies an effort of the human will which the determinism basic to Naturalism cannot admit. And when Crane grappled with the problem, he was forced to get beyond Naturalism; he was forced, perhaps, to fight the Naturalistic universe itself in his effort to get beyond.

Crane's *The Red Badge of Courage* is more complex and more confused than its critics have been willing to admit. The Naturalism for which it is usually admired—the neutralization of values consequent upon Crane's elevation of instinct and determinism as the twin bases of human action—does not begin to exhaust even the surface statement of this book; and the levels below the surface teem

† From *University of Kansas City Review*, XVII (Winter, 1950), 123–29, *passim*. Shroeder suggests a moral unity in Crane's work, resulting from the conflict between naturalistic laws and human values—a unity suggested in *The Red Badge* but climaxed in certain of the short stories. *Cf.* Stallman's conception of a mystical unity and Geismar's claim for a unity to be found in Freudian psychology (the two following essays).

with life. Its complexity renders impossible any attempt to pene-
trate far into its meaning in these pages. Its confusion indicates that
such a penetration might be of little value anyway; *The Red Badge*
may represent the assembly of the elements necessary for the definition of a problem rather than the final definition itself. But I think
it will be useful to us to extract a portion of the book's apparent
meaning, remembering, as we do so, that this portion is very likely
contradicted in other parts of the same book.

The most striking thing in *The Red Badge* is the peculiar equa-
tion constantly maintained by its imagery. Anything pertaining to
warfare in this book of war is apt to be visualized in terms of the
natural universe, and this universe itself is constantly personified.
The note is struck in the opening sentence, which speaks of the
cold of night as passing "reluctantly" from the earth. And the conclusion of the first paragraph gives us—with another personification
—a remarkable transmutation of the Confederate watchfires:

"A river, amber-tinted in the shadow of its banks, purled at the
army's feet; and at night, when the stream had become of a sorrowful blackness, one could see across it the red, eyelike gleam of hostile
camp fires set in the low brows of distant hills."

These eyes are still "peering" across the river on the day when the
regiment of Henry Fleming (Crane's youthful protagonist) leaves
camp; they seem to this youth "like the orbs of a row of dragons."
Moving columns of troops are represented as "serpents crawling from
the cavern of night," as "huge crawling reptiles." Tents spring up
on a campsite "like strange plants." Fires undergo a new metamorphosis to become "red, peculiar blossoms." A classical reference to
Cadmus's sowing of the dragon's teeth permits Crane to fuse his
flower and serpent imagery; on the day of attack, "regiments burst
into view like armed men just born of earth." Overtones of something actively diabolic in nature reinforce the suggestions of these
images. Artillery smoke drifts by "like observant phantoms." A shell
screams "like a storm banshee."

At times the imagery becomes even more suggestive. Crane's riflemen shoot "at thickets and at distant and prominent trees" as often
as at enemy riflemen. Fleming (who feels "threatened" by a landscape) fires "an angry shot at the persistent woods." As he moves
up to the line, the youth reflects that his "advance upon Nature" is
somehow too calm.

As we review these mutations and metaphors, we begin to suspect
that the theme of *The Red Badge* is not simply the youth's relation
—particularized by metaphors of nature—to battle. We suspect
that there is something more beyond this; and to define this some-

thing more, we might turn our first theme around and say that behind it we find Crane describing a relation—the battle as his metaphor—to nature. I must not pretend that our mutations and metaphors alone are adequate to this interpretation. They are runic signatures which run through the whole body of Crane's writings, and we will find them, though far less often, in even "Death and the Child," a tale in which war as a man-made blasphemy is carefully distinguished from nature's pattern of serene wisdom. But our war-nature equations occur in *The Red Badge* with such frequency as to force our attention on their possible implications. And other evidence can be adduced in support of my notion as to what the implications are.

The theme of the relation to nature is developed through event as well as through imagery. In a highly important chapter, Fleming, fled from battle, enters a wood:

"This landscape gave him assurance. A fair field holding life. It was the religion of peace. It would die if its timid eyes were compelled to see blood. He conceived Nature to be a woman with a deep aversion to tragedy.

He threw a pine cone at a jovial squirrel, and he ran with chattering fear. High in a treetop he stopped, and, poking his head cautiously from behind a branch, looked down with an air of trepidation.

The youth felt triumphant at this exhibition. There was the law, he said. Nature had given him a sign. . . . The youth wended, feeling that Nature was of his mind."

Here, certainly, is a rather different nature than that incarnate in the field of war. And the youth's immediate response to it boils down to the confusion of law for thing with law for man; we are involved with a Naturalistic response to a Naturalistic universe. Perhaps we are to read the youth's retreat (he ran from battle "like a rabbit") as an attempt to placate nature by submission to her. But whatever the case, nature will not be placated; the battle rages here as well as elsewhere. The youth passes a swamp and sees, "out at some black waters, a small animal pounce in and emerge directly with a gleaming fish." Nature, patently, has no aversion whatever to blood and tragedy. Indeed, as the youth immediately discovers, she flourishes on them. The youth enters a clearing in the wood:

"Near the threshold he stopped, horror-stricken at the sight of a thing.

He was being looked at by a dead man who was seated with his back against a columnlike tree. . . . Over the gray skin of the face ran little ants. One was trundling some sort of a bundle along the upper lip."

And this fearsome vision is succeeded, as the youth hastens from the forest, by a personification vastly different from that which earlier characterized nature as a gentle lady:

"Sometimes the brambles formed chains and tried to hold him back. Trees, confronting him, stretched out their arms and forbade him to pass. After its previous hostility this new resistance of the forest filled him with a fine bitterness. It seemed that Nature could not be quite ready to kill him."

This is no simple pathetic fallacy; it has its roots in those incidents in the forest which displayed in action the antagonisms basic to our battle of man and nature. We cannot rest in nature or in the Naturalistic universe. Whatever salvation is possible for man can be evolved only by the transcendence of (by battle with) thing, and Crane wafts his youth out of the haunted forest and back to the field where the battle can be fought. Very well; but *how* is the battle fought? Crane, I am afraid, gives two mutually contradictory answers. The youth does it by a Naturalistic response to the threat; by becoming "a barbarian, a beast"; by developing "teeth and claws." He also does it by sinking his own personality in the greater corporate personality symbolized by his regiment (which is envisioned as "a subtle battle brotherhood," as "a mysterious fraternity"). The youth senses the higher values involved in this identification when he first enters the battle:

"He suddenly lost concern for himself, and forgot to look at a menacing fate. He became not a man but a member. He felt that something of which he was a part—a regiment, an army, a cause, or a country—was in a crisis. He was welded into a common personality. . . . For some moments he could not flee, no more than a little finger can commit a revolution from a hand."

This finger, of course, does manage to detach itself, a phenomenon in which the youth finds matter for self-gratulation:

"He had done a good part in saving himself, who was a little piece of the army. He had considered the time, he said, to be one in which it was the duty of every little piece to rescue itself if possible."

The position in the book of this bit of sophistry is noteworthy. It comes at the beginning of the chapter in which the whole fabric of the youth's notion of nature—which includes the essential rightness of his spiritual amputation from his fellows—is struck to bits. The idea of the mystic brotherhood occurs several times more, but I see no reason to pursue it. Crane himself, as the book draws to its close, seems to grow less and less certain as to whether it represents a system of higher values or merely the instinct of the herd.

"The youth," Crane tells us early in his book, "had been taught that a man became another thing in a battle. He saw his salvation in such a change." It is undeniable that the youth found such a salvation, although the confusion as to whether he found it by turning nature's weapons back on the enemy or by an identification with a system of human values outside of and above nature makes it somewhat dubious that Crane himself was quite as fortunate as was his hero. The book has flaws apart from this odd indecision. The putting off of the Old Man (Crane parallels this theological desideratum in the youth's wish to "throw off himself and become a better"), since it is largely a matter of accident, lacks the authority of a consciously willed readiness to work out the hard way of salvation. Crane I think, had his own doubts about the validity of Henry's transformation. In a later short story, Henry, now grown old, dies while rescuing two colts from a burning barn. The incident seems to be both afterthought and act of expiation; Crane was moved, perhaps, to give Fleming a second chance. And we would prefer not to encounter this pretty description of nature at the end of the battle: "He turned now with a lover's thirst to images of tranquil skies, fresh meadows, cool brooks—an existence of soft and eternal peace." The picture smacks too strongly of the youth's early impression of the haunted forest; Crane seems to have forgotten everything that has gone before in his own book.

As a definitive study of that salvation which Crane expressly makes his theme, *The Red Badge* . . . is a promise rather than a fulfill-ment. . . . But if it is only a promise, . . . the intensity of the vision is itself good warrant that the artist will persist in the direction of such an act.

And Crane did. In two later and lengthy short stories— "The Open Boat" and "The Monster," both written in 1897—he recapit-ulated the antagonisms basic to *The Red Badge*. The haunted vision is still there. It is possible to detect in "The Monster" (par-ticularly in the powerful scene in which Henry Johnson rescues little Jimmie Trescott from the fire) precisely the same elements which went into the battle-imagery of *The Red Badge*. Here are our strange blossoms again:

"The room was like a garden in the region where might be burning flowers. Flames of violet, crimson, green, blue, orange, and purple were blooming everywhere."

Here is our serpent, this time as a flame:

"It coiled and hesitated, and then began to swim a languorous way down the mahogany slant. . . . in a moment, with a mystic impulse, it moved again, and the red snake flowed directly down into Johnson's upturned face."

* * *

The link between Johnson's "battle" (the term is Crane's) with nature incarnate in the flame and Fleming's battle with nature incarnate in the Civil War seems fairly solid in view of all this. . . . But all the idiosyncrasies of the vision, all the false directions and incoherencies, have been purged. Compare, as an instance typical of Crane's advance, the unhappy invocation in *The Red Badge* to nature as "an existence of soft and eternal peace" to the famous delineation in "The Open Boat":

"This tower was a giant, standing with its back to the plight of the ants. It represented in a degree, to the correspondent, the serenity of nature amid the struggles of the individual—nature in the wind, and nature in the vision of men. She did not seem cruel to him then, nor beneficent, nor treacherous, nor wise. But she was indifferent, flatly indifferent."

In one sense, this is yet another of those Naturalistic tags which I have condemned, in the bulk, as Crane's worst foes. But the difference between this achieved definition and the mere tag is crucial. In the first place, what might have been a tag has been transfigured by its successful animation of a precise image; it is, I repeat, an achieved insight. We feel that Crane had to work for it. And in the second place, Crane does not permit himself to rest in this statement. * * * This, conversely, serves as a stimulus; it dictates further definition: an effort to get beyond or at least to find out what the real implications are.

* * *

Logically, I suppose, a vision of nature's indifference should cancel out the equally powerful vision of Nature as somehow possessed by forces deadly to man. * * * The answer, of course, is that Crane reacted to the indifference as strongly (and in much the same way) as did Melville to his more direct vision of nature as actively evil. Crane felt the subtle threat implicit in the indifference so forcibly that he was moved to characterize it as positively malignant. The logical force of such a reaction is probably slight; the poetic force, on the other hand, is extreme. To nature's deadly indifference, Crane, in "The Open Boat," again and conclusively opposes "the subtle brotherhood of men." The opposition is much the same in "The Monster," which records two attempted salvations—each having those metaphysical overtones which we by now expect—

.n from nature: the first, Henry Johnson's rescue of Jimmie
scott from the fire; the second, Dr. Trescott's rescue of Henry
urned and maimed by the flames) from death. * * *

My intentions (which have dictated a certain inattention to the
artistic totalities of these works) are limited to an indication of how
these two stories advance beyond the partial achievement of *The
Red Badge:* . . . from a diffuse and inchoate response to the central problem to an integrated and final literary mastery of it. In *The
Red Badge* we seem to have the record of a running battle, and it
is, to be sure, a battle of heroic dimensions. But in these two short
stories (and I must add to them "Death and the Child," which
fights the same battle with a different emphasis) we have the artistic
victory. Very few of Crane's works are without some effectiveness.
The stories and novels that I have condemned would quite likely
suffice to make a decent literary reputation. But Crane's claim to a
place among the significant American writers, I think, must depend
upon these three short stories. And in view of their achievement, I
incline to believe that we must allow that claim.

R. W. STALLMAN

Notes Toward an Analysis of *The Red Badge of Courage*†

That Crane is incapable of architectonics has been the critical
consensus that has prevailed for over half a century: "his work is a
mass of fragments"; "he can only string together a series of loosely
cohering incidents"; *The Red Badge of Courage* is not constructed.
Edward Garnett, the first English critic to appraise Crane's work,
aptly pointed out that Crane lacks the great artist's arrangement of
complex effects, which is certainly true. We look to Conrad and
Henry James for "exquisite grouping of devices"; Crane's figure in
the carpet is a much simpler one. What it consists of—the very
thing that Garnett failed to detect—is a structure of striking contrasts. Crane once defined a novel as a "succession of sharply-out-

† Reprinted from the Introduction by
Robert Wooster Stallman to the Modern Library Edition of *The Red Badge
of Courage.* Copyright © 1951 by Random House, Inc. Reprinted by permission. Pp. xxii–xxxvii.

We here reprint the third section;
an excerpt from the second part will
be found in our "Backgrounds and
Sources." The Introduction carries as
its first note, "Done with the research
assistance of Mr. Sy Kahn of the
University of Connecticut." Mr. Stallman has asked the editors of the
present volume to represent his 1961
revisions, which are substantive corrections and do not alter his expression of critical opinion. These revisions appear as footnotes in italics,
and are identified by the date, "1961."

lined pictures, which pass before the reader like a panorama, leaving each its definite impression." His own novel, nonetheless, is not simply a succession of pictures. It is a sustained structural whole. Every Crane critic has concurred in this mistaken notion that *The Red Badge of Courage* is nothing more than "a series of episodic scenes," but not one critic has yet undertaken an analysis of Crane's work to see *how* the sequence of tableaux is constructed.

The form of *The Red Badge of Courage* is constructed by repetitive alternations of contradictory moods. The opening scene establishes the same despair-hope pattern as the very last image of the book—"a golden ray of sun came through the hosts of leaden rain clouds." This sun-through-rain image, which epitomizes the double-mood pattern dominating every tableau in the whole sequence, is a symbol of Henry Fleming's moral triumph and is an ironic commentary upon it. Crane is a master of the contradictory effect.

The narrative begins with the army immobilized—with restless men waiting for orders to move—and with Henry, because the army has done nothing, disillusioned by his first days as a recruit. In the first picture we get of Henry, he is lying on his army cot—resting on an idea. Or rather, he is wrestling with the personal problem it poses. The idea is a third-hand rumor that tomorrow, at last, the army goes into action. When the tall soldier first announced it, he waved a shirt which he had just washed in a muddy brook, waved it in bannerlike fashion to summon the men around the flag of his colorful rumor. It was a call to the colors—he shook it out and spread it about for the men to admire. But Jim Conklin's prophecy of hope meets with disbelief. "It's a lie!" shouts the loud soldier. "I don't believe the derned old army's ever going to move." No disciples rally around the red and gold flag of the herald. A furious altercation ensues; the skeptics think it just another *tall* tale. Meanwhile Henry in his hut engages in a spiritual debate with himself: whether to believe or disbelieve the word of his friend, the *tall* soldier. It is the gospel truth, but Henry is one of the doubting apostles.

The opening scene thus sets going the structural pattern of the whole book. Hope and faith (paragraphs 1–3) shift to despair or disbelief (4–7). The countermovement of opposition begins in paragraph 4, in the small detail of the Negro teamster who stops his dancing when the men desert him to wrangle over Jim Conklin's rumor. "He sat mournfully down." In this image of motion and change (the motion ceasing and the joy turning to gloom), we are given the dominant leitmotif of the book and a miniature form of its structure. The opening prologue in Chapter I ends in a coda (paragraph 7) with theme and anti-theme here interjoined. It is the picture of the corporal, and his uncertainties (whether to repair his house) and shifting attitudes of trust and distrust (whether the army is going to move) parallel the skeptical outlook of the wrangling men. The same anti-theme of distrust is dramatized in the episode which follows this coda, and every episode throughout the remaining sequence of tableaux is designed similarly by one contrast pattern or another.

Change and motion begin the book. The army, which lies resting upon the hills, is first revealed to us by "the retiring fogs," and as the weather changes so the landscape changes, the brown hills turning into a new green. Now as nature stirs so the army stirs too. Nature and men are in psychic affinity; even the weather changes as though in sympathetic accord with man's plight. In the final scene it is raining but the leaden rain clouds shine with "a golden ray" as though to reflect Henry's own bright serenity, his own tranquility of mind. But now at the beginning, and throughout the book, Henry's mind is in a "tumult of agony and despair." This psychological tumult began when Henry heard the church bell announce the gospel truth that a great battle had been fought. Noise begins the whole mental *mêlée*. The clanging church bell and then the noise of rumors disorder his mind by stirring up legendary visions of heroic selfhood—dreams jolted by realities. The noisy world is clamoring to Henry to become absorbed into the solidarity of self-forgetful comradeship, but Henry resists this challenge of the "mysterious fraternity born of the smoke and danger of death," and withdraws again and again from the din of the affray to indulge in self-contemplative moods and magic reveries. The paradox is that when he becomes activated in the "vast blue demonstration" and is thereby reduced to anonymity he is then most a man and, conversely, when he affects self-dramatizing picture-postcard poses of himself as hero he is then least a man and not at all heroic. Withdrawals alternate with engagements, scenes of entanglement and tumult, but the same nightmarish atmosphere of upheaval and disorder pervades both the inner and the outer realms.

Henry's self-combat is symbolized by the conflict among the men and between the armies, their altercation being a duplication of his own. Henry's mind is in constant flux. Like the regiment that marches and counter-marches over the same ground, so Henry's mind traverses the same ideas over and over again. As the cheery-voiced soldier says about the battle, "It's th' most mixed up dern thing I ever see." Mental commotion, confusion, and change are externalized in the "mighty altercation" of men and guns and nature herself. Everything becomes activated, even the dead. The corpse Henry meets on the battlefield, "the invulnerable dead man," cannot stay still—he *"forced* a way for himself" through the ranks. And guns throb too, "restless guns." Back and forth the stage-scenery shifts from dream to fact, illusions pinpricked by reality. Disengaged from the external tumult, Henry's mind recollects former domestic scenes. Pictures of childhood and nursery imagery of babes recur during almost every interval of withdrawal. The nursery rhyme which the wounded soldiers sing as they retreat from the battlefront is at once a travesty of their own plight and a mockery of Henry's mythical innocence.

> Sing a song 'a vic'try
> A pocketful 'a bullets,
> Five an' twenty dead men
> Baked in a—pie.

Everything goes awry; nothing turns out as Henry had expected. The youth who had envisioned himself in Homeric poses, the legendary hero of a Greeklike struggle, has his pretty illusion shattered as soon as he announces his enlistment to his mother. "I've knet yeh eight pair of socks, Henry. . . ." His mother is busy peeling potatoes, and, madonnalike, she kneels among the parings. They are the scraps of his romantic dreams. The youthful private imagines armies to be monsters, "redoubtable dragons," but then he sees the real thing—the colonel who strokes his mustache and shouts over his shoulder, "Don't forget that box of cigars!"

The theme of *The Red Badge of Courage* is that man's salvation lies in change, in spiritual growth. It is only by immersion in the flux of experience that man becomes disciplined and develops in character, conscience or soul. The book is about a battle, but it is a symbolic battle. A battle represents life at its most intense flux, and it, therefore, exploits the greatest possible potentialities for change. To say that *The Red Badge of Courage* is a study in fear is as shallow an interpretation as to say that it is a narrative of the Civil War. It is not about the combat of armies; it is about the self-combat of a youth who fears and stubbornly resists change and spiritual growth. It probes a state of mind and analyzes the gradual transformation of this psychological state under the incessant pinpricks and bombardments of life. From the start Henry recognizes the necessity for change but wars against it. But man must lose his soul in order to save it. The youth develops into the veteran—"So it came to pass . . . his soul changed." Significantly enough, in stating what the book is about Crane intones Biblical phrasing.

Spiritual change, *that* is Henry Fleming's red badge. His red badge is his conscience reborn and purified. Whereas Jim Conklin's red badge of courage is the literal one, the wound of which he dies, Henry's is the psychological badge, the wound of conscience. Just as Jim runs into the fields to hide his wound from Henry, so Henry runs into the fields to hide his "wound" from the tattered man who asks him where he is wounded. "It might be inside mostly, an' them plays thunder. Where is it located?" The men, so Henry feels, are perpetually probing his guilt-wound, "ever upraising the ghost of shame on the stick of their curiosity." The unmistakable implication here is of a flag, and the actual flag which Henry carries in battle is the symbol of his conscience. Conscience is also symbolized by the forest, the cathedral-forest where Henry retreats to nurse his guilt-wound and be consoled by the benedictions which nature sympathetically bestows upon him. Here in this forest-chapel there is a churchlike silence as insects bow their beaks while Henry bows his head in shame; they make a "devotional pause" while the trees chant a soft hymn to comfort him. But Henry is troubled; he cannot "conciliate the forest." Nor can he conciliate the flag. The flag registers the commotion of his mind, and it registers the restless movements of the nervous regiment—it flutters when the men expect battle. And when the regiment runs from battle, the flag sinks down "as if dying. Its motion as it fell was a gesture of despair." Henry dishonors the flag not when he flees from battle but when he flees from himself and he redeems the flag when he redeems his conscience.

Redemption begins in confession and absolution—in a change of heart. Henry's wounded conscience is not healed until he confesses to himself the truth and opens his eyes to new ways; not until he strips his enemy heart of "the brass and bombast of his earlier gospels," the vainglorious illusions he had fabricated into a cloak of pride and self-vindication; not until he puts on new garments of humility and loving-kindness for his fellow men. Redemption begins in humility—Henry's example is the loud soldier who becomes the humble soldier. He admits the folly of his former ways. Henry's spiritual change is a prolonged process, but it is signalized in moments when he loses his soul in the flux of things; then he courageously deserts himself instead of his fellow men; then, fearlessly plunging into battle, charging the enemy like "a pagan who defends his religion," he becomes swept up in a delirium of selflessness and feels himself "capable of profound sacrifices." The brave new Henry, "new bearer of the colors," triumphs over the former one. The flag of the enemy is wrenched from the hands of "the rival colorbearer," the symbol of Henry's own other self, and as this rival colorbearer dies Henry is reborn.[†]

† Author's note (1961): *Wilson, not Henry, wrenches the flag. In com-* *plaining that the phrase "is wrenched" is "highly misleading," S. B. Green-*

Henry's regeneration is brought about by the death of Jim Conklin, the friend whom Henry had known since childhood. He goes under various names. He is sometimes called the spectral soldier (his face is a pasty gray) and sometimes the tall soldier (he is taller than all other men), but there are unmistakable hints—in such descriptive details about him as his wound in the side, his torn body and his gory hand, and even in the initials of his name, Jim Conklin—that he is intended to represent Jesus Christ. We are told that there is "a resemblance in him to a devotee of a mad religion," and among his followers the doomed man stirs up "thoughts of a solemn ceremony." When he dies, the heavens signify his death—the red sun bleeds with the passion of his wounds:

"The red sun was pasted in the sky like a wafer."

This grotesque image, probably the most notorious metaphor in American literature, has been much debated and roundly damned as a false, melodramatic, and non-functional figure, but it has seemed artificial and irrelevant to Crane's critics only because they have lifted it out of its context. Like any other image, it has to be related to the structure of meaning in which it functions. I do not think it can be doubted that Crane intended to suggest here the sacrificial death celebrated in communion. Henry and the tattered soldier consecrate the death of the spectral soldier in "a solemn ceremony," the wafer signifies the sacramental blood and body of Christ, and the process of his spiritual rebirth begins at this moment when the wafer-like sun appears in the sky. It is a symbol of salvation through death. Henry, we are made to feel, recognizes in the lifeless sun his own lifeless conscience, his dead and as yet unregenerated selfhood, and that is why he blasphemes against it. His moral salvation and triumph are prepared for, (1) by this ritual of purification and religious devotion and, at the very start of the book, (2) by the ritual of absolution which Jim Conklin performs in the opening scene (page 1). It was the tall soldier who first "developed virtues" and showed the boys how to cleanse a flag—wash it in the muddy river! That is the way! The way is to immerse oneself in the destructive element!

Theme and style in *The Red Badge of Courage* are organically conceived, the theme of change conjoined with the fluid style by which it is evoked. Fluidity and change characterize the whole

field makes a point in his PMLA *essay (December, 1958). The first edition of my* [1951] *Introduction reads:* "He wrenches the flag of the enemy"—*my error. It is corrected in subsequent reprintings by the phrase* "is wrenched," *and it stands that way because my correction phrase had to fit letter-wise into the given letter-space of the original in the revised text.*

book. Crane's style, calculated to create confused impressions of change and motion, is deliberately disconnected and disordered. He interjects disjointed details, one non sequitur melting into another. Scenes and objects are felt as blurred; everything shifts in value. Yet everything has relationship to the total structure; everything is manipulated into contrapuntal cross-references of meaning. Crane puts language to poetic uses, which, to define it, is to use language reflexively and to use language symbolically. *It is the works which employ this use of language that constitute what is permanent of Crane.* Crane's language is the language of symbol and paradox. For example, the grotesque symbol and paradox of the wafer-like sun, in *The Red Badge;* or, in "The Open Boat," the paradox in the image of "cold comfortable sea-water," an image which calls to mind the poetry of W. B. Yeats with its fusion of contradictory emotions.† This single image evokes the sensation of the whole experience of the men in their wave-tossed dinghy. But, furthermore, it suggests another telltale significance, one that is applicable to Crane himself. What is readily recognizable in this paradox of "cold comfortable sea-water" is that irony of opposites which constituted the personality of the man who wrote it. It is the subjective correlative of his own plight. It symbolizes his personal outlook on life—a life that was filled with ironic contradictions. The enigma of the man is symbolized in his enigmatic style.

October, 1950‡
Storrs, Connecticut

† Author's note (1961): *My reading of this image as paradox is disputed by Philip Rahv in* Kenyon Review *for Spring, 1956, and defended in* Kenyon Review *for Spring, 1957: "Fiction and Its Critics," reprinted in expanded form in my* Houses That James Built and Other Literary Studies (1961).
‡ Author's postscript (1961): *"Notes Toward an Analysis of* The Red Badge of Courage" *was reissued in my essay "Stephen Crane: A Revaluation," in* Critiques and Essays on Modern Fiction: 1920–1951, *edited by John W. Aldridge (1952). It next appeared in my* Stephen Crane: An Omnibus *(November, 1952), again almost without any alterations except that much new matter was here added to my interpretation of Crane's war novel, and finally in my* Houses That James Built *(1961), again almost precisely as first published in 1951.*

In PMLA *(1958) Prof. S. B. Greenfield opines: "It is interesting to observe that Stallman, after examining the earlier manuscripts of* The Red Badge of Courage, *seems to have had a change of mind about Henry's 'sal-*vation.' He sees the 'images of tranquil skies' at the end of the novel as flatly sentimental and feels that they are given an ironic turn by the sun-through-clouds image: '[Henry] has undergone no change, no real spiritual development' (Omnibus, p. 221)." But contra Greenfield, there was no need for changing my mind about Henry's salvation as I had already spelled out —prior to seeing the manuscripts— the ironic double viewpoint about Henry's "salvation." I said in my* Critiques *essay, which was in the press prior to receiving photocopy of the manuscripts (the gift of Mr. C. W. Barrett in December, 1951), that "this sun-through-rain image, which epitomizes the double mood pattern that dominates every tableau in the whole sequence, is a symbol of Henry's moral triumph and it is an ironic commentary upon it" (Critiques, p. 259). As for "earlier manuscripts," as Greenfield puts it, there are two manuscripts, of which only one is an early and short version, the other being the final handwritten draft.*

MAXWELL GEISMAR

[The Psychic Wound of Henry Fleming Crane]†

* * * Crane's own behavior remained highly enigmatic; and
he * * * was suffering from tuberculosis. In the legends of his own
time he was viewed as a drunkard, a dope addict, a follower of loose
women; a notorious spokesman, in short, for a new literary movement that would have very similar charges thrown at some of its
other exponents. While recent scholarship has tended to clear
Crane of these charges, Thomas Beer still views him as another romantic figure of the Mauve Decade, and Berryman's study was actually the first one to suggest the true dynamics of this artist's in-
voluted temperament. . . . For we shall see that all of Crane's best
work sprang in effect from one dominant emotional experience: the
episode of childhood and infancy. It followed these emotions so
closely—in such an absolutely classical form of "sin" and atonement
—or of revolt and then surrender to the tribal law—as to provide us
with a new light on Crane's achievement.

His "realism," brilliant as it was, was related mainly to the tex-
ture of his fiction. Its true action was symbolic of the single experience in his own mind and heart. But what is fascinating, of course,
is to follow the disguised and diverse forms of this action as the
artist projected it outward into the universals of art: from the red
wound which his first young hero sought to the mutilation by fire, or
death by the sword of his final literary spokesmen.

"He knows nothing of war, yet he is drenched in blood," said a
discerning western critic of the period.‡ But, there was something
sweet, tender, lyrical which was the other side of horror in Crane's
work. There was something very touching in the purity of this artist's feeling which set him off, too, as a transitional figure both from
the sentiment of his own period, which he despised, and from the
savage code of the dawning Darwinian cosmos, which he refused
to accept. Perhaps it was [an] irony of literary history that the new
realism of the 1900's was, in this case, deeply rooted in the sheltered
and affectionate world of the nursery; but in a larger sense also

† From *Rebels and Ancestors*, copyright 1953 by Houghton Mifflin Company. Reprinted by permission. Pp.
73–79, 81–89. *Cf.* note on Schroeder's
article above. But, among theories of
homogeneous motivation for *The Red*

Badge, Geismar's Freudian approach
may suggest comparison also with a
naturalistic interpretation; *cf.* Hartwick, Walcutt, and others.
‡ Ambrose Bierce [Editors].

Crane's work was to stand at a halfway point between the old and the new.

"He had rid himself of the red sickness of battle," so Crane had described his innocent young farmer at the close of the Civil War story. "The sultry nightmare was in the past. . . . He turned now with a lover's thirst to images of tranquil skies, fresh meadows, cool brooks—an existence of soft and eternal peace."

Nothing could be lovelier than such passages in the writer's craft, or more untrue to the reality of his own obsessive and tragic career.

* * *

And there were very typical undertones in Stephen Crane's first book. Maggie's father was a sullen figure whose entrance was marked by the kicks he directed into "the chaotic mass on the ground" (the two battling children of Devil's Row). He then kicked his own son again for good measure, while the infant swore luridly at his parent. "For he felt that it was degradation for one who aimed to be some vague kind of soldier, or a man of blood with a sort of sublime licence, to be taken home by a father." The strain of parental conflict in Crane's story was supplemented at the outset by a touch of the demonic—by the violence suggested in the opening view of child-hood, by the horrors of proletarian life to which a somewhat fanciful view of the New York slums was adapted. * * * It was a scene closer to Daumier (or to Gustave Doré) than to the realities of the native scene. * * * The massive shoulders of Maggie's mother heaved with anger, so Crane said. "Grasping the urchin by the neck and shoulder she shook him until he rattled." The boy, a little later, ran to the hall, "shrieking like a monk in an earthquake," staggering away from a rain of parental blows and curses. The mother was viewed as a Besotted Fury with tangled hair and a mouth set in lines of "vindictive hatred."

* * *

And in such episodes as those in the "hilarious hall" on the Bowery, or of Maggie, after her seduction—"she was a-cryin' as if her heart would break"—the note of the Morality Play that was hidden beneath the shocking surface of the new realism became dominant. Maggie was certainly not the prostitute of the European novels of this genre; she was not even a "loose woman" in the sense that Dreiser's poor, innocent, pleasure-loving little Sister Carrie found herself to be. There was no trace of sexuality and few hints of warmth or affection—or even of mutual attraction—in her relationship with Pete. She was punished, as in the most devastating religious tract, immediately after the "deed" was done. * * * Her ending was brief and inevitable in the darkness of the final block, where the shutters of the tall buildings were closed like grim lips and some hidden factory sent up a yellow glare against the deathly black hue of the river.

The Darwinian moral in contrast to the accepted moral standards which Crane actually followed here, was obvious, too. Maggie was not fit to survive in the world of animal drives or true human passions. She is as a matter of fact a curiously wooden, graceless and unsympathetic figure when compared with Carrie Meeber or even the Trina of *McTeague*. His heroine, Crane said, had "blossomed in a mud puddle." * * * But it is actually Maggie's brother Jimmie, a more typical product of the slums, who is a more credible human being. "After a time his sneer grew so that it turned its glare upon all things. He became so sharp that he believed in nothing. To him the police were always actuated by malignant impulses, and the rest of the world was composed, for the most part, of despicable creatures who were all trying to take advantage of him. . . . He himself occupied a down-trodden position, which had a private but distinct element of grandeur in its isolation." They were revealing and prophetic lines in Crane's own history—this 'urchin's' world of malignant impulses and a private grandeur at war with authority. * * * The underlying turbulence of Crane's emotions carried the narrative forward in spite of fundamental flaws in the story. It is still a bright and exotic piece in the annals of realism, and *The Black Riders*, a volume of verse, in 1895, was another illuminating document in the career of a writer who had started out with such a rebellious bias.

* * *

Amy Lowell said, . . . "A loathed and vengeful God broods over *The Black Riders*. Crane's soul was heaped with bitterness, and this bitterness he flung back at the theory of life which had betrayed him. . . . Crane handed the world the acrid fumes of his heart, and they howled at him for an obscene blasphemer, or patted him on the back as a 'cracker-jack' on whom they doted." * * * The Darwinian winds had already struck a rudderless "ship of the world" here, which persisted in "going ridiculous voyages/ making quaint progress/ turning as with serious purpose" before the blind forces of destiny. * * * The note of Crane's own revolt against the harsh Jehovah of the Old Testament was expressed over and over again in these verses. "Well, then, I hate Thee, unrighteous picture; Wicked image, I hate Thee."

* * *

The recurrent symbolism, and the true charm of *The Black Riders*, was that of an affectionate and diminutive world: the world of the nursery.

> Then came whisperings in the winds:
> "Good-bye good-bye!"
> Little voices called in the darkness:
> "Good-bye! good-bye!"

And one remembers, along with the little voices, the "little blades of grass," the "little men" upon whose innocent heads the divine wrath was distributed, the "babes" who clung to tradition blindly, so Crane said—and the "little rows" in which his poems had originally come into his consciousness. * * * There were lines where Crane flatly juxtaposed a Deity who thundered loudly, "fat with rage, and puffing," and the vision of his inner thoughts who looked at him "With soft eyes/ Lit with infinite comprehension,/ And said, 'My poor child!' " Or the verse where he was advised: "You should live like a flower, holding malice like a puppy, waging war like a lambkin": those charming verses in which even the lambs were reduced to an innocent and affectionate diminutive. This was a child's universe of angels, and flowers and puppies—where even the central conflicts were those of the kindergarten. * * * It was a central view that also betrayed a certain lack of sin or evil—or of knowledge—on a more mature level of human behavior, even while it stressed those forces in its own terms. And wasn't this an odd introduction to the novel which became a cornerstone of the new "realism" in American fiction and established Crane's position as the master of blood and wounds—the brilliant historian of war and manhood.

The Red Badge of Courage, in 1895, was that work. Described as an episode of the American Civil War, its result was final, as Joseph Hergesheimer said. "Therefore all novels about war must be different; the old pretentious attack was for ever obliterated," and the later writer was correct in viewing the tale as a series of "connected and momentary activities, one fading into the other in a march from dark to dark." One notices Crane's deliberate stress on the anonymous—the "youthful private," the "tall soldier"; on the incomplete—"the twisted news of a great battle"; and on the group, as in the famous first lines of the novel. "The cold passed reluctantly from the earth, and the retiring fogs revealed an army stretched out on the hills, resting. As the landscape changed from brown to green, the army awakened, and began to tremble with eagerness at the noise of rumours. It casts its eyes upon the roads. . . ."

The technical achievement of the *Red Badge* was the picture of war done absolutely from the inside. It was the fragmentary consciousness of impending battle from the common soldier's point of view, with no 'causes' for the action which he is to determine, no sense of direction on his part, no plan of action which he understands, not to mention the larger issues of the Civil War which are never touched upon in the entire novel. During all the preliminary marching, retreating, actions, waitings, we are hardly even conscious of the officers who are controlling this military organism. There are only the routines of camp life; the gossip, boasting, joking of these farm country types—"it ain't likely they'll lick the hull rebel army all-to-oncet the first time"; and the pageantry. "In the gloom before the break of day their uniforms glowed a deep purple hue. From across the river the red eyes were still peering. In the eastern sky there was a yellow patch like a rug laid for the feet of the coming sun; and against it, black and patternlike, loomed the gigantic figure of the colonel on a gigantic horse." And the wet grass which rustled like silk at night when the air was heavy and cold with dew, or the blue, pure sky and the sun gleaming on the trees and fields, while Nature went on "with her golden process in the midst of much devilment," remind us that this was almost the last agrarian and to some degree still individualistic war for American troops. The army sits down again "to think." The first dead soldier whom Crane's hero encounters—an "invulnerable" corpse with his ashen face and tattered shoes—announces a new theme.

Earlier, this hero had suddenly realized he was caught in the "moving box" of his regiment. "As he perceived this fact it occurred to him that he had never wished to come to the war." His conflict, of course, had been related to his own fear and panic while the battle came closer to him—the "red animal—war, the blood-swollen god." On the surface it was a highly realistic, ironic and humorous account of a young boy's struggle with cowardice in the midst of a larger and brilliantly rendered scene of battle, disorganized and incoherent: the complete opposite of standard descriptions of heroics, bravery and martial discipline. "No one seemed to be wrestling with such a terrific personal problem," Crane's hero thinks. "He was a mental outcast." When he realizes that he is in a trap from which he cannot escape, he is outraged and terrified. "He lagged, with tragic glances at the sky." When the raw troops break under the rebel attack—the shells swirling and exploding like "strange war flowers bursting into fierce bloom" —there came into the youth's eyes, Crane said, "a look that one can see in the orbs of a jaded horse." Directly "he began to speed to the rear in great leaps," and his was the work "of a master's legs."

Yet his expression was that of a criminal who thinks his guilt and his punishment great, and he went far, "seeking dark and intricate places."

He went indeed from "obscurity into promises of a greater obscurity." There is that curious little scene in the religious half-light of a forest chapel where another corpse was seated with his back against a columnlike tree. "The dead man and the living man exchanged a long look," and the youth, receiving a subtle suggestion to touch the dead body, "burst the bonds which had fastened him to the spot and fled, unheeding the underbrush." . . . This was at the center of the psychological action in *The Red Badge of Courage*; the chapel scene is perfect dream symbolism in the novel. From that point the narrative tension is based on the classic theme of sin and retribution—but a sense of sin that is in fact deeper and more mysterious in its overtones than the issue of the youth's cowardice, and a retribution that takes on a very curious aspect, too. In the first trauma of battle, had Crane's young soldier developed a "red rage" of impotency because his rifle could only be used against one life at a time, while he was suffocating in the smoke of death? "He fought frantically for respite for his senses, for air, as a babe being smothered attacks the deadly blankets."

Now he returned to the battle with an obscure but nevertheless overpowering compulsion. "He must go close and see it produce corpses." And there are the famous chapters which describe "the steady current of the maimed," and the "awful machinery" in which the men had been entangled. Crane's hero walks amid wounds, in a bleeding mob of men—

"At times he regarded the wounded soldiers in an envious way. He conceived persons with torn bodies to be peculiarly happy. He wished that he, too, had a wound, a red badge of courage."

The meaning of the title of the story becomes clear, of course. But the "red badge"—in this context of torn bodies—almost indicates as much of a yearning for the mark of mutilation as for a sign of bravery. The chapter of the maimed is suffused with references to the stigmata of suffering. There is the remarkable portrait of the spectral soldier, Jim Conklin, walking stiffly in his death throes, "as if he were taking infinite care not to arouse the passion of his wounds." And the famous tag line of this chapter: "The red sun was pasted in the sky like a wafer"—a line which became in its time the slogan of Crane's modernism—actually referred of course to the flesh and the blood of the martyred God, or the bleeding Son.

What fascinating imagery ran through these sections of the

novel, to be sure! Crane's youth desired to screech out his grief.
He was stabbed, but his tongue lay dead in the tomb of his mouth.
If he envies the corpses—the dead—and is lacking the red wound
of courage—and virility—he is confronted by the prospect of wearing
"the sore badge of his dishonour" through the rest of his life. "With
his heart continually assuring him that he was despicable, he could
not exist without making it, through his actions, apparent to all
men." His capacity for self-hate was multiplied, Crane added. And
the simple questions of the tattered man in this parable of guilt
and redemption now taking place on the battlefield of the mind
were like knife thrusts to the youthful hero:

"They asserted a society that probes relentlessly at secrets until all
is apparent. His late companion's chance persistency made him feel
that he could not keep his crime concealed in his bosom. It was sure
to be brought plain by one of those arrows which cloud the air and
are constantly pricking, discovering, proclaiming those things which
are willed to be for ever hidden. He admitted that he could not defend himself against this agency. It was not within the power of
vigilance."

Thus the maimed body was equated with the maimed spirit
in the central action of *The Red Badge of Courage*. It was Henry
Fleming's shame at his psychic wound which led him to yearn for
the physical wound—a wound which in a deeper psychological
sense might also block him from the maturity—the manhood—
which he sought in the area of moral values. (And it is almost
the first time we are conscious that Crane's anonymous youth had
a name at all.) Then in swift succession there are those happy
omens of his salvation: the "false" wound which he suffers in his
struggle with another deserter; the episode of his rescue by the man
of the cheery voice and of the warm and strong hand. "As he who
had so befriended him was thus passing out of his life, it suddenly
occurred to the youth that he had not once seen his face." There
is the loud young soldier who befriends him when he returns to
his regiment of war-torn veterans and is received into their community with tenderness and care,—and then the youth's deep sleep
of exhaustion. "When the youth awoke it seemed to him that he
had been asleep for a thousand years, and he felt sure that he opened
his eyes upon an unexpected world. Grey mists were slowly shifting
before the first efforts of the sunrays. An impending splendour could
be seen in the eastern sky."

An "unexpected" world of tribal acceptance, of course; of security
within the codes and conventions of society, of law, honor and authority—and the impending splendour of equality among men after
what has been really a kind of trial by ordeal. For the ceremonies

of pagan ritual were implicit beneath Crane's constant use of Christian allegory in the *Red Badge*. The controlling vision of the novel is actually mythic, animistic, primitive. The deep sleep of exhaustion, extending back a thousand years—a trauma of rebirth and moral resurrection—brings the primitive elements of the fable into focus. And the theme was stressed. "It was revealed to him that he had been a barbarian, a beast," Crane said after his hero's next battle. "He had fought like a pagan who defends his religion. Regarding it, he saw that it was fine, wild, and, in some ways, easy. . . . And he had not been aware of the process. He had slept and, awakening, found himself a knight."

But here, for the first time, the novel faltered. Having been accepted into the tribe—after the ordeal of suffering—Crane's protagonist must accept the tribal laws and customs, even the language. One notices the touches of lingering Victorian sentiment in the descriptions of the "quiet manhood, non-assertive, but of sturdy and strong blood" now possessed by the battle-tested hero. There is a note of adolescent heroics in the descriptions of the seasoned troops, the veterans. "They gazed upon them with looks of uplifted pride, feeling new trust in the grim, always confident weapons in their hands. And they were men." In their battle fury, too—a delirium which was heedless of despair and death, a "mad enthusiasm" which was incapable of checking itself before granite and brass—Crane fell, as he very seldom did, into the rhetoric of war. In those "hoarse, howling protests" with which the men supported a desperate attack of the regiment, or in the "vicious, wolf-like temper" of comrades in battle—or their "barbaric cry of rage"—this brilliant stylist even descended to the clichés of the Social Darwinism which would mark, and to some extent disfigure, the typical literary figures of the age.

The conclusion of *The Red Badge of Courage* was an anticlimax: the true tension of the novel had disappeared. The tragic potential of the narrative had shifted at the moment of the hero's "conversion" and acceptance of the tribal (or military) codes. The final note was that of an ironic comedy of heroism—still, however, haunted by the furies and horrors which persisted in Crane's mind if they had been exorcized from the literary work. . . . For this was ultimately a study in social appearance—or social approval—rather than a full study of conscience. At the moment of the hero's deepest conflict, the central fact was simply that he could not keep his 'crime' concealed in his bosom, and not the nature of the crime itself. The enemy was still a society which probed relentlessly at the individual's secrets and proclaimed "those things which are willed to be for ever hidden"—this quite malignant agency indeed against which Crane's youth could not defend himself. And even after his conversion and social acceptance, there were ambiguous elements in his thought. "Some arrows of scorn that had buried themselves in his heart had generated strange and unspeakable hatred. It was clear to him that his final and absolute revenge was to be achieved by his dead body lying, torn and guttering, upon the field." Ambiguous and bitter elements; familiar and desperate convictions.

For it almost appeared that Crane had sought mutilation and death quite apart from the purpose of his narrative; we shall notice also that odd communion with corpses which is a recurrent feature in his work. * * * Perhaps indeed the "false" wound which had enabled his isolated protagonist to return safely to the communal fold might turn out in the end to be the true wound of the artist's work. Or at least the psychic wound which lay still deeper in Crane's consciousness had found only a temporary catharsis. As in the episode of the screaming, terrified soldier and the godlike officer whose voice expressed a divinity—"stern, hard, with no reflection of fear in it"— there was no doubt also that the little parable of the Civil War concealed beneath its moral and social levels the same religious and oedipal conflict that had preoccupied Stephen Crane in *The Black Riders* and, though more obliquely, in *Maggie*, too.

From this source came the central tension and prevailing imagery of the military story. The rebellion of the youth against the God of Wrath, the Unjust Father, had been projected into the fable of the sinful boy and the tribal law. . . . But one wonders what "crime" had rendered it necessary, as in the ceremonial exorcisms of primitive religions, for the errant youth to offer up part of his virility in the very struggle to achieve manhood. What was the real meaning of the "torn and guttering body" toward which Crane was drawn? And were the purposes and experiences of maturity to be bounded only by that baptism of fire—that bar mitzvah of blood—which had surrounded and almost obliterated the innocent youth of his tale?

At any rate, much too much of Crane's career was spent in the attempt to validate the imaginary experience in *The Red Badge of Courage* by the test of battle itself. He was obliged, as he said, to prove (but to whom?) that his first, brilliant, immensely intuitive major work was really "all right."

JOHN E. HART

The Red Badge of Courage as Myth and Symbol†

When Stephen Crane published *The Red Badge of Courage* in 1895, the book created an almost immediate sensation. Crane had had no experience in war, but in portraying the reactions of a young soldier in battle, he had written with amazing accuracy. As one way of re-examining *The Red Badge of Courage*, we would want to read it as myth and symbolic action. Clearly, the construction of the story, its moral and meaning, its reliance on symbol follow in detail the traditional formula of myth.[1] Crane's main theme is the discovery of self, that unconscious self, which, when identified with the inexhaustible energies of the group, enables man to understand the "deep forces that have shaped man's destiny."[2] The progressive movement of the hero, as in all myth, is that of separation, initiation, and return.[3] Within this general framework, Crane plots his story with individual variation. Henry Fleming, a Youth, ventures forth from his known environment into a region of naturalistic, if not super-naturalistic wonder; he encounters the monstrous forces of war and death; he is transformed through a series of rites and revelations into a hero; he returns to identify his new self with the deeper communal forces of the group and to bestow the blessings of his findings on his fellow comrades.

Whatever its "realistic" style, much of the novel's meaning is revealed through the use of metaphor and symbol. The names of characters, for example, suggest both particular attributes and general qualities: the Tall Soldier, whose courage and confidence enable him to measure up to the vicissitudes of war and life; the Loud Soldier, the braggart, the over-confident, whose personality is, like Henry's, transformed in war; the Tattered Soldier, whose clothes signify his lowly and exhausted plight; the Cheery Man, whose keenness and valor prevent his falling into despair. Likewise, the use of color helps to clarify and extend the meaning. Red, traditionally associated with blood and fire, suggests courage, flag, life-energy, desire, ambition.

† *University of Kansas City Review*, XIX (Summer, 1953), 249–56. By permission of the author and the *University of Kansas City Review*. Hart's emphasis on the psychological authority of the myth may be fruitfully compared with the Freudian analysis employed by Geismar in the previous article.

1. See Joseph Campbell, *The Hero with a Thousand Faces* (New York, 1949), p. 3. Campbell defines myth as "the secret opening through which the inexhaustible energies of the cosmos pour into human cultural manifestation."
2. *Ibid.*, p. 256.
3. *Ibid.*, p. 30.

Black, traditionally associated with death, implies "great unknown," darkness, forests, and, by extension, entombment and psychological death. The whole paraphernalia of myth-religious and sacrificial rites —the ceremonial dancing, the dragons with fiery eyes, the menacing landscape, the entombment, the sudden appearance of a guide, those symbols so profoundly familiar to the unconscious and so frightening to the conscious personality—give new dimensions of meaning to the novel.

What prompts Henry to leave his known environment is his unconscious longing to become a hero. In a state of conscious reflection, he looks on war with distrust. Battles belonged to the past. Had not "secular and religious education" effaced the "throat grappling instinct" and "firm finance" "held in check the passions?" But in dreams, he has thrilled to the "sweep and fire" of "vague and bloody conflicts"; he has "imagined people secure in the shadow of his eagle-eyed prowess." As the wind brings the noise of the ringing church bells, he listens to their summons as a proclamation from the "voice of the people." Shivering in his bed in a "prolonged ecstasy of excitement," he determines to enlist. If the call has come in an unconscious dream-like state where the associations of wind, church bells, ecstasy, heroism, glory are identified with the "voice" of the "group," Henry, fully "awake," insists on his decision. Although his mother, motivated apparently by "deep conviction" and impregnable ethical motives, tries to dissuade his ardor, she actually helps him in the initial step of his journey. She prepares his equipment: "eight pairs of socks," "yer best shirts," "a cup of blackberry jam." She advises him to watch the company he keeps and to do as he is told. Underlining the very nature of the problem, she warns that he will be "jest one little fellow amongst a hull lot of others."

It is this conflict between unconscious desire and conscious fear that prevents Henry from coming to terms with his new environments. Consciously concerned with thoughts of rumored battle, he crawls into his hut "through an intricate hole that served it as a door," where he can be "alone with some new thoughts that had lately come to him." Although his apparent concern is over fear of battle, his real anxiety is that of his individuation. As far as his relationship to war is concerned, he knows "nothing of himself." He has always "taken certain things for granted, never challenging his belief in ultimate success, and bothering little about means and roads." Now, he is an "unknown quantity." If his problems merge into that of whether he will or will not run from an "environment" that threatens to "swallow" his very identity, he sees that it cannot be solved by "mental slate and pencil." Action—"blaze, blood, and danger"—is the only test.

In giving artistic conception to Henry's conflict, Crane relies on a pattern of darkness and light, but adapts such traditional machinery to his particular purpose. As we have seen, Henry achieves courage and strength in the "darkness" of his tent, where his unconscious mind faces the problems of his new surroundings openly and bravely. As he peers into the "ominous distance" and ponders "upon the mystic gloom" in the morning twilight, he is eager to settle his "great problem" with the "red eyes across the river"—eyes like "orbs of a row of dragons advancing." Coming from the darkness towards the dawn, he watches "the gigantic figure of the colonel on a gigantic horse." They loom "black and pattern like" against the yellow sky. As the "black rider," the messenger of death lifts "his gigantic arm and calmly stroke[s] his mustache," Henry can hardly breathe. Then, with the hazy light of day, he feels the consciousness of growing fear. It seems ironic that his comrades, especially the Tall Soldier, should be filled with ardor, even song—just as he was in the darkness of his room at home. With the "developing day," the "two long, thin, black columns" have become "two serpents crawling from the cavern of night." These columns, monsters themselves, move from darkness to light with little fear, for they move, not as so many individuals, but as group units. Clearly, if Henry is to achieve his ambitions, he must "see" and "face" the enemy in the light of day without fear, as well as "perceive" his relationship to the group, which is, in a sense, a "monster" itself.

Henry's growing concern is not for his comrades, but for himself. Although he must march along with them, he feels caught "by the iron laws of tradition." He considers himself "separated from the others." At night, when the campfires dot the landscape "like red peculiar blossoms (as communal fires which impregnate the landscape with "life" and "vitality," they suggest the life energy of the group), Henry remains a "few paces in the gloom," a "mental outcast." He is "alone in space," where only the "mood of darkness" seems to sympathize with him. He concludes that no other person is "wrestling with such a terrific personal problem." But even in the darkness of his tent he cannot escape: the "red, shivering reflection of a fire" shines through the canvas. He sees "visions of a thousand-tongued fear that would babble at his back and cause him to flee." His "fine mind" can no more face the monster war than it can cope with the "brute minds" of his comrades.

Next day as Henry, with sudden "impulse of curiosity," stares at the "woven red" against the "soft greens and browns," the harmony of landscape is broken when the line of men stumble onto a dead soldier in their path. Henry pauses and tries to "read in the dead eyes the answer to the Question." What irony it is that the ranks open "to avoid the corpse," as if, invulnerable, death forces a way itself. He notes that the wind strokes the dead man's beard, just as the black rider had stroked his mustache. Probing his sensations, he feels no ardor for battle. His soldier's clothes do not fit, for he is not a "real" soldier. His "fine mind" enables him to see what the "brute minds" of his comrades do not: the landscape threatens to engulf them. Their ardor is not heroism. They are merely going to a sacrifice, going "to look at war, the red animal—war the blood-swollen god." Even if he warned them, they would not listen. Misunderstood, he can only "look to the grave for comprehension." His feeling is prophetic, for it anticipates the death and transformation of personality that is about to occur.

Before he actually runs from battle, Henry experiences a moment of true realization. Impatient to know whether he is a "man of traditional courage," he suddenly loses "concern for himself," and becomes "not a man but a member." "Welded into a common personality" and "dominated by a single desire," he feels the "red rage" and "battle brotherhood"—that "mysterious fraternity born of the smoke and danger of death." He is carried along in a kind of "battle sleep." He rushes at the "black phantoms" like a "pestered animal." Then, awakening to the awareness of a second attack, he feels weak and bloodless. "Like the man who lost his legs at the approach of the red and green monster," he seems "to shut his eyes and wait to be gobbled." He has a revelation. Throwing down his gun, he flees like a "blind man." His vision of "selflessness" disappears; in this "blindness" his fears are magnified. "Death about to thrust him between the shoulder blades [is] far more dreadful than death about to smite him between the eyes." Impotent and blind (without gun and "vision"), he runs into the forest "as if resolved to bury himself." He is both physically and psychologically isolated from the group and hence from the very source of food and energy, both material and spiritual, that impels heroic achievement.

In the language of myth Henry's inability to face the monsters of battle in the "light," to identify himself with his comrades (both acts are, in a sense, identical), and thus to give up his individual self, which is sustained only in "darkness" and in isolation, so that his full self can be realized in the light of communal identification symbolizes a loss of spiritual, moral, and physical power, which only a rebirth of identity can solve. Only by being reborn can he come to understand that man's courage springs from the self-realization that he must participate harmoniously as a member of the group. Only then can he understand the "deep forces" from which his individual energy and vitality spring. Thus, Henry's entombment in the forest is only preliminary to the resurrection that will follow. Without his full powers, his transformation cannot be effected by himself, but requires the necessity of ritualistic lessons and the aid of outside forces or agents. His own attempts to expiate his feeling of guilt by logic only leave him lost and confused in the labyrinth of his limitations.

After the burial of himself in the forest, it is his unconscious awareness of the nature of death that restores the strength and energy he had felt in his dreams at home. As he pushes on, going from "obscurity into promises of a greater obscurity," he comes face to face with the very "act" from which he is running. It is a dead soldier covered with "black" ants. As he recoils in terror, the branches of the forest hold him firm. In a moment of blind fear, he imagines that "some strange voice . . . from the dead throat" will squawk after him in "horrible menaces," but he hears, almost unconsciously, only a soft wind, which sings a "hymn of twilight." This aura of tranquility, produced in a "religious half light"—the boughs are arched like a chapel—transfixes Henry. He hears a "terrific medley of all noises." It is ironic that he should be fleeing from the black rider only to encounter death and "black ants." His ego is deflated. Did he ever imagine that he and his comrades could decide the war as if they were "cutting the letters of their names deep into everlasting tablets of brass?" Actually, the "affair" would receive only a "meek and immaterial title." With this thought and the song of the wind comes a certain faith. "Pictures of stupendous conflicts" pass through his mind. As he hears the "red cheers" of marching men, he is determined: he runs in the direction of the "crimson roar" of battle.

Although Henry's old fears have not been completely overcome, his meeting with the Tattered Man clarifies the need and method of atoning for his guilt. Having joined the marching soldiers, Henry is envious of this mob of "bleeding men." He walks beside the twice-wounded Tattered Man, whose face is "suffused with a light of love for the army which [is] to him all things beautiful and powerful." Moving in the "light of love," the Man speaks in a voice as "gentle as a girl's." "Where yeh hit?" he repeatedly asks Henry. "Letters of guilt" burn on the Youth's brow. How can he defend himself against an agency which so pitilessly reveals man's secrets? How can he atone for his guilt? His wish that "he, too, had a wound, a red badge of courage" is only preliminary to the fulfillment of atonement, just as in the rites of some primitive tribes or as in Christ's crucifixion on the cross, "blood" plays an essential part in the act of atonement and in the process of transformation.

If the Tattered Man's questioning reveals the need and nature of atonement, meeting the Tall Soldier shows the quality of character needed to make the sacrifice. Justifying the "tall" of his name by his "supreme unconcern" for battle, Conklin accepts his role as part of the group with coolness and humility. Because he realizes the insignificance of self, he has no fear of a threatening landscape. Sleeping, eating, and drinking afford him greatest satisfaction. During meal time, he is "quiet and contented," as if his spirit were "communing with viands." Now, fatally wounded, he is at his rendezvous with death; his actions are ceremonial, "rite-like." He moves with "mysterious purpose," like "the devotee of a mad religion, blood-sucking, muscle-wrenching, bone-crushing." His chest heaves "as if an animal was within," his "arms beat wildly," "his tall figure [stretches] itself to its full height" and falls to the ground—dead. His side looks "as if it had been chewed by wolves," as if the monster war had eaten him and then swallowed his life. This "ceremony at the place of meeting," this sacrificial ritual of placating the monster has enabled him to find the ultimate answer to the Question, but it has consumed its victim in the process.

It is the receiving of the wound, a kind of "magic" touch, whatever its irony of being false, that actually enables Henry to effect atonement. As the army itself retreats, he is truly "at one" with the group ("at one" and atone have similar functions as the very words imply), for both are running from battle. Actually, Henry is not "conscious" of what has happened. Clutching boldly at a retreating man's arm, he begs for an answer. Desperate at being restrained, the man strikes the Youth with his rifle. Henry falls. His legs seem "to die." In a ritual not unlike that of Conklin's dying (it is Henry's "youth," his immature self dying), he grabs at the grass, he twists and lurches, he fights "an intense battle with his body." Then, he goes "tall soldier fashion." In his exaltation, he is afraid to touch his head lest he disturb his "red badge of courage." He relishes "the cool, liquid feeling," which evokes the memory of "certain meals his mother had cooked," "the bank of a shaded pool," "the melody in the wind of youthful summer." The association of blood with that of food suggests the identical function of each. Just as food is nourishment to the body, so blood is nourishment to his spiritual and moral self. Because the monster has "eaten" of him and thus destroyed his fears, he has achieved a moral and spiritual maturity, even, as his going "tall" implies, sexual potency. He feels the tranquility and harmony that has always characterized his dream state. But his wound is an actual fact, and the achieved atonement is not quite same as in a "pure" dream state. Yet it is still achieved under the aegis of "dusk," and can only be fully realized in the full "light" of group identification.

Henry is further assisted in his transformation by an "unseen guide." Wandering in the darkness, he is overtaken by the Cheery Man, whose voice, possessing a "wand of a magic kind," guides him to his regiment. Thinking of him later, Henry recalls that "he had not once seen his face."

It is important to note here what part food and eating play in Henry's atonement and rebirth. As we have seen, food has both physical and spiritual significance. From the first, Henry has observed that "eating" was of greatest importance to the soldiers. After the Tall Soldier's death, he has speculated on "what those men had eaten that they could be in such haste to force their way to grim chances of death." Now, he discovers that he has "a scorching thirst," a hunger that is "more powerful than a direct hunger." He is desperately tired. He cannot see distinctly. He feels the need "of food and rest, at whatever cost." On seeing his comrades again, he goes directly towards the "red light"—symbol of group energy. They fuss over his wound and give him a canteen of coffee. As he swallows the "delicious draught," the mixture feels as cool to him as did the wound. He feels like an "exhausted soldier after a feast of war." He has tasted of and been eaten by the great monster. By the wound (the being eaten), he has atoned for his guilt with blood. In eating and drinking with his comrades (the communal feasting), he has achieved both literal and spiritual identification with the group. Through his initiation, he has returned as a "member," not an isolated individual. By "swallowing or being swallowed," he has, through atonement and rebirth, come to be master of himself and, henceforth, to be master of others. The Loud Soldier gives up his blankets, and Henry is, in sleep, soon "like his comrades."

In the language of myth, Henry has become a hero. When he awakes next morning from a "thousand years'" sleep, he finds, like Rip Van Winkle, a new "unexpected world." What he discovers has happened to the Loud Soldier is actually the same change that has come over him. For the first time Henry is aware that others have been wrestling with problems not unlike his own. If the Loud Soldier is now a man of reliance, a man of "purpose and abilities," Henry perceives in imagery that recalls the "blossoming campfires" of his comrades that

"a faith in himself had secretly blossomed. There was a little flower of confidence growing within him. He was a man of experience."

Again like the Loud Soldier, he has at last

"overcome obstacles which he admitted to be mountainous. They had fallen like paper peaks, and he was now what he called a hero. He had not been aware of the process. He had slept and, awakening, found himself a knight."

Having overcome the obstacle of self, Henry has at last discovered that the dragon war is, after all, only a gigantic guard of the great death.

If the hero is to fulfill the total requirements of his role, he must bring back into the normal world of day the wisdom that he has acquired during his transformation. Like the "knight" that he is, Henry is now able to face the red and black dragons on the "clear" field of battle. He performs like a "pagan who defends his religion," a "barbarian," "a beast." As the regiment moves forward, Henry is "unconsciously in advance." Although many men shield their eyes, he looks squarely ahead. What he sees "in the new appearance of the landscape" is like "a revelation." There is both a clarity of vision and of perception: the darkness of the landscape has vanished; the blindness of his mental insight has passed. As with the wound and the coffee, he feels the "delirium that encounters despair and death." He has, perhaps, in this "temporary but sublime absence of selfishness," found the reason for being there after all. As the pace quickly "eats up the energies of the men," they dance and gyrate "like savages." Without regard for self, Henry spurs them forward towards the colors.

In the language of myth, it is woman who represents the totality of what can be known. As "life," she embodies both love and hate. To accept her is to be king, the incarnate god, of her created world. As knower (one who recognizes her), the hero is master. Meeting the goddess and winning her is the final test of the hero's talent. Curiously, it is the flag that occupies the position of goddess in the story. The flag is the lure, the beautiful maiden of the configuration, whose capture is necessary if Henry is to fulfill his role as hero. Crane writes:

"With [Henry], as he hurled himself forward, was born a love, a despairing fondness of this flag which was near him. It was a creation of beauty and invulnerability. It was a goddess, radiant, that bended its form with an imperious gesture to him. It was a woman, red and white, hating and loving, that called him with the voice of his hope. Because no harm could come to it he endowed it with power. He kept near, as if it could be a saver of lives, and an imploring cry went from his mind."

As Henry and his comrade wrench the pole from the dead bearer, they both acquire an invincible wand of hope and power. Taking it roughly from his friend, Henry has, indeed, reached heroic proportions.

In his role as hero, Henry stands "erect and tranquil" in face of the great monster. Having "rid himself of the red sickness of battle," having overcome his fear of losing individual identity, he now despises the "brass and bombast of his earlier gospels." Because he is at-one with his comrades, he has acquired their "daring spirit of a savage religion-mad," their "brute" strength to endure the violence of a violent world, the "red of blood and black of passion." His individual strength is their collective strength, that strength of the totality which the flag symbolizes. As Crane says:

"He felt a quiet manhood, nonassertive but of sturdy and strong blood. He knew that he would no more quail before his guides wherever they should point. He had been to touch the great death, and found that, after all, it was but the great death. He was a man."

At last he has put the "somber phantom" of his desertion at a distance. Having emerged into the "golden ray of sun," Henry feels a "store of assurance."

Following the general pattern of myth with peculiar individual variations, Crane has shown how the moral and spiritual strength of the individual springs from the group, and how, through the identification of self with group, the individual can be "reborn in identity with the whole meaning of the universe." Just as his would-be hero was able to overcome his fears and achieve a new moral and spiritual existence, so all men can come to face life, face it as calmly and as coolly as one faces the terrors, the odd beings, the deluded images of dreams. If it is, as Campbell points out, the "unconscious" which supplies the "keys that open the whole realm of the desired and feared adventures of the discovery of self," then man, to discover self, must translate his dreams into actuality. To say that Henry accomplishes his purpose is not to imply that Crane himself achieved the same kind of integration. Whatever the final irony implied, he certainly saw that the discovery of self was essential to building the "bolder, cleaner, more spacious, and fully human life."

CHARLES C. WALCUTT

[Stephen Crane: Naturalist and Impressionist]†

* * *

My thesis is that naturalism is the offspring of transcendentalism. American transcendentalism asserts the unity of Spirit and Nature

† From *American Literary Naturalism, A Divided Stream* by Charles C. Walcutt. University of Minnesota Press, Minneapolis. Copyright 1956 by the University of Minnesota. Reprinted by permission. Pp. 66–82, *passim*. Aspects of this subject or its siblings can be found for comparison in Åhnebrink, Hartwick, Geismar, Hart, and others in this collection.

and affirms that intuition (by which the mind discovers its affiliation with Spirit) and scientific investigation (by which it masters Nature, the symbol of Spirit) are equally rewarding and valid approaches to reality. When this mainstream of transcendentalism divides, as it does toward the end of the nineteenth century, it produces two rivers of thought. One, the approach to Spirit through intuition, nourishes idealism, progressivism, and social radicalism. The other, the approach to Nature through science, plunges into the dark canyon of mechanistic determinism. The one is rebellious, the other pessimistic; the one ardent, the other fatal; the one acknowledges will, the other denies it. Thus "naturalism," flowing in both streams, is partly defying Nature and partly submitting to it; and it is in this area of tension that my investigation lies, its immediate subject being the forms which the novel assumes as one stream or the other, and sometimes both, flow through it. The problem, as will appear, is an epitome of the central problem of twentieth-century thought.

* * *

The works of Stephen Crane (1871–1900) are an early and unique flowering of pure naturalism. It is naturalism in a restricted and special sense, and it contains many non-naturalistic elements, but it is nevertheless entirely consistent and coherent. It marks the first entry, in America, of a deterministic philosophy not confused with ethical motivation into the structure of the novel. Ethical judgment there is, in plenty. To define Crane's naturalism is to understand one of the few perfect and successful embodiments of the theory in the American novel. It illustrates the old truth that literary trends often achieve their finest expressions very early in their histories. *Mutatis mutandis*, Crane is the Christopher Marlowe of American naturalism—and we have had no Shakespeare.

Crane's naturalism is to be found, first, in his attitude toward received values, which he continually assails through his naturalistic method of showing that the traditional concepts of our social morality are shams and the motivations presumably controlled by them are pretenses; second, in his impressionism, which fractures experiences into disordered sensation in a way that shatters the old moral "order" along with the old orderly processes of reward and punishment; third, in his obvious interest in a scientific or deterministic accounting for events, although he does not pretend or attempt to be scientific in either the tone or the management of his fables. Crane's naturalism does not suffer from the problem of the divided stream because each of his works in so concretely developed that it does not have a meaning apart from what happens in it. The meaning is always the action; there is no wandering into theory that runs counter to what happens in the action; and nowhere does a character operate as a genuinely free ethical agent in defiance of the author's intentions. Crane's success is a triumph of style: manner and meaning are one.

* * *

A perennial controversy about naturalism concerns whether it is optimistic or pessimistic—whether it dwells in the horrors it portrays or believes it can correct them. The problem achieves an epitome in *Maggie:* however stark the horror, no reader can feel that Crane is scientifically disinterested or unconcerned. Where his method does, through its fascinated concern with detail, achieve a ghastly fixation, it is the quality of Goya rather than the cold form of Velasquez. The story shows that nothing can be done for Maggie and her family, for they are lost; but it presents the exact reality with an intensity that defies indifference. I say the exact reality. It seems exact, but it would be more accurate to say that Crane objectifies and renders exactly his spirited and intentional distortion of the grotesque world that he has exactly seen.

* * *

Crane's naturalism is descriptive: he does not pretend to set forth a proof, like a chemical demonstration, that what happened must have happened, inevitably. This is what Zola was forever saying he did, and it is for these pretensions of scientific demonstration and proof that he has been chided by later critics. Crane simply shows how a sequence of events takes place quite independently of the wills and judgments of the people involved. The reader is convinced that it happened that way, and he sees that the ordinary moral sentiments do not adequately judge or account for these happenings. The writer does not have to argue that he has proved anything about causation or determinism: he has absolutely shown that men's wills do not control their destinies.

The Red Badge of Courage (1895), Crane's Civil War story, is the most controversial piece in his canon. It has been much discussed and most variously interpreted, and the interpretations range about as widely as they could. Is it a Christian story of redemption? Is it a demonstration that man is a beast with illusions? Or is it, between these extremes, the story of a man who goes through the fire, discovers himself, and with the self-knowledge that he is able to attain comes to terms with the problem of life insofar as an imperfect man can come to terms with an imperfect world? It is tempting to take the middle road between the intemperate extremes;

but let us see what happens before we come to the paragraphs at the end that are invoked to prove each of the explanations:

"He felt a quiet manhood, non-assertive but of sturdy and strong blood. He knew that he would no more quail before his guides wherever they should point. He had been to touch the great death, and found that, after all, it was but the great death. He was a man.

So it came to pass that as he trudged from the place of blood and wrath his soul changed. He came from hot plowshares to prospects of clover tranquilly, and it was as if hot plowshares were not. Scars faded as flowers.

. . . He had rid himself of the red sickness of battle. The sultry nightmare was in the past. He had been an animal blistered and sweating in the heat and pain of war. He turned now with a lover's thirst to images of tranquil skies, fresh meadows, cool brooks."

It is not obvious whether the young man who thinks these thoughts is deluding himself or not. To judge the quality of his self-analysis we must look in some detail at what he has been through. The book opens with a scene at a Union encampment in which the uninformed arguments of the soldiers are described in a manner that recalls the mockery of "infantile orations" in *Maggie*. The phrase pictures a squalling child colorfully, while it conveys the author's private amusement at the image of a shouting politician. In *The Red Badge* there is continually a tone of mockery and sardonic imitation of men who are boisterous, crafty, arrogant, resentful, or suspicious always in an excess that makes them comical, and the author seems to delight in rendering the flavor of their extravagances. An element of the fantastic is always present, the quality apparently representing the author's feeling for the war, the situations in it, the continual and enormous incongruities between intention and execution, between a man's estimate of himself and the way he appears to others, between the motivations acknowledged to the world and those which prevail in the heart. It is with these last that the book is centrally concerned—with the problem of courage—and it is here that the meaning is most confusingly entangled with the tone.

In the opening scene the men are excited over a rumor that the troop is about to move, for the first time in months, and immediately the tone of mockery appears. A certain tall soldier "developed virtues and went resolutely to wash a shirt. He came flying back. . . . He was swelled with a tale he had heard from a reliable friend, who had heard it from a truthful cavalryman, who had heard it from his trustworthy brother. . . . He adopted the important air of a herald in red and gold." Another soldier takes the report "as an affront," and the tall soldier "felt called upon to defend the truth of a rumor he had himself introduced. He and the loud one came near to fighting over it." A corporal swears furiously because he has just put a floor under his tent; the men argue about strategies, clamoring at each other, "numbers making futile bids for the popular attention."

From this outer excitement we turn to the excitement in the heart of the youth who is to be the hero of the tale. He has crept off to his tent to commune with himself and particularly to wonder how he will act when he confronts the enemy. He has "dreamed of battles all his life—of vague and bloody conflicts that had thrilled him with their sweep and fire. . . . He had imagined peoples secure in the shadow of his eagle-eyed prowess." He had burned to enlist, but had been deterred by his mother's arguments that he was more important on the farm until—the point is sardonically emphasized—the newspapers carried accounts of great battles in which the North was victor. "Almost every day the newspapers printed accounts of a decisive victory." When he enlists, his mother makes a long speech to him—which is presented by Crane with no trace of mockery—but he is impatient and irritated. As he departs, there is a tableau described, for almost the only time in the book, with unqualified feeling:

"Still, when he had looked back from the gate, he had seen his mother kneeling among the potato parings. Her brown face, upraised, was stained with tears, and her spare form was quivering. He bowed his head and went on, feeling suddenly ashamed of his purposes."

Vanity and dreams of Homeric glory occupy him thenceforth —until battle is imminent. Then he wonders whether he will run or stand; and he does not dare confide his fears to the other men because they all seem so sure of themselves and because both they and he are constantly diverted from the question by inferior concerns.

* * *

Approaching the first engagement, the youth perceives with terror that he is "in a moving box" of soldiers from which it would be impossible to escape, and "it occurred to him that he had never wished to come to the war . . . He had been dragged by the merciless government." He is further startled when the loud soldier, a braggart, announces with a sob that he is going to be killed, and gives the youth a packet of letters for his family. The engagement is described with terms of confusion: the youth feels "a red rage," and then "acute exasperation"; he "fought frantically" for air; the other men are cursing, babbling, and querulous; their equipment bobs "idiotically" on their backs, and they move like puppets. The assault is turned back, and the men leer at each other with dirty smiles; but just as the youth is responding in "an ecstasy of self-satisfaction" at having passed "the supreme trial," there comes a second charge from which he flees in blind panic: "He ran like a blind man. Two or three times he fell down. Once he knocked his shoulder so heavily against a tree that he went headlong." As he runs, his fear increases, and he rages at the suicidal folly of those who have stayed behind to be killed.

Just as he reaches the zone of safety, he learns that the line has held and the enemy's charge been repulsed. Instantly he "felt that he had been wronged," and begins to find reasons for the wisdom of his flight. "It was all plain that he had proceeded according to very correct and commendable rules. His actions had been saga-cious things. They had been full of strategy. . . . He, the enlight-ened man who looks afar in the dark, had fled because of his superior perceptions and knowledge. He felt a great anger against his comrades. He knew it could be proved that they had been fools." He pities himself; he feels rebellious, agonized, and des-pairing. It is here that he sees a squirrel and throws a pine cone at it; when it runs he finds a triumphant exhibition in nature of the law of self-preservation. "Nature had given him a sign." The irony of this sequence is abundantly apparent. It increases when, a mo-ment later, the youth enters a place where the "arching boughs made a chapel" and finds a horrible corpse, upright against a tree, crawling with ants and staring straight at him.

From this he flees in renewed panic, and then there is a strange turn. A din of battle breaks out, such a "tremendous clangor of sounds" as to make the engagement from which he ran seem trivial, and he runs back to watch because for such a spectacle curiosity becomes stronger than fear. He joins a ghastly procession of wounded from this battle, among whom he finds Jim Conklin, his friend, gray with the mark of death, and watches him die in throes that "caused him to dance a sort of hideous hornpipe." The guilt he feels among these frightfully wounded men, in this chapter which comes precisely in the middle of the book, should be enough to make him realize his brotherhood, his indebtedness, his duty; but his reaction as he watches the retreat swell is to justify his early flight—until a column of soldiers going *toward* the battle makes him almost weep with his longing to be one of their brave file. Increasingly, in short, Crane makes us see Henry Fleming as an emotional puppet controlled by whatever sight he sees at the moment. He becomes like Conrad's Lord Jim, romanc-ing dreams of glory while he flinches at every danger. As his spirits flag under physical exhaustion, he hopes his army will be defeated so that his flight will be vindicated.

The climax of irony comes now, when, after a stasis of remorse in which he does indeed despise himself (albeit for the wrong reason of fearing the reproaches of those who did not flee), he sees the whole army come running past him in an utter panic of terror. He tries to stop one of them for information, and is bashed over the head by the frantic and bewildered man. And now, wounded thus, almost delirious with pain and exhaustion, he staggers back to his company—and is greeted as a hero! Henry is tended by the loud soldier, who has become stronger and steadier. Henry's reaction to his friend's care and solicitude is to feel superior because he still has the packet of letters the loud one gave him a day before, in his fear: "The friend had, in a weak hour, spoken with sobs of his own death. . . . But he had not died, and thus he had delivered himself into the hands of the youth." He condescends to his loud friend, and "His self-pride was now [so] entirely restored" that he began to see something fine in his conduct of the day before. He is now vainglorious; he thinks himself "a man of experience . . . chosen of the gods and doomed to greatness." Remembering the terror-stricken faces of the men he saw fleeing from the great battle, he now feels a scorn for them! He thinks of the tales of prowess he will tell back home to circles of adoring women.

The youth's reaction to his spurious "red badge of courage" is thus set down with close and ironical detail. Crane does not comment, but the picture of self-delusion and vainglory is meticulously drawn. In the following chapter Henry does fight furiously, but here he is in a blind rage that turns him into an animal, so that he goes on firing long after the enemy have retreated. The other soldiers regard his ferocity with wonder, and Henry has become a marvel, basking in the wondering stares of his comrades.

The order comes for a desperate charge, and the regiment responds magnificently, hurling itself into the enemy's fire regardless of the odds against it; and here Crane devotes a paragraph to a careful and specific analysis of their heroism:

"But there was a frenzy made from this furious rush. The men, pitching forward insanely, had burst into cheerings, moblike and barbaric, but tuned in strange keys that can arouse the dullard and the stoic. It made a mad enthusiasm that, it seemed, would be incapable of checking itself before granite and brass. There was the delirium that encounters despair and death, and is heedless and blind to the odds. It is a temporary but sublime absence of selfishness. And because it was of this order was the reason, perhaps, why the youth wondered, afterward, what reasons he could have had for being there."

Heroism is "temporary but sublime," succeeded by dejection, anger, panic, indignation, despair, and renewed rage. This can hardly be called, for Henry, gaining spiritual salvation by losing his soul in the flux of things, for he is acting in harried exasperation, exhaustion, and rage. What has seemed to him an incredible charge turns out, presently, to have been a very short one—in time and distance covered—for which the regiment is bitterly criticized by the General. The facts are supplemented by the tone, which conveys through its outrageous and whimsical language that the whole business is made of pretense and delusion: A "magnificent brigade" goes into a wood, causing there "a most awe-inspiring racket. . . . Having stirred this prodigious uproar, and, apparently, finding it too prodigious, the brigade, after a little time, came marching airily out again with its fine formation in nowise disturbed. . . . The brigade was jaunty and seemed to point a proud thumb at the yelling wood." In the midst of the next engagement, which is indeed a furious battle, the youth is sustained by a "strange and unspeakable hatred" of the officer who had dubbed his regiment "mud diggers." Carrying the colors, he leads a charge of men "in a state of frenzy, perhaps because of forgotten vanities, and it made an exhibition of sublime recklessness." In this hysterical battlefield the youth is indeed selfless and utterly fearless in "his wild battle madness," yet by reading closely we see that the opposing soldiers are a thin, feeble line who turn and run from the charge or are slaughtered.

What it all seems to come to is that the heroism is in action undeniable, but it is preceded and followed by the ignoble sentiments we have traced—and the constant tone of humor and hysteria seems to be Crane's comment on these juxtapositions of courage, ignorance, vainglory, pettiness, pompous triumph, and craven fear. The moment the men can stop and comment upon what they have been through they are presented as more or less absurd.

With all these facts in mind we can examine the Henry Fleming who emerges from the battle and sets about marshaling all his acts. He is gleeful over his courage. Remembering his desertion of the wounded Jim Conklin, he is ashamed because of the possible disgrace, but, as Crane tells with supreme irony, "gradually he mustered force to put the sin at a distance," and to dwell upon his "quiet manhood." Coming after all these events and rationalizations, the paragraphs quoted at the beginning of this discussion are a climax of self-delusion. If there is any one point that has been made it is that Henry has never been able to evaluate his conduct. He may have been fearless for moments, but his motives were vain, selfish, ignorant, and childish. Mercifully, Crane does not follow him down through the more despicable levels of self-delusion that are sure to follow as he rewrites (as we have seen him planning to do) the story of his conduct to fit his childish specifications. He has been through some moments of hell, during which he has for moments risen above his limitations, but Crane seems plainly to be showing that he has not achieved a lasting wisdom or self-knowledge.

If *The Red Badge of Courage* were only an exposure of an ignorant farm boy's delusions, it would be a contemptible book. Crane shows that Henry's delusions image only dimly the insanely grotesque and incongruous world of battle into which he is plunged. There the movement is blind or frantic, the leaders are selfish, the goals are inhuman. One farm boy is made into a mad animal to kill another farm boy, while the great guns carry on a "grim pow-wow" or a "stupendous wrangle" described in terms that suggest a solemn farce or a cosmic and irresponsible game.

If we were to seek a geometrical shape to picture the significant form of *The Red Badge*, it would not be the circle, the L, or the straight line of oscillation between selfishness and salvation, but the equilateral triangle. Its three points are instinct, ideals, and circumstance. Henry Fleming runs along the sides like a squirrel in a track. Ideals take him along one side until circumstance confronts him with danger. Then instinct takes over and he dashes down the third side in a panic. The panic abates somewhat as he approaches the angle of ideals, and as he turns the corner (continuing his flight) he busily rationalizes to accommodate those ideals of duty and trust that recur, again and again, to harass him. Then he runs on to the line of circumstance, and he moves again toward instinct. He is always controlled on one line, along which he is both drawn and impelled by the other two forces. If this triangle is thought of as a piece of bright glass whirling in a cosmic kaleidoscope, we have an image of Crane's naturalistic and vividly impressioned Reality.

M. SOLOMON

[Social Responsibility *vs* Freedom: *The Red Badge*]†

* * *

Nietzsche had shouted: "God is dead," but the small voice of this poor American novelist, son of a Methodist preacher, humbly asked: "If I should cast off this tattered coat, and go free into the

† From "Stephen Crane, A Critical Study," *Masses and Mainstream*, IX (January, 1955), 32–41, *passim*. Reprinted by permission.

mighty sky; If I should find nothing there . . . what then?" There was more than a tendency toward disintegration of Crane's religious belief, but he feared the death of God, and so could not countenance it. Dostoevsky's Kirilov summed up the problem: "If God did not exist, everything would be allowed." When Crane posed the question in this way ("God lay dead in heaven") it plunged him into depths of dread; he saw "monsters livid with desire" emerging from "caverns of dead sins" to wrangle over the world. This is the torment of an unbeliever who would believe, or vice versa. Belief remained in Crane, but unbelief lingered. And so Crane's art veers away from religion, he deals with people in human and social terms, but does not seek to impose transcendental solutions on their problems.

* * *

It must be said at the outset that *The Red Badge of Courage* is a study in the meaning of social responsibility and freedom. It is the story of a youth, Henry Fleming, who enters into the world of war with a dream of glory in battle, and who flees from the reality of war, killing and death. From the point of his desertion he embarks on a Dantesque Pilgrim's Progress through the hell of the rear-lines and of his soul, eventually attaining a consciousness of his sin, and gaining motivation for his return to his comrades at the front. It is in his return that he learns the meaning of freedom and responsibility, and joins the common struggle for victory.

It is in this treatment of the theme of the hero's search for humanity and freedom that *The Red Badge of Courage* belongs to the great tradition of classic literature, from the *Book of Job* and the *Oresteia* to *Hamlet* and *Egmont*. It marks the return to American literature of this vein which was explored by *Moby Dick* and *Ethan Brand*. Seen in this light, Henry Fleming becomes a figure of true heroic proportions in a literature which has since been largely dominated by animal nihilists and depersonalized imbeciles.

Crane makes his break with naturalism here (although he retains much of Spencerian terminology). His hero has the capacity to find freedom through defeat of his fear. His is no automatic absolution for sin, no greased entry into heaven; he must fight his way in. Nor is defeat inevitable, for he triumphs. This is Garland's realism applied to human motivations and actions. What it is not is the positive value of *Maggie*, its critical realism and treatment of social evil; for in casting out the determinism of *Maggie*, Crane casts out its criticism of society. A fusion will have to be effected, but this will come later.

The novel opens in innocence: "He had, of course, dreamed of battles all his life—of vague and bloody conflicts that had thrilled him with their sweep and fire. In visions he had seen himself in many struggles. . . ." Henry's mother brings the story out of the mind and into reality with the keynote of the story:

"I don't know what else to tell yeh, Henry, excepting that yeh must never do no shirking, child, on my account. If so be a time comes when yeh have to be kilt or do a mean thing, why Henry, don't think of anything 'cept what's right, because there's many a woman has to bear up 'ginst sech things these times, and the Lord'll take keer of us all."

* * *

As [Ambrose] Bierce remarked [of Crane], "He knows nothing of war, yet he is drenched in blood." * * * Knowing "nothing," Crane sees the crucial fact of desertion and cowardice: "Since he had turned his back upon the fight his fears had been wondrously magnified. Death about to thrust him between the shoulder blades was far more dreadful than death about to smite him between the eyes."

Crane now takes his hero through seven stages of hell. Chapters six through twelve of the novel each contains a lesson in the nature of sin and the sense of humanity. But this is no Sunday-school catechism: it is a novel of blood and fire in which the ethic of loyalty and brotherhood arises out of the action seen through the reeling mind of the young deserter.

The first lesson strips the youth of his rationale for desertion— the regiment had not fallen under fire, but had stood fast. "He had fled, he told himself, because annihilation approached. . . . He had considered the time . . . to be one in which it was the duty of every little piece to rescue itself if possible. . . ."

* * *

Well, so be it. The coward will seek solace in the forest, away from the rumble of death, in the lap of Nature "where the high, arching boughs made a chapel" with green doors and a gentle brown carpet. And there he learns the second lesson, that there is no escape. In the chapel sat a dead man dressed in a uniform that had once been blue. "The dead man and the living man exchanged a long look."

* * *

The youth joins the grisly procession of the wounded returning from the front. Here is shown his instinctive desire to be with his fellows, to rejoin the living. But the dying soldiers in the march are more alive than the untouched coward. He meets the "tattered man," a soldier ". . . fouled with dust, blood and powder stain from hair to shoes . . . ," his head bound with a blood-soaked rag and his arm dangling like a broken bough. He believes in his cause: "His homely face was suffused with a light of love for the army which was to him all things beautiful and powerful. . . ." In a brotherly tone he asks the youth: "Where yeh hit, ol' boy?" and the question pierces like a sword of vengeance. The youth has received his third lesson, that he has lost the sense of belonging—the social sense—he is isolated.

* * *

This wound motif, the desire for mutilation which appears here and throughout Crane's war stories, has given Freudian critics a field-day opportunity to expound on "castration complexes" and subconscious "Oedipal repressions," as though Crane were not a conscious author, but an unthinking instrument through which instinctual and emotional patterns are poured into a fixed mould.

* * *

Actually, the "red badge" theme is a miracle of realistic insight into the workings of Henry Fleming's mind, his desire for kinship with the wounded soldiers whom he has deserted, his reverence for their courage. It is an insight which illuminates the genius of Crane, an insight which, however, would have been impossible without the precept of Tolstoy, from whose *Sevastopol* stories it is in part drawn.

* * *

Sevastopol in December, moreover, pictures "an old, gaunt soldier" whose "sufferings inspire you over and above the feeling of profound sympathy, with a fear of offending and with a lofty reverence for the man who has undergone them," and even contains the question "Where are you wounded?" * * * And later in *The Red Badge* we will see Crane echoing the central thesis of *War and Peace* on the question of who wins battles—strategy or soldiers. So the sources of Crane's novel reside in life and literature (in knowledge, not instinct).

The following chapter contains one of the most powerful scenes in American literature—the description of Jim Conklin's death. Here the lesson of the fruits of betrayal is brought home by the ghastly death of a comrade whom he had known in the ranks, wherein Henry appears to us as a repentant Cain, Judas or Paul, conscious at last of his sin. "The youth cried out to him hysterically: 'I'll take care of

yeh, Jim. I'll take care of yeh. I swear t' Gawd I will.'" In his encounter with the tattered man in the previous chapter, the youth
knew that he was alienated, but not yet that he was responsible;
here the personalization of his sin provides Henry with the seeds of
knowledge that he must be responsible as well as guilty.

It is one of Crane's great ironies that Henry's furthest penetration
into hell, his largest sin, occurs so soon after the death of Jim. Henry
is not yet ready to become his brother's keeper. He again meets the
tattered man, now on the verge of death, and, unable to endure the
"simple questions of the tattered man" he flees, leaving him to a lone,
agonizing death. * * * Henry knows that he has assisted in a personal murder, and this is the fifth lesson, that social guilt is individual guilt.

The sixth lesson deepens this idea. Crane shows that the youth's
one act of desertion, a seemingly small action, almost inevitably leads
him to become an enemy of his own people, his own cause: he
watches his army retreating— "There was an amount of pleasure to
him in watching the wild march of this vindication. He could not
but know that a defeat for the army this time might mean many
favorable things for him. The blows of the enemy would splinter
regiments into fragments. Thus, many men of courage, he considered, would be obliged to desert the colors and scurry like chickens.
He would appear as one of them."

* * *

The Union army is routed. The youth rushes among the wounded
men. "He had the impulse to make a rallying speech, to sing a battle
hymn, but he could only get his tongue to call into the air: 'Why—
why—what—what's the matter?'" He is seeking a way out of his
shame, a redemption. He clutches a soldier by the arm, who, confused and enraged, crushes his rifle against the youth's head. Thus,
in the midst of his atonement, Henry receives the final lesson—crude
justice. He has been repaid for his betrayal, crushed by his own army.
He has received his red badge of courage—from his own comrade.

Henry was not the only young soldier who deserted from the ranks
and then returned. While he is being watched over with "tenderness
and care" by his comrades in the regiment, he hears the many others:
"They'd been scattered all over, wanderin' around in th' woods,
fightin' with other reg'ments, an' everything. Jest like you done."
Henry's story is therefore not unique, it is typical. The crucial question is why did he desert?

Henry deserted because war is hell, the most monstrous activity de-
vised by human beings. * * * Because it sets brother against
brother, destroys the home, the land, the culture. Above all, because

it brings death, destroys people who want to live, and kills them with brute force, with bullets and bayonet.

* * *

However, Crane also tries to show us that there is an ethic in fighting—the ethic of solidarity, the common struggle for a common goal. Rising from this is the desire to "belong," not to let the others down, the soldier's desire to prove himself the equal of anyone in heroism. Crane reveals the deserter as an outcast from the group. * * * And as Henry Fleming learned during his pilgrimage through the rear-lines, he became cut off, a renegade, a man without a cause, friendless, soulless. Crane's hero deserts, and Crane would have us believe that he returns because the bonds of brotherhood and loyalty are stronger than cowardice and fear.

This is all very good, Crane's affirmation of humanist ethics, his profound insight that man is a social animal whose responsibility is to his fellows and whose degradation lies in his desertion into crude individualism and a "save your own skin" morality. * * * The new step in *The Red Badge* is the possibility of salvation, the return, the acceptance of responsibility. Henry knew that he had fled for self-preservation alone; he learned that there could be no life for him outside of his community, his society; and thus he returned to the regiment, with the lessons of comradeship, loyalty and dedication engraved on his soul. Once more, Henry Fleming "belonged."

A worthy theme, this, but when placed in the context of war it leaves *The Red Badge* open to an interpretation which the rebel, iconoclastic Crane would hardly have relished. Henry's return to the regiment can "logically" be regarded as an acceptance, as Maxwell Geismar put it, of "the martial standards as a kind of absolute." In other words, on the face of it, Henry's flight can be interpreted as a blind rebellion against authority, against war, and his return as a submission to arbitrary power and to the military. What lends weight to this view is the undeniable fact that throughout the novel Crane never refers directly to the great issues involved in the Civil War. There is no concrete sense of history in *The Red Badge*, no exploration of the causes and meanings of the war.

* * *

Henry "felt that something of which he was a part—a regiment, an army, a cause, *or a country*—was in a crisis." (Italics added.) This feeling never leaves him, for it was part of the consciousness of every decent Union soldier during the war, deeply ingrained, taken for granted. It may be said that it is this sense of collective crisis which causes Henry's individual remorse during his desertion. "Tales of great movements shook the land," and Henry had burned with the desire to enlist. This consciousness of a cause motivates him throughout the novel. Call it a vague consciousness if you will, but it was present, and Crane's use of this motif was no accident. He reflected the typical Union soldier's view, and it is this view that gives content to the patriotism and love of country, symbolized by Crane in his recurrent references to the flag:

"Here and there were flags, the red in the stripes dominating. They splashed bits of warm color upon the dark lines of troops." "The youth felt the old thrill at the sight of the emblem. They were like beautiful birds strangely undaunted in a storm."

And in the final, climactic battle, Henry bears the flag, proudly and with dignity:

"Within him, as he hurled himself forward, was born a love, a despairing fondness for this flag. . . . It was a creation of beauty and invulnerability. It was a goddess, radiant, that bended its form with an imperious gesture to him. It was a woman . . . that called him with the voice of his hopes."

This, of course, is only symbolic patriotism. The deepest patriotism of Crane's novel is found in his devotion to and confidence in the common people, who are the heroes of *The Red Badge*.

Thus can we establish the specific, historical and, in germinal form, *partisan* character of Crane's book. The timelessness here is the true "timelessness" which comes from a deep and correct insight into an age, not from an abstraction out of history. That Crane did not document the background fully is only a weakness, which enables the meaning of his book to be distorted today. Another novelist, a greater one, would have conceived his war novel more grandly, more maturely, as a web of profound and varied ideas on life and history woven together by the movement and counter-movement of many characters. Crane was no Tolstoy. Indeed, he had not quite grown up as a writer and thinker, and his insights in *The Red Badge* are the flashes of young genius rather than the considered discoveries of a mature artist. Hence the use of an impressionistic technique, with brief chapters and sharp, vivid, but often adolescent images ("His tongue lay dead in the tomb of his mouth"). It is not surprising that Crane should have stripped the novel bare of everything except the central situation in order to highlight his main ideas and to simplify the structural problem. He even had a rationale for this process: "I try to give to readers a slice out of life; and if there is any moral or lesson in it . . . I let the reader find it himself."

PHILIP RAHV

[The Symbolic Fallacy in Crane Criticism]†

The novel is at the present time universally recognized as one of the greater historic forms of literary art. Its resources and capacities appear to be commensurate with the realities and consciousness of the modern epoch, and its practitioners, having inherited a good many of the functions once exercised by poetry and the drama, no longer feel the slightest need to engage in the kind of apologetics that were quite common even as late as a hundred years ago, when in respectable quarters novel-writing and novel-reading were still looked upon as activities falling below the level of true cultural aspiration. But if the novel was then still widely regarded as a thing somewhat effeminate and moonshiny, fit mainly for the consumption of young ladies, it was at the same time quickly impressing itself upon the mind of the age as a newfangled form full of rude plebeian energy, unruly, unpredictable and ungovernable in its appropriation of materials from unprocessed reality—"the conscience of a blackened street impatient to assume the world." Much of the life the novel contains is defined by these contrary reactions, one pointing to its origin in romance and the other to its revitalization through the new principle of realism.

Among the last apologies for the novel—an apology in which we fully sense, however, the surge of confidence and power generated by the phenomenal rise of this relatively new genre—is the preface that the Goncourt brothers wrote for their novel *Germinie Lacerteux* (1864). "Now that the novel," they observed, "is broadening, growing, beginning to be a great, serious, impassioned living form of literary study and social research, now that by means of analysis and psychological inquiry it is turning into contemporary moral history, now that the novel has imposed upon itself the investigations and duties of science, one may again make a stand for its liberties and privileges." This memorable formulation is in the main still acceptable to us. The one dated element in it is of course the reference to science, a reference all too patently of its period and

† From "Fiction and the Criticism of Fiction," *Kenyon Review*, XVIII (Spring, 1956), pp. 276–87 *passim*. Copyright 1956 by *Kenyon Review*. Reprinted by permission of the author and *Kenyon Review*. This essay is a revised version of an address delivered at the School of Letters of Indiana University in July, 1955. Probably the most noted rebuttal of the extravagant extension of the symbolic interpretation. The last section of the essay, not dealing with Crane, is omitted.

linked to the development of the naturalistic school in French fiction. At the time not a few writers were so impressed by the triumphs of scientific method as to want to borrow some of its magic for themselves, yet at bottom it was not so much a matter of faith in science (though doubtless that played its part too) as of an intention to gain prestige for the novel by means of an honorific association. But apart from that the formulation I have cited has scarcely lost its cogency. The one question arising in connection with it is whether it is still necessary at this late date again to make a stand for the novel's liberties and privileges. So far as the intelligent reader at large is concerned such a stand may well be redundant. But it is not in the least redundant, I think, so far as some present-day critics of fiction are concerned and the reading-practices to which they have been habituating us.

My argument rests on a premise that most of us will surely accept, and that is that 20th Century criticism has as yet failed to evolve a theory and a set of practical procedures dealing with the prose-medium that are as satisfactory in their exactness, subtlety and variety as the theory and procedures worked out in the past few decades by the critics of poetry. It may well be, as is so frequently said, that in art there is no such thing as progress. But, then, criticism is only partially an art, so little of an art perhaps as to admit in some periods not only change, as all the arts do, but also gradual development toward a more accurate knowledge. One is certainly disposed to think so when comparing the present state of poetry-criticism with its state, say, forty or fifty years ago. The criticism of poetry has of late acquired a rich consciousness which may be defined objectively as the self-consciousness of the medium —an historic acquisition that, acting as a force in its own right, has already considerably affected the writing of poetry and may be expected to affect it even more in the near future.

In fiction the prevailing situation is quite different. Is it not a curious fact that while we have had in this century novelists as fully accomplished in their métier as the poets we all esteem are in theirs, none of these novelists have made a contribution to the theory of fiction that comes anywhere near what the poets have attained in their critical forays? You can go through all the essays of Thomas Mann, for instance, without finding anything of really clinching interest for students of the novel as a form; and Mann is surely an exceptionally intellectual and self-conscious artist. Nor will you find, in this respect, any truly close insights in Joyce or Proust. Both *The Portrait of the Artist* and *Ulysses* contain some discussions of aesthetic structure on a fairly abstract level, and these are of no help to us if we are on the lookout for the differentia distinguishing the prose-narrative from the other verbal arts. In Proust you encounter a metaphysical theory of the aesthetic meaning of time that generalizes the author's creative experience, but it scarcely yields the kind of concrete illumination of the novelistic form that we gain in poetic theory from the discursive writings of poet-critics like Valéry, Eliot, Pound, Empson, Ransom and Tate. As for American novelists of our time such as Fitzgerald, Wolfe, Faulkner and Hemingway, they have influenced fictional modes solely through their practice, steering clear of theoretical divagations.* * *

I am inclined to think that it is precisely the fact of signal progress that we have witnessed in the criticism of poetry that accounts in some ways for the observable lag in the criticism of fiction. * * * For the commanding position assumed by poetic analysis has led to the indiscriminate importation of its characteristic assumptions and approaches into a field which requires generic critical terms and criteria of value that are unmistakably its own. Just as Zola, the Goncourt brothers and other pioneers of the naturalist school associated the novel with science for the sake of the prestige that this conjunction seemed to confer upon their literary ambitions, so now critics of fiction are attempting to assimilate it to the poem, thus impeding an adequate inspection of the qualities and effects of the prose-medium. This effort to deduce a prosaics from a poetics is *au fond* doomed to fail, for it is simply not the case that what goes for a microscopic unit such as the lyric poem goes equally well for the macroscopic compositions of the writer of narrative prose.

In this paper I wish to isolate three biases that can be traced directly or indirectly to this recent infection of the prose-sense by poetics. The first bias is manifested in the current obsession with the search for symbols, allegories and mythic patterns in the novel —a search conducted on the unanalysed assumption that to locate such symbols in a fictional work is somehow tantamount to a demonstration of its excellence. The fact that the same symbols and patterns are just as easily discoverable in the worst as in the best novels counts for nothing among the pursuers of this type of research. The second bias, even more plainly deriving from the sensibility of poetry, is the one identifying style as the "essential activity" of imaginative prose, an identification that confuses the intensive speech proper to poetry with the more openly communicative, functional and extensive language proper to prose. The third bias is that of technicism, which may be defined as the attempt to reduce the complex structure and content of the novel to its sum of techniques, among which language is again accorded a paramount place.

* * *

In examining this bias toward symbolism, allegory and mythic patterning in the reading of fiction, one is first of all struck by its debilitating effect on the critical mind. There was a time not so long ago when it was clearly understood among us that allegory is an inferior mode scarcely to be compared to symbolism in imaginative efficacy; it was also understood that myth and symbol are by no means synonymous terms. But by now all such elementary though essential distinctions have gone by the board. The younger critics have taken to using all three terms almost interchangeably and always with an air of offering an irrefutable proof of sensibility, with the result that they have been nearly emptied of specific meaning and turned into little more than pretentious counters of approbation.[3] But the more these terms lose their reference to anything concrete beyond themselves, the easier becomes their conversion into verbal symbols in their own right, symbols of admission and belonging to a school at present academically and critically dominant. And if you add to this sacred triad the famed pair of paradox and irony your initiation is well nigh complete.

An example is wanted. There is Mr. Robert W. Stallman, for instance, who rather unnerves one with his literal passion for up-to-date notions in criticism. In an essay on Stephen Crane, he writes that

"like Conrad, Crane puts language to poetic uses, which, to define it, is to use language reflexively and to use language symbolically. It is the works which employ this reflexive and symbolic use of language that constitute what is permanent of Crane. It is the language of symbol and paradox; the wafer-like sun [the reference is to Crane's memorable sentence in *The Red Badge of Courage*: 'The red sun was pasted in the sky like a wafer']; or in 'The Open Boat' the paradox of 'cold, comfortable sea-water,' an image which calls to mind the poetry of W. B. Yeats with its fusion of contradictory emotions. This single image evokes the sensation of the whole experience of the men in the boat. . . . What is readily recognizable in this paradox of 'cold, comfortable sea-water' is that irony of opposites which constituted the personality of the man who wrote it."[4]

And preceding this paragraph with its wholesale disgorgement of shibboleths lifted from contemporary poetry-criticism, there is a

3. The word "myth" in particular is being put to such multiple and varied use these days—as when people speak of the myth of racial superiority, or of the myth of the proletariat, or of the mythology of Americanism—that if any sense at all is to be made of the mythic concern in literature, then the least a critic can do is to discriminate sharply between the broad,

popular, loosely analogical employment of the term and what Robert Graves rightly, I think, calls the "true myth," which he defines as "the reduction to narrative shorthand of ritual mime."

4. Cf. "Stephen Crane," p. 269, in *Critiques and Essays in Modern Fiction*, edited by John W. Aldridge (New York, 1952).

passage in which Mr. Stallman bares his fixation on the sentence previously quoted ("The red sun was pasted in the sky like a wafer"), in which he professes to see the "key to the symbolism of the whole novel." Why? Because the initials, J. C., of Jim Conklin, the tall, spectral soldier who dies in so grotesque a fashion, ineluctably suggests to Mr. Stallman that he represents Jesus Christ. Thus *The Red Badge of Courage*, which is something of a *tour de force* as a novel and which is chiefly noted for the advance it marks in the onset of realism on the American literary scene, is transmogrified into a religious allegory. All that is lacking in this analysis to give it the final certification of the *Zeitgeist* is the word "myth." Observe, too, that the evidence for this thesis is drawn, not from a study of the narrative progression of Crane's novel as a whole, but from a single image and the amalgam of the initials of the tall soldier's name with the name of Jesus Christ. It is entirely characteristic of Mr. Stallman's approach (and of the critical school to which he is attached) that it never even occurs to him that to speak of "the symbolism of the whole novel" is perhaps in this case a piece of sheer gratuity, that the novel is actually "about" what it seems to be, war and its impact on human beings moved by pride, bravado, fear, anxiety and sudden panic. If it is symbolic, it is in the patent sense in which all good art, in so far as it opens out to the world at large by transcending its immediate occasions and fixed, exclusive meanings, can be said to be symbolic. But to attribute a symbolic character to Crane's novel in this universal sense has nothing whatever to do with Mr. Stallman's idea of symbolism, an idea indistinguishable from the "fallacy of misplaced concreteness," systematically applied to works of literature.

The absurdity of Mr. Stallman's reading of Crane becomes all too apparent when you look up the text to check on his quotations. He professes to see a poetic paradox in the phrase "cold, comfortable sea-water," but in point of fact within the context of the story the juxtaposition of "cold" and "comfortable" cannot strike us as paradoxical but rather as wholly natural. The situation is that the four shipwrecked men in the tiny boat—the captain, the correspondent, the oiler, and the cook—are dog-tired, not having slept for two days. It is night, and three of them are sleeping in the water-drenched bottom of the boat while the correspondent is rowing:

"The wind became stronger, and sometimes a wave raged out like a mountain cat, and there was to be seen the sheen and sparkle of a broken crest.

"The captain, in the bow, moved on his water-jar and sat erect. 'Pretty long night,' he observed to the correspondent. . . .

" 'Did you see that shark playing around?'

" 'Yes, I saw him. He was a big fellow all right.'

". . . Later the correspondent spoke into the bottom of the boat. 'Billie!' There was a slow and gradual disentanglement. 'Billie, will you spell me?'

" 'Sure,' said the oiler.

"As soon as the correspondent touched the cold, comfortable sea-water in the bottom of the boat and had huddled close to the cook's life-belt he was deep in sleep."

Now obviously the water *in* the boat feels "comfortable" as against the waves beating *at* the boat, pictured throughout the story as black, menacing, sinister. In contrast the water at the bottom of the boat, in which the men have been sleeping, seems positively domesticated. Hence the adjective "comfortable." Only by carefully sequestering the phrase "cold, comfortable sea-water" from its context can you make it out to be paradoxical.

As for the sentence ending Chapter IX of *The Red Badge of Courage*—"The sun was pasted in the sky like a wafer"—it would seem to me that the verb "pasted" is quite as important to its effect as the substantive "wafer." Moreover, in the first edition of the novel "wafer" was preceded by "fierce," a modifier hardly suggestive of the Christian communion. Crane liked to speak of himself as an impressionist, and as a stylist he was above all concerned with getting away from the morbidly genteel narrative language of his time; the daring colloquialism "pasted in the sky" must have appealed to him on the well-known avant garde principle of "make it new." More particularly, this concluding sentence of Chapter IX illustrates perfectly what Conrad described as "Crane's unique and exquisite faculty . . . of disclosing an individual scene by an odd simile." Conrad's remark has the aptitude of close critical observation, whereas Mr. Stallman's far-fetched religious exegesis is mere *Zeitgeist* palaver.

No wonder that this critic is quite as partial to allegory as he is to symbolism. Thus in a study of Conrad he claims that "The Secret Sharer" is a double allegory—"an allegory of man's moral conscience and . . . of man's aesthetic conscience. The form of 'The Secret Sharer,' to diagram it, is the form of the capital letter L—the very form of the captain's room. (It is hinted at again in the initial letter of Leggatt's name.) One part of the letter L diagrams the allegory of the captain's divided soul, man in moral isolation and spiritual disunity. The other part of the letter represents the allegory of the artist's split soul. . . . The captain stands at the angle of the two isolations and the two searches for self-hood." [5] It is the inescapable logic of this obsession with symbols

5. Cf. "Life, Art, and 'The Secret Sharer'," p. 241, in *Forms of Modern Fiction*, edited by William Van O'Connor (Minneapolis, 1948).

and allegories that it is bound to decline into a sort of mechanistic Kabbala that scrutinizes each sign and letter of the printed page for esoteric or supernal meanings. The plain absurdity of Mr. Stallman's reading of "The Secret Sharer" should not, however, deter us from recognizing that this mode, which he carries to an extreme, is a fairly representative one nowadays and that it is greatly favored by abler critics who at times still manage to retain some sense of proportion. My concern is not with Mr. Stallman's absurdities as such. I cite him only because his very excess brings to light the fantastication inherent in the approach he shares with a good many other people.[6]

What, at bottom, is the animating idea behind this exaltation of symbolism in current critical practice? As I see it, its source is not directly literary but is to be traced to an attitude of distaste toward the actuality of experience—an attitude of radical devaluation of the actual if not downright hostility to it; and the symbol is of course readily available as a means of flight from the actual into a realm where the spirit abideth forever. If the typical critical error of the 'thirties was the failure to distinguish between literature and life, in the present period that error has been inverted into the failure to perceive their close and necessary relationship. Hence the effort we are now witnessing to overcome the felt reality of art by converting it into some kind of schematism of spirit; and since what is wanted is spiritualization at all costs, critics are disposed to purge the novel of its characteristically detailed imagination working through experiential particulars—the particulars of scene, figures and action: to purge them, that is to say, of their gross immediacy and direct empirical expressiveness.[7] It is as if critics were saying that the representation of experience, which is the primary asset of the novel, is a mere appearance; the really and truly real is to be discovered somewhere else, at some higher level beyond appearance. The novel, however, is the most empirical of all literary genres; existence is its original and inalienable datum; its ontology, if we may employ such a term in relation to it, is "naïve," com-

6. The payoff of the rage for symbolism is surely Mr. Charles Feidelson's recent book, *Symbolism and American Literature*, the fundamental assumption of which is that "to consider the literary work as a piece of language is to regard it as a symbol, autonomous in the sense that it is quite distinct both from the personality of the author and the world of pure objects, and creative in the sense that it brings into existence its own meaning." In this curious work the interest in symbolism has quite literally consumed the interest in literature.

7. An amusing confirmation of this mood has been provided by Lionel Trilling in a recent essay. Mr. Trilling reports that students have now "acquired a trick of speaking of money in Dostoevsky's novels as 'symbolic,' as if no one ever needed, or spent, or gambled, or squandered the stuff—and as if to think of it as an actuality were sub-literary." But this is a "trick" which young people, in a society as powerfully dominated by the cash-nexus as ours is, would hardly be capable of inventing for themselves. They must have learned it from their readings in contemporary criticism.

monsensical, positing no split between appearance and reality. "The supreme virtue of a novel," as Henry James insisted, "the merit on which all its other merits . . . helplessly and submissively depend," is its truth of detail, its air of reality or "solidity of specification." "If it be not there, all other merits are as nothing, and if these be there, they owe their effect to the success with which the author has produced the illusion of life." It is an illusion in the sense that what is recounted has not really happened but has been imagined by the author; but this cannot mean that it is an illusion in relation to itself too, that the novel dreams itself as it were. There is not some other novel, composed of spiritual and moral integers, hovering somewhere behind the illusion of life with which the novelist has sought to infuse his fictive world. We are of course free to interpret that world and to approach it from different angles and on different levels. But to interpret a fiction is one thing; to dissolve it is something else again, and we do dissolve it when treating it as a mere appearance, of the senses only, of interest only to the extent that it provides a domicile for symbols, supersensible forms comparable to Plato's Ideas. Such a notion has little in common with the literary theory of symbolism, though on the surface it may look like a logical extension of it. It belongs rather to metaphysics. The obsession with symbolization is at bottom expressive of the reactionary idealism that now afflicts our literary life and that passes itself off as a strict concern with aesthetic form.

This is not to say, to be sure, that fiction excludes symbolization. On the contrary, works of fiction abound in symbolic devices and the more significant among them have symbolic import. But when we speak of the symbolic import of a novel what we have in mind is nothing more mysterious than its overplus of meaning, its suggestiveness over and above its tissue of particulars, the actual representation of which it is comprised; and that is scarcely the same thing as treating these particulars as "clues" which it is the ingenious critic's task to follow up for hidden or buried meanings that are assumed to be the "real point" of the text under examination. In the long run this procedure cannot but make the text itself dispensable; it ceases to be of use once you have extracted the symbols it contains. The text, however, is not a container, like a bottle; it is all there is; and the symbol-hunting critics are unwittingly reasserting the dichotomy of form and content which they ostensibly reject. *Moby Dick*, for instance, is a work of which certain basic elements, such as the whale, the sea and the quest, have both symbolic and direct representational value. There is no consensus of opinion among commentators as to what the symbolic value of those elements comes to in specific, exact terms; and it is a proof of the merit of this work that no such consensus is in fact possible. The narrative, not being an allegory, has no meanings that can be mentally tabulated and neatly accounted for. Its symbols are integrally a part of its fictive reality, and it is precisely their organic character that renders them immune to purely intellectual specification.

* * *

EDWARD STONE

The Many Suns of *The Red Badge of Courage*†

The red sun in Chapter IX of Stephen Crane's *Red Badge of Courage*, whether because or in spite of its being the most celebrated metaphor in American literature before the supine evening of T. S. Eliot's *Prufrock*, seems to have blinded critics to the question of its relative importance, story-wise.[1] Certainly a close reading reveals that the wafer in question is merely the most striking manifestation of the sun in a story on which the sun almost literally never sets. And what is more, therein lies an insight into both the artistry and the theme of the *Red Badge*.

With regard to the sun, although by no means the sun alone, Crane's story is carefully scored for color. Rarely is the sun represented objectively in its function as light bearer, as when, early in Chapter III, rising it spreads "disclosing rays" on the regiments seeming to burst into view. Generally, when it appears or Crane calls attention to it, he does so for dramatic and symbolic purposes. There are as many as six specific instances of this, and it seems noteworthy that:

(1) with one exception they occur at the end of the chapter where they occur—are, in fact, usually the very last words;

(2) in each instance the color with which Crane invests the sun is related to, and thus underscores, the overall mood of the actors on whom it looks down;

(3) these fairly varied appearances are spaced almost precisely, and thus in turn suggest that they are meant to provide a supplementary interpretation of the stages of the interior action of the story.

† From *American Literature*, XXIX (November, 1957), 322–26. Reprinted by permission.

1. For an enumeration and appraisal of the various source studies of this metaphor see Robert W. Stallman, "The Scholar's Net. Literary Sources," *College English*, XVII, 20–27 (Oct., 1955).

The first of these appearances is in the middle of Chapter II. It follows the pre-dawn striking of camp. Untried, the soldiers are tense, suspicious, excited, and fearful. The inner debate of the central one of them, Henry Fleming, about his future conduct under fire has left him spiritually troubled and anxious. To them all, the awesomeness of the enemy troops across the river is heightened by the fact that it is black night, that the "red eyes" of the Confederates are still "peering" threateningly at them. But a striking alteration of mood suddenly comes about as a result of the daybreak, of the culmination of the "rushing yellow of the developing day" going on behind their backs as they march: "When the sunrays at last struck full and mellowingly upon the earth, the youth saw that the landscape was streaked with two long, thin, black columns. . . ." The effect of this first climactic sunrise on the troops in general is almost instantaneous. It is a *mellowing* experience in that it reassures the men and raises their spirits. Gloom and tension —the "muttering speculations"—of pre-dawn darkness give way to laughter, jest, even high jinks. The troops have been freed from the spell of the red eyes of the night along the opposite hillside: they have the assurance of the day's light that they have been singled out to attack from the rear, rather than possibly to be attacked themselves on the campsite. (Henry, to be sure, continues in his introspective, sullen mood; but here, as elsewhere, Crane's point of view is almost carelessly flexible, and is at different times that of Henry, of his comrades, of both, or possibly of Crane himself.)

The five other times attention is called to the sun occur at the very end of the chapters. Of Chapter V, first. In the lull after the North has repelled the enemy charge, Henry has time for the luxury of indulging "his usual machines of reflection." These lead him to several surprising, related conclusions—conclusions that comprise an underlying theme of the novel. The first of these is that, so far from fighting a private war, he has been a mere eddy in a huge current ("lighter masses [of troops] protruding in points from the forest . . . were suggestive of unnumbered thousands. . . . Heretofore he had supposed that all the battle was directly under his nose"). But even more noteworthy, the current itself is of no importance, relatively speaking. For we are told that "As he gazed around him the youth felt a flash of astonishment at the blue, pure sky and the sun gleaming on the fields. It was surprising that Nature had gone tranquilly on with her golden process in the midst of so much devilment." Here, then, the sun is the sun of Henry's naturalist creator. Its *gleam* now is ironic to Henry, a synonym of indifference, of unconcern with human travail, however grim: aloof, it has gone about its *golden* business of maturation. And therein lies for Henry the first awareness of the important truth that one's role in battle is neither noble nor ignoble, but merely anonymous —of no importance, *sub specie aeternitatis.* (And this, note, in victory. But, no matter: in defeat, too. For the cautious "So?" which closes Chapter XIV betokens the much later awareness in Henry of a corollary, namely that individual shame is unimportant. If, as it turns out, as much as half of the regiment became "lost" the preceding day, then cowardice needs redefinition; for when treason, as it were, succeeds, then 'tis no longer treason.)

The sun that appears close to the end of the very next chapter (VI) is presented indirectly and very briefly: ". . . the general beamed upon the earth like a sun." This sun is the same as that of the preceding chapter without the perspective of irony. Here its benevolent *beams* match the general's feelings. He is excited and merry at the realization (self-deception, doubtless in the mind of the runaway scrutinizing him) that his troops have withstood the second enemy charge. Consequently his reactions suggest to Henry the sun in its golden aspect, the Powers That Be looking down glowingly upon human endeavor.

But the "red sun . . . pasted in the sky like a wafer" at the end of Chapter IX is like no other sun in the book. The reason is that by now Henry's involvement in the battle has reached a stage whereat no less striking an apparition can express it. He has stood by watching as his champion Jim Conklin danced his strange, horrible dance of death, and in a "livid" but almost inexpressible rage he gestures defiantly, presumably toward the battlefield. The sun that now shines down may be, incidentally, red even to the casual observer, if one supposes that it is westering and that the air is very yellow with smoke and dust. But it seems red to Henry at this moment because it is now the symbol of a celestial partisan, of an *enemy*, agent of man's misery and violent ends. It is red in the *sense* that it (*war,* that is) was in Chapter III and will be again in Chapter XII—"the red animal, war, the blood-swollen god."[2] At such moments as these Henry no longer sees the sun as an unconcerned spectator to human action or a well-wishing one, but as a monster gorged on human flesh and blood.[3] When seen in such wide compass, this representation of the sun gains in symbolical emphasis at the same time as it rises above the impressionistic journalistic level of its much debated seemingly single appearance.[4]

2. For a widely different interpretation, see Stallman, *op. cit.*, p. 22, and his introduction to the Modern Library College edition, pp. xxiii–xxv.
3. Even, inferentially, on his own; for as the next chapter opens Henry is represented as "stabbed" and his tongue as lying "dead in the tomb of his mouth."
4. And if one may add to these three explicit visualizations of war as a carnivorous celestial horror a further, speculative one, there is the final sentence of Chapter II. Here, at night, after tor-

As Chapter XVII closes, however, Crane reintroduces the aloof, devil-may-care celestial eye of Chapter V. Now, as then, the sun appears so to Henry because at the time he views it there is a lull in the bloody fighting that permits philosophizing, and the philosopher (whether in the maturing youth or in Crane is not clear) finds this sermon in colors: "A cloud of dark smoke, as from smoldering ruins, went up toward the sun now bright and gay in the blue, enameled sky." The funereal signal of mortal anguish calls supplicantly to an orb gaudily bright in her tranquil background of blue—a symbol of frivolous unconcern even more impressive than in its similar appearance earlier because Crane is content now to leave its symbolical function implicit.

In its final appearance, in the final words of the book, the sun shines through the clouds in both the literal and the over-familiar metaphorical sense: "Over the river a golden ray of sun came through the hosts of leaden rain clouds." This is the mellowing, comforting sun of Chapter II, although we now see only one striking ray, a coda of the piece as a whole. The battle is at last over, and Henry's initiation is complete. Death, he now knows, is merely death; and with this intimate assurance to strengthen his spirit, he can now turn his thoughts to images of peace and tranquillity. Every gray cloud indeed does have a golden lining, tiny though it may be.

On this peaceful note the story closes. Like the correspondent in "The Open Boat," Henry has finally come ashore, so to speak, in spite of all hazards, and only after the sacrificial offering of someone close to him. Like him, too, the chart of his spiritual course can be read in the sky. Both now know its color intimately. For the correspondent, the spirit of the universe as represented by the stars had been alternately, as hope waxed and waned, a friend, a cruel foe, or merely indifferent. For Henry Fleming, all of these possibilities had radiated from a daytime planet.

---

turing himself with "visions of a thousand-tongued fear" of cowardice, we are told, Henry "stared at the red, shivering reflection of a fire on the white wall of his tent until, exhausted and ill from the monotony of his suffering, he fell asleep." It is a permissible flight of analysis to see in the serrate ("shivering") red image of the campfire's reflection against a white background a foreshadowing of the famous later symbol, for both are imaginative projections in color of a fearful object consonant with human death.

STANLEY B. GREENFIELD

From The Unmistakable Stephen Crane†

In a letter to a friend early in his brief writing career, Stephen Crane wrote, "I always want to be unmistakable"; and, at a later date, to another friend he explained retrospectively that "My chief-test [sic] desire was to write plainly and unmistakably, so that all men (and some women) might read and understand."[1] There is an irony in the critical fate that has befallen Crane's writings that perhaps that master ironist himself might have appreciated. For though the best criticism of his own time reveals a careful reading and understanding of his works, most recent criticism has seen Crane through a glass darkly.

I refer particularly to the body of commentary on Crane's war novel, *The Red Badge of Courage*, though the criticism of his other works is also lacking in clarity. An examination of the criticism of the novel reveals errors ranging from inadvertent though disturbing misstatements of fact to quotations out of context and gross distortion of sense. We find, for example, V. S. Pritchett avowing that Henry Fleming is never given a name, and Charles Walcutt, in the most recent study of the novel, completely forgetting the tattered man, saying that Henry deserts the dying Jim Conklin instead of this forlorn figure.[2] These are indisputably simple lapses of memory. But we read elsewhere, with more apprehension than comprehension, remarks to the effect that Henry has "a complete lack of appetite for glory," and that he deserts in protest "because war wrenches young people out of their path of life, thwarting their aspirations for work, education, love, marriage, family, self-development."[3] Such interpretations are not only patently wrong but too simple, for the human condition of the typical Crane character, as John Berryman has pointed out (p. 280), is a combination of pretentiousness and fear, as in the Swede of "The Blue

† From, "The Unmistakable Stephen Crane," *PMLA*, LXXIII (December, 1958), 562–72. Reprinted by permission of *PMLA*. The second (of three parts) has been omitted as relating primarily to the tales of Crane. The article may usefully be compared with Rahv's as an attack on the symbolic critics, in favor of realistic imagery.
1. Cited by John Berryman, in *Stephen Crane* (New York, 1950), p. 99. In all fairness, it should be noted that Crane elsewhere expressed an artistic credo to the effect that the meaning of a story should not be made *too* plain. (See Robert Wooster Stallman, *Stephen Crane: An Omnibus*, New York, 1953, p. 218).
2. *The Living Novel* (New York, 1947), p. 174; *American Literary Naturalism: A Divided Stream* (Minneapolis, 1956), p. 81.
3. George D. Snell, *Shapers of American Fiction* (New York, 1947), pp. 225–226, M. Solomon, "Stephen Crane: A Critical Study," *Masses and Mainstream*, IX (Jan. 1956), 38.

Hotel," or the New York Kid of "The Five White Mice," or Henry
Fleming, who throughout almost the entire novel is vainglorious
and, when he deserts, scared stiff. In another analysis we find the
novel as a whole regarded as defective because Henry's becoming a
man "is largely a matter of accident, [and] lacks the authority of a
consciously willed readiness to work out the hard way of salvation,"[4] a critical remark that suggests a confusion of ethics with
aesthetics and, in the context of the whole article, a failure to perceive or understand irony. In still another article we find the author
confidently proclaiming at the outset: "As one way of re-examining
The Red Badge of Courage, we would want to read it as myth and
symbolic action."[5] We may well wonder why we would or should.

I must examine at greater length the criticism of Crane by Robert Stallman. We are indebted to a great degree to Stallman for
the revival of an interest in Crane. But his critical method and interpretation I find very disturbing. His symbolic reading of *The
Red Badge of Courage*, with Jim Conklin emerging as Jesus Christ,
appears in his edition of the novel for the Modern Library and,
with some additional material, in his essay on Crane in *Critiques
and Essays on Modern Fiction* (ed. John W. Aldridge), and in his
Stephen Crane: An Omnibus; if I read aright the "For Members
Only" section of *PMLA*, it is now appearing in a Greek edition of
the novel. And this perseverance of the same argument and method
of criticism has led to converts.[6]

As an example of Stallman's method in his analysis of the novel,
we may look first at his purported objective summary of the action,
which precedes the explicit formulation of his theory of salvation
and redemption. In reviewing the sequence of events in the opening chapter, he describes the reception of Jim Conklin's rumor that
the army is going into action the next day (italics, save for the
word *tall*, are mine):

"But Jim Conklin's *prophecy* of hope meets with *disbelief*. 'It's a
lie!' shouts the loud soldier. 'I don't believe this derned old army's
ever going to move.' No *disciples* rally round the red and gold flag
of the herald. A furious altercation ensues; the *skeptics* think it just
another *tall* tale. Meanwhile Henry in his hut engages in a *spiritual*
debate with himself: whether to believe or disbelieve the word of
his friend, the *tall* soldier. It is the *gospel truth*, but Henry is one of
the *doubting apostles*."[7]

4. John W. Shroeder, "Stephen Crane
Embattled," *UKCR*, xvii (1951),
126.
5. John E. Hart, *"The Red Badge of
Courage* as Myth and Symbol," *UKCR*,
xix (1953), 249.
6. See, e.g., James T. Cox, "Stephen
Crane as Symbolic Naturalist: An Analysis of 'The Blue Hotel'," *Modern Fiction Studies*, iii (Summer 1957), 147–
158.
7. Pages xxiv–xxv of the Modern Lib.
edition.

There are several comments this account calls for. There is an error of fact that is *not* negligible: Jim Conklin's rumor is *not* the gospel truth, or any truth at all, for the first sentence of Chapter ii clearly states that "The next morning the youth discovered that his tall comrade had been the fast-flying messenger of a mistake."[8] Another error of fact: Henry is not debating, spiritually or otherwise, about believing or disbelieving his friend; he has a more serious concern, trying "to mathematically prove to himself that he [will] not run from battle." Finally, consider the words I have italicized in the above quotation: not one of them appears in the part of the novel Stallman is describing. In brief, there is not the faintest hint of a religious question of faith versus doubt. Religious phrasing unfortunately predisposes the reader toward an interpretation of spiritual redemption.

This is not the only instance of such distortion. Let us consider a passage describing the climax of the book, the end of Chapter ix, where Henry watches Jim Conklin die: "[Henry] curses the red sun pasted in the sky 'like a wafer.' Nature, we are told, 'had given him a sign.' Henry blasphemes against this emblem of his faith, the wafer-like red sun" (*Omnibus*, p. 223). First, the Crane quotation about Nature giving Henry a sign is not from this part of the novel at all: it is from Chapter vii, and is *Henry's* reaction to the squirrel's running when he threw a pine cone at him—a phrase, in other words, that is to be construed ironically in its proper context! Moreover, the text of the novel at this point is as follows:

"The youth turned, with sudden, livid rage, toward the battlefield. He shook his fist. He seemed about to deliver a philippic.
'Hell—'
The red sun was pasted in the sky like a [fierce] wafer."

Surely an unbiased reading of this passage reveals that Henry is blaspheming against the battlefield, against war. The shift in point of view from Henry to an observer ("He seemed about . . .") suggests that Henry is not even aware of the sun.

Again, this time in connection with the last part of the novel, Stallman makes a statement about Henry's so-called spiritual change: "The brave new Henry, 'new bearer of the colors,' triumphs over the former one. The flag of the enemy is wrenched from the hands of 'the rival colorbearer,' the symbol of Henry's own other self, and as the rival colorbearer dies Henry is reborn." The implication in this passage is that Henry has done the wrenching; otherwise the comment is pointless. But it is Wilson who has

8. All quotations from Crane are from *The Red Badge of Courage and Selected Prose and Poetry*, ed. William M. Gibson, Rinehart Eds. (New York, 1956).

actually grabbed the flag. The ambiguous passive voice ("is wrenched") is highly misleading.

Although there are many other points at which Stallman's theory about *The Red Badge of Courage* may be attacked,[9] I wish to consider briefly only one more instance of the weakness of his critical approach, this time in his salvation theory about "The Open Boat." This interpretation of the Crane short story appears in *Stephen Crane: Stories and Tales,* in *Stephen Crane: An Omnibus,* and in Aldridge's *Critiques and Essays on Modern Fiction.* The distortion here is again partially the result of misplaced quotation. For example, Stallman writes, "At the end 'they [the survivors] felt that they could *then* be interpreters.' Life—represented by the ritual of comfort bestowed on the saved men by the people on the beach—life now becomes 'sacred to their minds'."[10] What is the context of the quoted phrase "sacred to their minds?" Crane writes, "It seemed that instantly the beach was populated with men . . . and women with coffee pots and all the remedies sacred to their minds." That is, sacred to the women's minds, and it is remedies that are sacred. Even more damning to Stallman's "salvation" is the following: "The rescue of the men from the sea has cost them 'a terrible grace'—the oiler lies face-downward in the shallows." Where does the "grace" quotation appear in the story? On the second page, in the following context: "There was a terrible grace in the move of the waves, and they came in silence, save for the snarling of the crests."[11]

"I always want to be unmistakable." Poor Crane.

I should like to suggest that a clearer understanding of Crane's art, especially of *The Red Badge of Courage,* may be achieved if we examine the novel in conjunction with Crane's two most famous short stories, "The Open Boat" and "The Blue Hotel." For these three masterpieces have much in common, and their very differences are illuminating. For instance, all of them give promi-

---

9. A few of these will be mentioned in the course of my analysis of the novel, but I should like to mention here the lengths to which Stallman's critical method forces him. For example, when Henry, discovering that the wounded 'spectral soldier' is none other than his friend, the tall soldier, exclaims, "Gawd! Jim Conklin," Stallman comments that this "suggests an identification of Jim Conklin with God" (*Omnibus,* p. 282, n. 2). Must even swearing lend itself as evidence of religious symbolism?

10. *Stories and Tales,* p. 212.

11. Critics who follow Stallman's method—and this applies to critics in other areas than American Literature —should acknowledge that Biblical phrasing in a work is not *necessarily* a sign that Christian symbolism or allegory is also present in the work. The phrasing may simply be part of the language of a particular period or a particular writer, and though it may give a religious flavor to the work in question, it may have no more specific significance. Further, those who seek symbolic meanings on the strength of such phrasing are in danger of ignoring tone and context. As far as Crane's Biblical phraseology is concerned, we should remember that after all Crane was a minister's son.

nence to Nature and to man's impressions of her benevolence or malevolence, though the role of Nature in each work varies: it is *the* antagonist in "The Open Boat"; it should be but isn't the antagonist in "The Blue Hotel"; and it is a fancied antagonist in *The Red Badge of Courage*. Further, all of them are concerned with man's inflated sense of his own importance, but Crane's attitude toward man's pretentiousness ranges from sympathy in "The Open Boat" to sarcasm or bitterness in "The Blue Hotel." All of them emphasize the need for understanding and interpreting; but in them, again, Crane makes somewhat different suggestions about the possibility of man's evaluating his experience. But what this novel and these stories most strikingly reveal is the Crane artistic formula at its most complex and richest. None of them gives an answer to the mystery of life and death: man's fate is shown as neither the result of deterministic or naturalistic forces nor as an achievable salvation. Instead, Crane maintains an aesthetic perspective on all the elements that contribute to man's destiny: circumstance, instinct, ethical motivation, ratiocination, chance; he refuses to guarantee validity to any of them.[12] This balance between the deterministic and volitional views of life and between a sense of destiny and the haphazard workings of chance is, it seems to me, the secret of Crane's mature art; and I hope to demonstrate in the following pages that the meaning of these works is involved in this balance.

* * *

The nature of heroic behavior and the state of mind of the courageous man lie at the heart of *The Red Badge of Courage*. The majority of critics accept the point of view that the novel is a study in growth, whether that growth be spiritual, social, or philosophic. These critics "concede" that the novel, especially in its earlier parts, has a strong naturalistic bias which tends to vitiate, most of them feel, its aesthetic integrity, though Berryman, a believer in Henry's ultimate heroism, asserts that it is the end of the novel that is deficient, since it fails to sustain the irony (p. 107).[15] Two critics, notably, depart from this opinion. Shroeder sees evidence of growth but feels it is inconsequential: he complains that the novel fails because Henry's heroism is largely accidental and because the pretty picture at the end "smacks too strongly of the youth's early impressions of the haunted forest; Crane seems to have forgotten everything that has gone before in his own book" (p. 126). Walcutt, on the other hand, claims that Henry, at the end of the novel,

12. Cf. Berryman, pp. 287–288.
15. Berryman's interpretation of Crane as a whole is vitiated by his peculiar psychoanalytical view of Crane.

is back where he started from, naturalistic man still swelling with his ignorant self-importance (pp. 81–82).[16] I submit that neither interpretation of the novel—the heroic, with or without qualifications, or the antiheroic—gives proper credit to Crane's aesthetic vision. For though earlier than "The Open Boat" and "The Blue Hotel," *The Red Badge of Courage* exhibits the same interplay of deterministic and volitional forces as the two short stories, and the same pervasive irony binding the heroic and the anti-heroic themes. It reveals the same ultimate refusal to guarantee the effectiveness of moral behavior or the validity of man's interpretative processes, while simultaneously approving of the moral act and the attempt to gain insight into the meaning of experience.

To understand the novel, then, we must analyze Crane's handling of *behavior* and *attitude*. We may begin with the former. Its deterministic side has so often been commented on that a brief summary will suffice. It is enough to note that, like Scully's presumptuous behavior in "The Blue Hotel," Henry's presumption to patriotic motivation and ethical choice, in the guise of enlistment in the army, is ironically punctured by the circumstance of his enlistment, the "twisted news of a great battle";[17] to observe that Henry moves from tradition-conditioned behavior ("the moving box" of "tradition and law") to instinct-conditioned behavior as the atmosphere of battle overwhelms him; and to recall that Henry *awakes* to find himself a *knight* because he had gone on "loading and firing and cursing without the proper intermission," and had acted like "a barbarian, a beast."

The use of animal imagery to reinforce the determinism of the novel and to deflate man's pretensions to heroic conduct has also often been noted. The similar use of eating and drinking, both in deed and in imagery, has not, however, been given sufficient attention. What is most interesting is the variety of ways in which Crane stresses the survival theme by his handling of food and drink.

When Henry returns home with the news of his enlistment, his mother is milking the brindle cow, and when he departs, "she . . . doggedly [peels] potatoes." Here, food and drink are shown on the simple level of existence, as staples of life, and they point up by understatement the contrast between normality and the excited

---

16. It is interesting to observe that Stallman, after examining the earlier manuscripts of *The Red Badge of Courage,* seems to have had a change of mind about Henry's "salvation." He sees the "images of tranquil skies" at the end of the novel as flatly sentimental and feels that they are given an ironic turn by the sun-through-

clouds image: "[Henry] has undergone no change, no real spiritual development" (*Omnibus,* p. 221). I'm not sure where this "conversion" leaves the rest of Stallman's theory about Henry's rebirth when the rival colorbearer dies, but he himself has let it stand.

17. Cf. Walcutt, pp. 76–77.

Henry's impressions of war. As the men march along, they shed all superfluous equipment: " 'You can now eat and shoot,' said the tall soldier to the youth. 'That's all you want to do'." Here, war as an eat-or-be-eaten affair is stated explicitly. When Jim Conklin and Wilson dispute about the running of the army, the former eats sandwiches "as if taking poison in despair. But gradually, as he chewed, his face became again quiet and contented. He would not rage in fierce argument in the presence of such sandwiches. During his meals he always wore an air of blissful contemplation of the food he had swallowed. His spirit seemed then to be communing with the viands." This passage is almost pure comedy, with its emphasis on the power of food to condition man's frame of mind. In contrast is the tragedy in the description of Jim Conklin's death: "As the flap of the blue jacket fell away from the body, he [Henry] could see that the side looked as if it had been chewed by wolves." According to Stallman, this wound is supposed to be an unmistakable hint, among others, that Jim Conklin is Jesus Christ, but clearly it is part of the same eat-or-be-eaten concept that pervades "The Open Boat" and that we find in the melon image in the description of the Swede's death. Still another way in which food and drink contribute to meaning is found in the scene in which Henry and Wilson, at a significant lull in the battle after Henry has awakened a knight, go looking for water. Instead of finding the water, which is only an illusion on Wilson's part, they discover their own insignificance. Finally, at the end of the novel, Henry turns "with a lover's thirst" to images of peace. . . .

If Henry's and the other soldiers' behavior is conditioned by tradition and the instinct for survival, their fate, unlike Maggie's in Crane's earlier novel, is not the product of circumstance and the cumulative effect of other people's behavior. Their destiny involves other elements.

For one thing, there is Nature or the Universe. Henry visualizes Nature as being most concerned with his fate. She sympathizes or is hostile according to his mood and circumstance; and this impressionism is part of the philosophy and aesthetic of the novel. But Nature's involvement in the affairs of man is really, as in the two stories, noninvolvement, though in *The Red Badge of Courage* she is not flatly indifferent as in "The Open Boat," or malevolently indifferent as in "The Blue Hotel," but cheerfully so. Regularly throughout the book Crane provides glimpses of this cheerful reality, so that the reader does not lose sight of the illusions and delusions of Henry's limited perspective. The reader of the novel will recall the surprising "fairy blue" of the sky and the references to

Nature's "golden process" and "golden ray" of the sun.[19] Henry sees this indifference, but he does not understand it.

Another element is man's will. Jim Conklin, for one, demonstrates that man has and makes ethical choices. Before the battle, he states that he will probably act like the other soldiers; but when many of them run, he nonetheless stands his ground. Wilson, too, feeling as the battle joins that it will be his death, does not run. And there is a decided growth in Henry's moral behavior as the novel progresses. From running away and rationalizing his cowardice as superior insight, Henry moves through a series of actions in which he does the right thing. When he and Wilson, on their mistaken expedition for water, overhear the officer say that not many of the "mule-drivers" will get back, both keep the secret and do not hesitate to make the charge. When the two friends grab the flag from the dead colorbearer, Henry pushes Wilson away to declare "his willingness to further risk himself." And in the final charge, Henry "saw that to be firm soldiers they must go forward. It would be death to stay in the present place, and with all the circumstances to go backward would exalt too many others." Henry at these moments is more than an animal.

Ethical choice, then, is part of the novel's pattern: the moral act is admired. Yet Crane refuses to guarantee the effectiveness of moral behavior, even as he refuses in the two short stories. For there is the element of chance, finally, as in those stories, that makes the outcome unpredictable. Jim Conklin, for all his bravery, is killed. The tattered man, who watches with Henry Jim's death struggle and who is concerned over Henry's "wound," has acted morally, but he is dying and is, additionally, deserted for his pains. Wilson, on the other hand, who has also done the right thing, is rewarded by chance with life and praise; but Henry's immoral behavior, not only in running but later in lying about his head wound, is equally rewarded.

The complexity and withal the simplicity in the nature of man's behavior and its effect upon his destiny is crystallized, it seems to me, in the figure of the cheery soldier. This man, before whom obstacles melt away, guides Henry back to his regiment after Henry has received a "red badge" from the rifle butt of one of his own men. As they move along, he talks blithely of the mixup in the battle and of another's death; he comes out of nowhere but takes

---

19. As for the hotly-debated wafer image, although it cannot be said to be cheerful, it seems to me that Scott C. Osborn is perfectly right when he suggests that it is the seal of Nature's indifference to Jim's (and man's) fate ("Stephen Crane's Imagery: Pasted like a Wafer," *AL*, XXIII, 1951, 362). I believe it was to insure this meaning that Crane deleted the "fierce" from his final revision of this passage.

Henry "firmly by the arm"; and as he leaves, whistling audaciously, the youth realizes that he has not once seen his face. This disembodied jovial voice is, like Nature, cheerfully indifferent. His materialization out of the blue seems to be an element of chance. His bringing Henry back to his regiment willy-nilly suggests a deterministic pattern. Finally, he seems to represent Henry's own will, arriving as he does at that point in the action when Henry really desires to return to his regiment.

Man's behavior, then, as viewed in *The Red Badge of Courage*, is a combination of conditioned and volitional motivation. Man has a freedom of choice, and it is proper for him to choose the right way; at the same time, much of his apparent choice is, in reality, conditioned. But even acting morally or immorally does not guarantee one's fate, for the Universe is indifferent and chance too has scope to operate. Crane is interested, however, in more than man's public deeds. He probes in addition the state of mind of the heroic man and the possibility of his interpreting experience. Again, as in the short stories, the light of his irony plays over the presentation of man's attitude toward life.

The heroic attitude is given to us in the early part of the novel at a relatively simple level. Jim Conklin, the tall soldier, exhibits a serene faith in himself and his opinions, even when he is wrong. He will not run like Henry's squirrel. If the other soldiers stand firm, he will. Self-confidence, that is the keynote of the heroic temperament. The reader is made to admire Jim's attitude and subsequent bravery, to approve his calm acceptance of the incomprehensible movements of the army forcing him to build and then abandon three breastworks, "each of which had been an engineering feat worthy of being made sacred to the name of his grandmother." At the same time, however, as this last quotation reveals, Jim's self-confidence is slightly pretentious. We first see Jim developing virtues by washing a shirt, and he is "swelled with a tale he had heard from a reliable friend, who had heard it from a truthful cavalryman, who had heard it from his trustworthy brother." When this rumor is proved false the following morning, Jim feels called upon to beat severely a man from Chatfield Corners. And in a passage I have cited above, we see there is comic deflation in Jim's blissful and righteous eating of sandwiches.[20]

Wilson demonstrates this confidence in a somewhat different key. The loud soldier is brash, first in his optimism, then in his pessimism. But whether he is supremely confident that he will not

20. Stallman sees this shirt washing as a sign of the way to achieve spiritual salvation . . . Crane's ironic attitude toward Jim Conklin in instances I have cited certainly militates against our seeing him as a Christ figure.

be killed or, raising "his limp hand in a prophetic manner," that he will, his is the attitude of the hero. The bravura deflation involved in Wilson's switch from one kind of brashness to another is obvious. Even later, however, when Wilson has become non-assertive and more humbly and quietly confident, when we feel for him, as we did earlier for Jim, a warm approval, there is something a little too self-humiliating, at first, in his new relationship with Henry.

The tattered man furnishes a third glimpse of the heroic attitude. Although he has just seen Jim Conklin die, and he himself is badly wounded, he is very sure of his own destiny: "Oh, I'm not goin' t'die yit! There's too much dependin' on me fer me t'die yit. No sir! Nary die! I *can't!*" He is more concerned over Henry's "wound" than over his own. But his mind wanders and we know he is going to die as Henry deserts him in the fields. Again we find a mixture of admiration for and ironic puncturing of this state of mind, though the ultimate effect in this scene is one of pathos.

* * *

Most of the critics of this novel, as I have observed, note a fading away of the irony as the novel draws to an end. But Walcutt, in his dissenting theory, claims that if we take Henry's thoughts about his new manhood in the context of the whole novel, we see that his motives always have been and still are vain; that he "has never been able to evaluate his conduct," and he is still deluded about himself (pp. 81–82). There *is* irony in the end of the novel; in fact, if one examines the longer version in the earlier manuscript of *The Red Badge of Courage*, he can have no doubt that there is. For there are long passages there, later excised by Crane, which clearly reveal a delusion in Henry's thoughts.

* * *

But at what is this final irony directed? Not, as Walcutt would have it, at Henry's evaluation of his conduct, but at the presumption in his false impressions of Nature and the Universe; at his *philosophical* self-confidence. Just as earlier Jim Conklin's, Wilson's, and the tattered man's supreme confidence in themselves had been held up to ironic scrutiny, so here is Henry's, only on a befittingly larger scale. But even as the minor characters' confidence has its approbation from Crane, even as in "The Blue Hotel" man's conceit was shown to be the very engine of life, so was Henry's. It seems to me that what Crane was trying to do in his revision was to eliminate the too obvious irony and redress the tonal balance of the novel.

This tonal balance is seen in Crane's handling of Henry's final evaluation of his conduct. Shifting from the apparency of things to positive statement in Henry's recapitulation of his conduct, Crane abandons the word *seems,* so pervasive in the novel. "His mind was undergoing a subtle change. . . . Gradually his brain emerged from the clogged clouds, and at last he was enabled to more closely comprehend himself and circumstance." As Henry reviews his deeds, Crane writes: "From his present viewpoint he was enabled to look upon them in spectator fashion and to criticize them with some correctness, for his new condition had already defeated certain sympathies." No *seems* here; the tone is entirely sympathetic, though the refusal to guarantee interpretation is still here with "to more closely comprehend" and "with some correctness." There is no vain delusion about the past. As for the future—well, that is a different matter, highly ambiguous: "at last his eyes *seemed* to open to some new ways," and he "thirsts" for the obviously impossible, unchanging, "eternal peace." But however insecure the basis of Henry's thoughts about his future actions may be, Henry still has emerged from his experience with a new assurance of which Crane obviously approves: "He felt a quiet manhood, non-assertive but of sturdy and strong blood." [21]

The achievement of Crane in *The Red Badge of Courage* may be likened, it seems to me, to Chaucer's in *Troilus and Criseyde,* despite the lesser stature of the novel. Both works are infused with an irony which neatly balances two major views of human life—in *Troilus and Criseyde,* the value of courtly love versus heavenly love; in *The Red Badge of Courage,* ethical motivation and behavior versus deterministic and naturalistic actions. Both pose the problem, "Is there care in Heaven?" One is concerned with human values in a caring Universe, the other in an indifferent Universe. It is the age-old question of human values appearing in both, though the context varies. Too many critics of both works have suffered from an inability to see the validity of both of the conflicting sets of values. Chaucer shows us earthly love at its best. Alas that it is ephemeral against the backdrop of eternity and Christ's love for us and ours for Him: the perdurable quality of the poem that teases

21. I must dispute Walcutt's interpretation of this famous passage: "With all these facts [the juxtaposition of courage, ignorance, vainglory, etc.] in mind we can examine the Henry Fleming who emerges from the battle and sets about marshaling all his acts. He is gleeful over his courage. Remembering his desertion of the wounded Jim Conklin, he is ashamed of the possible disgrace, but, as Crane tells with supreme irony, 'gradually he mustered force to put the sin at a distance,' and to dwell upon his 'quiet manhood' " (p. 81). The mistaken identification of character is negligible. But two points are, I think, crucial: Henry is not gleeful about his courage, but "He was gleeful when he discovered that he now despised [the brass and bombast] of his earlier gospels." And Henry doesn't *dwell* upon his quiet manhood (the word is, I feel, prejudicial): "He felt a quiet manhood . . ."

us out of our senses (and provokes so much critical commentary) is precisely the interplay throughout the poem of the two sets of values, so that even though Chaucer "guarantees" in his palinode that the love of "thou oon and two and three eterne on lyve" is ultimately more rewarding, the lovely though perishable quality of human love is not effaced. Crane's magnum opus shows up the nature and value of courage. The heroic ideal is not what it has been claimed to be: so largely is it the product of instinctive responses to biological and traditional forces. But man does have will, and he has the ability to reflect, and though these do not guarantee that he can effect his own destiny, they do enable him to become responsible to some degree for the honesty of his personal vision. It is this duality of view, like Chaucer's, that is the secret of the unmistakable Crane's art.

MORDECAI and ERIN MARCUS

Animal Imagery in *The Red Badge of Courage*†

There is extensive use of animal imagery in Stephen Crane's *The Red Badge of Courage*.[1] This imagery largely takes the form of similes and metaphors. Excluding all of the numerous sunken metaphors which imply animal-like action, this short novel contains at least eighty figures of speech employing animals or their characteristics. These images occur in the narrative itself, in the dialogue, and in the thoughts of the central character. However unaware Crane may have been of the abundance and patterning of this imagery, the consistency with which it is used often furthers his characterization and presentation of ideas, and constitutes a significant method of communicating meaning.

The imagery employs domestic, wild, and imaginary animals, and also makes reference to undefined animal-like characteristics. References to domestic animals occur most frequently. With very few exceptions they are applied to people rather than to things, and they always refer to the enlisted men rather than to the officers. Wild animals, on the other hand, are used to describe things as well as individuals. Imaginary animals and vague animal comparisons tend to be used to describe groups of men.

† From *Modern Language Notes*, LXXIV (February, 1959), 108–11. Reprinted by permission.
1. The only other mention of this point is a brief notation by Professor William M. Gibson in his introduction to Stephen Crane, *The Red Badge of Courage and Selected Prose and Poetry* (New York, 1956), viii.

The Red Badge of Courage is the story of Henry Fleming's initiation into manhood through a resolution of fear, and it is also a bitterly anti-romantic treatment of war—one which shows elements of naturalistic philosophy. Crane's use of animal imagery lends considerable support to the novel's themes and viewpoint. It is frequently used to describe the youth's feelings and actions as he passes through progressive stages of apprehension, terror, conquest of fear, and acceptance of the human situation. During the first thirteen chapters the animal imagery helps to portray his apprehensions about the enemy and his early behavior in battle. During this part of the novel the youth struggles with shame and terror. Feeling that he is inadequate to cope with the coming battle, he reflects that he and his comrades are all sure to be "killed like pigs." His shame about these feelings will not allow him to "warn" his comrades because he fears that a wrong declaration would "turn him into a worm." The youth's terror determines his perception of certain things. On the march at night he perceives the enemy campfires as "the red eyes . . . of a row of dragons," and with at least a suggestion that the point of view is Henry's, his own regiment and army are several times described as a row of monsters, dragons, and wild horses, and he and his comrades are identified with familiar animals such as terriers and chickens. In the thick of battle Henry becomes a "well-meaning cow," and there is in his eyes the look that can be seen in those of a "jaded horse."

The culmination of his terror comes when he observes a fellow soldier throw down his gun and run "like a rabbit," whereupon Henry's fear makes him like "the proverbial chicken" which runs wildly about in all directions in its efforts to escape from danger. Later in the story of his flight, after many harrowing experiences, Henry pauses to consider his situation, and he realizes that he has acted like a worm and "a craven loon." Nevertheless, he cannot leave the scene of battle because of a "certain mothlike quality" within him. His terror, and the animal imagery which accompanies it, contrast sharply with his romantic feelings about war shown in the opening of the novel, when he saw himself full of "eagle-eyed prowess."

After the youth has begun to overcome his fear of battle, his attitudes about himself and about war alter, and the animal imagery which describes him also changes. After he and his regiment have participated successfully in a battle, they are described by the lieutenant as having fought like "hell-roosters" and "wild cats." Henry plunges at the enemy flag like a "mad horse." He now sees his comrades in a different light. He notices their "vicious wolf-like temper." Wilson, his friend, springs "as a panther at prey." The novel consists of twenty-four chapters: in the first twenty-three Henry has changed from a worm and a chicken to a wild cat; in chapter twenty-four he realizes that he has been an animal all the time that he was fighting, and his new acceptance of his precarious lot as a man is shown by his realization that he is a man and not an animal. "He was a man. . . . He had been an animal blistered and sweating in the heat and pain of war."

Crane's conclusion does not clearly suggest that the youth comes to understand that fear made him act like a terrified animal and newfound pride and courage subsequently helped him to act like a fierce animal. Nevertheless, Crane's attitude toward war, as we see it throughout the novel, suggests that he is critical of both fear and aggression. This critical attitude, and Crane's criticism of war, are partially communicated by animal imagery. As we have noted, much of this imagery appears in the representation of Henry's feelings. Armies are often seen as monsters and serpents, and men at war are shown as the victims of strange and vicious forces which either make them timid and cowardly, or brave and reckless. In addition to these images, war is twice described as "the red animal —war." Although Crane's ironic treatment of Henry's cowardice suggests more approval for Henry's actions when he behaves with courage, Crane still communicates the idea that it is as bad to kill like a beast as it is to run like a rabbit. Thus Crane's animal imagery contributes to his moral judgment of war.

The animal imagery also contributes to Crane's naturalism. This, however, is somewhat complicated by his attitude as shown in a scene rather early in the novel in which Henry seeks to justify his cowardice by comparing his behavior to that of a squirrel who runs when a pine-cone is thrown at it. In the squirrel's flight Henry sees the law of Nature at work. Nevertheless, Crane's intention here seems to be at least partially satirical, which suggests that he is perhaps more critical of cowardice than he is of fierceness. In any case, Henry's assumption of manhood leads from an animal-like cowardice to an animal-like fierceness. Crane's inability to lead Henry to manhood by any means other than a release of contrasting animal-like forces in his soul may account for the charge of failure to convince which has often been made of Henry's assumption of manhood. Yet Crane's consistency may be defended by claiming that he has shown two similar but opposing forces which lead to the hero's realization that he is not an animal but a man. For Henry's manhood consists of a final courage which has stemmed from his earlier terror and wild courage. Nevertheless, Crane does not clearly show that his hero understands the ordeal he has experienced, and the fact that he has passed out of the realm where natural forces rule into a realm where will-power functions. Thus Crane is trapped in the dilemma of the determinist who wishes to assert the existence of will-power, but sees change only as the result of natural forces.

Crane's naturalistic tendency is perhaps most clearly visible in references to the soldiers as sheep. The men are driven about and "nobody knows what it's done for." The officers are like "critical shepherds struggling with their sheep." The "sheep" are controlled by forces they cannot understand, just as—in the determinist's viewpoint—man's life is shaped by forces beyond his comprehension or control.

In addition to conveying certain ideas about man and war, Crane's animal imagery makes a considerable contribution to his impressionistic method of description. Many of the images we have cited add to the colorful and imaginative description which permeates the novel. Two particularly vivid and apt pieces of description employing animal images deserve special notice: "the bugles called to each other like brazen gamecocks," and "the blue smoke-swallowed line curled and writhed like a snake stepped upon."

We have cited only a rather small proportion of the numerous animal images in *The Red Badge of Courage*. More intensive examination of them would reveal additional vivid description, further support of leading ideas, and several ironic juxtapositions. Animal images and animal comparisons are used throughout the novel to convey changes in states of mind and the pattern of their development. Most important is Crane's use of them in presenting the theme of change from cowardice to wild courage, and finally from immaturity to manhood.

JAMES TRAMMELL COX

From The Imagery of *The Red Badge of Courage*†

"The red sun . . . pasted in the sky like a wafer" of Stephen Crane's *The Red Badge of Courage* continues to generate more critical heat than light. Since the publication in 1951 of R. W. Stallman's much-debated introduction to the Modern Library edition of the novel and his later expansions of this reading, contemporary criticism has been sharply divided on at least three issues:

† From *Modern Fiction Studies*, V (Autumn, 1959), 209–19. Reprinted by permission of the Purdue Research Foundation. The most comprehensive essay on the subject.

the significance of the religious imagery, the closely related problem
of Henry Fleming's development or lack of it, and the question of
Crane's fictional method, naturalist or symbolist. Seldom however
are these fundamental points of disagreement recognized as such;
all too frequently they are obscured or simply avoided in a dispute
over critical method. If the imagery gets re-examined, the examination is likely to limit itself to this single image in isolation. Only a
single article is devoted primarily to a study of the imagery as a
whole.[1] Another look is urgently needed.

Of what has been done, the best on the significance of the religious imagery is Bernard Weisbarger's recent suggestion that
"There is going to be rebirth, indeed, but not a supernatural one.
Here is a negation of the Christian conversion."[2] This obvious
obverse significance of the Christian symbolism, noted but misin-
terpreted by Stallman and quite consistent with Henry Fleming's
naturalistic re-education, seems to have occurred to no one but Mr.
Weisbarger. On the problem of Henry Fleming's development,
more specifically on its significance in the naturalistic universe depicted in the novel, Stanley B. Greenfield's summation is thoughtful and valuable, especially to the extent that it reconciles what
seems a discrepancy between Crane's determinism and the manifest
value he attaches to individual insight and moral behavior:

"Crane's magnum opus shows up the nature and value of courage.
The heroic ideal is not what it has been claimed to be: so largely is
it the product of instinctive responses to biological and traditional
forces. But man does have will, and he has the ability to reflect, and
though these do not guarantee that he can effect his own destiny
they do enable him to become responsible to some degree for the
honesty of his personal vision."[3]

Closer textual analysis—a method Mr. Greenfield inconsistently
ridicules and utilizes at will—reveals a need for considerable qualifi-
cation of the cheerful indifference of Nature and of the "decided
growth in moral behavior"[4] he finds in Henry Fleming's development. For the imagery suggests that this cheerful appearance of
Nature is a part of its treacherous hostility. As Crane expresses the
idea in an expunged passage from an earlier manuscript version,

1. John E. Hart, *"The Red Badge of
Courage* as Myth and Symbol," *University of Kansas City Review,* XIX
(Summer 1953), 249–257. The value of
Mr. Hart's analysis is limited by his
purpose, which is to compare Henry
Fleming to the mythic hero, thus reflecting more the anthropological interests
of 20th century criticism than the naturalism of late 19th century fiction.

2. Bernard Weisbarger, *"The Red
Badge of Courage,"* *Twelve Original
Essays on Gr at American Novels,* ed
by Charles Shapiro (Detroit, 1958).
pp. 104–105.
3. Stanley B. Greenfield, "The Un
mistakable Stephen Crane," *PMLA*
LXXIII (December 1958), 572.
4. *Ibid.,* 569.

"It [Nature] could deck a hideous creature in enticing apparel."[5] The imagery also insists upon the irony of Henry's discovery of unselfishness and courage through the wounded vanity of egocentrism, so that the decided growth toward moral manhood posited by Greenfield ignores this basic irony, as well as its chief philosophical implication: that man's relationship to his universe is paradoxical. He becomes least an animal when most an animal. On the question of Crane's fictional method, Stallman is still significantly right in his recognition of the extent to which "Crane puts language to poetic uses, which is to use it reflexively and symbolically."[6] And it is past time that this fundamental question be considered apart from any given interpretation, for a full understanding and appreciation of the better works of Stephen Crane are absolutely dependent upon an awareness of this method.

What makes this awareness so very important, in particular, to a reading of *The Red Badge of Courage* is that the novel is an initiation story, the account of a young man's discovery of the nature of reality; and the definition of this reality, symbolically presented to the reader through the imagery, provides Henry Fleming's slow discovery with a pervasive dramatic irony as essential to a full appreciation of the work as, for example, a foreknowledge of Oedipus' origin is in *Oedipus Rex*.

Briefly paraphrased, the definition Crane provides us with is largely the same naturalism to be found in "The Blue Hotel." The earth and all life on it originated from the fierce fire of the sun, which continues ultimately to determine both life and death on the earth in the dependence of all life here upon its warmth and light for existence. It is this condition of things, further, which requires that all life—specifically man, animal, and plant, as enumerated by Crane—must alike struggle to survive. Whatever the decking or coloration for the plant or animal, whatever the disguises for man—which would include all the myths of man's mind that obscure this conception of himself and his universe, notably his pretense to honor and glory, his romantic concept of nature, and his belief in eternal life—all are engaged in an endless struggle to survive that necessitates a conflict relation to environment. For this reason the inner nature of all life is hostile. Its battles are for existence, and the essence, in fact, of existence is a battle. This being true, all attempts either to escape or to deny this conflict are doomed to meaninglessness. For meaning, man's only recourse in such a universe is to heed the general's exhortation, "t' go in—everlastingly—like blazes—anything"; that is, to embrace life as con-

5. R. W. Stallman, *Stephen Crane: An Omnibus* (New York, 1952), p. 292.   6. *Ibid.*, XLV.

flict. In so doing man achieves a paradoxical harmony with his hostile universe that allows him, like the regiment, to proceed "superior to circumstances until its blazing vitality fades." It also allows him to know, for a moment, "a temporary but sublime absence of selfishness" and the undeceived brotherhood which his nature, his condition, and his disguises otherwise preclude. And with full knowledge comes, finally, a certain dignity, nothing more.

* * *

Consistently overlooked, even by Edward Stone,[7] in the long wrangle over the wafer image is the central role of the sun, metaphorically and philosophically, in the novel as a whole. It is set up in the beginning of the novel in the account of Henry's misconceptions as a youth: "There was a portion of the world's history which he had regarded as the time of wars, but it, he *thought*, had been *long gone over the horizon* and had disappeared forever" (6).[8] To this Crane adds, "He had long despaired of witnessing a Greek-like struggle. Such would be no more. Men were better, or more timid. Secular and religious education had effaced the throat grappling instinct, or else firm finance held in check the passions." Furthermore, this whole idea, with the last two sentences verbatim, is repeated on page 13. Consequently, it cannot be without significance and irony that the general who is in charge of the fighting that Henry has deserted on the first day of battle is described first as "much harassed" with the appearance "of a business man whose market is swinging up and down" (84), secondly, as having in his eyes "a desire to chant a paean" (86), and thirdly as one who "beamed upon the earth like a sun" (86).

Here is ample evidence, indeed, manifest in the action and explained in the imagery, that the time of wars is anything but "long gone over the horizon." As a Greek, an ironically unfirm representative of firm finance, and a sun, this general as the immediate cause of the conflict that ensues is still very much on Henry Fleming's horizon. The explanation provided by the imagery is first of all that finance is neither firm nor capable of holding in check men's passions. Further, in their common identity through metaphor, the imagery also calls attention to the common relation both the general and the sun have to the conflict which follows: it is causal, the general immediate and the sun ultimate. This is again the chief significance and the chief irony in the timely reappearance of the "red sun . . . pasted in the sky like a wafer" (115) when Henry

7. Edward Stone, "The Many Suns of *The Red Badge of Courage*," *American Literature*, XXIX (November 1957), 322–326.

8. Italics mine. All text references are to the Modern Library edition.

has just observed in Jim Conklin's fall that his "side looked as if it had been chewed by wolves." The time of wars has still to go over the horizon because religious education has also failed to efface "the throat grappling instinct."

* * *

The red badge that Henry Fleming wears is seed and sign of this same sun. For in the necessity imposed by the sun on all life to struggle for survival, man retains within a fiery hostility as revealed in the description of his hut, where it is not surprising that we find a fire in a "flimsy chimney of clay and sticks [that] made endless threats to set ablaze the whole establishment" (5). Philosophically, it is the same fire. It is the same fire that disturbed Henry when he "burned to enlist" (6). In the heat of battle, with existence threatened, it is this fire that has now emerged upon Henry's "red and inflamed features" (207) and upon the general's face, "aflame with excitement" (85). The regiment itself is a "firework that, once ignited proceeds superior to circumstances until its blazing vitality fades" (65).

* * *

Confirming the determining role of the sun as overhanging or providing the conditions under which man, so defined, exists, the sun appears here too: "The sunlight, without, beating upon it [the folded tent which serves as a roof] made it glow a light yellow shade" (5). Thus besides giving the fire necessary to existence, it demands finally as a consequence of this fire death. For yellow is consistently associated with death. The first corpse Henry sees is dressed in a suit of "yellowish brown" (43), and the mouth of the corpse in the chapel of the trees has changed from red "to an appalling yellow" (92). And overhanging the battle area Henry flees from exactly as it overhangs his quarters is "a yellow fog [that] lay wallowing on the treetops" (87).

* * *

A further aspect of man's nature is symbolically revealed in this interior: his tendency, deriving from his hostility, to screen from himself his inner nature, wreathing it in constructs of belief and value which only obscure the truth, as the smoke from the fire here "at times neglected the clay chimney and wreathed into the room" (5), obscuring this fire as the smoke of battle so often obscures the flames of the enemy guns, making it "difficult for the regiment to proceed with intelligence" (212). A part of this tendency is laziness and ignorance, qualities frequently associated with smoke:

"some lazy and ignorant smoke curled slowly. The men, hiding from the bullets, waited anxiously for it to lift and disclose the plight of the regiment" (224). Primarily however it is the fear of death which leads man to construct his own smokescreens, as suggested in the frequent linkage of smoke with the color gray. For the face or prospect of death is gray in each of the deaths that Henry has occasion to observe closely: in the "ashen face" (44) of the first, in "the gray skin of the face" (92) of the corpse in the chapel of the trees, and in "the gray appalling face" (106) of Jim Conklin. Also revealing is its identification with phantom: "Smoke clouds went slowly and insolently across the fields like observant phantoms" (52). For both Jim Conklin and the guilt Henry feels over his desertion of Jim are repeatedly referred to as a "specter" or "somber phantom." The implication of the linkage would seem to be that the guilt Henry feels is a part of the "clogged clouds," from which Henry's brain must emerge before his eyes are opened to new ways and the old sympathies are defeated. It derives from those systems of false belief and value which only obscure from man the fiery essence of the naturalistically conceived universe finally recognized and accepted by Henry Fleming. As such, this "sin" may be put "at a distance" by Henry with somewhat less callousness.

Aside from the false concept of heroism and the emptiness of its values, honor and glory, which it is the obvious purpose of the story to expose as so much smoke obscuring the true nature of man and his conflicts, a romantic concept of Nature, as a part of Henry's secular education, must also be included in this smoke. This romanticism is especially apparent in the sentimental pantheism which leads him to see in the landscape he comes to in his flight "a religion of peace" (90), where the arching boughs in a grove of trees "made a chapel" (92), with the sunlight in them providing "a religious half light" (92) and the wind "a hymn of twilight" (95). The low branches are "green doors" (92) to this chapel and the pine needles "a gentle brown carpet" (92). But exactly as the sentimentality of his earlier reaction to "the gentle fabric of softened greens and browns" which "looked to be a wrong place for a battlefield" (43) is revealed when it becomes the scene of the holocaust he flees, so here are his illusions shattered: within these green doors, resting on this gentle brown carpet is a rottening corpse, its uniform, once blue, now faded to a "melancholy shade of green" (92). However gentle green and brown may seem to the miseducated Henry Fleming, Crane makes it shockingly clear to the reader here and elsewhere that green and brown are the colors of the earth which requires death and decay for its fertility.

In the further relation of image to incident, Crane tells us a great deal more about Nature in this particular passage. The eyes have the "dull hue to be seen on the side of a dead fish" (92), linking the corpse to the frequently noted fish devoured previously by the small animal. The corpse, in other words, is like the fish in its failure to survive. What is not so frequently noted is that on five other occasions we are reminded of this resemblance. Henry, for example is a " 'Fresh fish!' " (15) and the courageous Lieutenant Hasbrouck "a whale" (265). Also war is twice a "red animal" (46 and 137) and more than twenty times either war or the enemy is a monster about to devour the men, whose frequent fear is " 'We'll git swallowed' " (205). Thus through its connection with this meal of the small animal and the corpse, the conflict that takes place on the battlefield becomes itself a symbol of the struggle for survival. And the connection is repeated, emphasizing that all life is involved in this struggle, in the detail of the ant on the lip "trundling some sort of bundle" (92), for again through simile and metaphor Crane elsewhere identifies this bundle as the soldiers being devoured by the red animal, war: they are "Grunting bundles of blue" (247) that drop here and there "like bundles" (69). Henry himself is "a parcel" (154).

Also significant in this passage is the threat of the branches "to throw him over upon it [the corpse]" (93), symbolizing Henry's involvement in the natural order which demands ultimately a return to the earth like that of the corpse. Furthermore this involvement is carefully elaborated through the tree symbolism. Not only are Henry and the men frequently entangled in Nature's trees or her "brambles [which] formed chains and tried to hold him back" (97), but they are repeatedly likened to a tree to reveal the identity of their mutual struggle, as in the song of the soldiers:

> A dog, a woman, an' a walnut tree,
> Th' more yeh beat 'em th' better they be (96)

If they survive, that is. The tattered soldier, whose wounded arm dangles "like a broken bough" (102) and Jim, whose body swings forward as he goes down "in the manner of a falling tree" (114), can hardly be described as "better." To indicate that this bit of homely naturalism is to be taken seriously, incidentally, Crane frequently repeats the beating or thrashing imagery like this picture of Henry, who sprawls in battle "like a man who had been thrashed" (193), and compares the soldiers also to women and dogs.

The idea of entanglement is also carried over into the machine imagery, which is used more than fifteen times to describe the battle, suggesting both the deterministic inevitability of this struggle and its destructive power. For instance, as Henry joins the column of the wounded: "The torn bodies expressed the awful machinery in which the men had been entangled" (101). And this machinery is not only the battle but the fixed processes of the natural order demanding conflict and death: "The battle was like the grinding of an immense and terrible machine to him. Its complexities and powers, its grim processes, fascinated him. He must go close and see it produce corpses" * * * Over seventy comparisons of the men to animals contribute to this significance of the battle, and in this line, its immediate source is defined as the animal-like hostility of the inner man: "A dull animal-like rebellion against his fellows, war in the abstract, and fate grew within him" (89). To suggest that man is as helpless as a babe in the grinding machinery of the natural order and his fury against it as foolish as that of a child, there are over twenty-five comparisons like these of the men to infants and children: An officer displays "infantile features black with rage" (211) and another "the furious anger of a spoiled child" (59), while Henry before his first battle feels "in the face of his great trial like a babe" (41). This is Nature as it really is—hardly the "woman with a deep aversion to tragedy" (91) Henry Fleming conceived it to be.

* * *

As a further aspect of the miseducation which obscures from Henry Fleming the fiery essence of his naturalistic universe, his religious education is also responsible. It too is a part of the "clogged clouds" and the old sympathies, as revealed not only in the imagery depicting Jim Conklin's death but also in the inferno imagery and in the imagery of the primitive warrior-worshiper. In the ironic resemblances of Conklin to Christ, Crane is perhaps naïvely, but clearly and powerfully saying that in this red world Jesus Christ is a grim joke. It is to this climatic conclusion that Crane builds in this crucial chapter exactly as he built up to the shattering revelation of the corpse in the trees. Only here it is the reader who gets the shock instead of Henry, for to have had Henry consciously perceive the resemblance would have been both too obvious and too implausible.

The resemblances are manifestly here however. Since Stallman has noted many of them, I would call attention only to the principal resemblance he's missed: when Jim Conklin falls, his "body seemed to bounce a little way from the earth" (114–15). Here, the point of this carefully and subtly prepared resemblance to Christ, with eight preceding hints, becomes clear. We know why, as Henry rushes to the fallen body, he discovers that "the teeth showed in a laugh" (115). It is because this death, which is all too real, makes of the other a palpable absurdity with its Ascension to the right hand of God. The only ascension here is a grotesque bounce "a little way from the earth." And when then the ultimate source and seal of this grimly naturalistic death appears in the sky in the shape—of all things—of a wafer, the irony is devastating and the significance no less: this red wafer symbolizes that there will be *no* miraculous transubstantiation from this mangled and meaningless corpse. Rather, it is a reminder of what we have seen of another corpse: the "red animal, war" and the ants will be the unholy communicants that devour this quite untransubstantiated and unrisen body which is left "laughing there in the grass" (118)— laughing at the appalling joke Henry Fleming's religious education has perpetrated upon him in its promise of eternal life.

What has confused some readers in this resemblance is that Crane does the same thing with his religious imagery here that he does in the short story, where Scully is at one moment God and Satan the next. Jim Conklin is *also* compared to the imps of hell in his "hideous hornpipe," his arms flailing about "in expression of implike enthusiasm" (114), and the "'God!'" that the tattered soldier exclaims upon the fall is starkly changed to "'Hell—'" (115). The significance of this apparent inconsistency is simply that all of heaven and hell man will ever know is here on earth, the product of his own efforts to obscure from himself the truth of his hostile nature in a hostile universe. And inferno imagery, like this line linking Jim to these imps, abounds throughout the text: "The black forms of men, passing to and fro before the crimson rays made weird and satanic effects" (31). They dodge "implike around the fires" (32). War, like life, is hell.

It is in the interesting sense in which Crane uses "enthusiasm" that the religious imagery becomes most revealing, for this enthusiasm is "the daring spirit of a savage religion mad" (251). Again it may be traced from the very beginning of the novel in the "enthusiast" (8) who rings the church bell with news of battle. In Henry too we see it on the march where for a moment "The thrill of his enthusiasm made him . . . fiery in his belief in success" (33–34). Finally, it is this religious enthusiasm of the pagan worshiper and warrior that defines the state of mind necessary for the performance of unselfish or heroic deeds:

"The men, pitching forward insanely, had burst into cheerings, moblike and barbaric. . . . It made a mad enthusiasm. . . . There was the delirium that encounters despair and death, and is heedless and blind to the odds. It is a temporary but sublime absence of selfishness." (209)

In a sense Crane seems to be saying that the Dionysiac fury of the pagan worshiper, who at least recognized his universe as hostile, was closer to a valid view of man and his universe than the Christian is with his humanistic veneer and false promise of eternal life. If the general, who gives us the central thematic statement of the novel—"t' go in—everlastingly—like blazes"—were to chant his paean, it would with more validity be addressed to the red sun than to the Heavenly Father.

This pattern is further revealing if we examine the source of this enthusiasm more closely. For it is in the flames of man's inner egotism, stirred up through wounded vanity to a pitch of hatred that is repeatedly described as "a dream" (191), a "delirium" (209), and a "state of frenzy" (251), precluding the consciousness necessary to will. As Crane tells us on the occasion of Henry's first experience of it, from which he awakes a knight or hero, "he lost sense of everything but his hate, his desire to smash into pulp the glittering smile of victory which he could feel upon the faces of his enemies" (191). And it is not only his enemies "his greater hatred was riveted upon the man, who, not knowing him, had called him a mule driver" (220). The friendly jeers of the veterans produce the same reaction, the praise of the lieutenant an infantile swelling of the same vanity. Before the final charge of the enemy it is again the recollection of being called mud diggers that determines the men to hold and again "some arrows of scorn" (246) that generate "the strange and unspeakable hatred" in Henry, who desires nothing so much as "retaliation upon the officer who had said 'mule drivers' and later 'mud diggers'" (246). To see in this childish hatred with its subsequent "enthusiasm of unselfishness" (250) a "decided growth in moral behavior" is a misreading quite as mistaken as a Christian redemption. Both interpretations miss the point of the paradox Crane *labors* throughout the latter half of the book: that the selfless behavior of heroism paradoxically emerges only from the grossest, most infantile, animalistic, fiery hatred born of the vanity of egocentrism. Though in his non-conscious "enthusiasm" he may be temporarily a man (see 227), it is only after Henry Fleming's "eyes seemed to open to some new ways" (265) that he feels "a quiet manhood" (266). Awareness—the ability to perceive truthfully the nature of this symbolically revealed, hostile universe—alone confers this new quiet, this new dignity.

ERIC SOLOMON

From The Structure of *The Red Badge of Courage*†

In spite of the abundance of war novels produced by two world conflicts, *The Red Badge of Courage* is still the masterwork of war fiction. Stephen Crane's novel is the first work in English fiction of any length purely dedicated to an artistic reproduction of war, and it has rarely been approached in scope or intensity since it was published in 1895.

Any judgment of the influence of *The Red Badge of Courage* on later war fiction would of necessity be conjectural. The circumstance that Ford Madox Ford and Ernest Hemingway worshipped at the Crane shrine does not in itself prove that *No More Parades* or *A Farewell to Arms* was directly affected by Crane's book. But the novel became part of the literary heritage of the twentieth century, and whether or not a war writer consciously recalls Crane's performance, the fact remains that *The Red Badge of Courage* is a touchstone for modern war fiction. Stephen Crane gave the war novel its classic form.

Crane, however, made no great innovation in style or subject matter. Realism, irony, detail, the emotional impact of combat— all these had appeared somewhere in earlier war fiction. The contribution of Stephen Crane to the genre of war fiction was twofold. First, he defined the form in his novel that deals with war and its effect upon the sensitive individual who is inextricably involved; war is treated as neither journalism nor autobiography nor dashing romance, but as a test of mind and spirit in a situation of great tension. Crane also constructed a book that still stands as the technical masterpiece in the field.

Crane accomplishes in the longer form of the novel what Ambrose Bierce attains in the short story. *The Red Badge of Courage* creates a single world, a unique atmosphere where war is the background and the foreground. * * * Like the painters of the Italian Renaissance who conceived the *tondo,* a form that forced the artist to choose and manipulate his subject matter to fit a small, circular canvas, Crane chooses to restrict his novel to war and its impact upon his hero. There is no mention of the causes or motives of the war or of any battle; Crane's war is universal, extricated from

† From *Modern Fiction Studies,* V (Autumn, 1959), 220–34, *passim.* Reprinted by permission of the Purdue Research Foundation.

any specific historical situation. We may gain an impression of how a literary artist makes war his *tondo* by an analysis of the structure of *The Red Badge of Courage*. For Crane approached the subject of war as an artist, picking his materials for their fictional value. He was not reliving an experience, but creating one.

* * *

It is true that many of Crane's effects are gained by recourse to an impressionistic method, a technique used by previous war writers to convey the sense of a vast battle scene. His combat descriptions are swiftly shifting impressions of action. Furthermore, he shows the influence of the impressionists in his dependence on color, the contrasts of light and shade. And his characters have a certain anonymity. Although Crane shows many of the realities of war, there is not as much careful detail in his novel as in De Forest's *Miss Ravenel's Conversion*. It is possible to apply the term impressionistic to one aspect of *The Red Badge of Courage*; certainly intensity and expressiveness are stressed—but not necessarily at the expense of symmetry and neatness. For an example of a fully impressionistic war novel, we need only consider Andreief's *The Red Laugh*, where disjointed and blurred fragments of combat are joined together to give a vast vision of horror.

It is equally an oversimplification to think of Crane's book merely in terms of naturalistic fiction. There are, to be sure, certain naturalistic doctrines that Crane follows. Some details appear to be chosen for their shock effect, like the corpse Henry finds in the forest—a sight that makes the dead bodies in Bierce seem pleasant by comparison. But the presence of the corpse is not arbitrary. It fits into the youth-to-experience theme, teaching Henry to understand death as something ghastly—not noble. Henry's salvation comes from a newfound sense of dedication to life and beauty after he has understood the ugliness of death. When he finally risks his life in battle, after having viewed the disgusting corpse, he knows what death involves.

One aspect of naturalism that had already appeared in the war fiction of Bierce and Rudyard Kipling is the double process of animation of mechanical objects and depersonalization of human beings. Crane's novel is packed with parallels between the animal and human worlds. His picture of war shows the iron and steel weapons in the role of flesh-and-blood inhabitants of the combat world. Even the battle flag, normally a symbol, takes on a more human dimension here. The flag struggles to free itself from an agony and finally falls with a gesture of despair.

The machines are humanized, and an abstraction like war itself is described as a red animal. Men, for their part, become either animals or machines. It is interesting to note how consistently Crane avoids physical descriptions of his characters and uses animal imagery to tell how men look in war. The regiment seems like "one of those moving monsters" or "crawling reptiles"; men are pigs, worms, cows, rats, kittens, etc. Fear makes Henry look like "a jaded horse," "a craven loon." War seems so brutally deterministic to Crane that it robs man of the free will and intelligence that differentiate him from the animals. For this reason the use of animal imagery is fitting for the naturalistic interpretation of war. The images reflect the belief that combat is the most savage pattern of human existence.

Crane's vision is basically ironic, perhaps not as sardonic as that of Bierce, but certainly bitter. He understands war in the naturalistic sense of involving the loss of individual initiative and motivation. The fatalism of war seems for a time to crush Henry. He compares himself to a squirrel who automatically must run away from danger in order to obey the law of survival of the fittest. Nature is apparently allied with the superior, intangible force that rules the world of war. One of the most illuminating passages that Crane cut out of the final version of the novel represents war in naturalistic terminology. "From his pinnacle of wisdom, he regarded the armies as large collections of dupes. Nature's dupes who were killing each other to carry out some great scheme of life." But when Henry succeeds in war, nature shines upon him benignly, and the book closes with a lyric description of the sun breaking through the clouds. Neither impressionism nor naturalism is the dominant mode for dealing with the world of war. We shall see that Henry's actions are those of a free individual.

* * *

II

Robert Wooster Stallman comes closest to understanding the nature of the novel's structure. He describes *The Red Badge of Courage* as a series of fluctuations between hope and despair, a group of withdrawals and engagements.[6] This is accurate, and we shall notice how Crane follows war's own pattern in his alterations between action and inaction.

There is evidence of much tighter control in Crane's war novel, however. Like the careful symmetry of *The Scarlet Letter*—which

6. Robert Wooster Stallman, "Stephen Crane: A Revaluation," *Critiques and Essays on Modern Fiction*, selected by John W. Aldridge (New York, 1952), pp. 263–265.

has scenes on the scaffold in chapters one, twelve, and twenty-four —so in the twenty-four chapters of *The Red Badge of Courage* there is a careful unfolding of plot; in the latter work there is a triple development.

The first section of the novel shows the dilemma of the youthful hero who feels, and then actually becomes, isolated from the group in war. Crane portrays the psychological journey of Henry Fleming from a foolish romantic pride, through the depths of fear, the first qualms of conscience, and a realization of his place in the military scheme—marked by his return to the regiment following the climactic wound he received in Chapter Twelve.

The same cycle is repeated, once he has rejoined his comrades. Now he interacts with the group as the regiment undergoes *its* test of fear and the recapture of confidence in combat. Finally, the regiment and Henry act as veterans in a successful skirmish. The *Bildungsroman* ends, on the scaffold, as it were, with the young man from the provinces altered and matured by war but still an ambiguous figure who has come to terms with the realities of the world through which he has made his picaresque way to knowledge. Like a lesser Melville, Crane deals with the ambiguities of character, and the battlefield, instead of a ship, is his world.

Henry Fleming's progression, on the most obvious level, is from fear to courage. Crane also extends the meaning of war and its impact upon the hero to a more involved moral nexus. Before he joins the army, Henry is a romantic dreamer, inspired by visions of a chivalric type of warfare in which he becomes a mighty hero. The immediate shock of training destroys any Homeric view of war, but Crane shows, in the book's only flashback out of the immediate war situation, the pre-war dreams of the youth. Like the child in Bierce's "Chickamauga," Henry has been brought up on books and pictures of battle. Crane fixes the pattern of the esthetic young man off to the wars—a figure that was to become a stereotype in the fiction of two world conflicts. Henry enlists in a haze of glorious aspiration that is undercut only by his mother's sober, sad advice. Through Henry's posturing, his ability to conjure a vague smile from a female student into an idealized vision of the girl he left behind him, Crane establishes the character of a sensitive, highly imaginative youth. As Herman Melville wrote, "All wars are boyish and are fought by boys." It is to be expected that Henry's illusions will die hard.

When the rumor of impending action reaches the waiting army, Henry withdraws to worry about the necessity of proving his courage, since he knows nothing about himself as far as war is concerned. He must prove himself in the heat of combat, in the destructive element. Just before the first engagement, Henry gives way to pure hysteria, believing that he is in a trap and being led to certain death. His feeling of persecution is replaced by a wild, animal rage, once the actual combat commences; when the first lull comes, Henry believes he has passed his test. The mercurial youth is in an ecstasy of self-satisfaction. "So it was all over at last! The supreme trial had been passed. The red, formidable difficulties of war had been vanquished."

The author, however, equates war to life, and the reality of battle is made to parallel the reality of human existence where the mere passing of one test does not remove the possibility of other tests being imposed. In war the process is speeded up. Under the shock of the enemy's second attack, Henry protests, gives in to panic, and finally flees in fear. He reaches his low point of cowardice here. From this point on his emotional movement is forward, to a rebirth of courage.

After his communion with nature in the forest, Henry starts back towards the holocaust, fully realizing the irony involved in such a return to danger. He still retains his vague dreams of leading heroic charges, but once he has come back to his regiment—half way through the novel—the fear motif of *The Red Badge of Courage* is completed. For the remainder of the book the hero is sure of himself, even overconfident; and by the end of the story he has become a war devil, exulting in action, capturing a flag, and receiving praise from his superiors. Taken as simply a "psychological portrayal of fear,"[7] the novel is not only ironic, it is amoral. The successful hero has only learned that he is not particularly cowardly. Incisive as his probing of the hero's neurotic fright is, Stephen Crane has much more to say about the influence of combat upon the inexperienced participant.

III

The essential quality of Crane's novel cannot be derived from the study of one man's response to war. War has presented, among other things, a highly developed social problem ever since the days of individual combat were over. The gradation of the army system and its rigid chain of command combine with the massive troop movements of modern warfare to make combat a reflection of a special society with its own precise rules of conformity. And as Mark Schorer has pointed out, any novel must find a form that will encompass both the individual and social experiences.[8]

7. Stephen Crane, "Letter to John N. Hilliard," *The Academy*, LIX (August 11, 1900), 116.

8. Mark Schorer, "Foreword," *Critiques and Essays on Modern Fiction* (New York, 1952). p. xviii.

It may not be immediately obvious that *The Red Badge of Courage* is more than the story of the young soldier who is Crane's hero and point-of-view character. The author does not try to describe his individuals fully. We do not even know the youth's whole name until Chapter Twelve. Taking Crane's novel on its own terms, we need not expect rounded figures, logically described, having past histories; neither should we overlook Henry Fleming's comrades in the war situation.

Henry comes into close contact with five other soldiers in his passage from apprenticeship to mastery. Of these, the tall soldier, Jim Conklin, is most important. Henry identifies with Conklin's calm attitude when faced with combat and attempts to accept his steadying advice. The death of Conklin has particular meaning to the hero; just as in Crane's story, "The Open Boat," the stronger personality does not survive the test. The loud soldier, Wilson, a foil to Henry's fears at the start, undergoes a similar, and even more rapid, growth to manhood through the ordeal. The attitude of the somewhat anonymous lieutenant, Hasbrouck, reflects the hero's place in the military society. When Henry is a coward, the officer strikes at him with a sword, but when the youth is fighting well, he and the lieutenant are filled with mutual admiration.

Two more figures, shadowy ones to be sure, but still vividly realized, provide a commentary on the soldier's progress. Direct opposites, the tattered soldier whom Henry leaves wandering blindly in a field, and the cheery stranger who guides Henry back to his regiment, signify respectively betrayal and comradeship. The interaction of the hero with these five characters and the regiment as a whole furnishes the fundamental theme of *The Red Badge of Courage*. The standards by which Henry's development is measured are those of group loyalty rather than fear and courage. Although the secondary characters are typed, and meant to be so, and not sharply individualized, they are still effectively presented.

The novel opens on the large picture of the entire fighting force. "The cold passed reluctantly from the earth and the retiring fogs revealed an army stretched out on the hills, resting." As in a motion-picture opening, the scene gradually focuses on a particular group of soldiers—Conklin doing his washing, Wilson arguing violently, and then on Henry in a solitude of self-mistrust.

The key to Henry's development, and the essential meaning of war for him, comes in the flashback to his farewell from his mother. The importance of this scene is not in his mother's adjuration to do his duty bravely, nor in the general anti-romantic atmosphere of cows and socks, but in her words that remind the youth of his own insignificance in the larger scheme. " 'Yer jest one little feller amongst a hull lot of others, and yeh've got to keep quiet an' do what they tell yeh. I know how you are, Henry.'" She knows, but he must learn in battle what kind of a man he is.

Henry's vanity does not allow him to be a little fellow among a whole lot of others except in the rare moments of rationalization when he comforts himself with the consideration that he is part of a vast blue demonstration. Because abstract judgment fails him in his fear, he is isolated. Crane stresses Henry's feeling of solitude. He has no one with whom to compare suspicions; he is different, "alone in space," "a mental outcast." Both the calm competence of the tall soldier and the brash assurance of the loud soldier convince Henry that his is a unique weakness.

When the regiment advances for its baptism of fire, Henry is a part of the group, albeit unwillingly. He feels himself carried along by a mob. The image Crane uses to signify Henry's attitude of helplessness is important. ". . . there were iron laws of tradition and law [sic] on four sides. He was in a moving box." He is doing exactly what his mother warned him against, considering himself an important individual. He hates the lieutenant and believes that only he, Henry, knows that the entire regiment is being betrayed. In other words, the youth revolts against the iron laws of the war world, the traditions of obedience and humility in the ranks. Crane plays off Henry's condition of rage against Jim Conklin's faithful acceptance of the new environment. The other soldiers are shadowy figures in Henry's mind, since his ego has denied him the comforts of military friendships. He is too wrapped up in himself to realize that others are in the same condition of doubt and fear.

A sudden shift in emphasis takes place when the battle starts, as Henry rapidly adjusts to reality. Losing concern with himself for the moment, he becomes "not a man but a member," a part of a "common personality," a "mysterious fraternity." Whereas in his isolation and doubt he was trapped in a moving box, now, by sinking his personality into the larger personality of the group, he regains control of himself. Crane describes Henry's combat activity with the same box image as before, but there is one important difference. Henry is now in charge. "He was like a carpenter who has made many boxes, making still another box. . . ."

Crane transfers the point of view from Henry to the regiment at this juncture. In the impressionistic battle scene, the focus is on "the men," "they," "a soldier" while the regiment goes about its grim business. An integral part of Henry's development is the realization that even the regiment is not the only important participant in the battle. He understands that the fighting involves many regiments and momentarily grasps the idea of his own relative unimportance. But Crane is too acute a psychologist to conceive such a rapid character change and have Henry learn the soldier's hardest lesson easily. When the break in the combat comes, Henry reverts to his pride and considers his rather petty action to have been magnificent. He must undergo a more serious test before he can reap the full benefits of his war experience.

The second attack is too much for him. Henry cannot comprehend the rules of war that are so irrational as to impose another test so soon. He deserts the group, and by this act he breaks all the rigid rules of war. The sight of the lieutenant, angrily dabbing at him with his sword, symbolizes for Henry his new role as an outcast. The youth is no longer, in the Conradian sense, one of them. He asks himself, "What manner of men were they anyhow?", those fools who stayed behind to meet certain death.

The novel is not merely a portrait of fear; it is the portrait of a mind that learns to come to terms with itself and to live down an act of cowardice. Henry Fleming must become a man according to the rules war sets forth. Therefore, he must cast off the egoism that made him run, and gain a true perspective on his importance.

The book is often ironic, since his growth is neither particularly moral nor is it without fluctuations. Henry's failures and successes in war are those of a hero *manqué*, if we are to measure them by the usual Christian ethic. But *The Red Badge of Courage* is a war novel, and Henry Fleming should be judged by the ideals of a war world. The lesson Henry has to learn is basic to combat. The individual cannot depend on his personal reasoning powers. Henry's mind has seen the danger and he has fled, while his stupid comrades have stayed and shown courage. The beginning of wisdom comes with the comprehension that his own judgment is insufficient. He is in the position of a criminal because of his enlightened intellect. Henry feels the bitterness and rage of an outcast, a sensitive dreamer who, trapped between romance and reality, can make the best of neither world. Caught in a box of his own making, Henry faces the age-old problem of the individual at odds with society. He has not only indulged in an act of self-betrayal, he has thrown over his responsibilities to and for the others. He does not yet understand that his own salvation (physical and spiritual) must be the product of his dedication to universal salvation. Henry's story is not tragic, because, unlike Lord Jim, the young soldier manages to compensate for his anti-social action and work his way back to the fellowship of men which, in the world of war, is represented by the regiment. But the road back is not easy.

After his dark night of the soul passed in the forest where nature appears to second war's cruelty, Henry commences his return to the battle—to life or death. The physical isolation of the youth ends when he meets a line of wounded soldiers staggering towards the rear, soldiers coming out of the active world from which Henry had fled. Henry joins the crowd, but he remains an outsider, for he has no wound. Crane reverses the symbolism of Hawthorne's *The Scarlet Letter* or "The Minister's Black Veil." Henry is distinguished by his *lack* of any mark. "He was continually casting sidelong glances to see if the men were contemplating the letters of guilt he felt burned into his brow. . . . He wished that he, too, had a wound, a red badge of courage." Ironically enough, he desires to be marked by the red death he had feared. Honor, or the appearance of honor, is his new goal.

As if to emphasize his sin, Henry remains with the denizens of the strange world of wounded. He meets the tattered man, one of Crane's most brilliant portraits of a nameless figure. We know nothing about the tattered man except that he is wounded, and that he is a rather naïve and gentle soul. He is the antithesis of the young soldier in every way. The tattered man has been hit; he talks proudly of his regiment and its performance; he is humble and loves the army. In other words, he stands for the simple man who has done his duty and received his mark of honor. The tattered man represents society, and to the conscience-stricken Henry the wounded soldier is a reminder of guilt. Henry cannot remain with the tattered man when he asks the probing question, " 'Where yeh hit, ol' boy?' ", that emphasizes the youth's isolation.

A greater shock is in store for Henry Fleming. After he leaves his tattered companion behind, he meets the spectral soldier—the tall soldier, Jim Conklin—transformed by a fatal wound. Henry's feeble wish for a little wound pales into the realm of bathos in comparison to Conklin's passion. The dying man's expression of sympathy and concern for Henry adds to the acute discomfort of the youth's position. In his walk through the valley of the shadow of death at Conklin's side, Henry's education advances. Conklin's death brings home to Henry the true nature of war, brutal and forbidding, more than the sight of an unknown corpse in the forest could do. The body of his friend stretched out before him, Henry curses the universe that allows such things to be. He shakes his fist at the battlefield and swears, but his insignificance in the larger scheme is indicated by Crane's most famous line, "The red sun was pasted in the sky like a wafer."

Despite his genuine grief at Conklin's death, Henry is unable to accept responsibility for the tattered man, who has returned to pry at Henry's guilty secret, the crime "concealed in his bosom." He deserts the tattered man a second time, and in denying him the young soldier commits his real sin. He breaks both a Christian and a military ethical rule ("Greater love hath no man. . . ."). Like his original act of cowardice, this desertion goes unpunished. If we are to read the novel as a study in irony, there is no confusion; Henry is a sinner who succeeds in war without ever changing his ways. Crane's attitude towards his hero is ambiguous throughout the novel, however, and the betrayal of the tattered man is essential to Henry's growth to maturity. Although the tattered man himself says that " 'a man's first allegiance is to number one,' " Henry realizes what he has done. His later heroism is a successful attempt to wipe out his cowardice. While he eventually rationalizes his betrayal, the memory of the tattered man blocks any real return to the egocentric immaturity that marked his character at the outset of the novel.

He heads back to the "furnace" of combat, since the heat of that purgatory is clearly more desirable than the icy chill of solitude. His progress is halting. Henry is unable to throw off his romantic visions; he imagines his new self in a picturesque and sublime role as a leader of lurid charges. Once again the reality of war breaks his dreams apart, reality in the forms of physical exhaustion, thirst, and the memory of his cowardice. No longer a visionary, Henry can now make his way through the war world.

Crane's bitterness comes to the surface in this part of the novel. Henry is really worried about appearance. How can he pretend to be something he is not—a hero? It is when the self-centered youth is concerned with the difficulty of fabricating a lie effective enough to account for his disappearance that his full name is given for the first time by the author. The young soldier mentions it in apprehension of the name, "Henry Fleming," becoming a synonym for coward. Names and appearances are his only concern.

Henry Fleming's actions must be judged by the standards of war. While he is planning his lie (a sin, from a normal ethical viewpoint), fate, in the form of a hysterical soldier who clubs Henry out of the way, provides the wound that not only preserves the appearance of his integrity but also opens the way for his attainment of genuine honor. It is ironic, even cynical, for war to help Henry after he has broken the rules, and for the coward to pass as a hero. Two other points must be kept in mind, however. Crane constantly refers to his hero as "the youth," and despite his transgressions, Henry is still an innocent fumbling for the correct path, not a hardened sinner. Furthermore, he does not receive his wound in flight, but in the performance of an act of courage! Henry is struck down (by a coward) while inarticulately striving "to make a rallying speech, to sing a battle hymn." He is in a position to suffer such a wound because he has originally fled from his regiment, but he is going against the current of retreating infantry, *towards* the battle, when he gains the red badge. The wound, then, may be seen as the result of heroism, not cowardice, and the irony is vitiated. Henry has escaped from his nightmare of weakness before he is wounded. His own efforts have proved him not completely unworthy of the saving grace granted him by the fate of war.

The wounded Henry is again part of the fellowship of armed men. "The owner of the cheery voice," who plays Mr. Strongheart in Henry's progress, guides the dazed youth through the forest wasteland back to the regiment. The gratuitous support of the cheery man is in direct contrast to Henry's earlier refusal to accompany the tattered man. The first twelve chapters of the novel come to an end with Henry outlined in the reflection of his regiment's campfires. The return to the company, which in war fiction has stood for homecoming from Kipling's "The Man Who Was" to Jones's *From Here to Eternity*, marks the completion of Henry Fleming's isolation and the start of the conquest of glory for himself and the regiment.

The hero of Crane's war novel has not yet learned what the author is in a later story to call "virtue in war." His relief at the arrival back into the "low-arched hall" of the forest (a suggestion perhaps of the mead hall of the Old English epics, the symbol of the fellowship of strong warriors) is intense. He views the sleeping company with complacency because to all appearances he is one of them, since he performed his mistakes in the dark. In the second part of the novel Henry will come to understand war and his own nature. For the present, it is enough to go to sleep with his fellows. "He gave a long sigh, snuggled down into his blanket, and in a moment was like his comrades."

IV

Only Joseph Conrad, of the multitude of Crane's critics, grasps the essential duality of *The Red Badge of Courage*. Conrad seems to realize that Henry Fleming *and* the regiment are in the same position. "In order that the revelation should be complete, the young soldier has to be deprived of the moral support which he would have found in a tried body of men matured in achievement to the consciousness of its worth."[9] Conrad pinpoints the idea that the maturation process does not affect the hero alone. "Apart from the imaginative analysis of his own temperament tried by the emotions of a battlefield, Stephen Crane dealt in his book with the psychology of the mass. . ."[10] The remainder of the novel treats the group that Henry has rejoined.

9. Joseph Conrad, "His War Book," *Tales of Hearsay and Last Essays* (London, 1955), p. 121.
10. Joseph Conrad, "Introduction," Thomas Beer, *Stephen Crane* (New York, 1923), p. 3.

Although Crane's narrative technique still enforces the use of Henry as the point-of-view character, the youth is attentive to others as well as himself. Wilson, the former loud soldier, has been altered by his day of combat from a blatant, self-confident boy to a calm, quietly self-reliant soldier who is proud of the regiment. In order to perfect his relationship with Wilson and the other soldiers, Henry must try to understand their sources of fear and courage.

When the regiment goes into action on the second day, Crane focuses on the whole body, giving equal space to anonymous soldiers' complaints, the lieutenant's anger, and the serious determination of Wilson and Henry. The young soldier sinks himself completely into the business of battle and transfers his doubts and dreams into a savage hate of the enemy. If Crane indicated the importance of Henry's wound by giving his full name for the first time, here he emphasizes the youth's continuing growth as a human being by describing him physically. As Henry thinks less of himself, he becomes more of an individual in the pages of the novel. He fights well in this battle and becomes a hero in the eyes of his regiment.

The personal insignificance that Henry discovered applied to himself in the first section of the novel, now appears to fit the regiment which Crane describes in terms similar to those he earlier utilized for the young soldier. "The world was fully interested in other matters. Apparently, the regiment had its small affair to itself."

Henry and the regiment undergo another severe exposure to fire in their first charge. Crane describes the mass movement brilliantly, transferring the attention from the youth to the men, and back. The crucial episode is the same for all of them, "a temporary but sublime absence of selfishness."

The regiment falters in the confusion of the attack; the men go through Henry's former mental turmoil. "Here, crouching and cowering behind some trees, the men clung with desperation . . . the whole affair seemed incomprehensible to many of them." The advance is saved by the courage and leadership of three men: the lieutenant, Wilson, and Henry. They lead the regiment forward, and symbolically Henry takes over as flag-bearer, participating in the combat in the absolute center of the group, the one position that more than any other represents the mass spirit. When the regiment is forced to retreat, Henry feels *their* shame as acutely as he felt *his* earlier. (Formerly he was selfish enough to pray for the army's defeat so his cowardice might go unnoticed.) He harangues his comrades, striving to save the regiment's reputation.

The regiment turns and drives the enemy back; it passes its test. Henry is free from doubt and fear because he has committed himself to the larger unit. By losing himself in the mass, he has found himself. To the same extent, the regiment has conquered its panic and irresolution. "The impetus of enthusiasm was theirs again. They gazed about them with looks of uplifted pride, feeling new trust in the grim, always confident, weapons in their hands. And they were men."

The final stage of development in war for Henry and the regiment involves the learning of the veterans' virtues—calmness and workmanlike efficiency. The young soldier is an observer in the last attack, a tiny player in a huge, impressionistic drama. Before, as a coward, he was the god-like center of a tiny stage; now, as a good soldier, he is absorbed into the regimental chorus. Henry loses all sense of individuality. "He did not know that he breathed; that the flag hung silently over him, so absorbed was he."

Crane makes much of the fact that when the regiment is pinned down by enemy fire, Henry—the veteran—knows that the only thing to do is to return to the attack. To hang back would mean annihilation; to retreat would build up the enemy's spirit. Henry has assimilated the rules of war. Now his thoughts and emotional responses are the proper ones, forgetful of self in the face of duty. His companions, too, respond automatically to the necessities of battle, the facts of military life. The climax of *The Red Badge of Courage* comes as the regiment and its flag-bearer, without regard to vanities, charge once more and victoriously overrun the enemy's position. They have all passed the test.

The last chapter of the novel is an artfully contrived anticlimax. The regiment marches on; the author's attention is again directed to his hero. Henry has proved his courage; he has even been singled out for praise by the colonel. "He had dwelt in a land of strange, squalling upheavals and had come forth. He had been where there was red of blood and black of passion, and he was escaped." Were the novel to end here on this note of rejoicing and pride, an ironic reading of the book would be justified. Henry would be a mock hero, a Jonathan Wild. Henry cannot forget the tattered soldier, however, whom Crane characterizes in lyrically sentimental language, ". . . he who, gored by bullets and faint for blood, had fretted concerning an imagined wound in another . . . he who, blind with weariness and pain, had been deserted in the field." Again Henry considers himself a moral leper. He is filled with concern lest his comrades realize his secret sin.

Crane cancelled the passage that explains Henry's final rationalization of the betrayal, but these omitted words help to explain the moral construction of the book. "At last, he concluded that he saw in it quaint uses. He exclaimed that its importance in the aftertime would be great to him if it even succeeded in hindering the workings of his egotism. . . . He would have upon him often the consciousness of a great mistake. And he would be taught to deal gently and with care. He would be a man."

These last words, a repetition of those applied earlier to the regiment, show that Henry has matured as an individual and a member of society. Henry has learned the nature of fear and battle. "He had been to touch the great death, and found that, after all, it was but the great death." More important, he has learned the essence of man's duty to man, as well as the fact that life (like war) is not a romantic dream but a matter of compromises. Perhaps there is an element of irony, since he has not become a "good" man, but he has done a "good" act—in the terms of the war world —by displaying courage and self-abnegation in the final skirmish. At least war has shown the young soldier his real self, and the acquisition of self-knowledge is no small accomplishment. Henry has become a new man who views life in a fresh framework, aimed not towards glory but a job to be done. Glory is pleasant but irrelevant. In the final scenes of *The Red Badge of Courage,* Henry takes full responsibility for his life; he is no longer an automaton. His properly disciplined ego comprehends the nature of obedience and action. And the development of his inner life is paralleled by that of the regiment.

The novel ends with a sweeping peroration, hailing Henry as a part of the procession of weary soldiers, a part of the regiment that has proved itself worthy of the army just as he has proved himself an individual worthy of inclusion in the group. They have all succeeded in the war which telescopes such a tremendous amount of experience into a brief moment. "Over the river a golden ray of sun came through the hosts of leaden rain clouds."

JAMES B. COLVERT

From Structure and Theme in Stephen Crane's Fiction†

In a passage in Stephen Crane's "The Open Boat" the narrator describes the predicament of the men in the ten-foot dinghy as they precariously navigate the heavy seas.

"As each slaty wall of water approached, it shut all else from the view of the men in the boat, and it was not difficult to imagine that this particular wave was the final outburst of the ocean, the last effort of the grim water. There was a terrible grace in the move of the

† From *Modern Fiction Studies,* V (Autumn, 1959), 199–208, *passim.* Reprinted by permission of the Purdue Research Institute.

waves, and they came in silence, save for the snarling of the crests.
. . . Viewed from a balcony, the whole thing would doubtless have
been picturesque."

To the men in the boat the horizon of jagged waves at which their
eyes glance level marks the extreme limit of the universe. "None of
them knew the colour of the sky." The waves shut all else from
view, and as they sweep down upon the dinghy they seem to
threaten the very nucleus of all visible creation, the men in the
open boat. But suddenly the perspective changes. The narrator
intrudes to suggest that the plight of the men might seem from a
different point of view something less than cosmic in its significance.
"Viewed from a balcony" their situation might seem simply
"weirdly picturesque."

A brilliant passage in "The Blue Hotel" shows clearly how the
distancing effect of the speaker's point of view is achieved through
metaphor and imagery. The Swede, crazy with rage and terror after
a ferocious fight with old Scully's son at the blue hotel, is making
his way through town in a howling blizzard.

"He might have been in a deserted village. We picture the world as
thick with conquering and elate humanity, but here, with the bugles
of the tempest pealing, it was hard to imagine a peopled earth. One
viewed the existence of man then as a marvel, and conceded a
glamour of wonder to these lice which were caused to cling to a
whirling, fire-smitten, ice-locked, disease-stricken, space-lost bulb."

The imagery suggests a cosmic distance between the narrator and
his subject. The speaker sees the Swede as if from a balcony in
space, and both the crazy Swede and his world seem indeed pathetically small and insignificant.

These passages throw light on the characteristic structural pattern of the Crane story. The narrative design of Crane's best fiction
is defined by the tension between two ironically divergent points
of view: the narrowing and deluding point of view of the actors
and the enlarging and ruthlessly revealing point of view of the
observer-narrator. To the men in the boat the universe seems to
have shrunk to the horizon and to have concentrated within its
narrow limits all the malignant powers of creation; but the longer
view of the narrator reveals this as a delusion born in the men's
egoistic assumption that they occupy a central position in Nature's
hostile regard. The correspondent sees the waves as "wrongfully
and barbarously abrupt," but in the very act of passing moral judgment upon Nature, he implicitly asserts his superior worth and
significance. He errs in the judgment because his perspective, unlike the narrator's, is limited by his acute self-consciousness. And
the Swede's point of view, again in contrast to the narrator's,
admits no "glamour of wonder" in his clinging to an "ice-locked

. . . space-lost bulb," for in the flush of his victory over young Scully, he is "elate and conquering humanity" who can say to the bartender in the saloon, "Yes, I like this weather. I like it. It suits me."

In Crane this handling of point of view is more than a technical expediency for bringing order and clarity into the narrative structure. It is a manner of expression which grows inevitably out of his vision of the world. One sees by means of this double perspective the two polar images of the Crane man. In the narrator's view man is insignificant, blind to his human weakness and the futility of his actions, pathetically incompetent in the large scheme of things. But from the limited point of view originating in his aspiring inner-consciousness, the Crane hero creates a more flattering image of himself and the world. Trapped within the confining circle of his swelling emotions of self, he sees himself as god-like, dauntless, heroic, the master of his circumstances. The two images mark the extreme boundaries of Crane's imaginative scope—define, as it were, the limits of his vision of the world. For the Crane story again and again interprets the human situation in terms of the ironic tensions created in the contrast between man as he idealizes himself in his inner thought and emotion and man as he actualizes himself in the stress of experience. In the meaning evoked by the ironic projection of the deflated man against the inflated man lies Crane's essential theme: the consequence of false pride, vanity, and blinding delusion. The sentence which follows the passage quoted from "The Blue Hotel" goes to the thematic dead center of his fiction: "The conceit of man was explained by this storm to be the very engine of life."

* * *

. . . The motif of false self-estimate emerges everywhere—in gesture, statement, act, situation—weaves into structural units, and finally fuses into an implicit statement of theme: that human incompetency—comic in the Sullivan County sketches, tragic in *Maggie*—finds its source in vanity, delusion, and ignorance of self.

This theme Crane developed more maturely and significantly in *The Red Badge of Courage*, begun in the spring of 1893 shortly after the stillbirth of *Maggie* and published in the newspaper version in December, 1894. The hero of the novel, Henry Fleming, is essentially "the little man," the deluded people of *Maggie*, and the Swede, for the "engine of his life," too, is pride, vanity, and conceit, the moral consequences of which *The Red Badge* explores. But like the correspondent in "The Open Boat" Henry is redeemed by a successful adjustment of his point of view, and for the first time Crane admits into his theme the working out of a solution to his hero's dilemma.

The novel treats four stages in Fleming's growth toward moral maturity. In the beginning he is unable to distinguish between his heroic dreams and hopes and the actual condition of war. Then follows a period of confusion and doubt as reality begins to intrude upon his dream world. Next he goes through a period of desperate but futile struggle to preserve, through deceit and rationalization, his pseudo-heroic image of himself and the world. In the end he solves his problem when he learns to see the world in its true light, when he is finally able to bring his subjectivity into harmony with the reality which his experience makes clear to him.

The structure of the novel is characteristically a series of loosely related, ironic episodes built up in the contrast between two points of view toward reality, a subjective interpretation originating in vanity, pride, and illusion juxtaposed against an "objective" reality originating in the superior long view of the narrator. So long as Henry is under the influence of his swelling vision of himself, he is incapable of acting morally and honestly. But in the end the disparate worlds of illusion and reality are brought into meaningful relationship, and in the resolution of the ironic tension between the two, the meaning of Henry's experience is made clear to him.[6] Only then is he morally capable of facing up to war and life.

As the novel opens, Henry is troubled by the conflict he vaguely senses between his heroic image of self and fleeting glimpses of cold reality. He dreams of thrilling conflicts and his own "eagle-eyed prowess;" "his busy mind had drawn for him large pictures extravagant in color, lurid with breathless deeds." But from the first this heroic image is disturbed by dim, fleeting images of reality. His mother could "with no apparent difficulty give him many hundreds of reasons" for not enlisting, and "she had certain ways of expression that told him that her statements of the subject came from a deep conviction." Yet Henry is blinded by conceit: he rebels firmly "against this yellow light thrown upon the color of his ambitions."

The story continues to unfold as a variation on this basic idea. Henry plans a fine speech after his enlistment. He imagines sentences "which . . . could be used with touching effect." Actually, his noble oration turned out as a pathetically inadequate, "Ma, I've enlisted." At the seminary, where he goes to say goodbye to his old school mates, he struts; but one girl makes "vivacious fun at his

6. Mr. Robert W. Stallman, in his *Stephen Crane: An Omnibus* (see "Notes Toward an Analysis of *The Red Badge of Courage*," pp. 191–201) makes a similar point about the structure of *The Red Badge*. But by his reading the religious symbolism that "radiates outwards from Jim Conklin" is the key to the structure of the novel. The difference between my reading and Mr. Stallman's is a matter of emphasis at this point, but the implications of Mr. Stallman's claim for religious symbolism leads away, in my opinion, from the core of Crane's true meaning.

martial spirit." His illusion that "real war was a series of death struggles with small time in between" is pricked momentarily by the reality of the monotonous camp life. Veterans bolster his romantic conception when they talk much of smoke, fire, and blood and the "bewhiskered hordes" who were the enemy; yet he talks across the river to an enemy picket who says, "Yank, yer a right dum good feller." The real world makes constant inroads upon his innocent and egotistical dreams, until at last these opposing images burst into open conflict in his mind.

"He contemplated the lurking menaces of the future, and failed in an effort to see himself standing stoutly in the midst of them. He recalled his visions of broken-bladed glory, but in the shadow of the impending tumult he suspected them to be impossible pictures."

Henry's problem is the re-discovery of himself, for he now knows that "whatever he had learned of himself was here of no avail. He was an unknown quantity. He saw that he would again be obliged to experiment as he had in early youth."

Deprived abruptly of the security of his false views, he can at first find no meaning in anything. Refracted through the thick prism of his ego, reality appears to him irrational, incoherent, terrible in its nightmarish disorder. The actions of his officers, who have "no appreciation of fine minds," are unreasonable. There is no purpose in the movements of the regiment. Nature appears to him in confusing guises—sometimes placid and friendly, now formidable and menacing, again neutral and indifferent. Determined by the immediate demands of his self-regard, his reading of events is shifting and inconsistent, providing one moment a basis for self-glorification, proving the next the falseness of his private world order. Thus in a moment of despair after he runs from battle, he can see nature's law of self-preservation as the justification of his ignoble flight. He is in perfect harmony with a law of nature. But later, when he experiences the horror of Jim Conklin's death, he sees in nature the power of a menacing fate, of which the baleful red sun, hanging over the carnage, is the hateful symbol.

Next, he desperately seeks solace in bold deceit. Indeed, the pretense that his wound was honorably received forms a basis for the reconstruction of his old vainglorious image of himself. "When he remembered his fortunes of yesterday, and looked at them from a distance he began to see something fine there. He had license to be pompous and veteran-like." But as always, the constructions of his vanity are destroyed. He overhears a more objective estimate of a staff officer, who refers contemptuously to Henry's regiment as "muledrivers."

In the end he is forced to abandon his search for comfortable justifications. When he throws himself into battle, blind with rage and despair, he symbolically accepts the world for what it is and tries to come to terms with it. In the thick of reality, so to speak, he undergoes a change; he experiences for the first time "a sublime absence of selfishness" and emerges a triumphant victor over falseness. Liberated from his imprisoning ego, he can marshal all his acts and from a new point of view "look at them in spectator fashion and criticize them with some correctness. . . ." He sees himself, as it were, from a balcony—from the same point of view, in the same perspective, as the observer-narrator sees him. And his "new condition had already defeated certain sympathies." He sees "that those tempestuous moments were of the wild mistakes and ravings of a novice who did not comprehend." In his new humility he finds that he can "look back upon the brass and bombast of his earlier gospels and see them truly." And he has a truer measure of his personal insignificance. He sees that he is "tiny but not inconsequent to the sun," that "in the space-wide whirl of events no grain like him would be lost."

He can understand now that his experience from the first has been pointing toward these conclusions, even when he was least capable of realizing it. Had he not been blinded by his overweening sense of self, he might have been less surprised, looking up after the ordeal of his first battle, to see that "Nature had gone tranquilly on with her golden process in the midst of so much devilment." Had he been able to see through the screen of his vanity, he might have realized that the flaming red sun which hung so ominously over Conklin's death scene was menacing only in his fancy that nature regarded him and his affairs as important. He comes to realize that the sun—as the symbol of nature, of course—is after all "imperturbable" and shines indifferently upon "insult and worship." Or he might have seen that the tattered man, "who loaned his last of strength and intellect for the tall soldier, who, blind with weariness and pain, had been deserted in the field," was a living reproof of Henry's vanity and selfishness. Or again, he might have noted the change in Wilson, the "loud soldier," after the first battle.

"He [Wilson] seemed no more to be continually regarding the proportions of his personal prowess. He was not furious at small words that pricked his conceits. He was no more a loud young soldier. There was about him now a fine reliance. He showed a quiet belief in his purposes and his abilities."

But earlier he could not assimilate these experiences; they appeared to him as discontinuous fragments in a welter of meaningless events. Only when he sees them in spectator fashion do events in reality seem to fit into a comprehensible order.

Bibliography

STEPHEN CRANE: WORKS, LETTERS, BIOGRAPHY

The Work of Stephen Crane, ed. Wilson Follett, 12 vols., New York, 1925–27.
The Collected Poems of Stephen Crane, ed. Wilson Follett, New York, 1930.
Twenty Stories by Stephen Crane, selected by Carl Van Doren, New York, 1940.
The Sullivan County Sketches of Stephen Crane, ed. Melvin Schoberlin, New York, 1949.
Stephen Crane: An Omnibus, ed. R. W. Stallman, New York, 1952.
Stephen Crane, The Red Badge of Courage and Selected Poetry and Prose, ed. William M. Gibson, New York, 1956.
Stephen Crane: Letters, ed. R. W. Stallman and Lillian Gilkes, New York, 1960.
Berryman, John. *Stephen Crane,* New York, 1950.
Crane, Stephen. *Love Letters to Nellie Crouse,* ed. Edwin H. Cady and Lester G. Wells, Syracuse, 1954.
Garland, Hamlin. *Roadside Meetings,* New York, 1930.
Garland, Hamlin. "Stephen Crane: Soldier of Fortune," *Saturday Evening Post,* CLXXIII (July 28, 1900), 16.
Garland, Hamlin. "Stephen Crane as I Knew Him," *Yale Review,* III (April, 1914), 494.
Gilkes, Lillian. *Cora Crane: A Biography of Mrs. Stephen Crane,* Bloomington, 1960.
Linson, Corwin K. *My Stephen Crane,* ed. Edwin H. Cady, Syracuse, 1958.

STEPHEN CRANE: GENERAL CRITICISM

Åhnebrink, Lars. *The Beginnings of Naturalism in American Fiction,* Upsala and Cambridge, 1950.
Beer, Thomas. *Stephen Crane: A Study in American Letters (with an Introduction by Joseph Conrad),* Garden City, 1923.
Colvert, James B. "Structure and Theme in Stephen Crane's Fiction," *Modern Fiction Studies,* V (Autumn, 1959), 199.
Colvert, James B. "The Origins of Stephen Crane's Literary Credo," *University of Texas Studies in English,* XXXIV (1955), 179.
Conrad, Joseph. *Last Essays,* Garden City, 1926
Follett, Wilson. "The Second Twenty-eight Years: A Note on Stephen Crane, 1871–1900," *Bookman,* LXVIII (January, 1929), 532.
Ford, Ford Madox. *Portraits from Life,* Boston, 1937.
Garnett, Edward. "Stephen Crane and His Work," *Friday Nights: Literary Criticism and Appreciations,* New York, 1922.
Geismar, Maxwell. *Rebels and Ancestors: The American Novel, 1890–1915,* Cambridge, 1953.
Greenfield, Stanley B. "The Unmistakable Stephen Crane," *PMLA,* LXXIII (December, 1958), 562.
Gullason, Thomas A. "Tennyson's Influence on Stephen Crane," *Notes and Queries* (April, 1958), 164.
Hartwick, Harry. *The Foreground of American Fiction,* New York, c. 1934.
Kazin, Alfred. *On Native Grounds,* New York, 1942.
Kwiat, Joseph J. "Stephen Crane and Painting," *American Quarterly,* IV (Winter, 1952), 331.
Mankiewicz, Herman J. "The Literary Craft of Stephen Crane," *New York Times Book Review* (January 10, 1926), 7.
Munson, Gorham B. *Style and Form in American Prose,* New York, 1929.
Nye, Russel B. "Stephen Crane as Social Critic," *Modern Quarterly,* XI (Summer, 1940), 48.
Schneider, Robert W. "Stephen Crane and the Drama of Transition," *Journal of Central Mississippi Valley American Studies,* II (Spring, 1961).

Shroeder, John W. "Stephen Crane Embattled," *University of Kansas City Review*, XVII (Winter, 1950), 119.

Solomon, M. "Stephen Crane: A Critical Study," *Masses and Mainstream*, IX January, 1956), 25

Spiller, Robert E., *et al.*, eds. *Literary History of the United States*, 2 vols., New York, 1948.

Stallman, Robert W. "Stephen Crane: A Revaluation," *Critiques and Essays on Modern Fiction, 1920–1951*, ed. John W. Aldridge, New York, 1952.

Stevenson, John W. "The Literary Reputation of Stephen Crane," *South Atlantic Quarterly*, LI (1952), 286.

Stewart, Randall. *American Literature and Christian Doctrine*, Baton Rouge, 1958.

Van Doren, Carl. *The American Novel* (rev. ed.), New York, 1940.

Walcutt, C. C. *American Literary Naturalism, A Divided Stream*, Minneapolis, 1956.

Wells, H. G. "Stephen Crane from an English Standpoint," *North American Review*, CLXXI (August, 1900), 233.

Westbrook, Max. "Stephen Crane: The Pattern of Affirmation," *Nineteenth Century Fiction*, XIV (December, 1959), 219.

Winterich, John T. "Stephen Crane: Lost and Found," *Saturday Review of Literature*, XXXIV (February 3, 1951), 21.

THE RED BADGE OF COURAGE: CRITICISM AND SOURCES

Carlson, Eric W. "Crane's *The Red Badge of Courage*," *Explicator*, XVI (March, 1958), 6.

Chase, Richard. "Introduction," *The Red Badge of Courage*, New York, 1960.

Colvert, James B. "The Red Badge of Courage and a Review of Zola's *La Débacle*," *Modern Language Notes*, LXXXI (February, 1956), 98.

Cox, James T. "The Imagery of *The Red Badge of Courage*," *Modern Fiction Studies*, V (Autumn, 1959), 209.

Eby, Cecil D., Jr. "The Source of Crane's Metaphor, 'Red Badge of Courage,'" *American Literature*, XXXII (May, 1960), 204.

Gibson, William M. "Introduction," *The Red Badge of Courage and Selected Prose and Poetry*, New York, 1956.

Gullason, Thomas A. "New Sources for Stephen Crane's War Motif," *Modern Language Notes*, LXXII (December, 1957), 572.

Hart, John E. "*The Red Badge of Courage* as Myth and Symbol," *University of Kansas City Review*, XIX (Summer, 1953), 249.

Hergesheimer, Joseph. "Introduction," *The Red Badge of Courage*, New York, 1925.

Hinman, Wilbur F. *Corporal Si Klegg and His "Pard,"* Cleveland, 1887.

Hoffman, Daniel G. "Introduction," *Stephen Crane: The Red Badge of Courage and Other Stories*, New York, 1957.

Klotz, Marvin. "Crane's *The Red Badge of Courage*," *Notes and Queries*, VI (February, 1959), 68.

Lively, Robert A. *Fiction Fights the Civil War*, Chapel Hill, 1957.

Marcus, Mordecai and Erin. "Animal Imagery in *The Red Badge of Courage*," *Modern Language Notes*, LXXIV (February, 1959), 108.

O'Donnell, Thomas F. "DeForest, Van Petten, and Stephen Crane," *American Literature*, XXVII (January, 1956), 578.

O'Donnell, Thomas F. "John B. Van Petten: Stephen Crane's History Teacher," *American Literature*, XXVII (May, 1955), 196.

Osborn, Scott C. "Stephen Crane's Imagery: 'Pasted like a Wafer,'" *American Literature*, XXIII (December, 1951), 362.

Pratt, Lyndon Upson. "A Possible Source of *The Red Badge of Courage*," *American Literature*, XI (March, 1939), 1.

Pritchett, V. S. *The Living Novel*, New York, 1947.

Rahv, Philip. "Fiction and the Criticism of Fiction," *Kenyon Review*, XVIII (Spring, 1956), 276.

Rosenfeld, Isaac. "Stephen Crane as Symbolist," *Kenyon Review*, XV (Spring, 1953), 311.

Solomon, Eric. "The Structure of *The Red Badge of Courage*," *Modern Fiction Studies*, V (Autumn, 1959), 220.

Solomon, Eric. "A Gloss on *The Red Badge of Courage*," *Modern Language Notes*, XXXV (February, 1960), 111.

Solomon, Eric. "Another Analogue for *The Red Badge of Courage*," *Nineteenth Century Fiction*, XIII (June, 1958), 63.

Stallman, Robert W. "'The Red Badge of Courage': A Collation of Two Pages of Manuscript Expunged from Chapter XII," *Papers of the Bibliographical Society of America*, XLIX (1955), 273.

Stallman, R. W. "The Scholar's Net: Literary Sources," *College English*, XVII (October, 1955), 20.

Stallman, R. W. "Introduction," *Red Badge of Courage*, New York, 1951.

Stallman, R. W. "Fiction and Its Critics: A Reply to Mr. Rahv," *Kenyon Review*, XIX (Spring, 1957), 290.

Stone, Edward. "The Many Suns of *The Red Badge of Courage*," *American Literature*, XXIX (November, 1957), 322.

Stone, Edward. "Crane's 'Soldier of the Legion,'" *American Literature*, XXX (May, 1958), 242.

Van Doren, Carl. "Introduction," *The Red Badge of Courage*, New York, 1944.

Webster, H. T. "Wilbur Hinman's *Corporal Si Klegg* and Stephen Crane's *The Red Badge of Courage*," *American Literature*, XI (November, 1939), 285.

Weisberger, Bernard. "The Red Badge of Courage," *Twelve Original Essays on Great American Novels*, ed. Charles Shapiro, Detroit, 1958.

Werner, W. L. "Stephen Crane and *The Red Badge of Courage*," *New York Times Book Review* (September 30, 1945), 4.

Wyndham, George. "A Remarkable Book," *New Review*, XIV (January, 1896), 30.

Wogan, Claudia C. "Crane's Use of Color in 'The Red Badge of Courage,'" *Modern Fiction Studies*, VI (Summer, 1960), 168.

6